Praise for *Nine Kinds of Naked*, by Tony Vigori

"Part quirky love story, part philoso
part metaphysical mystery, *Nine*
more musical dance than written w

—*Sa* *Review*

"Will remind many readers of such mischief-makers as Tom Robbins, Douglas Adams, Kurt Vonnegut, and Robert Anton Wilson."

—*Austin-American Statesman*

"Channeling the spirited humor of Douglas Adams…, Vigorito's is a crisp, sardonic voice."

—*Texas Monthly*

"A whimsical tale of time, space, coincidence, and cause and effect. The author displays most of the linguistic acrobatics and playful rumination that made his debut a cult classic."

—*Kirkus Reviews*

"Vigorito's style makes for a lyrical adventure that complements the surreal plot."

—*Daily Texan*

"Think of the late David Foster Wallace, or the early novels of TC Boyle… Wild, gleeful abandon… Like riding a roller coaster that's threatening to careen off the tracks."

—*The Philippine Star*

"Linguistic gymnastics abound... Vigorito demonstrates once again that he's a wild stylist... startlingly original... an entertaining anarchist..."

—*Chicago Sun-Times*

"A beautiful book, absolutely wonderful... hilarious... can't recommend it enough."

—*Ink & Quill.*

"A rambunctious romp through time and synchronicity, and a hilarious present-day parable on our brinksmanship existence."

—*Reality Sandwich*

"A narrative roller coaster... delicately and masterfully interweaving numerous plot lines and an odd cast of characters... all described in chaotic, exuberant language."

—*Austin Monthly*

"Filled with style and sarcasm... This is one of the few novels one could pick up at any arbitrary page and enjoy... a surprisingly fun read."

—*Knight News*

"Displays Vigorito's incomparable imagination... and his trademark quirky brilliance."

—*Minneapolis Books Examiner*

"Have a ball with this hyperactive, zany novel."

—*Publishers Weekly*

"Like those maverick classics, *Alice in Wonderland* and *Gargantua*, *Nine Kind of Naked* is as fanciful and inventive in its form, its structure, as it is in its observations... It fed tasty crackers to all the hungry parrots in my mental aviary."

—TOM ROBBINS

"Offers ten distinct varieties of literary satisfaction, including metaphysical highjinks, libidinous lowjinks, hermeneutic mind games, Gordian plot twists, cognitive estrangement, linguistic surrealism, stylistic pyrotechnics, laugh-out-loud jokes, scrappy extrapolations, and the synergistic sum of the above."

—JAMES MORROW

"With this strange carnival of a book, Vigorito has scored himself a permanent plot in the neighborhood of the American surrealist novel. The breadth of his imagination and the sheer exuberance of his writing cannot be ignored."

—NEAL POLLACK

"Like scuffling with a naked and unreasonably cheerful version of yourself."

—BILL FITZHUGH

Read more reviews and an extended sample at TonyVigorito.com

Praise for *Just a Couple of Days*, by Tony Vigorito

"An apocalyptic vision worthy of Kurt Vonnegut... the narrative pops with linguistic acrobatics... consistently dazzling... An underground cult classic."

—*Kirkus Reviews*

"A lyrical, thoughtful, viral meme of a book. Read it!"

—CHRISTOPHER MOORE

"A master of contradiction... displays a talent for tackling serious matters... and making them absurd and funny in a way that seems to release the reader from the weight of the issue."

—*Minneapolis Books Examiner*

"Vigorito laces his writing with a satirical touch, adding levity to the heady subject matter."

—*Columbus Alive*

"Vigorito's narrative style is a fun, lyrical experience."

—*Montgomery Advertiser*

"Unpredictably adventurous and singularly ambitious."

—*Wisconsin Bookwatch*

"Vigorito's... irreverent, whimsical style... has attracted a cult following... The final apocalyptic vision is a twist not seen since Kurt Vonnegut's *Cat's Cradle*. **Recommended**."

—*Library Journal*

"Tony Vigorito's brilliant novel is a *Dr. Strangelove* for the biotech century, a witty and wise end-of-the-world romp that manages to be optimistic—even joyous—yet cynically dystopian at the same time. *Just a Couple of Days* is savvy, wickedly funny, and profoundly disturbing. An absorbing, thought-provoking read."

—RICHARD HEINBERG

"I'd go so far as to say that this novel is 'folk heroic' and should be read by anyone who still values their capacity to think for themselves… Real writing speaks for itself—and to us. This does."

—KRIS SAKNUSSEMM

"May be the most unusual, the most original novel I have ever read."

—TOM ROBBINS

Read more reviews and an extended sample at TonyVigorito.com

LOVE AND OTHER PRANKS

Also by Tony Vigorito

Just a Couple of Days
Nine Kinds of Naked

LOVE AND OTHER PRANKS

TONY VIGORITO

MÖBIUS
SAN FRANCISCO

www.TonyVigorito.com

Publisher's Cataloging-in-Publication Data

Vigorito, Tony.
Love and other pranks/Tony Vigorito.
        p. cm.
        LCCN 2016907121
        ISBN 978-0-9701419-5-8
        ISBN 978-0-9701419-6-5
        ISBN 978-0-9701419-7-2
        ISBN 978-1-945213-03-8
        1. Man-woman relationships—Fiction. 2. Pirates—Fiction.
3. Romance fiction. 4. Action and adventure fiction.   I. Title.

    PS3622.I48L68 2016   813'.6
                        QBI16-600072

Layout and cover design by Damonza

Printed in the United States of America.

For the beautiful Christina.
So much more than I could have imagined.

What has been will be again,
what has been done will be done again.
—*Ecclesiastes 1:9*

———————

History does not repeat itself,
but it does rhyme.
—*attributed to Mark Twain*

LOVE AND OTHER PRANKS

Prologue:
In the Beginning

THE FIRST TIME Adam kissed Eve, she was brandishing a Granny Smith in her grin as if she had just bobbed it out of a cider barrel. Obviously, Adam could not proffer a proper kiss so long as Eve wielded that apple between her incisors, so clever Adam settled for lodging his teeth into the open end of her apple. Then he growled.

They had been flirting famously, and Adam had just announced his incipient kiss. Eve's immediate response had been to wedge the fruit between her grinning teeth, presumably as an impregnable barrier. Not exactly a come-hither, but Adam chose to receive it as a dare, and really, there didn't seem to be another option in any event.

Certainly, Adam could have accepted it as a cruel rejection and crept away, but that would have been unbearably craven. He also could have slapped the apple out of her sassy lips, though of course that would have been frightfully belligerent. Or, he could kiss her anyway—inasmuch as the circumstances would permit—and let neither fruit nor folly come between them.

Adam chose wisely. He knew this as soon as Eve overcame

his apple-begotten audacity and growled right back at him. Actually, she snarled and tugged at the apple like a starving wolf, but Adam held on and gnashed back as if this frothing apple was indeed the last desperate scrap of carrion. Immediately, Adam realized that Eve's apple-grappling technique was impressive, twisting her head and yanking suddenly sideways in her fierce attempts to rip the apple from his teeth. It was everything Adam could do to keep up, adjusting his pressure and pull against her ferocity and finding little opportunity to assert his own assault until an impulse suggested he cease the struggle and yield to that which he had been resisting. Thus informed, Adam pitched his face forward in instinctive jujitsu, slacking her yank and loosing her clench just long enough to successfully tear the apple free, at which point he crunched through his end triumphant and taunted the twice-bitten apple in his grasp.

Defiant, Eve chewed her chunk of apple like it was a wad of chaw in a quick draw. Adam flashed his teeth and imitated her in turn and they glared at each other eyes aflame until Adam tossed the fractured apple heavenward. Their eyes unwavering captured the pulse of one another's lips swollen in mutual anticipation, and as the airborne apple touched the apogee of its ascent they at last dared mingle the nectar sweetening their tongues. Kissing their way into one another's hearts, he sucked her upper lip and she nibbled his lower as the apple bonked off both of their skulls, though this kiss would not be dissuaded.

If their eyes had yet been open, they might have spied an angel and a devil toasting their kiss, eyes wild with mischief as if they had just lit a strip of firecrackers in a henhouse.

If only it had been so pointless a prank.

PART ONE:

YES, AND NECTAR

1

San Francisco, early 21st century

RUTH BE TOLD, Adam's name was Merlin—Merlin Otherwise—and he had been calling himself Adam that night only because that is how a couple costumed as an angel and a devil had earlier that evening addressed him. And truth again be told, Eve's name was Lila—Lila Louise—and Lila was just being coy when she introduced herself as Eve in response to Merlin's allegation of Adam on top of a gigantic and shimmering opalescent king cobra float on Halloween night in San Francisco. Lila and Merlin were in the Castro, atop the lead float in an illegal parade that had successfully revived the traditional Halloween-in-the-Castro street party banned by the city so many years ago, and when they kissed, a roaring cheer erupted from the assembled throngs. Naturally, it is possible and even probable that the crowd was cheering not their kiss but the fact that the flamethrower mounted in the king cobra's mouth had just belched a tremendous blast of fire, but listen, who among us would question the mythos of love?

Certainly not a pirate, which is how both Lila and Merlin were dressed. Merlin had swashbuckled his way onto the exclusive Bay Area hipster cobra float, uninvited and knowing nobody whatsoever but leaping aboard nevertheless as though he were its belated captain, black pirate shirt billowing open in the breeze, chest and face painted for the glory of Poseidon. Lila noticed him immediately, though when he eventually approached she pretended otherwise.

"We've met before, I'm certain," Merlin opened, doing everything he could to avoid examining this redhead's pirate getup, her own white pirate shirt billowing also wide-open to reveal a seashell bikini top, though even that enchantment was not so seductive as the golden pendant she mesmerized about her neck.

"I'm certain we have not," Lila replied, tossing a Granny Smith in her grasp, an apple she'd been contemplating crunching into for the last half hour.

"I'm certain that we have," Merlin insisted. "It was the eighteenth century, wasn't it? Aboard that bastard Goldtooth's man-o'-war? Somewhere off the coast of Bermuda?"

Lila toyed with her golden pendant, smiling, as she turned to face Merlin completely. "What is this nonsense which now confronts me?" she demanded.

"Yes," Merlin pursued his bullshit concoction, encouraged. "I remember it all now. You jumped ship off Hispaniola with a group of runaway slaves, and so swift was your cutlass that no man dared touch you uninvited, let alone defy your assumed leadership. Then, the motley lot of you found your way back aboard your pig husband's ship and overthrew him, for he was just an imperialist tool who'd kidnapped you from your village in Ireland and treated you like chattel. Plus, you wanted your own ship with which to make an honest living undermining the slave trade. Yar, always the principled pirate, you were. Flaming Jane, they called you. I'd recognize that flame of red hair anywhere, and still flaunting that Möbius band pendant, no less."

Lila again touched her pendant, impressed that he knew of its geometry. "Perhaps your story is true," she played along, "but you still haven't told me from whence I should know you. A swaggering hotspur like yourself, for all I know you could be one of Goldtooth's scoundrels."

"Savvy this," Merlin grinned. "If I were one of his scoundrels, I would not have then warned you of his murderous intentions. And I have to say," Merlin drew in close and lowered his breath. "Yours was a brilliant gambit, my lovely."

Lila smiled, smitten. "And what was your name?"

"Crow, they called me then, though tonight I go by Adam. And what of you, Flaming Jane? What are you called in this go-round?"

"I suppose you can call me Eve," Lila lied. "But one question remains unanswered."

"And what might that be?"

Grinning sly, Lila pointed her apple at him. "I'm curious why I would have told some tangle-bearded traitor all of this?"

"Because." Merlin straightened himself dignified. "We became lovers."

2

Somewhere in the Caribbean, early 18th century

THE GENTLE PITCH of the ship oscillating across the waves
that had lulled Crow into a fever-befuddled delirium
now blindsided him wide awake. A rogue wave slammed
into starboard like the pelt of a blue whale flung by a drunken
pissed-off Neptune, cascading seawater everywhere and leaving
cries of curse and alarm in its wake. Crow bolted upright and
happened to catch a toppling hourglass just as Flaming Jane
came banging into the captain's quarters, though when Flaming
Jane met Crow's eyes, instead of apprehension and confusion
she found only wonder.

"Tempt me with your outlaw apple," Crow whispered the
lyrics of the song that had serenaded his dreamscape into the
waking world. *"With eyes that flash so wild—"*

"You're okay," Flaming Jane observed breathless, illuminating him with her lantern and steadying herself against the
creaking moaning hull. "Your fever's broken."

"Answer me it's oh so good with lips that dare and smile,"
Crow continued reciting his dreamsong, embracing the hourglass as the ship's thirty-pound Maine Coon mouser named

Catface nuzzled against him. Pausing, Crow grew a smile. *"As we lick yes, and nectar!"*

Since Flaming Jane believed in the oracular power of dreams, she indulged his dreamsaying, though not his poetry. "No more poetry!" she demanded. "Tell me your dream! Quickly now, before it dissolves!"

Crow complied, still blinking wonder. "We were riding a white snake across the sea, and there was an angel—no, a devil—and I told you my name was Adam and you told me your name was Eve and you had an apple and we kissed and you told me you were a pirate and then I told you this wasn't really happening."

"What wasn't really happening?"

"Life." Crow paused, the dream vanishing into perplexity. "And then I told you there was something worth more than even gold."

3

T HOUGH HE OBVIOUSLY possessed the moxie somewhere within himself, Merlin was rarely so Casanova with women as he had been with Lila that Halloween, and was so that evening only because a couple of recently reunited matchmakers just in from New Orleans and costumed as an angel and a devil had earlier stepped in front of him, addressed him as Adam, handed him a bumper sticker upon which was printed the phrase ARGUE NAKED, and placed a little white pill impressed with a heart into his palm.

"What's this?" Merlin inquired as he peered at the presumed tab of Ecstasy.

"Love," purred the angel perfect.

"Chaos," dared the devil baritone.

Merlin shook his head, an excessively bacchanalian youth having turned him off to drugs—or medicines, as they are euphemized in the Bay Area. "Thanks, but I don't—" He offered the pill back to them.

The angel and the devil declined, chiming "Have a beautiful night!" as they disappeared into the crowd, leaving Merlin alone to consider whether he should pop a pill given to him unsolicited by total strangers. He did not consider for long, for though he was in general grossed out by drugs and mistrustful of pressed pills in particular, and though it had been several years since he'd abandoned any experimentation with MDMA due to the effervescent terror of sadness it too often left in its heartbreaking wake, he had freshly lost the group of acquaintances with whom he'd come to the illegal Halloween parade and discovered immediately afterward that his cell phone battery had decided to take the night off. Having been wandering alone through the crowds wondering what he was supposed to do now, Merlin suddenly possessed an intriguing diversion.

However, despite the fact that the San Francisco Bay Area has maintained a tremendous appetite for its magical mystery medicines in the decades since its flower children wilted, the pill Merlin had been given was actually nothing more than a miniature vitamin C tablet supposedly enhanced with a single drop of a homeopathic dilution of a love potion whose molecular structure had been tuned to the mystical resonance of the angel's favorite Tibetan singing bowl. Whether or not that potion had anything at all to do with how the evening then transpired may never be known for certain, but the fact remains that within an hour Merlin was blasting around, rolling like he invented the wheel, uncontainably enthused as he drew smiles from everyone who witnessed him dance his way toward the front of the illegal parade. In his Tibetan singing bowl–tuned, placeboic intoxication, Merlin felt certain there was only one way to witness an illegal parade, and that was from the deck of its lead float. No barricade could convince him otherwise, and even the policewoman who stood in his path attempting to manage the crowds was so enchanted by his shining grin that she agreed to grant him passage, but only if he let her write the word passion across his chest with her fire-engine-red lipstick. Merlin consented yes of course, and though he could not have fathomed what this would eventually imply, there was but a moment's retrospect before he understood that it was both invitation and invocation. But Merlin never paused to consider the nature of what it was he was inadvertently inviting and invoking upon himself that night. For that matter, he never even turned the pill over before he swallowed it.

If he had, he would have found another heart, broken in two.

4

"QUIVER ME TIMBERS," Lila murmured moments after her apple-sweetened kiss with Merlin had dissipated. Opening her eyes, she leaned in toward Merlin's ear. "There *is* something you should know about me, however," Lila whispered mischievous. "I sometimes hear music boxes in my mind." In truth, Lila's music boxes had fallen suddenly silent when they kissed, and it was precisely this that caused her to notice the resumption of their faraway, plinking chorus.

Merlin blinked, amused. "I shan't be deterred."

"Also," Lila continued, "an imp has possessed me on this Halloween." The imp she was referring to here was a little white pill impressed with a heart that the couple costumed as an angel and a devil had also given to her, but Lila did not elaborate her metaphor, and thus Merlin and Lila would not realize the coincidence for quite some time.

Merlin smiled nonetheless at her revelation. "That's nothing," he shrugged. "I've been possessed by an imp since I was nine years old."

Lila grinned. "I can't *wait* to hear that story."

"As it happened," Merlin launched, unhesitant upon her prompt, "I had recently finished reading *Tom Sawyer*, and I was thinking about how that rascal Tom had so much more fun than I did. Up until then, see, I was a well-behaved, straight-A teacher's pet, obviously a precocious reader, and lying in bed one night I somehow came around to the conclusion that I needed more mischief in my life. I'm nine years old, remember, and this was some kind of a major epiphany for me. I even said it out loud, announcing it into the nighttime, and the next thing I knew my skin was crawling with goose bumps and this jolt of fright shot through me as I all of a sudden imagined that I saw a jaguar lunge at me out of the darkness of the night—"

"A jaguar?" Lila interrupted.

"Some kind of a jaguar," Merlin nodded. "But all its spots were like eyes. And that of course yelped me right out of bed and bawled me down the hallway, where it took my parents a half an hour to calm me down." Merlin leaned in close and lowered his voice to a whisper. "But from that night forward, an imp seemed to have possessed me. I became an unmanageable terror to my parents and teachers, a real hellion."

"A hellion, huh?" Lila nodded with faux gravity.

"I tell you."

"Have you considered an exorcism?"

Merlin shook his head. "Not a chance. I'm having way too much fun."

Lila grinned again. "There's something else you should know about me."

"Anything, my lovely."

"My name isn't really Eve," Lila confessed. "It's Lila. Lila Louise."

"The beautiful Lila," Merlin smiled. "Well," he matched

her, "I suppose I should mention as well that my name isn't really Adam. In fact it is Merlin. Merlin Otherwise."

Lila's smile broadened. "Aren't we just a couple of pranksters?"

"You have no idea," Merlin cautioned. "Laughter *is* our highest prayer, after all."

"Oooo," Lila cooed. "And aren't the children snickering in the pews the holiest people in church?"

Merlin raised his eyebrows. "Blessed are the pure in heart—" he began.

"For they shall see God," Lila finished his beatitude.

Merlin blinked, and smiled through his words. "God be praised, and who has time for church?" They beamed at one another, speechless for several moments, until Merlin bowed handsome. "And how do you spell the beautiful Lila?"

"With as many *l*'s as thou darest lilt off thy sapling tongue."

"A poetess as well?" Merlin grinned. "Since we're being so ruthlessly honest here, there is one other thing you should know about me."

"Pray tell."

"I don't believe this is really happening."

"What's this?"

"Life."

"Life?"

"This mortal apparition."

"Ah, if by life you mean the ego's denial of death, then life *is* an impermanent prank at the end of the day, isn't it?" Lila smiled.

"The ego's denial of death," Merlin repeated, nodding. "A vital clarification."

"Only a fool would take such a tawdry tale for the truth," Lila continued. "And we are not fools."

"No, we are not fools. But I am a pirate."

"As am I."

"I don't always dress like this, though."

"Subterfuge is essential."

"Subterfuge *is* essential," Merlin nodded. "Of course, once you realize that the ego's pretense at life isn't really happening, you discover that there's really nothing but subterfuge."

Lila nodded noncommittal. "Actually," she corrected, "there *is* something that's really happening, and it is ever so much more than subterfuge. Wouldn't you agree?"

Merlin paused a moment before nodding in comprehension. "Of course, my lady. And worth ever so much more than gold."

5

IT'S NOT EASY being a redheaded pirate. The sun was merciless on Flaming Jane's fair skin in the first place, and became all the more so when reflecting off the sea. Flaming Jane knew Providence was with her, however, when she happened to salvage a barrel of shea butter from a merchant ship on one of her earliest plunders. This—along with a collection of pirated parasols and a practice of war-painting their bodies flamboyant spectacular—sufficed for her sun protection.

Far more problematic than the sun, however, was the instant notoriety Flaming Jane's red hair conveyed upon her. They could scarcely port anywhere without some seaman spying her sea-sprayed and tangled mane and recognizing her as the notorious Flaming Jane. Certainly, she could have shorn her flame of hair or taken care to hide it, but Flaming Jane was not one to capitulate to the dictates of lesser men. She embraced the epithet they dubbed upon her, and it only pleased her that the reward for her capture was twice and thrice that of far more successful buccaneers. Flaming Jane was no toothless and swill-sipping scoundrel, after all. She was an educated woman who defied her proper place as the property of her admiral husband who had kidnapped her from her village in Ireland, overthrowing his command and turning a stolen man-o'-war into a pirate ship full of runaway slaves, deserters, and other such ne'er-do-propers. Such matrimonial and nautical treachery could not go unpunished. Not in these imperial seas.

But none of these concerns fazed Flaming Jane now. She hastily unrolled a weathered goatskin and spread it upon the drawing table. "Look at this," she said, stabbing her knife into the leather to hold it in place against the roll of the waves. Crow laid the hourglass he was still hugging on the bedding and balanced himself upright. He peered at the goatskin illuminated by her lantern.

"That's a map," Crow observed.

"Hell have mercy!" Flaming Jane sassed loud. "Is that what this is?"

"Where did you get it?" Crow asked, ignoring her sarcasm.

Flaming Jane did not answer his question. "Look at *this*." She instead tapped her index finger urgently, and Crow followed it to discover a serpent moving to swallow its own tail.

"That's a serpent," Crow observed again.

"Yes, lover. Your powers of observation are extraordinary."

"Hey!" Crow retorted, raising his voice. "Cut me some slack, wench! This is the first I've stood in a bloody week!"

Flaming Jane smiled. She despised men who were spineless with women, and she constantly tested Crow on this. Much to her delight, he never failed to slap the sass off her lips—figuratively, of course, for she would have severed any hand that so much as cut a breeze across her freckled face. "Fair enough," she granted. "But there's hardly call to play hell about it."

Crow pursed his lips and pointed to the map. "I suppose you also noticed that the serpent has twisted upon itself a hundred and eighty degrees, just like your pendant there?"

Flaming Jane instinctively touched the pendant around her neck, a pendant she had salvaged from a chest of plundered jewels. It was a simple band of gold with a half twist that gave it the curious property of having only one side. In fact Flaming Jane had *not* noticed this, though she did not let on, merely nodding instead. "And look at *this*," she changed the subject, pointing earnestly to the top of the map, where it was scripted in French: *Le Trésor de Tous les Trésors.* Another hand had scrawled its English translation directly beneath, in a darker, more recent ink than the rest of the faded map: The Treasure of All Treasures.

"The treasure of all treasures," Crow murmured, then looked at Flaming Jane. "Worth more than even gold?"

Flaming Jane nodded, pointing to the right-hand side of the map. "Now look at *this*."

"An angel?"

"Yes," she coaxed. "And *this*." She pointed to the left-hand side of the map.

"A devil." Crow paused. "Just like in my dream."

"Just like in your dream," Flaming Jane affirmed, her eyes sparkling sapphire in the light of the lantern as she quickly rolled up the map, but not before Crow's eyes had caught a warning scripted in French across the open sea, another hand having scrawled its English translation alongside it:

Prends Garde au Pré des Merveilles.

Beware the Meadow of Marvels.

6

ENERALLY SPEAKING, Merlin didn't know what the fuck he was doing. He felt certain that there must have been an entrance ramp somewhere along the road to adulthood that he'd long ago whizzed past oblivious, and now, feeling lately betrayed by the carpe diem philosophies that had fueled his twenties, he had no idea how to turn around or even where this bumpy road less traveled by might be taking him.

In the first place, his degree in environmental studies had convinced him that the industrial civilization into which he'd been thrown was bound to collapse, and so rather than fasten his fortune onto a sinking ship, he'd focused instead on sucking the proverbial marrow out of life. But in his vain attempts to follow his bliss and get free, and really, to flee his own heartbreak at being trapped in so tragic a culture, Merlin had stayed in the world of partying, international-backpacking twenty-somethings into his thirties, long enough to see the fluorescent house lights go on, essentially, illuminating how hedonistic and sordid the whole lifestyle had been. But by then he had already drifted far too far afield for the flimsy, hopelorn script of conventional socialization to hold any possible interest—as if being approved for thirty years of debt and a vacant life of swollen desperation were the highest ambitions of the human experience.

In the second place, Merlin had bounced all over the planet on whatever cash he could capture chasing down epic treks and spectacular experiences, ostensibly for the purpose of finding himself, but mainly because he wanted to get his Jim Morrison kicks before the whole shithouse went up in flames. Lately disenchanted by the hypocrisies of his own lifestyle, however, Merlin gradually realized that industrial civilization wasn't going anywhere anytime soon. And now, as a consequence of his pessimistic hedonism, he had little more to show for the last decade of his life than a stash of ill-gotten cash that was fading apace with his memories.

Ultimately, it was on a raft upon a river deep within the virgin rain forests of Borneo, on his way back from visiting the world's largest bat cave, where the guide had boasted of the cave's three-hundred-foot-tall mound of guano—the surface of which, he'd explained, writhed perpetually with cockroaches and maggots—and had gone on to explain how if some unfortunate bat pup were to lose its grip from its roost upon the ceiling and fall, the pup would be stripped to its skeleton within minutes by swarms of flesh-eating bugs, you see, and it was on that raft upon that river deep within the virgin rain forests of Borneo, contemplating this as a curtain of bats billowed across the dusking sky, that Merlin realized just how lost he had truly become.

Travelers on the international backpacking circuit are fond of paraphrasing a line from Tolkien: *Not all who wander are lost.* Maybe not, Merlin mused, but he sure as hell was, and he blamed the Bay Area. From Santa Cruz to Mendocino, the entire region had been soaked by that "high and beautiful wave" of the 1960s, but when that transcendental tsunami finally broke and rolled back, it left a heartbreak of faded hopes and jaded dreams. Wading through the lingering countercultural flotsam left behind by that era, it remained all too easy to get caught up in the peacock, to feel like he was supposed to be a perfectly centered Zen master seizing every day, and if his eyes were a shadow less than shining then he was a miserable failure to his own spirit. And although the psychedelic supernova of a distant Summer of Love was yet reverberating throughout the artistic underclass of the Bay Area, the one love that is all you need had somehow gotten lost in the confusion of illusions across the ensuing decades, and like apocalyptic flash burns on a concrete wall, all that remained was a two-dimensional shadow of what was once a living pulsing thing, as if hedonism had hired mysticism as its decorator and designer, masking the depravity of its narcissistic ego beneath the aesthetics and accouterments of what might have been an enlightened civilization, like chimpanzees that figure out how to wear clothing but still fling their feces at one another.

San Narcisisco, Merlin sometimes called it, even though he knew that was probably an unfair cynicism. Still, despite the gentrifying invasion of Silicon Valley and its creeping, high-rent displacement of the city's traditionally bohemian inhabitants, and despite the despondent hypocrisies which had long ago corrupted the countercultural lighthouse and left so many lost souls sailing circles in a sea of egos inflated by runaway property values, there was no other American city in which he'd rather live—even if he could only afford to live across the Bay in Oakland anymore. Where else would it have seemed a perfectly reasonable lifestyle to work as a bicycle courier for two years in his postcollegiate twenties, he and his coworkers amusing themselves with an exotic underground drug called LP9 on any given day that they worked, for the dare, for the thrill, for the stamina and performance enhancement? This, they told each other, was in imitation of Zen masters who run down creek beds, hopping from rock to unpremeditated rock as a practice of compelling themselves into the full-blast present moment. Reckless drug abuse under the pretense of enlightenment—why not? This is California, baby! Let's see some saffron-robed Zen master breakneck his bicycle down Filbert Street's 31.5-degree gradient at rush hour while soaring the expansive heights of LP9, dodging cats and cars and craters and goddamned smartphone zombies—and then hold his holy shit together inside some humming office building all while interacting with the coffee-breathing stress-monsters whose precious financial instruments they delivered. It was a fact that not a single courier in their crew ever crashed—until, that is, one of them eventually did and the whole crew scattered disenchanted 'cause of course it's all fun and games till someone gets in a wreck on LP9—and the only enlightenment Merlin ever attained was a realization that automobiles were a mechanical manifestation of the gigantic American ego, bloated and bleating their way through traffic like sheep corralled into slaughter.

That, and a lingering, deeply amusing sensation that life—or the ego's pretense at life—is not really happening.

7

WHAT HAS COME to be called the Jolly Roger—the skull-and-crossbones flag pirates used to broadcast their intentions and inspire terror on the high seas—originated in Christian artwork from the Middle Ages. Symbolizing resurrection, a skull and two crossbones were frequently placed at the foot of Christ's crucifixion. The skull was supposed to be the skull of Adam, while the crossbones themselves were in the shape of a cross rather than an X. Eventually, ship captains took to drawing a little skull and crossbones in their logs next to the names of sailors who had died, as a way of blessing their death with the promised rebirth in the kingdom of heaven. Over time, however, this meaning was entirely forgotten and sailors came to associate the symbol only with death, and by the time pirates began using the Jolly Roger to identify themselves, it is safe to assume that they intended to threaten only murder, with nary a thought toward reassuring their victim's resurrection. And the name Jolly Roger, incidentally, itself derived from the French words *jolie rouge*, or "pretty red," since the earliest pirate flags were blood red, for the obvious homicidal reasons.

Crow knew nothing of this cryptic history as he shifted his weight on the folded Jolly Roger flag upon which he was sitting.

Feeling much refreshed after recovering from what seemed at the time to be an interminable breakbone fever, Crow sat upon the stool in his perch—an oaken rum barrel with the top removed, mounted high atop the ship's mainmast—enjoying the sun's kiss upon his skin and plinking idly at his cavaquinho as he surveyed the horizon. Because the crow's nest occupied a distant point from the ship's center of mass, every pitch and roll of the ship was amplified. Hanging out up there too long usually resulted in severe seasickness even for seasoned seamen, but it never seemed to squeam Crow in the slightest. In fact, the relative quietude and isolation of the crow's nest pleased him, providing him with ample time to daydream new songs, and because most sailors considered lookout duty a punishment, he never had to compete for a turn.

As a pirate, Crow wasn't so typical—having learned to read as a child at an orphanage, and having been a voracious autodidact ever since—but then neither was the rest of the crew of *Eleusis*, all of whom were runaways, fugitives, and ex-slaves just trying to stay alive and extract a life unencumbered by boss and command. As such, *Eleusis* was a ship of renegades even among pirates. Populated neither by the thieving mercenaries nor the sadistic drunken killers who crammed most ships flying the Jolly Roger, Flaming Jane had instead assembled an undomesticated, unaffiliated band of outlaws who were seeking not merely booty, but beauty—though this should hardly be taken to mean that *Eleusis* was not compelled by treasure. Quite the contrary, Flaming Jane had led an aggressive campaign of intercepting Spanish galleons laden with treasure looted from the remnants of the native Aztec civilization. In contrast to other pirates, however, their commandeered booty was not squandered on the next bar and brothel, but stowed away, stashed, and hidden. Having found that freedom is indistinguishable from life itself, the crew of *Eleusis* was determined to keep their freedom—and their lives—or die defending it. Every one of them was armed with multiple knives, swords, pistols, bows, and tomahawks, gleaming, polished, sharpened, and ready to loose unhesitant upon anyone who dared dangle a noose or jangle a chain in their general direction.

Crow observed the activity on deck, enjoying the fact that nobody—with the exception of Catface—ever looked up. Catface was entirely black excepting the ghost-white comet of fur that graced the entirety of his head from the lynx-tips of his ears to the base of his neck. Allegedly descended from cats crossbred with bobcats by eleventh-century Vikings to be large and fascinated by water, Catface could not have been happier hunting rats and mice aboard *Eleusis*. As for everyone else on board, there wasn't a great deal to be done these past few days as they sailed toward their destination, so most of the crew was either napping in hammocks or gathered in circles making music. A wakeful bunch were stump wrestling, a game in which two players faced each other standing on stumps and tried to shove one another off balance—made all the more difficult by the pitch of the ship itself, and excellent practice for the combat they sometimes faced at sea. It was all very idyllic, and as Crow surveyed the horizon he contemplated his fever dream and was moved to strum his new song:

Tempt me with your outlaw apple
with eyes that flash so wild
Answer me it's oh so good
with lips that dare and smile
> *as we lick yes,*
> *and nectar!*

Cast this day into the night
the wind it shivers cold
Cuddle with me closer trust
our spirit soars so bold

> *as we whisper yes,*
> *and nectar!*

Fend with me the taunt of dark
our fear will find repose
Dream with me discover light
the shining smile that knows

> *as we murmur yes,*
> *and nectar!*

Blinking into mourning sad
at life's forgotten hymn
Must we surely die my love
and fade into the dim

> *as we cry yes,*
> *and nectar!*

Find with me the love that's lost
the song that's long unsung
Sing with me abandoned words
unleashed upon our tongue

> *as we shout yes,*
> *and nectar!*

Kiss me by the candlelight
oh kiss me by the sun
Dance with me like hurricanes
and spin our souls undone

> *as we roar yes,*
> *and nectar!*

Crow might have continued on if Moby—a scarlet macaw he'd won in a dice game from some drunken sailor back on Goldtooth's galleon—hadn't suddenly appeared in his field of vision in a flash and a flutter of red, blue, and yellow. Crow had released the parrot immediately after he'd won it because he couldn't bear to see the chains chafing its ankles, but after he'd set the bird free he was surprised to discover that the macaw had taken a fondness to him and had hung around him ever since. Alighting now upon the barrel's edge, Moby bobbed his head and steadied himself before squawking, "Windward ho, Crow Smarty!"

Crow knew better than to smirk merely amused at the bird's greeting. Moby was smart as a smack and more than clever enough to see into the hearts of men, and only a fool taunting peril would dismiss his discourse as meaningless mimicry. Squinting in the direction of the wind, it wasn't long before Crow's sharp eyes caught a momentary glint of light flash on the eastern horizon. Swinging his cavaquinho over his shoulder and grabbing his spyglass in the same motion, he focused it in the direction of the glint. Scanning across the horizon, he saw nothing at first, but momentarily glimpsed a sail briefly peekaboo the horizon and knew that the glint of light he'd seen could only have been reflected off the spying lens of a pursuing telescope. Their position compromised, Crow located the speaking trumpet stashed on the floor of the rum barrel and sounded Moby's alarm to the crew: "Windward ho!"

The effect was immediate as leisure leapt into action. Everyone knew the stakes and everyone knew exactly what to do. Crow himself waited till he spotted Flaming Jane's red hair before chimping his way down the masting ropes to advise her. The glint of light told him everything he needed to know: They were being followed, and their pursuer was attempting to keep an invisible distance. It might be other pirates, it might be a Royal Navy ship, it might be Goldtooth himself. The consequences were the same in any event.

Nobody sneaks up on *Eleusis*.

8

ERHAPS THE WIND carried the stench of the Royal Navy's cowardice to within noseshot of Crow. Crow, touching a scar across his left cheek, sensed it was the Royal Navy that was following *Eleusis*, though we need suppose neither his olfaction nor his intuition supernatural. After all, it was no mere captain from whom Flaming Jane had commandeered *Eleusis*. Flaming Jane's estranged husband had been Admiral Jasper, formerly in command of Great Britain's entire Caribbean campaign, and her marital mutiny aboard his flagship vessel had shot a cannonball through his military career. Crow never understood why Flaming Jane didn't abandon Admiral Jasper and his crew on a sandbar at low tide and let the sea do its business. Instead, she marooned them on a deserted island, where Admiral Jasper not only survived but escaped, and the demoted Captain Jasper now devoted every vessel he could divert toward the capture of his estranged wife, the pirate Flaming Jane.

But Flaming Jane had her own way with the world and its lackeys, deeming death an unnecessary crudity when she could so easily outwit her opponents. Her mutiny on board *Eleusis* (originally named the *Queen Elizabeth*) was no exception. When she first vanished from her husband's ship, for instance, all the Admiral's atlases and sea charts, which detailed everything that was known of Caribbean coastlines, coves, sandbars, currents, and tides—basically all the nautical intelligence necessary for imperial navigational supremacy—vanished along with her. These were items of such tremendous tactical utility that—lest they fall into enemy hands—the Royal Navy had protocols in place for their destruction in the event of the *Queen Elizabeth*'s surrender.

Still, since a dozen African slaves had also disappeared from the ship that night, along with the captain's personal sloop, assumption ruled that the Admiral's wife was kidnapped by brutes, and shudder be her fate. But in fact, knowing that the *Queen Elizabeth* was ultimately headed to a remote naval outpost for provisions (and having taught herself to navigate by carefully watching her husband work and pestering him with as many questions as he would tolerate), Flaming Jane simply navigated ahead in the much swifter sloop. There, she and her crew of runaways hid the sloop in a shallow inlet off to the south of the bay's peninsula and busied themselves dying the sails pitch black and first boring and then plugging large holes in its hull as they waited for the *Queen Elizabeth* to finally come lumbering along.

After the *Queen Elizabeth* had restocked its provisions and the moon was new, they sailed the sloop alongside it under the cover of night and black sail. Then, her eyes roaring like hurricanes, Flaming Jane silently unplugged the holes in the hull of the sloop one by one. The implication was as clear as it was severe as seawater burbled around their feet: There would be no retreat, and if anyone had lacked resolve before, there could be no question now. They swiftly and silently boarded the *Queen Elizabeth*, overpowered the guards, and made straight for the weapons room, commandeering the cache and thereby seizing the entire ship by complete surprise. Striking sail before dawn, the other nearby naval vessels were never the wiser that the *Queen Elizabeth* had been hijacked by its own slaves.

Admiral Jasper snorted awake in his quarters to a pheasant feather tickling up his nose. Grogging open his molten eyes, he found Flaming Jane grinning over him at the far side of his own sword as Catface pawed playfully at the pheasant feather. Admiral Jasper scarcely had time to realize his own smoldering hangover before an immense African slave—an otherwise gentle giant by the name of Noa—pulled a burlap sack over Admiral Jasper's head and delivered a punishing thud that sent him back into unconsciousness. But a chamber remained in this unconsciousness, and it hammered with the intractable voice of his indocile wife.

"This is our ship now, you sonuvabitch."

9

ON THE AFTERNOON prior to Halloween night—and the
only reason Lila had been able to attend the outlawed
Halloween street party in the Castro in the first place—
Lila quit her job at the Octopus's Garden, the fine-dining seafood restaurant where she worked. Her departure was occasioned by the arrival of a loathsome ex-boyfriend who called
himself Ivan Humble. Lila had left Ivan over a year ago when
he forbade her from visiting her father after her father had suffered a debilitating heart attack. This prohibition was on the
supposedly selfless grounds that her presence at her father's
probable deathbed would trigger attachments that would result
in her father carrying his karma into his future lifetimes. Lila
hadn't spoken to her father in almost two decades, ever since
he'd walked out on her and her mother, but Lila laughed nonetheless in Ivan's face at his ludicrous logic and left to forgive her
father. Ivan Humble—or his devotees, of which he had many—
had been periodically stalking Lila ever since.

"Follow me, and let the dead bury their dead," Ivan had
said to Lila at the time. This was one of Ivan's favorite teachings. He lifted it right out of the book of Matthew, chapter 8,
verse 22, when Jesus blew off a disciple's request to attend his

father's funeral before following him. And since Ivan considered himself an awakened Master in the same league as Jesus and Mohammed, he felt entitled to this same attitude. When Ivan looked in the mirror after a tanning session, after all, he saw only the Buddha gazing back at him. Consequently and as far as he was concerned, anyone who disagreed with him was in their mind and thereby spiritually dead.

"Let the dead bury their dead," Ivan again reminded his inner circle during their Saturday walkabout that Halloween afternoon when they asked after Dalai, one of their own whom Ivan had publicly admonished that morning. The walkabout was reserved only for those Ivan deemed his most highly evolved aspirants after Saturday morning *satsang*, silent meditation in the presence of their guru. They were, as he constantly congratulated them, his inner circle, those most committed to the Holy Company of Beautiful People, and with whom Ivan promised to someday share the Wisdom. The walkabout essentially consisted of Ivan peacocking around town with an entourage of his most loyal followers, strutting about as if he were wearing a glittering cape, and all of them gazing intensely at others as if they were burning with an awareness at which others could only guess. "I can only guide her toward sarrendar," Ivan explained. "If Dalai rejects my guidance, she will continue to create her own karma and persist in samsara."

Lila overheard all this as she approached the table of six to reluctantly take their order, rolling her eyes at Ivan's peculiar pronunciation of *surrender*, always accenting the final syllable and pronouncing it *sarrendar*. Quite aside from that, it aggravated Lila to see Ivan, as she knew he was there only to taunt her. Lila had spent over a year with the Holy Company of Beautiful People, eventually as Ivan's would-be wife, before leaving out of revulsion for the manner in which Ivan deceived and manipulated his disciples, goading their fears and insecurities all while pretending to enlighten them. Like everyone else, Lila had been struck by the group's uncommon beauty when they swanned into the restaurant all pimp and peacock (physical beauty and a fashionista sensibility were prerequisite to being invited into the Holy Company of Beautiful People in the first place), but as soon as she overheard Ivan talk all she wanted to do was bounce an unscrewed pepper shaker off his head.

Consciousness is a field, Ivan sometimes explained. This is why just being in a guru's presence elevates your consciousness, and the implicit rationale for *satsang*. The Buddha-field, he called it. But despite his pretensions, Ivan was no spiritual Master, and the only field of consciousness he vortexed was a demon-field of narcissism, drawing everyone into a field of shallow pretense and tenuous identity. Lila had gradually realized that Ivan micromanaged every aspect of his appearance in order to flaunt his false bodhisattvic presence, and nothing made her liver quiver more than spiritual conceit. More than that, though, nothing gave her a greater sense of purpose than popping narcissistic egos—which, she had discovered, were every bit as fragile as overinflated balloons.

"Welcome to the Octopus's Garden." Lila grinned a good waitress, knowing she was about to sacrifice her tip for the satisfaction of goading her gurusional ex-boyfriend's narcissism.

"Welcome to the rest of your life," Ivan immediately interrupted her greeting, fixing a charming gaze upon her and flashing a smile that brandished a gold canine he polished to perfection every morning.

"My name is Lila," Lila gazed back dismissive, "and I'll be your server this afternoon."

"Your name is Rukmini," Ivan gazed on, insisting upon

the name he had once given her, "and your selfless service is appreciated."

"My name is *Lila*," Lila corrected him, smiling. "And since this is my job, my service here is not exactly selfless. You poking me in the third eye is appreciated neither."

The entire table fell still at this admonition, though Ivan's gaze was unfazed. "Your service, and your life, is as you wish it to be, Rukmini. You may leave your guru, but you cannot leave your karma. We create our own universe, and manifest our own destiny."

"You're very good at weaponizing a spiritual vocabulary," Lila responded, holding her gaze brazen. "But the truth becomes false when spoken by a liar, doesn't it?" She paused, never averting her eyes. "And that's quite the Svengali gaze you have there, by the way."

Still holding Lila's eyes, Ivan addressed the rest of the table. "Rukmini: Her name comes from Sanskrit. It means wife of the Lord Krishna." This elicited "ahh's" and "hmm's" from the rest of the table as they nodded knowingly at one another.

Ivan claimed to reveal his disciples' true natures with the names he bestowed upon them, but Lila obviously disliked the way Ivan presumed possession of her at the same time that he deified himself, wondering instead how to say *gimme a fucking break* in Sanskrit. Lila maintained her cool, however, continuing to meet Ivan's gaze as she addressed the rest of the table. "Svengali: The word comes from the name of a hypnotist villain in a nineteenth-century novel. It means a person who tries to completely dominate another, usually with sinister motives."

Despite the paralysis of his Botox-begotten brow, Ivan's eyes of practiced placidity momentarily darkened. Vengeance was vowed, and he wished to god that he'd lashed her less gently the time Lila had agreed to let him tie her to his king canopy, but he held his composure. "You are not among us," he dismissed and turned his eyes at last away from Lila so as to submit her to the group for instruction. "Witness the dim arrogance of the spiritually dead." He gestured in vast condescension. "Deserving of our compassion, but certainly not our attention."

Lila smiled. "Has it ever occurred to you, dear Ivan, that you are your own cult and your ego is your guru?"

"What are you speaking about now?" Ivan demeaned inattentive.

"You are your own cult," Lila pronounced again. "And your ego is your guru." Then she added cheerfully, "While you contemplate that, can I start you off with something to drink?"

Ivan smiled, his indifference feigning at the limit of its flexibility. In fact, all he wanted to do was to heap opprobrium upon this fresh-mouthed little tart of a traitor who presumed to see through his masks, but he had to keep up appearances for his disciples. "My only request, Rukmini my child, is that you realize the truth that your thoughts create your reality."

Lila paused long, blinking. "Yes," she nodded at last. "I've manifested this, haven't I? I attracted this into my life."

"Yes!" one of Ivan's disciples, Illuminata, whispered in earnest assistance, silenced immediately by a wave of Ivan's manicured hand.

Lila's eyes lit up. "That means you must have manifested *me*, that you attracted this into your life as well, isn't that right?" Hijacking a pitcher of ice water from a passing tray, Lila bowed graciously. "Thank you for this awakening, oh ascended Master."

Ivan, so narcissistic that he couldn't tell when he was being mocked, had time to nod in blessing and bliss before the liter of ice water splotched into his lap.

Jolted beyond any pretense of enlightened aplomb, Ivan

gasped "What—!?" before roaring undignified, "—the fuck are you doing!?"

Lila smiled wild as a storm of indignation shockwaved across the table, displacing the din of the restaurant with an awesome and head-swiveling rush of hush. Lila smiled wilder still when she realized her job would not survive Ivan's tantrum. Turning to leave, she blithely answered the wrath of Ivan. "I'm creating my own reality, of course."

10

I AM SO fucking enlightened, Ivan had congratulated himself earlier that Saturday morning, gazing out across the two hundred or so faces of his disciples gathered before him in *satsang.* Ivan was the only person in the room with his eyes open; everyone else's eyelids were scrunched in determined serenity, eyes turned up in desperately mystical contemplation of their third eye. Ivan's eyes were supposed to be closed in meditation as well, but he enjoyed spying on everyone this way. It left him free to ogle whomever he pleased.

Ivan was thus unavoidably startled when his eyes happened to meet the wide-open eyes of Dalai, one of his most contrary disciples. Thanks to the facial paralysis from his recent Botox injections, however, no sign of surprise revealed itself on his face. Ivan simply met Dalai's gaze with faux equanimity, gazing deeply into her suspicious eyes until she closed them in submission. Later, after leading his disciples in a closing round of *Oo-fa-kay-fa-lay-lay,* Ivan let everyone know that he had begun wearing a turban in order to contain his expanding crown chakra and delay his imminent dematerialization, and reminded them that there was a very good chance that he would ascend into the higher realms during an upcoming total solar eclipse. Then he said that he'd felt someone had "dark energy" that morning, and asked to speak with Dalai afterward. The implication was clear as all heads swiveled in Dalai's direction.

Oo-fa-kay-fa-lay-lay, by the way, was a Polynesian prayer of obscure origin that according to Ivan meant, "May we know ourselves!" It was sung in a round at varying octaves and with increasing enthusiasm, and went something like this:

What the Bible thinks it knows is how our spirit grows
Oooooooo…
Oo-fa-kay-fa-lay-lay!

What the Koran thinks it knows is how our spirit grows
Oooooooo…
Oo-fa-kay-fa-lay-lay!

What the Pope thinks he knows is how our spirit grows
Oooooooo…
Oo-fa-kay-fa-lay-lay!

What the Lama thinks he knows is how our spirit grows
Oooooooo…
Oo-fa-kay-fa-lay-lay!

What the Preacher thinks he knows
is how our spirit grows
Oooooooo…
Oo-fa-kay-fa-lay-lay!

What the Rabbi thinks he knows is how our spirit grows
Oooooooo…
Oo-fa-kay-fa-lay-lay!

And on and on until their collective effervescence had them
howling and cheering and dancing and convulsing in spiritual
ecstasy upon the floor. Ivan, especially, was invariably possessed
by the holy hysterical whenever this song was sung, for not only
had Ivan invented the song, but he was also the only one who
knew that *Oo-fa-kay-fa-lay-lay* was actually Hawaiian street
slang for "fucked in the ass."

11

IT'S A SIGN of a low level of evolution to open your eyes
during *satsang*," Ivan scolded Dalai as she knelt at his feet.
"But your eyes were open, Master."
"Yes, Dalai, but only because I sensed some dark energy."
"But Master," Dalai protested, "isn't all energy light? I don't
understand what you mean by dark energy."
Ivan smiled at her in lofty compassion. "You're in your
mind again, Dalai. If you want to experience the Wisdom, you
have to sarrendar your ego. This is not news to you," Ivan reprimanded. "The path to the Wisdom is very clear: Only by serving an awakened Master and accepting his guidance can you
defeat your ego and realize God. You have chosen me as your
guru, Dalai, and I tell you this: If you don't accept my guidance you will lose your shot at enlightenment and be reborn for
countless lifetimes."

"But you said God is within," Dalai responded despondent. "Why would the Wisdom come from without? And what's wrong with being alive? Master, I don't understand any of this."

Ivan made a show of closing his eyes momentarily, fluttering his eyelids as his pupils rolled back in his head as if he were fanning through the pages of the akashic records—the alleged universal library of all experience. "I cannot see clearly enough whether it is your karma to receive the Wisdom in this life, Dalai. Perhaps you are not yet ready for the Holy Company of Beautiful People. Perhaps you prefer the company of *the dead*." Ivan turned his eyes away in dismissal as he pronounced *the dead*. *The dead* was how Ivan referred to anyone who was not in the Holy Company of Beautiful People, but for Dalai, it also reminded her of the fact that she was sick with metastatic breast cancer, and Ivan had assured her that he could heal her, just as he had once healed another of his devotees—Chris Bliss—of his colorectal cancer, if only she would sarrendar her ego.

"No," Dalai replied, earnest. "I'm ready to accept your guidance, Master."

Ivan studied her apprehensive expression a long while before relieving her. "Some of the other aspirants are performing *seva* in my garden Monday morning. You should join them."

Seva, yes, selfless service to make life easier for others. "But Master," Dalai protested her selfless service, "I have to work on Monday, and I can't afford to lose my benefits. Master, you know I'm sick."

Ivan sighed and stood up, pausing to caress a thumb he'd dabbed with peppermint oil against Dalai's third eye before turning to go. This was how he gave *shakti*—primordial cosmic energy—to his disciples, as the cool burn of the peppermint oil assisted in the illusion that something was actually happening. "Follow me," he commanded as the peppermint oil tingled upon Dalai's forehead as if it were the sparkling echo of Ivan's divine touch, "and let the dead bury their dead."

12

T HE WISDOM, as Ivan explained to the Holy Company of Beautiful People, was nothing short of the Philosopher's Stone, the elixir of immortality and the fruit of the Tree of Life. According to Ivan, it was during a visit to the Great Pyramid at Giza years ago that a delegation of transdimensional extraterrestrial Egyptian deities revealed to him his bodhisattva nature and presented him with the Philosopher's Stone, a dollop of amber with a mosquito inside that had been fossilized from the sap of the Tree of Life. This amulet conferred immortality and an assortment of supernatural powers upon him and him alone, as well as revealing to him the wisdom of the sages. (For the record, incidentally, Ivan had actually shoplifted this amber amulet from a retired French shopkeeper in Hamelin, Germany, while he was backpacking across Europe many years ago, long before he'd snorted his oil brat trust fund up his nose—a trust fund that had served to assure him that he was born into a divine destiny as an enlightened Brahmin and thereby entitled to great wealth as a result of his holiness in a previous life.)

"Wisdom," Ivan defined, "is seeing what is normally hidden. I see the Vastness where you see the limited, and if you wish to receive the Wisdom you must follow my guidance." Claiming such expansive vision, Ivan succeeded in overriding all logic, suspicion, and common sense among his followers.

After all, if he could see the Vastness, and thereby see much more deeply and clearly into their spiritual journeys than they, then by following his guidance, they could succeed in one day attaining the Wisdom themselves.

And who but a fool would question the wisdom of a bodhisattvic ascended Master who could cure cancer?

13

THE HAPPIEST DAY of Chris Bliss's life was the day he met the bodhisattvic ascended Master who would one day cure him of his colorectal cancer.

Having relocated to the Bay Area during an earlier phase of the tech sector's relentless boom-and-bust cycles, Chris Bliss had accepted a job at an internet startup that offered a thin salary supplemented with generous stock options that they promised would eventually be worth millions—so long as everyone worked seventy-plus hours a week. Chris Bliss happily threw his fortune onto that improbable ship, grateful at least that the job enabled him to more or less avoid spending any time alone.

But the improbable ship did not prove itself seaworthy once the economy tanked, and his stock options ended up being worthless. Thereby, Chris Bliss found himself unemployed and gazing into the sewers of his own solitude for weeks on end. Motivational audiobooks monotoned any time he spent alone in his car, and he set his television to turn on with his morning alarm and again a half hour before he expected to be home in the evening. As for his days, he desperately located and scheduled free classes around the Bay Area—anything not to be alone with himself—and consequently wound up attending a free yoga class in Dolores Park every afternoon. As time went by, a lithe yogini by the name of Illuminata began striking up conversations with him after class, offering to trade massages, asking him out with the rest of the group for tea, and eventually inviting him to a secret yoga class led by a bona fide ascended Master. Illuminata made him promise not to tell anyone about the ascended Master, and she kissed him when he agreed.

The ascended Master, of course, was Ivan, and his secret yoga class was unlike anything Chris Bliss had ever experienced. Located in a palatial private residence in the Presidio Heights, Ivan led the group of fifty or so in a Polynesian chant that he said meant "may we know ourselves" as helpers circulated throughout, adjusting asanas, massaging tight muscles, and whispering words of blessing into the ears of the practitioners. When the class was over, Ivan personally welcomed Chris Bliss into their mystery school, underlining the importance of secrecy, and invited him to sit in the center of the circle for a game he called How Good Can You Stand It? The game was simple. For the next fifteen minutes, Ivan and the others showered him with compliments, and it was there that Chris Bliss, terrified of being alone, learned that he was actually brave. He also learned that he possessed a disarming smile, that he was a warrior, a great leader, and a hundred other hyperboles. Chris Bliss lapped it up, as happy as a stray cat over a saucer of self-esteem.

Based on his conversations with Illuminata, Ivan had already surmised that Chris Bliss was just about the loneliest sad sack he'd ever met. Consequently, within a year Ivan invited Chris Bliss into his inner circle, with all its attendant status advantages, and shortly thereafter—during a private, therapeutic session Ivan called a Healing—Ivan informed Chris Bliss that he believed him to be his successor. "This is your lifetime to ascend," Ivan assured him, his voice wavering with feigned emotion, "so long as you follow the guidance of your guru." Ivan turned away and began to weep softly. When Chris Bliss offered him a handkerchief and asked him what was the matter, Ivan explained that he was thinking of his own deceased Master, and of how much he loved him. Chris Bliss wept as well at this revelation, realizing how much he ought to love his Master if he were to ascend, and he promised that he would follow Ivan's guidance. Ivan smiled, and offered him the used handkerchief to keep as a relic.

During the next Healing, Ivan, looking gently concerned, explained to Chris Bliss that he could sense that Chris Bliss's anxiety had provoked a colorectal cancer to take hold in him. But not to worry, Ivan immediately reassured him, for he could cure him as long as he followed his guru's guidance. Alarmed, Chris Bliss again promised that he would, but then, during their next Healing, Chris Bliss reported that he'd seen a doctor who did not confirm the diagnosis. Ivan shook his head sadly and withdrew, saying only how disappointed he was in him before abruptly ending the session.

The following week found Chris Bliss strangely abandoned, as everyone in the Holy Company of Beautiful People who had been close to him—including Illuminata—had been warned by Ivan that it was perilous to their spiritual journeys to associate with Chris Bliss at this time. Of course, they were not to let him know about this directive, and as a consequence, in his next Healing, Chris Bliss broke down, tearfully confessing to Ivan that he was absolutely unable to control his anxiety, which had grown so large as to become paranoia. Ivan held him in a deep embrace for a long while, whispering "my child" again and again. At the close of the Healing, Ivan explained to Chris Bliss that anxiety is the sound of colorectal cancer in its early stages, and cautioned him to steer clear of Western doctors. "You may as well hire a mechanic to grow an orchid," Ivan chastised.

Then, Ivan announced Chris Bliss's colorectal cancer to the entire Holy Company of Beautiful People. "Passion refers to the passion of the Christ," Ivan explained, "and com-passion is short for community passion. What happens to one of us happens to all of us, and by sharing in one another's suffering we lessen the burdens that may befall any one of us." Under Ivan's direction, the Holy Company of Beautiful People offered Chris Bliss fountains of compassion, arranging daily massages, preparing all his meals, and sitting with him such that he would never be alone as he reflected upon his mortality and spiritual journey.

And two weeks later, in a miraculous Healing attended by the entire Holy Company of Beautiful People, Ivan healed Chris Bliss of the colorectal cancer that he never had.

14

USTOMARILY, a tankard of ale has a glass bottom. Tradition holds that this was useful to the British peasantry for checking to see if a shilling had been dropped into their tankard unawares by an agent of the Royal Navy. In this case, if some poor sop drank his ale before finding the shilling, he was considered to have accepted the King's shilling and thereby to have volunteered to serve in the Royal Navy, and he would find himself at sea by morning.

Thus it was that most of the men sailing under His Majesty's flag had been pressed into service in the first place, either kidnapped from their farms by press-gangs or drunk under the table in a pub only to awaken miles out to sea and suddenly subject to the unforgiving rigors of military discipline. Except when he pitied them, Crow loathed the Royal (and any other colonial) Navy. There was a time when Crow hesitated to kill such victims of circumstance, but that was a long time ago. Now he considered them a bunch of ankle-grabbing cowards for not revolting against their kidnappers, and regardless of how they had found themselves in their situation, and regardless of any consequences they might suffer, they still had to choose to follow orders, and if those orders had anything to do with killing another person for trying to get free, then Crow had no qualms about releasing them from their feeble-minded fates.

After all, Crow had hardly had an easy run in life himself, and knew that any man was only as free as he insisted on being. Orphaned at an early age due to his parents' confinement in debtor's prison, he'd grown up in an orphanage under the tutelage of Mother Marie, a nun who reminded the orphans under her care every single morning after the rosary that they should have never even been born, that they were a burden on the rest of society, and that they should be grateful that they got anything at all. Mother Marie was not one to spare the rod, and Crow suffered the ducking stool for every minor infraction, even being hung by his thumbs when he persisted in his sass and smartassery. But he did learn to read.

Crow twice ran away from the factory in which he was forced to work as a teenager, had his first taste of a grommeted belt the second time, and promptly escaped again the next morning. Finding his way to a port, he volunteered as a redemptioner, signing and biting a contract with a ship's captain who would allow him indentured passage to the West Indies. Once landed, according to the contract, he would have a set number of days to find a redeemer—a planter who would buy his passage paper and for whom Crow could then work off his indentured servitude. Crow had examined his bite mark—the *indenture*—that notched every copy of the contract, ostensibly as positive identification, and had every intention of honoring this arrangement, but once they neared port, the ship's captain had Crow placed in the brig, forcibly detaining him until his contract had lapsed so that he could sell him for greater profit at auction.

Enraged and despising anyone who presumed to direct the

course of his life, Crow ran away from the plantation owner who purchased him. After some days of hunger, the Fates found favor upon him and he fell in with a tribe of surviving Arawak living free in the jungle and ambushing Spaniards for livelihood and vengeance. Indeed, in crossing their path Crow would likely have been killed himself if he had not charmed them by being able to play a cavaquinho one of them carried, and being himself faster than the cleanest pair of heels, it was not long before he ran as free as they and as free as he'd ever been, though not before enduring their initiation ceremony.

The initiation ceremony consisted of painting Crow's face with mud, and once the mud had dried, the itinerant shaman named Joe tattooed their totem—an intricately designed cross inspired by the Arawak's early contact with Western missionaries—upon Crow's back. During this ordeal, the remaining men of the tribe leveled their spears upon Crow with the warning that they'd run him through if the slightest single crack appeared in the mud mask now dried upon his face. The tattoo was excruciating, but the mask upon Crow's face remained indifferent.

It was among such wild company that Crow eventually learned the spear, and also there that Crow learned of their oral history, of how two centuries earlier a quarter million of their peaceable ancestors had been wiped out within two decades of opening their arms to the *Niña*, the *Pinta*, and the *Santa María*, half of them within the first two years. They told him unimaginable tales of slavery and slaughter, stories of starving women drowning their own infants when they could no longer produce milk, and of men worked to death digging for gold that was never there while their captors boasted the sharpness of their blades to one another by casually slicing their captives' bodies.

Horrifying, but none of it really surprised Crow. He had

suffered inexcusable abuses himself, and in his short time on Haiti he had already observed morbidly obese landowners being hauled around by sedan chair–bearing slaves while other slaves shaded them with banana leaves and fanned at the grease oozing from the aristocrat's overfed pores. It was all just another day in hell, and he was used to it. No, what surprised Crow were the stories his Arawak brethren told of the lives their ancestors led before the arrival of the Europeans, lives of purpose in service to one another, of hospitality, of sharing, and of love. Here was the human nature Crow had always sensed, and why he had been so baffled by the world in which he found himself.

Crow lived with the Arawak for years, accepting the name they gave him and adopting their view of the Spaniards, enthusiastically participating in their traps, ambushes, and attacks on any soldiers who ventured into the jungle interior of the island. Crow quickly became a valued asset to their tribe, mastering the cane spear to such a degree of excellence that he could snatch clean out of the air any spear thrown at him with the palm-out side of his right hand, instantly rotate it 180 degrees, and send it sailing back at his assailant all in one lethal motion.

Thus would they arrange their ambushes: Crow, having taught himself some Spanish, would dress in the costume of the Spanish gentry. Then, with a jug of rum in his fist, Crow would confront a company of soldiers and loudly announce that he was impervious to the spear. Thence predictably followed much scoffery and a general brouhaha, but in the end they were always sport to slaughter a fool, and some rum-stinking cretin would venture to hurl his spear at Crow only to discover his own death before his exertion had even exhaled. Then, before the surrounding astounded could finish a blink, a hail of spears and arrows fell upon them from every direction, the

Arawak having enveloped the party while it was distracted with Crow's quixotic braggadocio.

When asked how he managed this trick so effortlessly, Crow attributed it to some mythical Viking heritage he imagined himself as having. This wasn't true, probably, and meant nothing to the Arawak in any event, but the itinerant shaman Joe nonetheless rewarded his contributions to the tribe by giving him a honeycomb-encrusted pair of dice he'd allegedly pulled out of an angry beehive without suffering a single sting. These dice, the itinerant shaman Joe said, would always land dogs—a pair of ones—and a worthless, losing roll in the sailor's dice game of hazard.

But only, the itinerant shaman Joe shouted as he slapped Crow's forehead and broke into a roaring guffaw, when he pitched them with his left hand.

15

LIFE ON A Royal Navy ship was about as far removed from life on *Eleusis* as an ocean could ever imagine. Before Flaming Jane had rechristened the *Queen Elizabeth* as *Eleusis*, it was little more than a floating prison, kidnapped men pressed into naval service and compelled under the whip into grueling work to serve the interests of a distant Crown that cared nothing for their welfare.

Admiral Jasper, captain of the *Queen Elizabeth*, certainly cared nothing for his men—whom he considered mere pawns serving his own rancid ambition of ensuring his place in English society—any more than he cared for his wife, whom he had kidnapped and educated only so that she might be well mannered upon his arm. A ruthless privateer, Admiral Jasper sailed under a letter of marque that gave him permission to plunder Spanish ships, seizing any cargo that provided him and the Crown profit, and sharing very little of it. Naturally, such arrangements would not long resist mutiny if he didn't distribute some of the wealth to his officers, which he did, and they in turn violently repressed any resistance from growing within the ranks of the remaining crew. The remaining crew, in turn, had greater privileges than any slaves who had been taken aboard, and imagined that they would one day ascend the hierarchy themselves. In such fashion was gross inequality maintained across a ship and throughout an empire.

Indeed, it was widely regarded aboard the *Queen Elizabeth* that the true captain of the ship was not Admiral Jasper, but the "captain's daughter," otherwise known as "the cat." The cat was a cat-o'-nine-tails, a flogging whip unbraided into nine thrice-knotted tails. The cat was hung in a blood-red baize bag on the main mast for all to see (and the origin of the phrase, "who let the cat out of the bag," incidentally), and Admiral Jasper made certain that the crew assembled at least once a week to witness the flogging of some offender of military discipline. In the event that there were no recent infractions, he would simply have a slave tied to a cannon and their back opened with lashes, all the while taunting the crew to object—"What's the matter, swabbies, the cat got your tongue?!"—just to ensure that discipline was properly prodded.

Once, after several weeks of no breach of discipline from the crew, Admiral Jasper grew paranoid that a mutiny was brewing. Once his officers had tied one of the slaves to a cannon and his first mate was about to mete out a dozen lashes, Admiral Jasper seized the cat-o'-nine-tails from his hands and stalked back and forth in front of the crew, glaring at them as if he were about to lash the lot of them across their faces right there. Then, without warning, he drew his sword and beheaded the slave with a hack and a half.

Flaming Jane (still a merely tame Jane at the time) had been petting a purring Catface and anxiously watching all this transpire from the portal of the Admiral's quarters—the room from which she was forbidden to leave unescorted by him, since superstition held that it was bad luck to have a woman at sea. She observed her husband clumsily chase after the slave's head as it tumbled across the deck, eventually seizing hold of it by the hair to display its still-twitching face to his men as he roared reprobation upon them.

Turning away in horror as Catface jumped from her lap, Jane felt the first spasm of an immense sob begin to overtake her. But it was a grief much too deep to permit, and in its stead she bit her lip until it bled as her eyes narrowed upon the Admiral's maps and charts spread upon the table and she began to plan her mutiny.

16

ON THE MONDAY following the illegal Halloween parade, Lila kept thinking it was Sunday.

"I keep thinking it's Sunday," Lila said to Merlin, who had spent the last couple of days attending to Lila's pleasure, leaving only when she dispatched him for more wine, chocolate, ice cream sandwiches, and celery, the staples of her kitchen, though Merlin supplemented it with quinoa, Tuscan kale, sprouted almonds, grass-fed buffalo, Romanesco broccoli, wild-caught Alaskan salmon, ginger kombucha, pink Himalayan salt freshly ground upon bananas drizzled with pomegranate molasses, and sundry other organic provisions.

"It *is* Sunday," Merlin assured her, even though it was not. "If it was Monday, I'd be at work. There's the pudding if you're looking for the proof."

"Pudding?" Lila replied brightly. "Did you buy pudding?"

"I did not," he admitted as Lila pouted dramatic, only to be interrupted by her dog, a Tanzanian zebra shepherd that looked just exactly as you might imagine. The Tanzanian zebra shepherd, Lila had explained to Merlin, was a rare breed developed by the Tanzanian government to herd zebras and keep them from wandering outside the boundaries of Serengeti National

Park. They were illegal to export, but she had managed to smuggle a puppy out by dyeing it completely black. Merlin had blinked momentarily at her story and immediately declared a grinning bullshit, impressing the heck out of Lila, as he was the first person she'd met since dyeing zebra stripes on her white shepherd mix a week ago for Halloween who had seen through her ludicrous account—everyone else just gushed oh my god that's so awesome. The truth of the pigmentation is that Lila's dog was completely white but for a jet-black face that looked as if it had stuck its head out the window of a speeding car under a new moon and stained its face a windblown midnight. Dogface, Lila had named her—Mutatananda Digbert Dogface, actually—and Dogface jumped onto the bed all wag and pant.

"Dogface," Lila cooed, wiping the boogers from her dog's eyes as Merlin looked on. Merlin was enamored of Lila, the beautiful Lila, but he remained uncertain of how he felt about Dogface. For one thing, Dogface had sat next to the bed, whining and growling every time they'd made love that weekend, falling quiet upon reprimand only to proceed to lick herself into auto-cunnilingual leg spasms. And now, here was Dogface happily lapping her own eye boogers off Lila's fingertips.

Merlin's cell phone vibrated on the table, interrupting his contemplation and swiveling all of their heads. Glancing at the caller ID, Merlin furrowed his brow and turned it off. "Work?" Lila inquired, a note of dismay flattening her voice.

"I hope it doesn't offend you to discover that I've never been much of a worker." Merlin yawned and tossed his phone aside. "At least insofar as working for somebody else. As a matter of holy fact," he jerked a demonstrative thumb toward his own chest, "I've been fired or quit on a day's notice from every job I've ever held." He smiled as if this were a point of pride, which for Lila, it was. This was, after all, two mornings after she'd tossed that liter of ice water into Ivan's lap and abandoned her waitress job, the tale of which Merlin had thoroughly applauded. "Besides," Merlin went on, "They should know better than to call me on a Sunday. It's the Sabbath, for fuck's sake. Let's keep it goddamn holy." Merlin paused and glanced at Lila. "I hope my indelicate language doth not wound thy gentle ears."

"Uh, what-the-fuck-ever," Lila snorted. "I already told you I was a gawdamn sailor, a pirate, I tell ye."

"I'm just sayin'," Merlin sassed. "I've been known to cuss the pistols off pissed-off pirates."

Lila's eyes sparkled in a copulatory gaze. "I adore you."

"You *adore* me?" Merlin sat up. "Adore?" Standing, he grabbed a heavy dictionary off the top of Lila's bookcase. "It should be interesting to discover what *that* means." Plopping down on the bed again, he fanned through a few pages before settling on one.

"You don't know what *adore* means?"

"*Adore*," Merlin pronounced, reading, "'To like or admire very much. To regard with the utmost esteem and affection.'" He looked at her, grinning idiotic.

"Yes," Lila grinned back. "I regard you with the utmost esteem and affection."

"It also says," Merlin continued, "'to worship as a deity.'"

Lila rolled her eyes in recollection of her ex-boyfriend Ivan's unparalleled spiritual narcissism. "Yes, well, despite your manscaped chest, don't go chiseling an idol of yourself just yet. We'll just go with the first meaning."

Merlin regarded his manscaped chest. "You have to keep a clean temple if you want to host a proper Dionysian debauch from time to time," he explained.

"A *proper* Dionysian debauch," Lila repeated, reaching

forward and teasing one of his nipples. "I suppose a little vanity in the name of a good party never hurt."

"I'm not vain." He brushed her hand away.

"Everybody's vain." Lila reached for his other nipple. "Ask any plateglass window on a busy sidewalk. So tell me, dear Dionysus, how tall is your cock?"

"How should I know?" Merlin snorted, brushing her hand away again. "What, you think I've measured it or something?"

"Uh, yes."

Merlin waved her off, grinning as he returned his attention to the dictionary.

"I'll bet you smirk at the clerk when you buy your Magnums," Lila pronounced, continuing her teasing.

Merlin ignored her, pretending to study the dictionary. "Maybe you could *revere* me, how about that?"

"*Revere?*" Lila chided. "Why Merlin, I thought you a proper prankster. Doesn't your handy dictionary there teach you that 'revere' comes from a Latin root meaning 'to be afraid of'?"

Merlin furrowed his brow and again fanned through the pages. "Comes from the Latin *revereri*," he confirmed. "'To stand in fear or awe,' and etymologically synonymous with wary." He shrugged his chin. "How about that?"

Lila nodded. "That's where the term *God-fearing* comes from, and who ever heard of a God-fearing child? As it turns out, reverence is cowardice and irreverence is courage, as a God-cheering prankster like yourself would doubtless agree."

Merlin closed the dictionary. "I knew there was a reason I kept you around."

Lila smiled. "As if you have any choice. But you're going to have to settle for adore."

"Adore," Merlin tested it upon his tongue.

"I adore you," Lila affirmed.

Merlin leaned forward and kissed Lila softly about her neck, and as Dogface first began to whine and then to masturbate, Merlin whispered, "And I adore you more."

17

OWING TO HIS TENURE as a bicycle courier, Merlin did lots of handstands. Unrestrained in their reasoning, his courier crew had developed a fervent theory among themselves that the ego was a simpleminded artifact of humanity's upright posture and consequent lack of sufficient blood flow to the brain. The ego, they reasoned, is nothing but the skeletal leftovers of true, enlightened consciousness, basically the carcass of brute survival we're left with when we drain the brain of all its visionary vitality, and probably also why humanity is so lacking in common sense. Allegedly, this is also why yogis stand on their heads to reach nirvana.

Merlin had long since doubted that any of their pole vaults of hypomanic reasoning were ever even remotely based in fact, especially since he specifically enjoyed grandstanding his Jedi Master handstand push-ups in public parks, and if that was supposed to be nirvana then nirvana certainly enjoyed looking like a badass. In any event, Merlin practiced his handstands every day, and this is precisely where he placed himself as Lila showered that morning. Intermittently, he returned Dogface's upside down gaze, vaguely wondering how such a silly beast could manage to simultaneously appear both regal and forlorn, but mostly he let his eyes roam about Lila's room as his mind roamed about its own recollections.

Just a couple of days ago, Merlin had returned from his
Borneo misadventure, ostensibly to witness the total solar
eclipse expected to shadow the Bay in a few weeks. He had been
vaguely pinning his redemption on the upcoming eclipse, hoping for something somehow transformative, or at least something greater than a wow and brow-furrowed appreciation of
celestial mechanics. But an unpleasant encounter in a parking
lot on the day he arrived back had underlined for Merlin just
how lost he'd gotten as he'd stumbled around the planet fleeing
the pain in his own heart.

Merlin had been circling the crowded parking lot at the
Berkeley Bowl for five minutes, surfing for a spot, feeling
lonely as the unavailability of parking spaces seemed to mirror his own solitude. Merlin was not one of those creepers
who stalk after someone returning to their car. He preferred
to just go with the flow till a space naturally opened up, and
so he enjoyed a minor victory when someone's reverse lights
suddenly illuminated just ahead of him. Flicking his turn signal on, Merlin mused that parking lots were like love: It only
appears as if all the spaces are already taken, but in fact cars
are constantly moving into and out of parking spaces, just
like people are constantly moving into and out of relation-
ships until they find their life partner, and therefore it's all
about timing, about going with the flow, and nobody likes a
creeper. Feeling pleased with his parking lot epiphany as the
car backed out of its parking space, Merlin was waiting for
it to pull forward so that he'd be clear to pull into the space
when another car came careening around the corner from the
wrong direction and screeched into the empty parking space.

Before he even knew what he was doing, Merlin had
slammed his car into park and gotten out, rapping upon the
driver's-side window of the car that'd stolen his spot. A teenager

sat in the driver's seat, now texting on his cell phone, and the teenager looked at Merlin and laughed, sliding out of his car with an entitled smirk upon his face. "Hey, man," the teenager drawled, taunting his car keys in front of Merlin's face. "What can I say, bro? You gotta be faster on the draw—"

Without a thought, Merlin slapped the keys out of the teenager's hand. "Is that fast enough for you?" Merlin yelled, his voice bellowing a greater roar with each sentence he spoke. "Now pick up your keys, get back in your car, pull out of that spot, and *wait your turn like everybody else!*" Startled, the teenager immediately did as Merlin commanded. That might have been a satisfying turn for some, but although Merlin could be physically imposing, he didn't get off on being an asshole, and the whole encounter only succeeded in irreparably souring his mood, disgusted that he'd been so diminished as to have to squabble over a parking space in the first place.

The next day was Halloween, and still suffering an anger hangover born of his own road rage, Merlin wandered across the face of Creation's ugly stepsister—his neighborhood in Oakland. The bleak East Bay landscape may just as well have been the lowest level of Dante's Inferno, though no flames could ever taunt that frozen lake of lovelessness. A relentless and unspoken mockery insisted upon narrating Merlin's point of view as he dodged bumshit on the sidewalk, unbearable hideousness assaulting him at every turn: Here a woman gimped her way past in high heels, pulling at her muffin-topped miniskirt as she broadcast for a boyfriend; here an old man bragged to his cohorts about how he used to be able to catch a fly out of midair, eyes bulging from the face draped over his skull, daring anyone to disbelieve how amazing he once was as his rickety arm lurched demonstrative at an imaginary fly and nearly toppled him off balance; here a child with chocolate frosting on his inflated face carried an orange tabby by the pits of its front legs, slinging it side to side as it mrowled its discontent; here an aged and hairy transvestite in Coca-Cola stretch pants goaded revulsion from passersby, nodding as he nonplussed them with his tennis-ball tits, and here a man with an attitude uglier than his car extended his middle finger at the pinnacle of his pipe-stem arm in a lethargic fuck-you salute toward another scowling driver.

Merlin put on his sunglasses, as if that would somehow shield him from the glare of his own misanthropy. *Bunch of knuckle-dragging mouth-breathers*, the cantankerous voice in his head groused as a street preacher across the way yelled, "If you would just listen to me!" before furrowing his brow and thumbing holy determined through his King James Bible as a young woman wearing a T-shirt proclaiming I Believe in Unicorns wandered past Merlin, pulling on her dreadlocks and chattering into her smartphone about how her dreads helped her "listen to Jah" as she looked away from a passed-out homeless man drooling on yesterday's newspaper pillow. Meanwhile, a morbidly obese man carrying a bag of fast food seeped along in front of him, and a hunch-shouldered hands-jammed-in-his-jeans twentysomething sauntered aimless and alone, the brim of his camouflage cap pulled so far down that his face was entirely obscured as he presumably counted chewing gum stains on the sidewalk upon which he slacked at the dust.

Not watching where he was going, the twentysomething in the camouflage cap almost collided with another pedestrian, some striding douchebag in a sweaty suit who alerted him with an annoyed "Watch it!" The twentysomething in the camouflage cap stopped short and glanced up, reflex unplugging his hand from his pocket in order to hide the now-visible scar tissue on his neck and lower face from offending the eyes of the douchebag in the sweaty suit, who happened to glimpse the burn scars anyway and startle away.

However roaring with cynicism Merlin's ill mood had been, his abject contempt flipped immediately into the deepest, most heartbreaking compassion at the sight of the twentysomething in the camouflage cap's single gesture of mortified concealment. Whatever war-torn mishap had caused his burns, it also managed to incinerate Merlin's cynicism as he witnessed the man's loneliness, his fear of being rejected, his isolation and alienation, and it was just the same as the woman crippling along in high heels hoping to please the ubiquitous male gaze, it was just the same as the old braggart trying to convince others of his continued worth, it was just the same as the piggish child finding consolation in the company of cats, it was just the same as the transvestite demonstrating his identity to himself through the eyes of others, it was just the same as the driver fending his way through a hostile world armed only with a defiant middle finger, it was just the same as the street preacher looking for truth in something that deceives as easily as words, it was just the same as the shallow young woman in dreadlocks seeking something more meaningful than materialism, it was just the same as the homeless man drowning his hopelessness in a bottomless bottle, it was just the same as the obese man nurturing himself with junk food, it was just the same as the douchebag distracting his existential terror with ambition, and it was just the same as Merlin's own contempt trying to convince himself that he was different from all these other lost souls. It was all just the same, the same crying shame, the same dying game, and it was all Merlin could do not to fall madly in love with the world and all its fools.

18

I<small>T WAS BUT</small> several hours after Merlin fell madly in love with the world and all its fools that he met Lila, and the timing of their rendezvous was not lost upon him. Merlin had made a different set of decisions than he otherwise would have made that day, and a different set of doors had consequently opened, and one of them was the door to the bedroom of the beautiful Lila—although, as it happened, Merlin actually had to pick the lock on her door since she had lost the key to her apartment amidst the Halloween festivities. Happily, Merlin's amateur locksmithing impressed the hell out of Lila and she did not hesitate to invite him in, and though the rumpus set a certain Tanzanian zebra shepherd a-snarl, Merlin did not hesitate to follow.

"Yes and nectar!" Lila had beamed two days ago once they were inside her apartment in Berkeley, raising her glass in toast to their first sip of cabernet together. *Yes and nectar.* Merlin had no idea what such an inspired toast was supposed to mean, but it had an immediate effect on him nonetheless, filling him with an awe, and an adoration, that remained two days later.

"Yes and nectar," Merlin now mumbled upside down in his handstand as Lila finished her shower, feeling like he was struggling to remember something he had never before heard. "What does that even mean, Dogface?" Dogface perked her ears and briefly panted, but there was no time to further this inquiry as a tap upon the window swerved their attention. Coming out of his handstand and shaking his arms, Merlin followed Dogface, whose wagging tail wiggled her entire torso and assured Merlin that there was no cause for alarm. And indeed there was not, for there, alit upon the fire escape outside the window, was a parrot ablaze in its flamboyant plumage of red, blue, and yellow.

"Yes and nectar," the parrot announced, ducking its head this way and that.

Astonished, Merlin said nothing. After a moment, a chuckle escaped his lips.

"Yes and nectar," the parrot said again, then let loose a cry that sounded perfectly orgasmic before fluttering off into the morning mist of Berkeley.

19

U PON RECOUNTING the details of an orgasmic parrot on the fire escape that twice pronounced her *yes and nectar* salutation, Merlin half expected that Lila would distrust the truth of his tale. This was not at all the case, however, as Lila simply smiled delighted and cried, "Moby is back!" as she ran dripping wet and naked to the window. Then she added, drawing upon the credibility the appearance of the parrot presumably lent her, "I told you I was a gawdamn pirate."

Moby, it turned out, was her nickname for the parrot, though as she explained it, he had really taken the name himself. As was usually the case when she was alone at home, Lila had been entirely naked the first time the parrot had appeared on her fire escape—naked, that is, except for her Möbius band pendant. After they'd assessed each other in silence for a few moments, the parrot had smartly proclaimed, "Möbius." Lila called him Moby for short.

Despite his own encounter with the uncanny parrot, Merlin was skeptical. "Möbius?" he repeated. "You're telling me Moby comprehends Euclidian geometry?"

"What a little voyeur," Lila happily continued. "He was probably watching us all weekend."

"He did sound exactly like your orgasms," Merlin admitted glumly. Between Dogface's masturbation and Moby's voyeurism, he was feeling uneasy with the bestial lust surrounding their sexuality.

"I don't doubt it," Lila replied, scanning the sky outside the window to her fire escape. "I've heard him make dozens of sounds, and he knows hundreds of words. In fact," she turned toward Merlin, "Moby first said *yes and nectar* the morning of the day we met."

Merlin regarded her in silence, blinking. "That's where you came up with that toast?"

Lila nodded, allowing a hesitant pucker to her lips, as if holding back the smile to a joke only she was in on.

"You didn't make that up?"

Lila shook her head.

"So what does *yes and nectar* mean?"

Lila shrugged as her lips puckered again. "I was hoping you could tell me."

20

WHEN ADMIRAL JASPER finally awoke from Flaming Jane's mutiny over the *Queen Elizabeth*, he was greeted with the horrific discovery that he had been marooned. Far more unfortunate than this discovery, however, was the fact that his lesser crew had held him responsible for their dire circumstance of being dumped on a deserted island as well. After executing all the officers as soon as one of them attempted to press an order, the lesser crew visited their vicious displeasure upon Admiral Jasper's unconscious body, beating him severely and going as far as to cut off his lips before leaving him for dead on the shore, several of them resolving privately to themselves to return later that night and extract his gold teeth.

But the rising tide of saltwater stinging across Admiral Jasper's disfigured mouth beckoned him back to breath, and when he staggered inland seeking freshwater he shortly came across his remaining crew assembled around a spring. Cowed by the Admiral's gruesome appearance and suddenly terrified of the potential consequences should they be rescued, a path immediately parted and he was assisted with water and breathless explanations of the cruelty that the mutinous slaves had pummeled upon him and his officers. Lies and treachery, of course, for the mutineers had used only as much force as was necessary to secure the ship, but it nonetheless came to be known that Jane had personally eviscerated the Admiral's lips, that his crew had screamed in protest of this violation of their captain, that she had only sneered and said she would salt and season his lips properly before eating them, and that her red hair had burst into flames as she laughed the mad maniacal and summoned a hellish gale to drive them onto the island.

"Flames as high as her hair is long, I tell yee!"

"A demon, Captain!"

"We thought yee was dead like the rest!"

"A succubus for certain!"

"Bloody consort to the devil hisself!"

"Flaming Jane, she called herself! Flaming Jane!"

"A pirate!"

"Flaming Jane!"

"A witch!"

"It's a miracle you're alive!"

"Flaming Jane!"

"Don't worry, Captain, we'll find 'er! We'll find Flaming Jane!"

Admiral Jasper listened intently to all this as he desperately refreshed himself, grinning ghastly with rage. Standing at last, stippled sunshine gleamed off the golden teeth now gritting rictus where his lips once were. Admiral Jasper knew his admiralty and any ambitions he'd held of securing his place in English society were finished. By any estimation, whatever vanity had compelled Admiral Jasper was now deader than it ever thought it could die, and though no voice had yet uttered the nom de guerre that would soon be feared throughout the Spanish Main, Goldtooth was born in his place. Wrath boiling behind his eyes, Goldtooth unhesitantly roared his vengeance, his lipless and spittling lisp doing nothing to drain the dread from its echo.

"Aye, 'ateys! 'Ind her I shall! 'Ind her I shall!"

21

PERHAPS IT WAS ludicrous that Lila would ever attempt to make an honest living, especially when an honest living implied little more than a life of uninspiring sycophancy in service to her student loans. Individually, she may have whittled her life away slinging desperately elegant dining experiences, but with Merlin, enrapturing into unexpected love, life was much too fantastic to dim into such murk and shadow, flickering into fluorescence like some stepped-on plastic geranium.

Lila liked to say she was a pirate, but until she so dramatically abandoned her job, Lila had worked as a waitress to support herself as an artist. Inasmuch as one can be, Lila had been successful in food service. She made more tips than anyone, but as she explained to Merlin, she did so not by touching the customers friendly, nor by squatting when she took their orders, certainly not by smiling obsequious, and never ever by putting thank-you happy smiley faces on the bottoms of the bill. Rather, she did the opposite, maintaining a coolly professional demeanor throughout, deflating her customers' attempts at flirtation into an insecurity which they would then resolve by attempting to prove their worth with a soaring tip.

"Life is performance art," Lila explained to Merlin one night shortly after they met as he massaged her feet. "At work, I give customers an opportunity to experience their own self-worth instead of seeking approval outside themselves. They miss the whole point by tipping me." She sighed. "But I suppose their lack of vision cannot be helped."

"Life is performance art," Merlin repeated, working his thumb through the contours of her arch. "I am blinded by thy brilliance."

Lila smiled weakly, appreciating the encouragement but not really believing it. Lately, she'd been realizing that the phrase *starving artist* was a real thing, that society truly intended to starve every free spirit into submission. It had been easy enough to coast on the enthusiasm of her life less ordinary throughout her twenties, but now she was twenty-nine—twenty-nine-and-a-half-and-counting—and still waiting tables for salaried professionals, and now she was unemployed on top of that. It wasn't that she wanted some uptight professional salary—not at all—she just couldn't comprehend how others accepted their lives so ordinary without complaint. What was wrong with her?

"I feel like I want to just lie down and die," Lila admitted, her voice breaking as tears flowed from her eyes and Merlin moved to comfort her. "I'm so tired of trying, working, struggling." She buried her face in Merlin's chest and wept softly. Once her grief had released, she continued, strugglesome in her words. "I feel like I was never properly domesticated, you know? Why can't I find my little corner of this inhumane world and just settle in and suffer silently like everyone else? Why do I think I'm special, that the rules don't apply to me? How is everybody so able to make these decisions that I can't? What's wrong with me? Why can't I just silence the song in my soul and play by the rules?" Her eyes narrowed and she raised her voice determined. "Because I *can't*, that's why, because the rules suck and the game is fixed, and I don't ever want to look back on my life and say that I wasn't there for it!" Lila shook her head as her anger fell again into its exhaustion. "I just want to give up, you know? I know everyone suffers this way, don't they? Wrestling with the world into which we're thrown, orphans of the universe, and most of us won't give up until the moment of our death, but wouldn't it be nice to just get it over with, to surrender *right now*?"

Merlin had been watching her expression, its shades of sorrow, exhaustion, and defeat blighting her beauty, and he decided right there that he would not stand idly by and watch this outstanding woman be trampled into someone else's human resource. "Well, I sure as hell ain't here to domesticate you," he responded, interrupting her angst with a gentle tug upon her pinky toe. "I just want to help you get your paw out of that trap." When her crestfallen eyes at last met his determined grin, he pulled a scarlet glass bottle out of his nearby backpack, bubbles of imperfection antiquing its surface, its edges etched smooth. "I wasn't going to show you this till tomorrow, but I cannot bear to see your spirit smothered by such emptiness. No, not for another second can I bear it."

Lila accepted the bottle and sat up. "What's this?" she asked, her voice chirping a cheerful octave already. "Where did you find such a lovely bottle?"

"I found it yesterday on the beach," Merlin responded.

Lila uncorked the bottle. "There's a note inside," she announced, attempting to shake the message through the narrow neck.

"Here." Merlin handed her a pencil.

Lila accepted it and used the eraser tip to draw a rolled-up piece of parchment out of the bottle. She opened it gingerly, its edges cracked and burnt by time or perhaps by Merlin's lighter, and her smile grew authentic when she read the words scripted upon it:

Live Your Dream.

The parchment also flaunted a signature, fearless and flamboyant in its lawless calligraphy—*Flaming Jane.*

22

COMBINED WITH HIS zombified appearance, the turkey vultures that perpetually circled the sky above Goldtooth aroused considerable superstition among his crew. Suspicions were private or shared in hushest whisper, for all remembered the lethal beating they'd unleashed upon the Admiral, and all had heard tales of Haitian voodoo, of supernatural forces possessing the newly dead and reanimating them for some evil purpose. Once the buzzards took to perching upon Goldtooth's shoulders, rumors swelled that they were whispering the secrets of the dead in his ears, and all lived in fear for their immortal soul.

Goldtooth took to wearing a black bandana over his dentulous and disfigured mouth, pulling it down whenever he wanted to bellow a greater terror in his crew. With such demanding discipline, it was not long before they succeeded in signaling a passing ship, a galleon recently captured from the Spanish by the Royal Navy. Goldtooth assured his surviving crew that they would become his officers once on board and he had assumed command under the presumption of his admiralship. When the existing captain balked at this and began to inform him that he was no longer the admiral as a result of his wife's mutiny,

Goldtooth knifed him in the throat before he could conclude his protestation and immediately ordered his crew to arrest the captain's officers for mutiny. Goldtooth's crew, themselves greedy for rank, had been told to anticipate a skirmish and already had the officers surrounded, overpowering them easily as Goldtooth alone faced the rest of the galleon's crew, pulling his bandana down and daring "any'un else?" as a buzzard alit upon each shoulder and Goldtooth broke into the mad cackles of a reanimated skull. More than one sailor promptly pissed their breeches.

As it happened, Crow and four of his Arawak brethren were aboard the galleon, having been captured under special commission by the original Spanish captain. They were en route to be tried and hanged when the Royal Navy took the ship, and they were given slave duties under the new captain. While Crow obviously had no love for the galleon's former captain, he was certain their circumstance would only worsen under Goldtooth's command. Crow watched as Goldtooth flaunted his teeth and cruelty, and wondered how long the totemic crosses he and his Arawak brethren had tattooed across their backs would continue to shelter them from the whip.

No sooner had he wondered this than one of Goldtooth's men offered the still-cackling Goldtooth a cat-o'-nine-tails he'd freshly located. Goldtooth seized the cat with sadistic nostalgia and—still intent on establishing his absolute authority over the rest of the hijacked crew—immediately ordered one of the slaves tied to the mainmast. A stumble of fortune placed Crow's Arawak brother Gabriel in immediate reach of Goldtooth's men, and within seconds Gabriel's shirt was stripped and his wrists were cinched to the mainmast. The intricately designed cross displayed across the full canvas of Gabriel's back—the totemic cross that all of them shared—had thus far spared the lot of them from suffering the full fury of any whip. This was due not to the intervening grace of God, but rather to a widespread superstition against cutting the cross of Christ. Having experienced the cruelties of Western missionaries firsthand, this is precisely why the surviving Arawak had chosen the cross as their totem in the first place. Any lashes received were thus hesitant in their flog, and never broke the skin.

As Goldtooth wielded the cat, however, Crow knew that no cross would dissuade this demon. In one vicious swipe Goldtooth split Gabriel's cross in nine places, and though Gabriel made no sound Crow could feel the sear of Gabriel's agony pulse through his own being. A few more of those and he'd flay the skin right off Gabriel's back. Crow was not about to let that come to pass.

"Enough!" Crow heard his own voice bellow tremendous, rendering silence across the ship as Goldtooth reeled off balance from the interrupted pitch of his whip. Crow himself was surprised by his command, realizing that he had no plan whatsoever a moment before remembering that he rarely did.

"'Oo dares?!" Goldtooth thundered as two of his men seized upon Crow. As the one on his left grabbed his arm Crow's hand found the hilt of a knife sheathed in his captor's belt. In one smooth swipe he unsheathed the blade and slashed it upward and lethal across his captor's neck before a wide arc planted the knife deep into the chest of his other captor. Catching the second captor's sword and retaining the bloodied knife as the man on his right collapsed sideways, Crow was now doubly armed, and no man made another move toward him.

"Admiral." Crow immediately bowed blades down before Goldtooth. "You have inadvertently rescued me, and I bear no loyalty to any captain save you." Gesturing to the corpses at his feet, Crow continued. "I have relieved you of two of your more

worthless swabs, and I offer myself as a more capable replace-
ment." Crow genuflected before Goldtooth, ready to sigh his
ghost if that be his fate.

"'Ut are ye called?" Goldtooth snarled, leveling his pistol at
Crow's head.

"Crow."

"Crow," Goldtooth repeated darkly. "'Ut do ye care 'or this
Injun, Crow?"

"I seek only to improve my own lot," Crow lied. "I care
nothing for this Indian. But spare him now, Admiral, and your
mercy will earn the respect of the others aboard this ship."
Crow paused, and looked directly at Goldtooth. "Respect is
worth more than fear in mutinous seas such as these, Admiral."

Goldtooth blinked, appreciating the Machiavellian expe-
dience of Crow's counsel. "I like yer kind 'a sailor, Crow."
Gesturing Crow to rise, Goldtooth addressed the rest of the
ship, hollering, "This is 'irst Lieutenant Crow." Then, before
he could stand, Goldtooth slashed a knife blade across Crow's
left cheek, startling him unawares. "And i' any'un e'er q'estions
'e again!" Goldtooth roared as his vultures screamed in bloodthirsty ecstasy, "I'll tie ye to this deck and let the 'uzzards eat
ye raw!"

23

SEA SPRAY MISTED across Crow's face, the salt stinging the
stitches still mending the gash Goldtooth had slashed
across his left cheek. Crow was standing redundant
guard outside Goldtooth's locked quarters, disgusting over the

muffled groans and wheezing flatulence that had been abusing his ears for the last fifteen minutes. Goldtooth demanded this detail of him every day, and Crow had shortly discerned that as first lieutenant he was essentially Goldtooth's seat of easement guard, standing watch until Goldtooth unlocked his door and handed him a horrifically heavy slop bucket of excrement to be pitched into the sea.

It need hardly be mentioned that Crow loathed Goldtooth, though this hatred was not without respect. Making Crow his first lieutenant, for example, was an obvious political gambit. Promote the troublemakers, give them a title, some spare privileges, and an interest in the status quo, and thereby keep them from rousing the rabble. Indeed, Crow had never encountered a man more cunning in his ability to manipulate and deceive those around him. Goldtooth sustained his command by crafting triangles of mutual mistrust among all the various parties aboard the ship—which he had rechristened the *Damnation*—and neither Crow nor anyone else on board could ever be certain that damnation was not the truth of their situation.

Goldtooth's flatulence turned suddenly explosive, and Crow took an involuntary step away from the door. Sighing, his revulsion was at least interrupted by some commotion now within his view, a circle of drunken sailors amusing themselves with the spectacle of Goldtooth's three buzzards terrorizing a parrot imprisoned by rings around its ankles chaining it to a perch. Crow winced at this and—glancing back at the door to the captain's quarters—a flatulent splat echoed by a helpless moan chased him farther yet. Guessing that he still had several minutes to bide, Crow wandered over to the fray, pushing his way to the center as the buzzards took flight.

"Whose bird is this?" Crow demanded.

"Mine!" One of the galleon's original crew stood up, stumbling.

"I'll toss you for it," Crow offered, pulling the enchanted dice the itinerant shaman Joe had given him out of a pouch around his neck, dice he had long ago sucked clean of their honeycomb crust.

"What're you putting up?"

Crow removed a sack of gold dust from his belt. Goldtooth had given this to him, presumably to purchase his loyalty, after occupying the former captain's quarters. Everyone knew what it contained, and the assembled drunken burst into laughter at this wager.

"Wager that sack of gold for a bloody stupid parrot?" the owner brayed. "Have you been smoking too much rope? You're on, matey! You're on!"

Crow offered him the dice to examine. The parrot's owner tossed the dice a few times experimentally, then muttered suspicious, "How do I know these bones isn't fixed?"

"Name the bet," Crow offered, knowing he would reason that loaded dice would be fixed to land high, since dogs—a pair of ones—is the worst possible roll in the sailor's dice game of hazard.

"Low roll wins," he answered as he pitched the dice. He sneered wide as they landed two and one.

Jeers and laughter surrounded Crow but he remained nonetheless poker. Crow observed that his Arawak brethren were at the ready as he waited for the gaggle to simmer. That was good, but there was probably no reason to blow his cover just now. Since he'd been careful to conceal the totemic cross tattooed on his own back, no one yet realized that Crow was allied with the Indian slaves aboard.

Glancing next to the macaw, he found it watching the game with apparent interest. Looking at Crow, the bird spoke to him. "Möbius," the parrot said, but his voice competed with the general din, and so Crow only heard him say *Moby*, and no one else could hear him in any event, preoccupied as they were with placing side bets on a long shot and passing swigs on a jug of rum spiced with gunpowder. After a minute, Crow shook his left fist demonstratively in the center of the circle, all falling quiet as someone called, "No more bets!" Crow pitched the dice onto the deck and in the same motion reached for his machete, unsheathing it before the dice rattled into a pair of ones. A roar went up from the assembled, except for the sailor who'd just lost his parrot, who had his hand on the hilt of his own blade before Crow discouraged him with a gesture of his machete. Crow retrieved his sack of gold dust and his dice, and—keeping his eyes narrowed upon his opponent—carefully picked up the parrot's perch. "Play nice," he cautioned, scolding with his blade as he backed away grinning. "Laughing bones are no cause for quarrel."

Having been gone for all of five minutes, Crow returned to his post outside the captain's quarters, now possessed of a parrot. Ignoring the ongoing blurt of Goldtooth's colon, Crow busied himself removing the rings from the parrot's ankles, now badly chafed from its efforts to defend itself from the buzzards' harassment. "Möbius," the macaw spoke again as it watched Crow succeed in releasing the rings from its ankles, although here again, having never heard the word Möbius (which as a matter of anachronistic fact had not yet even entered the English lexicon), Crow simply assumed he had said *Moby*.

"Moby," Crow repeated. "You can speak?"

"You can speak?" Moby replied.

"Can you talk?" Crow tried again.

"Can you talk?" Moby sassed.

Crow smiled. "My name is Crow, smarty," Crow introduced himself and stepped back. "Off you go, Moby."

Moby raised each of his feet in turn, examining them carefully. Looking again at Crow, Moby pronounced, "Thank you, Crow Smarty," before flapping himself aloft.

Crow grinned, gazing amazed as Moby flew high into the sky until he heard Goldtooth unlatching the door behind him. Turning suddenly cheerful toward his janitorial duties, Crow greeted Goldtooth, who emerged glistening in sweat, handed Crow his pail, and wordlessly returned to his stinking quarters. Unable to avoid noticing the coiled python of crap steaming fecal from the heavy pail in his grasp, Crow's mood soared nonetheless, and though he was heaving the fetid contents of Goldtooth's slop bucket overboard, his attention was consumed by Moby's ongoing ascent into the overwhelming immensity of the sky, and Crow remembered that he was, and he always had been, and he always would be, absolutely free.

24

"**D**O YOU THINK we're ever *not* acting?" Lila asked Merlin as she lay curled under his arm and across his chest five days after they met, five days they'd spent almost entirely together.

"Of course not," Merlin responded, yawning. "Life is performance art, isn't that what you said? *All the world's a stage, and all the men and women merely players.*"

"Yeah, but who's the actor?"

"Who's the actor?" Merlin repeated. "That's a good question."

Lila propped herself up on her elbows. "I think there's a difference between acting and being."

"That's doubtful," Merlin rubbed his eyes.

"But acting is inauthentic. I mean, are you acting right now?"

"Not in the sense of being intentionally inauthentic, but I'm hardly just being either."

"Why not?"

"I don't know, I just know I'm not, and you're not either, by the way. Everyone just acts how they're supposed to act, and that's not really authenticity, is it? You said it right the night we met, only a fool would take such a tale for the truth."

"Such a *tawdry* tale," Lila corrected.

"Such a tawdry tale," Merlin agreed. "The ego's pretense at life isn't really happening, but we sure act like it is."

"Right, but there are different levels of acting." Lila sat up and straddled him. "Maybe we act like life in all its sound and fury is really happening, but that's different than acting like something that you're not."

Merlin stroked her naked torso with a bright yellow spider mum he'd plucked from a vase on the nightstand. "You're going to have to prove that one to me," he said after thoughtfully sniffing the flower.

"Okay. Act like you're angry right now."

"What am I angry about?"

Lila shrugged. "It doesn't matter."

"Sure it does," Merlin protested. "If I'm going to act effectively, I can't just rage around for no reason at all, can I? Everything has a context. The best actors don't pretend anything, they *become* that which they are acting. That's why acting is no different from everyday life, acting like this is really happening."

"Fine. So act like you're angry because we're arguing."

Merlin shook his head. "Too vague. Why are we arguing?"

"You're just stalling."

Merlin paused. "We would at least need some kind of a safety word."

"A what?"

"A safety word, like with S&M, a word to suspend the fantasy, to remind us that this isn't really happening."

"S&M?"

"Sadomasochistic sex, you know."

Lila blinked, cringing inwardly in reluctant recollection of her sexual misadventures with Ivan's proclivities. "I didn't know you were into S&M."

"It's just an example."

"So you're not into S&M?"

"Uh, no, not particularly. Why, are you?"

Lila paused. "No."

"I mean, don't get me wrong." Merlin stroked her hips and idly snapped the elastic of her panties. "It's fun to play with dominance and submission. I'll tie you to the bed and give it to you hard slam any day of the week."

"Yeah."

"But I'm not into zipper masks and gag balls."

"Lovely. Thanks for clarifying."

"The point is, we need a safety word."

They fell silent as they looked around the room, searching for a word that might serve their purpose. "How about Möbius?" Lila reached across Merlin and plucked her Möbius band pendant off the bedside stand and dropped it around her neck. Tracing the half twist that gave the band the curious property of having only one side, she contemplated its geometry. "It only has one side," she murmured with satisfaction, and at that moment, Moby fluttered to rest on the fire escape outside the window.

Merlin grinned, appreciating the synchronicity of Moby's appearance. "Möbius. That's a decent safety word."

"Good. So are you angry now?"

Merlin tried to change the subject. "Has anyone ever told you that you look like Botticelli's Venus?"

"Yes." Lila plumed her mane, which she considered to be not so much red as turmeric. "So are you acting angry now?"

"No."

"So act like you're angry. I want to see if you can act."

Merlin shrugged his chin, considering. "I don't really want to act like I'm angry."

"Why not?"

"Because I don't want to, that's why not."

Lila pursed her lips and crawled off him, laying down as far away from him as she could and turning her back. "You're no fun," she protested.

Merlin looked at her. "It's adorable when you pout like a five-year-old, sweetie, unless that's the level of your emotional maturity."

Lila was silent awhile, then she repeated her assessment. "You're no fun."

"Why? Just because I don't do what you tell me to do? I hate to break it to you, but you're not the boss of me."

"I'm not trying to be the boss of you," Lila turned and slapped the bed between them.

"Sure you are." Merlin threw back the covers and got up. "It's always the same thing with you, isn't it?"

"What are you talking about?"

"Who knows?" Merlin pulled on his shirt. "Maybe you should ask yourself what I'm talking about. After all, it's all about you, isn't it? I'm just a figment of your imagination, apparently. God, you're so arrogant."

"*I'm* arrogant?" Lila sat up, hugging a pillow to her chest. "Oh, that's rich, mister. You suddenly have me all figured out, and how can anyone possibly call you arrogant? *I've been fired or quit on a day's notice from every job I've ever held,*" she imitated Merlin. "You *ooze* arrogance."

"Maybe so, but at least I admit it. You, on the other hand, you pretend you don't have any issues, like you're the ultimate evolved being, you and your Holy Company of Beautiful People."

"Hey!" Lila yelled. "I just want some serenity in my life!"

"I just want some serenity in my life!" Merlin mocked her. "You sound like a latte late for a yoga class!"

Lila ignored his insult. "Why are you getting all drama queen?"

"Maybe because you like to pretend there's no sand in the butter!"

"Sand in the butter?" Lila interrupted. "What are you talking about?" But Merlin was talking over her.

"Drama is inevitable, and the more you resist it the worse it gets!"

"What? Whatever happened to just going with the flow?"

"Uh, *nothing* happened to going with the flow, that's the whole problem. Where do you think the flow is, anyway? It's right here, right now, *this is* the flow, it can't possibly be otherwise. Does a river pout and pitch a fit every time it meets an obstacle? No, it just flows around it and it's because of the obstacles that the rapids and canyons and waterfalls are formed. It's *you* that's lost, aping at serenity and making that an excuse for yourself to not have to face any challenges. Going with the flow isn't the destination, it's the journey."

Lila snorted. "Oh, and who thinks they're the ultimate evolved being?"

"The only time you're not going with the flow," Merlin continued pontificating, "is when you stand in judgment."

"He said as he stood in judgment," Lila completed his sentence. "Way to dodge accountability, mister."

"Wow." Merlin regarded her in calm condescension. "You're one to talk about dodging accountability. That's the projection of the century. Tell you what, sister, why don't you go hammer your yammer on someone else's eardrum?"

"What?" Lila inflamed.

"Let's not get all sudsy and soap operatic." Merlin waved her away in dismissal. "Go lather your blather on someone else."

"What are you talking about?!" Lila raised her voice.

"Uh-oh! Look who flipped the bitch switch!" Merlin

angrily pulled on his pants. "I see how you are, sweetheart. I'm well acquainted with your walls and your bullshit ohmigod adolescent *what are you talking about?!* incredulity. Everyone else is crazy and what are they even talking about anyway? I see how you are. You've dealt with your issues, you have it all figured out, you take it all in so hippie-go-laid-back and holier-than-thou and how dare I call you arrogant? And I know you pride yourself on being high maintenance, but I've got news for you, sweetheart: I ain't your janitor. Now watch me go with the flow all the way outta here."

"What?" Lila was aghast. "At least I'm not acting *ass*holier-than-thou!"

"Keep on shouting at your shadow! I'm sure your anger will protect you! And I'll tell you something else—"

"Fuck you!"

"Möbius."

Lila froze, stunned. Merlin sat gently on the edge of the bed. "Möbius," he said again, stroking her hair away from her face as her fury fell into hurt. "You said you wanted me to act like I was angry, like I was arguing with you."

Lila hugged her knees to her chest as sadness overcame her. "No," she shook her head, whimpering softly as she looked away. Her eyes found Moby, staring at her from the far side of her bedroom window. Moby cocked his head.

"Hey," Merlin soothed, crawling onto the bed and wrapping his arms and legs around her as she initially resisted but ultimately released into his embrace. "Möbius, baby. It's okay, it's all right. It's just a game, this isn't really happening." After a moment, he added, "Do you really think I'm the kind of guy that would say 'Look who flipped the bitch switch'?"

Lila looked at him and smiled in spite of her tears. "Sudsy

and soap operatic?" she sniffled. "I told you to act like you were angry, not like you were a total asshole."

"I don't know that there's really much difference," Merlin chuckled. "Besides, anger is one letter away from angel."

Lila blinked, thinking his last remark rather cheesy. "Uh, did you really just say that?"

Merlin stroked her hair. "A momentary speech impediment is all it takes," he cooed, breathy and earnest, "but only in Engrish."

Lila blinked again and shook her head. "That's stupid," she said, before chuckling in spite of herself.

"And *assholier-than-thou*, by the way?" Merlin chattered amiably along. "That was very good. But just so you know, I would never ever get dressed during an argument. Quite the contrary, I follow the Jainist tradition of arguing naked. You've seen that ARGUE NAKED bumper sticker on my fridge, right? Gymnosophy, they called it in ancient Greece. I take that seriously."

Lila ignored him now, hugging him closer. "I didn't like that game."

"It was your idea."

"I know. But let's not play it again."

"All right. But if we ever forget, let's just remind one another that this isn't really happening."

"How?"

"Möbius, of course. Our safety word."

Lila's laughter at last overwhelmed her tears as she looked again at Moby. "You never answered my question."

"Which question?"

"Who's the actor?"

"Love is the actor, of course. Love isn't merely all you need—love is actually all there is. Everything else is subterfuge, remember? And if, as you say, life is performance art, then surely you must understand that you will not know the truth of your art until you release the love in your heart."

Lila gazed at him. "I adore you."

"I adore you more."

And they held each other closer than before, their breathing falling into calm synchrony, their smiles blossoming like morning glories at the break of dawn. After a time, Lila murmured, "It sure felt like it was really happening, though."

"I know. It always does. But it never is."

"Möbius," Lila sighed.

"Möbius," Merlin affirmed.

"Möbius," Moby repeated, and flapped away.

25

A LONG WITH ALL of Goldtooth's atlases and sea charts, Flaming Jane had inadvertently stolen a treasure map that'd been hidden among them during her mutiny over the *Queen Elizabeth*. Goldtooth—having drawn a parchment copy of the map that he kept sealed in his boot at all times, and guessing that Flaming Jane would eventually discover and attempt to decipher the original map herself—was thereby able to extrapolate her likely trajectory. Thus it was less than two moons before the *Damnation* caught up with *Eleusis*, although Goldtooth's crew suspected it was the buzzards that were guiding Goldtooth's apparent dead reckoning.

In order to camouflage his identity from Flaming Jane, Goldtooth ordered all his original crew belowdecks and hoisted a confiscated Jolly Roger along with a white flag to bluff a peaceful intention. Taking care to stay out of sight of any spyglasses himself, Goldtooth then ordered Crow and two Arawak slaves to row a hogshead of rum across to *Eleusis*. His mission, Goldtooth explained, was to arrange for a peaceful trade of provisions, and the barrel of rum would represent a goodwill gesture. Crow was to reveal nothing of either the ship's or Goldtooth's affiliation with the Royal Navy, but only to present themselves as fellow pirates under the command of the notorious pirate Goldtooth. Goldtooth also showed Crow a sack of rubies and permitted him to choose one. "Do this," Goldtooth encouraged, "and you can 'ave the 'ole sack." Crow nodded, sparkling his eyes greedy in order to assure Goldtooth that he could be trusted.

What Goldtooth did not tell Crow, however, was that he had stuffed the hogshead of rum full of pounds of wormwood leaves he'd harvested while marooned, and his intention was to poison the entire crew of *Eleusis*. The alcohol in the rum would extract thujone from the wormwood, a hallucinogen and nerve toxin that—at the extreme concentration he'd introduced into the rum—would result in a nightmarish madness leading eventually to lethal seizures. It made no difference to Goldtooth if Crow and the slaves happened to consume any of the poisoned rum themselves.

But there was really very little risk of that. No sooner had Crow, Gabriel, and another brother named Azriel lowered the barrel of poison rum into a rowboat and begun to row across to *Eleusis* than they were planning how they could get their two remaining Arawak brothers off the *Damnation* as well. Crow distributed various blades to the others, retaining a flintlock pistol and a saber for himself.

Nearing *Eleusis* after a solid hour of rowing, they were paid a hostile welcome. A couple of warning shots greeted them, and several arrows cut the air above their heads, sniped by an archer in the crow's nest. At these gestures, Crow and his brothers ceased rowing, and after a brief consult faced the company aboard the starboard side of *Eleusis*. It was a motley crew of African, European, and Native American faces, more women than men, and a red-haired woman standing on the maintop whose eyes were so wild that they shone even across the distance. All their faces and bodies were painted for battle, their hands brandished multiple blades, a white-faced black bobcat strolled mrowling across the gunwales, and Crow could not help but grin.

"What's in the cask?" someone's voice boomed.

Crow turned and patted the barrel. "Here thar be rum!" This announcement was met with derision and jetsam, but Crow only congratulated the catcalls, joined by his brothers.

"Ah, so yours is no ship o' fools!" Crow hollered as the hooting relented. "Strong water is the drink of the devil, for certain, softens the head and crazies the mind! Why I'd sooner drink seawater myself than—"

"Are these natives your slaves, then, white man?" It was Flaming Jane who interrupted him, her voice as severe as any saber.

"Stay your tongue, white *woman*!" Crow hollered back, matching eyes with her. "My name is Crow, and these men are my brothers." At that, Crow turned and stripped his shirt off, revealing the totemic cross tattooed upon his back. Then, each of his brothers announced their respective names—Gabriel and Azriel—displaying the totemic crosses tattooed on their backs in turn. Pulling his shirt on and turning back around, Crow addressed her again. "And what of you, white woman? You appear to leader half a ship of Africans. Is this ship your white woman's burden?"

This riposte invited an array of bows and harpoons to flex and aim in his direction, but Crow—sensing the smile prancing about the lips of Flaming Jane—failed to flinch. Crow continued. "If you wished us dead we would be so already, white woman."

At that remark, one of the pirates hollered "Yar!" and hurled his harpoon at Crow. Crow—unable to avoid catching it as he had done so many times with the cane spear—effortlessly flipped the harpoon and fired it immediately back upon his attacker, managing to merely graze the belligerent sailor's right shoulder. "I did not have to miss his heart!" Crow yelled in warning to anyone else contemplating an attack upon them.

Flaming Jane was smiling, her eyes sparkling. "As you can see," she replied, "I lead no one aboard this ship. If anyone follows me, it is their choice and not my command. And my name, dear Crow, is Jane, or as the scuttlebutt has come to call me in these seas, *Flaming* Jane. Who is your captain?"

"No man is our captain," Crow responded, pleased with the obvious intelligence of this Flaming Jane.

"I suppose that is well said," Flaming Jane granted. "And what of the others? Cannot they speak for themselves?"

At this, Gabriel—the leader of their tribe when they ran free— responded in his native Arawakan tongue, which Crow translated: "Though we understand you well, it is dangerous for us to speak the language of the white man."

"Dangerous why?" Flaming Jane inquired.

Gabriel again spoke via Crow: "Language is deep magic, and we are the last of our kind. Our ancestors assist when we speak the tongue of our mothers. And as to our captain, we stand brother and equal to Crow, and no man is our captain."

Flaming Jane thanked Gabriel before turning again to Crow. "I'll ask you once more, Crow, and do not be precipitous in your answer. Who captains your ship?"

"Goldtooth, my lady. The notorious pirate Goldtooth wishes me to arrange a peaceful trade of provisions. He offers this rum as a goodwill gesture, although I have gathered that this barrel of demonswill has done little to persuade you."

"The notorious pirate Goldtooth?" Flaming Jane repeated. "Do you suppose me stupid, dear Crow? Does this notorious pirate Goldtooth have any other name?"

Crow narrowed his eyes. "I bear no loyalty to Goldtooth, but neither do I bear any loyalty to you or anyone else on board your ship. I have been sent by Goldtooth as a trade ambassador, but I have no interest in trade negotiations, and forsooth, the only objective that concerns my brothers and me is how to get our two remaining brothers off his accursed ship. If you can offer us assistance, we can offer you ours in turn. Otherwise, and though I find this encounter most charming, we have nothing left to discuss."

Flaming Jane considered, immediately pleased with this Crow's intellect. "Do you have a pistol, Crow?"

Crow pulled the loaded flintlock out of his shoulder holster and displayed it before the array of flexed-again bows.

"Would you fire it into your barrel?"

Crow comprehended her intention immediately. "You suspect a Trojan horse?"

"Would you fire it into your barrel?" Flaming Jane repeated.

Having had to manage the ungainly sloshing of the liquid within the barrel while rowing, Crow did not hesitate to fire his weapon for fear of hidden men or gunpowder. He shot a hole into the side of the barrel, and rum instantly began to fountain out both sides, half of it into their rowboat. The rum smelled pungent and acrid, hardly uncommon among seafaring liquors, although Azriel—after collecting some of it in an emptied wineskin and cautiously tasting it—identified the offending smell as wormwood, a plant he had once used in thin dilutions as the itinerant shaman Joe's apprentice, and a frightful poison at higher concentrations. Azriel informed Crow that it was likely poisoned, and Crow nodded.

"Rum indeed!" Crow called out to Flaming Jane. "Though it appears your suspicions are not without foundation. Azriel tells me this rum smells of wormwood poison, and while I myself can identify nothing distinctive about its bouquet, never would I doubt the nose of Azriel nor the skulduggery of Goldtooth."

"Who is this Goldtooth?" Flaming Jane asked again, incensed. "What coward would ambush our ship with poison?"

After some consultation with his brothers, Crow answered.

"Promise us asylum and assistance and we will tell you everything we know about Goldtooth. We are able seamen and fearless in battle besides. But as I said, we must get our remaining two brothers off the *Damnation*. I have no doubt that a woman of your obvious cunning could assist us, but if you are not willing, then we must return to our brothers and await another opportunity."

Flaming Jane and her crew regarded them in silence. "They propose an alliance," she at last said to the crew. "What say you?" Scarcely had she spoken than every hand aboard *Eleusis*—vengeful against he who sought to ambush their sanctuary—raised aye. Every hand, that is, except for the pirate who had hurled his harpoon at Crow, but he was otherwise occupied tending to the wound upon his shoulder.

Flaming Jane nodded at this decision. "We have an accord!" she announced, and turning to Crow, she could not help but smile. "Welcome to *Eleusis*!"

26

BY EARLY AFTERNOON of the same day Goldtooth had sent him to poison the crew of *Eleusis*, Crow was spotted rowing back toward the *Damnation*, alone with the hogshead of rum. As both ships were careful to stay well out of range of one another's cannon fire, Crow was exhausted by traversing the distance between the two ships on his own. Breathless and parched, he was unable to offer any explanation until he was back on board and properly refreshed.

"I advise you to abandon any notion of trading provisions with the red witch who captains that ship," Crow cautioned

Goldtooth after gasping back half a gallon of freshwater. "Flaming Jane, she calls herself, as I suspect you already knew. She said she's never heard of the notorious pirate Goldtooth, scoffed at your generous goodwill offer, forced us to blow a hole into the side of the barrel, and emptied the rum into the sea."

"Into the sea?" Goldtooth grit his teeth.

"It's true, Cap'n," spoke a sailor who was helping haul the now-empty barrel out of the rowboat. He examined the holes in the sides and shook his head mournful, verging on tears as his voice broke. "All the rum done gone."

Crow nodded and continued. "Then she took the slaves and sent me back, her crew heckling me with their slingshots till I was out of range."

"That's it?!" Goldtooth roared, spraying spittle in every direction. "That's all?!"

"Her ship is short of crew, and all she needs are slaves," Crow went on, pulling a large sack out of his satchel. "She gave you this for the two slaves she kept." He opened the sack and displayed a small fortune in doubloons before dropping it onto the deck. "She promises twice as much for another two slaves."

Goldtooth fingered the gold coins, curdling with rage as he guessed they were from his own chest aboard the former *Queen Elizabeth*. He glared at his former ship, floating just out of range of his cannons. He had been hesitant to fire upon the ship for fear of damaging the *Queen Elizabeth*, but his hatred for Flaming Jane was fast outgrowing any attachment to his old vessel.

"If I may, Captain," Crow drew in close and lowered his voice to a whisper. "I've heard talk of this Flaming Jane and what she's done to you. Her ship is short of crew and vulnerable. We could easily overtake her."

Goldtooth eyed Crow for a few moments. "We'd ne'er catch

'er," he shook his head finally, knowing the man-o'-war at full sail to be a lighter, swifter ship than the galleon.

"We won't have to." Crow handed Goldtooth the ruby he'd earlier given him. "I've not yet earned my payment, Captain, but if you give me a chance, why I'll slay that pirate wench myself."

Goldtooth did not trust Crow—Goldtooth did not trust anyone—but he was nonetheless intrigued. "'Ow?"

"Send me back with the two more slaves she wants. Once I'm back on board, I'll detonate a cask of gunpowder next to the mainmast. Strike sail as soon as you hear the explosion, and you'll be upon her crippled ship in no time."

Goldtooth licked his teeth, nodding appreciation at Crow's duplicitous scheming. "And 'at do ye get outta this?"

Crow grinned. "You'll need someone to steward one of these ships once you captain them both, am I correct?"

"Aye," Goldtooth nodded, clapping Crow on the shoulder in ostensible appreciation of his ambition, though privately he considered Crow far too clever for his own good. "Yer a good sailor, Crow," Goldtooth encouraged, resolving to kill him as soon as he gained control of both ships. "Do this and you can 'ave this galleon."

27

R EFRESHED AND FED, Crow set off for *Eleusis* with his two remaining Arawak brothers by late afternoon. Goldtooth sent a small cask of gunpowder with them, hidden in a satchel, and figured there was a greater than even chance that Crow's plan might actually work. Crow was certainly motivated, believing he stood to gain his own ship out of this, and if he failed, well, Goldtooth didn't see how he had anything but a few Indian slaves to lose. Crow would surely be killed, and while Goldtooth knew his boats well enough to know that he would not likely catch his old man-o'-war in a full-sail chase, he could certainly keep on her until another opportunity arose. The hunt was on, and the hunter was patient.

Goldtooth had raised anchor as soon as Crow had departed, and already had men in place ready to drop the sails at the sound of the explosion. He watched through his spyglass as Crow and the slaves approached the former *Queen Elizabeth*. There appeared to be some discussion for several minutes, and then they began to board. He could not make out what happened after that, but soon afterward the anticipated explosion resounded across the waves. Goldtooth roared "Yar!" and watched as his sails dropped from their mainmasts like heavy veils against the heavens, ballooning as they seized the breeze and lurching the ship into motion moments before another explosion—this one much, much closer—rocked the *Damnation*.

Having dashed his head against the gunwales from the force of the blast, it took a moment for Goldtooth to fathom that the explosion was aboard his own ship and that the mainmast of the *Damnation* was engulfed in flames. Bewildered, Goldtooth looked toward *Eleusis* as its sails billowed pregnant with wind, and by the time he turned back toward his own sails a remorseless gasp of flame had instantly consumed the canvas, masts, and riggings entire, their blazing outlines roaring like the devil's own flagship.

28

ROW AND HIS Arawak brothers' successful sabotage upon the *Damnation* granted them instant notoriety aboard *Eleusis*, and having already proven themselves under fire and sail, he and his brethren were welcomed aboard without having to face the typical gauntlet of piratical hazing. Serendipity, too, ensured there would be two other Arawaks already aboard, Zedekiel and Lailah, who would vouch for them yet further, and that very evening they went on the account—joined *Eleusis* in its treasure-hunting expeditions—Crow and his brothers adding their signatures around the borders of the ship's contract in signification of their equality with everyone else on board.

It bears mentioning, however, that it was Flaming Jane who had insisted upon the irony of their plan, tempting Goldtooth into attempting to attack *Eleusis* by the same means that they would attack the *Damnation*. "Irony is a force in the world," Flaming Jane had explained to Crow. "And this will ensure our good fortune."

"Ensure our good fortune?" Crow amused. "You intend to prompt at Providence?"

"Yes I do," Flaming Jane affirmed. "God enjoys a good story as much as anyone, and we are nowhere if not within the story of God."

And thus would Crow lure Goldtooth into sending him back to sabotage *Eleusis*, all the while sabotaging the *Damnation*. While aboard the *Damnation*, Crow had tied a booby-trapped cask of gunpowder under a tarp along the maintop, rigging it with a twine he tied to the corner of a bound sail. Then he told his two remaining Arawak brothers, Seraph and Malakai, to saturate all the bound sails with kerosene. This they wicked into the sails by stuffing rigging rope into the rolled-up sails as they appeared to be going about their duties, and stuffing the other ends of the ropes into hidden containers of kerosene. Then, once they were all safely aboard *Eleusis* and Flaming Jane had detonated Goldtooth's cask of gunpowder in the rowboat on the far side of *Eleusis*, Goldtooth dropped his sails, causing the twine rigged to the cask of gunpowder to snap taut and trigger a flintlock inside the hidden cask of gunpowder, firing the weapon, detonating the cask, and creating an incendiary explosion that, in addition to crippling the mainmast, immediately consumed the kerosene-saturated rigging and sails.

The booby trap was far more successful than Crow had thought it would be. He blinked at the conflagration reflecting across the dusk-darkened water, regarding it in silent astonishment as everyone else aboard *Eleusis* whooped the war victorious as they dropped sail. Steadying himself on a cannon, Crow touched the scar on his cheek, the scar Goldtooth had given him, and happened to glance at Catface. Catface was gazing not at the inferno but at the sky, swishing his tail impatient, and following Catface's gaze heavenward Crow spied three buzzards tracing patient circles high above them, and Crow knew that this war had just begun.

PART TWO:

THE TREASURE OF
ALL TREASURES

29

EVER SINCE a sadhu on the banks of the Ganges bet Merlin his breakfast that he could best him in ten consecutive throws of rock-paper-scissors, Merlin found that he possessed an uncanny knack for the game. Though he lost his breakfast to the sadhu that morning, the sadhu offered him a smudge of silt upon his brow as a gesture of gratitude, and Merlin had scarcely lost another match since. Thus it was that he shook his head amused when Lila suggested a best-of-three match one morning in order to determine who would have the first shower.

"I should warn you," Merlin stretched his fingers in preparation for the match, "that I am regarded throughout the seventeen thousand islands of the Indonesian archipelago as a roshambo rockstar."

"Oh really?" Lila sat up. "The whole archipelago?"

"As a gentleman," Merlin shook his hands vigorously, "I would happily have allowed you to enjoy the first shower, or better yet, to have crowded right in there with you—"

"As would I, of course," Lila interrupted. "But now that you've gone and boasted in the face of a sportive invitation," she reached into a drawer and pulled out a pair of black leather gloves, "thrown down the roshambo gauntlet, as it were, we'll just have to see who is truly the better one among us."

"What the heck is that?" Merlin protested as Lila pulled on her gloves. "Those had better be regulation."

"Intimidated by leather, eh?" Lila grinned. "It's hardly my fault that you showed up to a soccer match without your shin guards, is it?"

Merlin regarded the gloves suspiciously. "To mask your tells, no doubt?"

"As if I have any tells," Lila demurred.

"This is simply delicious." Merlin grinned and readied his stance. "But gather your wits, oh beautiful Lila, for no gallantry will gentle my game upon you."

"Ah yes," Lila observed. "Pretend yourself a gentleman in order to protect against the humiliation of your defeat. Better to lay your chivalry to rest, grasshopper, and trust that I will mock you unmercifully as my rock shatters your scissors."

Merlin blinked. "It is clear that you, like me, understand very well that this match has long begun."

"But of course," Lila answered. "Only a rank amateur believes the game begins upon the throw. Humans are utterly incapable of making a truly random decision."

"So you try to enchant me with the belief that your rock will shatter my scissors? But you must know that I know this—"

"And therein lies the flaw in your Sicilian logic," Lila interrupted. "Shall we get on with this then?"

"Ah!" Merlin pointed. "Impatience. You presume to possess the high ground at this moment? You're an assertive lass, that much is certain, likely to lead with a rock for the illusion of strength it subconsciously implies."

"Oh dear," Lila rolled her eyes. "Do you truly deem me so daft?"

"Quite the contrary," Merlin assured. "I am certain I'm in the presence of the uncelebrated wit of our generation, the wicked wit of the West, to be certain."

"Your sarcasm will unravel you," Lila warned.

"Not a bit of it," Merlin shook his head. "I'm afraid I've already won; all that remains is this acting out of that which was long ago preordained." He held his hand up to ready the throw. "But you are correct; I'll most likely throw scissors in the vain belief that you won't throw rock."

"Whatever you say," Lila yawned. "It won't shift the fact that I'll be throwing rock. The decision is all yours."

"As you wish." Merlin readied his hands. "Here we go then, on three: one, two, *three*." And at each count they caught their left fists in their right palms, ultimately leaving them both with a rock, a tie.

"I told you I'd throw a rock," Lila grinned.

"Now you've revealed everything," Merlin smiled.

"Watch, I'll throw rock again. Ready? One, two, *three*."

Rock, and rock. And without pause they counted and threw again.

Rock, and rock.

And again. Rock, and rock.

And finally again: scissors, and scissors.

"Ooo," Merlin taunted. "You tried to draw me into throwing paper, didn't you?"

"You and I both know we are beyond such puerile tactics." Lila straightened her shoulders. "We are both learned in the dark arts of trash-talk and trickery, but this has clearly become a truly intuitive contest. Shall we do this?"

"Oh, I think we shall. But if I were you, I wouldn't throw paper. One, two, *three*." Paper, and paper.

"One, two, *three*." Paper, and paper.

"One, two, *three.*" Rock, and rock.

"One, two, *three.*" Scissors, and scissors. And on and on they went, the only sounds being the slap of their fingers and fists into their palms coupled with their breathless counts of one, two, *three*! At one point, Lila stopped curling her hand into a fist and instead slapped her paper palm on the first two counts in an attempt to throw Merlin off his game, but it had no effect upon their tie. Merlin responded by yelling his count, "Paper, scissors, *rock*!" while throwing scissors, but again, it had no effect upon their tie.

Lila paused, arms akimbo, and smiled.

Merlin held his hands at the ready. "Why are you smiling?"

"Because I know something you don't know."

"And what is that?"

With a flourish, Lila switched to throwing with her right hand. "I am not left-handed."

"One, two, *three.*" Paper, and paper.

Merlin interrupted their next throw, shaking his hands loose. "There's something I ought to tell you."

"Tell me." Lila licked her lips.

"I'm not left-handed either."

And their brows furrowed as they adjusted their stance, licking their lips and focusing their breath, neverminding the stakes enormous that whosoever broke this tie would win the bragging rights of the millennium.

"Zone play." Merlin smiled upon their umpteenth tie, after some five minutes of play.

"Give up?" Lila responded upon their next tie.

"You wish," Merlin replied as they tied yet again.

And on and on they went, and they may have gone on the rest of the morning if not for Dogface, who abruptly barked at the parrot who landed on the fire escape outside the window.

Moby startled away, but Merlin and Lila's attention veered grateful from their game.

"It appears you've met your match," Lila smiled upon a sigh.

"It appears you've met *your* match," Merlin replied in smile.

And there was nothing left to do but kiss.

30

THE FIRST TIME Crow and Flaming Jane got into an argument—which was but the morning after she welcomed him aboard *Eleusis*—she screamed in his face like a wildcat. Much to her astonishment, the unstoppable cannonball of her voice had just met the immovable post of Crow's as he bellowed right back, and within seconds blows were thrown and deflected, blades were drawn and slashed, and pistols were cocked and pointed as ferocity flared their nostrils, glared their eyes, and bared their teeth. The force of their confrontation was such that all who witnessed had to squint and take two steps back, and no one dared intervene. Neither Crow nor Flaming Jane nor anybody else could ever recall how the argument began, but regardless of that, it ended with the following words:

"Don't *ever* try to stand in my way!" Flaming Jane yelled. "Or I'll keelhaul your ass from here to Cuba!"

"Don't *ever* try to give me an order!" Crow roared right back. "Or down goes your shanty to the bottom of the sea!"

And they eyed each other warily, prowling the perimeter of the circle created by their shock wave, and Crow at last relaxed the hammer of his pistol. Flaming Jane followed suit, and, their boundaries satisfactorily established, they turned away from the encounter only to rendezvous later that evening in the captain's quarters, and tales would later tell tall that their lovemaking was so wild that it shivered the timbers of the entire ship as it rolled across the moonlit waves.

31

SCANNING THE STREET outside for any sign of Moby after
the rug burn wrestling sex that had followed her roshambo
stalemate with Merlin, Lila's eyes narrowed instead upon a
jet-black metallic Range Rover with privacy glass parked across
the street. Any question as to whom the Range Rover belonged
to was settled by its namaste vanity plate, though she doubted
it was Ivan himself who was staking out her apartment. Fishing
a cheap pair of binoculars from a nearby drawer, she confirmed
that it was merely one of his minions, though she could not
determine exactly who.

"What is it?" Merlin asked, peering over her shoulder.

Lila shook her head, exasperated. "I know that car," she
said, fumbling again through her drawer and pulling out a gross
pack of bottle rockets. "Ivan's having me followed."

"What?" Merlin scanned the street. "Are you serious?"

Lila paused, gritting five bottle rockets in her teeth. "See
the license plate on that Range Rover?"

"But why?" Merlin asked as he squinted at the license plate
across the street.

"Probably because I sent a mass email to everyone in the

Holy Company of Beautiful People detailing all of his criminal shenanigans after I left."

Merlin swiveled to look at Lila, impressed. "Damn, sister. You don't mess around, do you?"

"Yeah, well, a lot of good it did me. Ivan just made it out like I was insane with jealousy. Now I have over two hundred enemies."

Merlin looked again toward the street. "Namaste?" He laughed out loud once he'd discerned the license plate. "I honor the divinity within you? You've gotta be kidding me."

Lila smiled but did not answer. She was preoccupied with pulling a six-foot-long piece of half-inch galvanized conduit out from under her bed, itself duct-taped to a five-foot-long piece of one-and-a-half-inch-wide PVC pipe.

"It should be interesting to discover what the heck *that* is," Merlin observed.

Lila grinned and handed him the bottle rockets from her teeth along with a cigar lighter from the nightstand. "The length of the barrel ensures its accuracy," she explained. "And the PVC keeps the barrel perfectly straight. I could bounce a bottle rocket off the bill of a ball cap from fifty yards off with this baby. If I really wanted to."

"And why do you have this?"

"I made it back in college after some frat boy got me drunk and tried to take advantage of me," Lila stated matter-of-fact. "After that, I targeted the whole fraternity with bottle rockets for the rest of the year, since they had to walk down an alley next to my apartment in order to get back to their frat house." She examined her makeshift bottle rocket cannon as if it were an antique rifle. "I've just hung on to it ever since."

"Cripes," Merlin assessed. "You're quite the firecracker, aren't you?"

Lila shrugged. "Do you know anything about geopolitics?" she asked as she wiped the dust off her bottle rocket cannon.

"Plenty, I suppose," Merlin answered.

"Well, what do they call it when one nation doesn't respect the boundaries of another nation?"

"War?"

Lila nodded and hefted her makeshift bottle rocket cannon. "It works the same with people. By not respecting my boundaries, Ivan is waging war on me, and he's a fool if he thinks I won't defend myself."

"Good thing you still have all these bottle rockets." Merlin grinned smart-ass.

"It sure is." Lila smiled in such a way that assured Merlin that she wasn't taking this entirely seriously. "So, line up the fuses when you load them in the back," she instructed simply, as if she were teaching him nothing more severe than how to play house. "But don't light them till I say. Then just push them inside the pipe and replace the cork."

"Aye!" Merlin hopped to it, plucking the cork from the end of the pipe and prepping the rockets. "I'll buy you a green tea if you hit your target."

"Ready." Lila smiled as she adjusted her aim to account for the angle and the arc of the bottle rockets' descent. "Aim." She drew a deep breath. "Fire."

Merlin touched the torch lighter to the wicks of all five bottle rockets, pushed them inside the galvanized pipe, and replaced the cork. Lila corrected her aim once again as she exhaled, and seconds later all five rockets came zipping out of the open end of the steel pipe, thwooping one right after the other, tracing a trail of sparks across the street as they arced toward their target, bouncing directly off the windshield of the Range Rover before scattering across its hood and firecracking every which way. A *jeezus christ!* was heard to holler before the engine roared alive as its tires squealed out of there, the fleeing vanity of its license plate nonetheless honoring the divinity within them.

32

ACTING ON IVAN's behest, Chris Bliss had been tailing Lila ever since their encounter at the Octopus's Garden. Ivan occasionally requested such selfless service of Chris Bliss and the other aspirants in his inner circle, reminding him that the Holy Company of Beautiful People was a chosen people and as such it shone uncommonly bright, sometimes attracting the envies and resentments of outsiders. As Ivan decreed it, this warranted not only secrecy about their group, but also occasional black ops against anyone from whom Ivan sensed dark energy.

Last night, Ivan had called upon Chris Bliss to visit him in his quarters. Meditating in front of a candle, Ivan had fallen into a trance, claiming to see visions from a previous life. "Do you see?" Ivan whispered, breathless under the strain of the vision revealing itself through the candle flame. "It is us, my child! We have tread this path together before, as Master and disciple."

"I see!" Chris Bliss thrilled, though in truth he saw nothing more magnificent than the brazen licks of the flame itself.

Ivan shuddered, nearly collapsing sideways, and Chris Bliss caught him. "You failed me," Ivan groaned. "Failed to protect me."

"Master, never!" Chris Bliss panicked, desperately squinting at the flame.

"My child," Ivan drew a tormented breath. "Do not waste this life again. Only by protecting your Master will you attain the enlightenment you've sought for so many lifetimes."

"I will not fail again," Chris Bliss assured him. "I will do whatever it takes."

Ivan nodded as his labored breathing returned to normal. "I can see the strength in your spirit, my child. This will be your lifetime, I can feel it."

Chris Bliss beamed at this assessment.

"Tell me," Ivan went on. "Have you any word from our medicine carrier?"

Chris Bliss shook his head. "He's still saying he hasn't been able to source any LP9 for months. But he'll contact us the minute he turns some up." Chris Bliss reached into his pocket and pulled out a small Ziploc baggie of crystalline white powder. "But he says he has lots of MDMA though."

Ivan accepted the baggie and, after carefully opening it, dipped his pinky finger into it. This he offered to Chris Bliss, who fellated it gratefully into his mouth.

"Yes," Ivan smiled as Chris Bliss sucked on his pinky. "You are ready."

Ivan's pinky finger popped out of Chris Bliss's mouth. "Master?"

"For the Wisdom."

"I am ready, Master!"

"You can be the heir to this spiritual lineage, my child. But the Wisdom is translinguistic, and whether the translinguistic transference is successful is entirely up to you. You must follow my every guidance."

"Anything, Master."

Ivan regarded him for several solemn moments. "Remember,

my child, that ours is a mystery school by necessity. Just as Christ was crucified and the early Christians were fed to the lions, others just like us have been persecuted all throughout history. The shepherd must protect his flock, and always are we under threat."

Chris Bliss nodded. "Always are we under threat."

"Recently, the spiritually dead have succeeded in getting dangerously close to us."

Chris Bliss narrowed his eyes. "Lila."

Ivan nodded. "We must be ever vigilant. We cannot let that happen again."

"I will not fail again, Master. I will do whatever it takes."

Ivan reached toward his meditation altar and picked up a half-ounce amber vial. "Sometimes, our dharma calls upon us to release the spiritually dead from their mortal suffering." Ivan took Chris Bliss's hand and pressed the amber vial into his palm. "The bitterness of her coffee will mask the bitterness of this medicine. You must give *all* of it to her, my child."

Chris Bliss smiled. "Yes, Master."

Ivan reached forward and stroked Chris Bliss's face. "Pray for her."

33

A ND THUS IT WAS that Chris Bliss became the heir apparent to the spiritual lineage that Ivan claimed for himself. Chris Bliss styled himself an archangel defending enlightenment against the dark, and having witnessed Lila's impudent ice-water attack upon Ivan, Chris Bliss had no question that Lila was in the thrall of some kind of dark energy, and the Savior must be saved, bottle rockets be damned.

Besides which, Chris Bliss *loathed* Lila; he always had. Gorgeous in every proportion, Lila had swerved Ivan's and every other man's second chakra as soon as she showed up in the Holy Company of Beautiful People, sassing after *satsang*, pointing out hypocrisies and contradictions, and getting away with it for all her charm. A succubus of dark energy, Chris Bliss determined, and he was just the archangel to vanquish her. And that email she sent everyone, slandering Ivan, claiming that he was a fraud. Ah, that evil bitch. His duty was his pleasure.

Artemisia absinthium, read the label on the half-ounce amber glass vial in his palm, the cap of which he unscrewed and plugged with the pad of his pinky finger. It was pure worm-wood oil, the key ingredient in absinthe, the notorious liquor of Parisian bohemians in the 1800s. A stimulant at low doses, it was a potent nerve toxin at high doses. Chris Bliss was to secrete the entire contents of the vial into Lila's coffee at The Walrus—the coffeehouse she was known to frequent—a task that was soon presenting itself as he stood behind them in line, wearing a fake mustache and a pair of mirrored aviator shades. Since the barista prepared the drinks but left them on a tray for a server to bring to their table, all he would have to do is pass his hand over the cup and release the contents of the vial. The bitter of the coffee would mask the bitter of the wormwood, and if it didn't send her into lethal seizures within an hour, it would leave her with severe and permanent mental deteriora-tion. Delirium, coma, paranoia, psychosis—the list of derange-ments was delicious. "Pray for her," Ivan had said. He'd pray for her, all right—pray that she survived a twitching drooling psy-chotic retard.

Meanwhile, oblivious of these diabolical machinations,

Merlin was happily chatting up Lila on the wonders of green tea, of how studies had shown that its potent antioxidant properties could actually slow the aging process.

"What's wrong with aging?" Lila asked. "What're you, afraid of dying?"

"I ain't afraid of dying," Merlin retorted. "I'm afraid of not living. And nothing's *wrong* with aging, but nothing's wrong with staying sexy either, and I'd rather enjoy a hundred years of vitality than have to face fifty years of gradually declining health. Besides, who can afford health care?"

"Very well then," Lila sighed, indulging his fanaticism. "Green tea it is."

And thereby did Merlin order them each a matcha green tea coconut latte. "Matcha has a hundred thirty-seven times the antioxidant potency of regular green tea," Merlin boasted. "Because you're consuming the whole powdered tea leaf, not just the water it's been steeped in."

"Wow," Lila patronized, neither aware that Merlin's dorky enthusiasm had just saved Lila from permanent mental derangement, as a delicately flavored pale frothy green tea would not suffice to mask the brown and bitter wormwood oil.

Chris Bliss realized this immediately, silently cursing as he screwed the cap back on his wicked vial of wormwood oil. He ordered a croissant and a *Wall Street Journal*, and resolved instead upon Plan B, merely to observe and report.

34

TAKING A SEAT at an adjacent table to Lila and this Merlin, Chris Bliss stroked the used handkerchief Ivan had long ago given him as a relic and pretended to vex over the *Wall Street Journal.* Clearly, Lila and this Merlin were lovers, fresh lovers by the looks of them, and this Merlin was probably the source of Lila's dark intoxication. Chris Bliss made a few halfhearted notes, but his mind kept wandering toward a recollection of last night, when Ivan had at last permitted him to receive the "translinguistic emission" of the Master's penis. This was the Wisdom, Ivan had grunted as he irrumated himself into Chris Bliss's mouth, yes the ineffable, that which cannot be spoken, and the reward for his devotion. Chris Bliss had gone wild with enthusiasm, anticipating a rapturous explosion of enlightenment, and while there was indeed a burst of something, Chris Bliss had not guessed that enlightenment would taste so salty.

Not to worry, Ivan had reassured. Probably, he was still resisting the Wisdom, as evidenced by the fact that he had gagged on the translinguistic emission. "You're still experiencing the three-dimensional illusion," Ivan had explained. "Rather than the fourth-dimensional truth. You have to learn to identify with your spirit, my child, and not with your body. Patience, my child. It will come."

Chris Bliss could hardly wait to try again, and sitting here in the coffeehouse he felt certain that one of the baristas who smiled at him was secretly a Zen master sent to check up on him and observe his progress. The thought of this thrilled him, but for now, he had only to make sure Lila would not thwart his salvation. His attention seized when he heard Lila mention Ivan's name.

"I need to apologize for what I told you about Ivan yesterday," Lila sighed loud and remorseful as she toyed with some flowers in a small vase on the table, causing Merlin's eyebrows to stretch.

"What, you mean you don't actually think that he's a black hole of sociopathic narcissism?" Merlin clarified, grinning. Lila shook her head lightly, but Merlin carried on. "A personality utterly devoid of empathy, and so insecure not only about himself but about the mystery of existence that he has diabolically manipulated hundreds of people into feeding him the delusion that he's an enlightened Master?"

Chris Bliss nearly threw up his heart at this slander of his messiah—matters were much worse than he could ever have imagined—but was ultimately relieved to see that Lila was so obviously chastened. Lila shook her head sadly, murmuring, inexplicably, "Möbius." While Chris Bliss had no idea what that meant and would never even think to speculate, Merlin— after blinking a couple of times—certainly comprehended her meaning:

Möbius. *This is not really happening.*

"I see," Merlin responded, softening his tone and playing along improv. "Feeling a little regret, are we?"

Lila knew well the derangements of the Holy Company of Beautiful People, and had guessed that whoever had been staking out her apartment would not be scared off by mere bottle rockets. Besides, neither Chris Bliss's rodentine features nor the mewling nose whistle and rotten cabbage death breath of his chronic sinusitis were hidden by his plaid fedora and nasty trash 'stache disguise. Knowing that Chris Bliss could not see her face, Lila could not help but smirk. Taking a moment to regain her composure, she continued. "He's such a wonderful being," she gushed, as if helpless at the thought of Ivan. "An avatar, a messiah, I really don't know, but I hope you can meet the Master someday. Meeting him is like meeting the highest version of yourself, your own greatest potential. I'm so afraid that in a moment of weakness I've shut him out of my life forever."

"I'm sure the Master has already forgiven you," Merlin gently reassured.

"Do you really think so?"

"I *know* so."

"I hope so," Lila sniffled as Merlin grasped her hand earnest, and she smiled at the sound of Chris Bliss getting up behind her, who could hardly wait to report to Ivan that Lila had not fallen after all, that she was in fact stricken with grief that she would never see the Master again. Plus, Chris Bliss was eager to again attempt to receive the translinguistic emission of the Wisdom, so eager, in fact, that he inadvertently left the wicked vial of wormwood oil behind on the table.

35

MERLIN FOLLOWED Lila's grinning eyes as she watched Chris Bliss hurry away down the sidewalk. Chris Bliss snatched the fedora off his head along his way. "Who was *that*?" Merlin asked, his tone no longer artful.

"That would be Chris Bliss, the messiah's favorite minion," Lila snickered. "I'd recognize his testicular chin anywhere, plus he always has this distracted look on his face, like he's just suddenly realized that he didn't sufficiently wipe his ass."

Merlin smiled as he watched Chris Bliss stride away for a few moments. "Not to mention his hairline. Dear god, what happened there?"

"Oh jeezus," Lila rolled her eyes. "Ivan has his disciples guinea-pig various plastic surgeries before submitting to them himself. When Chris Bliss's hairline started receding, Ivan paid for his initial hair transplant procedure just to see how it would look. But Chris Bliss had aggressive male-pattern baldness, so he ended up looking like a Franciscan monk with a monastic crown of hair. Ivan says it's called a *tonsure*. Says it's a sign of holiness."

Merlin laughed out loud. "That's the most ridiculous thing I've ever heard!"

"Yeah," Lila shook her head, twirling the flowers from the small vase on the table, looking suddenly despondent. "The Holy Company of Beautiful People," she disdained. "What a bunch of *lunatics*."

Hoping to change the subject to something less obviously distressing, Merlin picked her keys up off the table. "Hey, did you know this is called a key fob?" he asked cheerfully, displaying the remote control device on the key chain. "And did you know that if I pressed the unlock button on your key fob two hundred and fifty-six times while it's out of range, I could permanently disable it?"

Lila looked up with some interest from her despondency. "Seriously?"

Merlin nodded and pointed to the fob in her hand. "So check this out: The way these work is that there's a pseudo-random number generator in the remote control as well as in a receiver inside the car. Every time any button on the key fob is pressed, it generates a pseudo-random forty-bit code. When the receiver on your car receives this signal, it compares it to its own pseudo-random code, and as long as their codes are synchronized, the car locks or unlocks." Merlin leaned forward, pleased to see that Lila was listening attentively. "However—and here's the trick—in order to protect against accidentally pressing a button on the key fob when it's out of range and accidentally desynchronizing their pseudo-random codes, the receiver will also accept any of the next two hundred and fifty-six expected pseudo-random codes in the sequence. But if I were to press it two hundred and fifty-six times while it's out of range, the receiver would no longer recognize the incoming code, the codes would be out of sync, and the remote would be useless." Merlin leaned back, nodding in satisfaction with himself.

Lila squinted at Merlin. "And how do you know this?"

"I told you I used to fancy myself an amateur locksmith. I learned all kinds of cool stuff like that. There's really no such thing as perfect security. If you practiced for just a few hours, you could defeat most locks out there fairly easily."

Smiling, Lila reached forward and took her keys from him. "Well, aren't you just Mr. Mystery?" Then she fell silent again, returning to twirling the flowers from the small vase on the table. After several moments, she gestured in the direction in which Chris Bliss had left. "I'm sorry if I seem distracted. I just can't believe I was ever a part of that nonsense. It really bothers me sometimes."

Merlin nodded compassionate. "Why don't you tell me more about it? I mean, I still don't get how this guy manages to con so many people."

"It's a subtle game," Lila said after a thoughtful pause. "First of all, you need to realize that I didn't even know Ivan existed until six months after I started making all these new friends through a yoga class I was taking. It's awesome to be a part of a community all of a sudden, right, and once they'd ensnared my identity, they started dropping details about an ascended Master that they knew about, and when I asked about it they said I might be able to meet him someday, just sort of goading my curiosity. Since they were all these attractive, intelligent, successful people, I just naturally assumed they must have known something I didn't, so I went along. And then when I met him, he seemed to have this supernatural insight into my life, but only because everyone had been reporting all these details I'd casually shared with them over the last few months. And of course, they were all expecting me to see him as this ascended Master as well. It's actually pretty difficult to resist others' descriptions of reality, especially when you identify with them. Plus, Ivan would host these extended therapeutic healing sessions with individuals and small groups—which of course we had to pay for—in which everyone was supposed to reveal their issues and insecurities. Supposedly, doing so would release us from our fears, but really he just used our fears and insecurities to further manipulate us. And then on top of all that, the longer you're in the cult the more all your social and economic resources are invested in it, and since your identity is really just your social location, and since your social location is ultimately based on access to resources, you eventually become entirely dependent on the illusion being real. Controlling people's identities by controlling their access to resources is the number-one way to compel compliance. So anyway, it took awhile for the truth to trickle through."

Merlin was listening intently. "It's actually kind of impressive. Disturbing and deranged, but nonetheless impressive that he's able to manipulate so many people that way."

"I suppose," Lila shrugged. "Same as any politician, really.

His real talent was in mesmerizing people with flattery, and then revoking it. The unspoken currency of social interaction is approval, and after gracing you with his and all these uncommonly attractive people's love and acceptance, he'd strategically withhold it. Everyone seeks approval from the world at large, some assurance that they are loved and accepted. By occasionally withholding his approval, he created a magnetic presence for himself, causing people to project their abandonment issues onto him and casting himself as the solution. Since everyone wants to relieve themselves of the traumas of their childhood, and because he re-stimulates feelings of disapproval and abandonment, he becomes your makeshift parent, your guru."

"God," Merlin wrinkled his nose. "What an antichrist."

"Yeah, I'd find myself thinking things like *Why won't he smile at me?* or *What can I do to win his attention?* Plus, remember, he's already surrounded himself with all these other attractive people, so you know, you want to be accepted by your community of friends as well, and that only happens through him, because if he turns on you then they turn on you. But of course, the entire phony community is only held together by the insecurity and low self-esteem of its members and the dependency upon him that he's manufactured. Like for example, he would advise one guy in the group that another woman in the group was his soul mate and that he should stop at nothing to fulfill his karma with her, while at the same he was telling that same woman that she should avoid that guy at all costs if she was to have any hope of transcending her karma in this lifetime. That sort of thing."

"What a monster."

Lila nodded. "Anyway, as long as you don't question him, no matter how absurd or even criminal things get, your self-esteem and your financial situation feel promising. But it relies utterly upon the worldview he creates for you. It's brainwashing."

Merlin nodded. "And then when he ties it up with spirituality, the entire thing becomes a surrogate for the existential abandonment of being thrown into life in the first place."

Lila paused, considering. "Yeah, that's exactly right. And he makes himself impervious to criticism as well, since if you try to call him out on any of his BS, he just claims some Zen master crazy wisdom smackdown. 'Don't get mad at me,' he'd shrug. 'Get mad at God.'"

Merlin chuckled, and Lila continued. "It's the ultimate alibi. You know those stories of Zen masters who supposedly slap their students into enlightenment? Well, that's how he styled himself, digging on your self-esteem, taking your money, manipulating you, *molesting* you, all just for your growth, just trying to get you over your attachments, just giving you what you need to slap you into enlightenment. Like it's some kind of a favor." She shook her head in disgust and fell silent.

Merlin nodded for a few moments. "Hey," he touched her arm. "Nice choice on the coffeehouse, by the way." He looked around appreciatively. "I especially like the tunes," he said, nodding. "'I Am the Walrus.'"

"It's totally my favorite coffeehouse." Lila smiled as she idly toyed with the flowers in the small vase on the table. "They actually only ever play the Beatles here. That's why they call it The Walrus—"

"Hang on, hang on," Merlin interrupted. "And you used to work at a seafood restaurant called the Octopus's Garden?"

Lila shrugged. "The Beatles are kind of a thing for me. Their music reminds me of something."

"What does it remind you of?"

"I can't quite remember," Lila replied, her gaze drifting faraway.

"Well," Merlin chuckled and shook his head, "I can't imagine why I know what you mean."

"I know, right?" Lila's gaze returned from its sojourn, and she resumed toying with the flowers in her hand, idly counting their petals. "Do you know what kind of flowers these are?" Merlin glanced at them. "Looks like some kind of a daisy?"

"Blackfoot daisies, actually," Lila corrected, privately pleased that all of them were invariably possessed of an odd petal count that would inevitably end on *he loves me.* "See, the petals are much larger than your common daisy. Plus, there's nowhere near as many. These must come from a nursery, though. Blackfoot daisies are not native to this area."

"A horticulturalist too?" Merlin observed.

Lila shrugged and fell into a pensive pause. "Anyway," she sighed. "Thanks for letting me vent."

"Of course."

"You want to know the strangest thing about Ivan, though?" Lila continued. "I *am* more aware than I used to be, but that doesn't make *him* an ascended Master. It actually just makes him a demented pervert." She paused, still fingering her flowers. "After all, a true seeker will find enlightenment even following a jackass."

Merlin grinned. "So you tossed a liter of ice water in his lap. I've always wanted to do something like that."

"Yeah," Lila smiled. "It was pretty awesome."

"So are you going to try to get your job back?"

"Nah," Lila shook her head. "I'd turn to a life of crime before I'd go back to that job. There are far worse things to lose in life than a *job.* Your soul, for instance. Your self-respect. Your freedom. Your integrity. Your faith." She paused. "Tonight's a full moon, isn't it?"

"I think so," Merlin shrugged. "Why? What're you gonna do now?"

"Gosh, I don't know." Lila moved to get up, taking her bouquet of blackfoot daisies with her. "I'll probably get robbed and beaten and run over by an ambulance as I'm starving to death." She grinned spectacular. "But at least I won't be slaving my life away for someone else's seafood." She paused, standing, toying with her keys, an idea glimmering her eyes. "Besides, I have an idea."

"You have an idea?" Merlin said, leaning in to kiss her. "That sounds dangerous."

"It *is* dangerous," Lila responded and met his kiss. "*We're* dangerous. Möbius, remember? The ego's pretense at life is an illusion. It isn't really happening." She ran her tongue across his lips, shivering him. "That's a dangerous thing to realize." Turning to go, Lila's eyes caught sight of the half-ounce amber glass vial that Chris Bliss had inadvertently left behind on his table and her hand deftly swiped it into her purse for later investigation. Merlin noticed nothing.

"You know," Merlin cautioned as he licked the tingle from his lips, "calling something an illusion doesn't necessarily mean it isn't real."

"I know *that*," Lila smiled as they turned to go. "It just means it can be whatever we want it to be."

36

WHEN FLAMING JANE was still a child in Ireland, a traveling merchant from France had once captivated her imagination with the story of Joan of Arc. The merchant told of how—when Joan of Arc was just seventeen—she was trying to persuade one of her generals to attack an English fortress. She was rebuffed as an illiterate peasant and dismissed, but instead of capitulating, she held her conviction steadfast and announced that she would lead the men over the walls herself, to which the general dryly responded, "Not a man will follow you." Undeterred, Joan of Arc drew her sword and shouted, "I will not look back to see if anyone is following or not!" Her defiant ferocity inspired courage in all who witnessed and ultimately she succeeded in leading the charge victorious.

Flaming Jane had smiled a private mischief when she first heard that story, and now, the day after Crow had awoken from his fever dream—and just fifteen minutes after he'd resounded Moby's *Windward ho!* warning that they were being followed— that same private mischief smiled itself across her face as she prepared to address the entire crew from fifteen feet up the main rigging, patiently awaiting the cacophony of voices to satisfy themselves into silence.

"Behold, the Spanish colonial real!" Flaming Jane began at last, holding a silver coin at arm's length between her thumb and forefinger. "And see that there is nothing real about it! The very word *real* is a contraction of the word *regal*, as if some inbred royalty has dared to dictate the reality we inhabit!" She pitched the coin into the sea to a swelling revelry of *Ho!*

"But we have no interest in the lies of royalty!" Flaming Jane yelled, sea breeze billowing her hair around her face like flares of wild sunshine as every sentence she spoke now found its punctuation in an enthusiastic *Ho!* from the crew:

"They plunder the poor under the pretense of law while we rob the rich under the cover of nothing save our own courage!"

Ho!

"We are called thieves because we take what they steal!"

Ho!

"We are called outlaws because we liberate the people they enslave!"

Ho!

"We are called pirates because we do not buccaneer on their behalf!"

Ho!

"But we work for no crown!"

Ho!

"We do not require a king's permission to sail these seas any more than we require his permission to draw our next breath!"

Ho!

"We are kings and queens each of us, and as free as he who commands an armada!"

Ho!

"We take orders from no one and we give orders to no one!"

Ho!

"*I* govern only myself, and *I* have no patience for the

hen-hearted wimps who allow themselves to be governed by others!"

Ho!

"This is *my* life, and if your life follows my life, then that's your choice and *never* my command!"

Ho!

Flaming Jane paused long, her gaze daring anyone to defy her anarchy. But none spoke a word, and even the gulls had ceased their squawk and quarrel to attend to her words. When she continued, her voice had settled:

"As you know, my friends, our position has been discovered. There is little doubt that we will face our enemy soon, and I sense the same as you that it is an enemy we have faced before. I can offer you no certainty save this: All of us will die someday, and until then the only business of life is merry adventure. Death is the dance our lives have implied. Play it safe and we'll be dead years before we die. But play it dangerous and death won't even slow us down." These words were met with another roistering swell of *Ho!*, and Flaming Jane doubled her volume to finish her address. "Oppression is spring-loaded, brothers and sisters, and this is our advantage over everyone who would obstruct us!"

Ho!

"*We* are fearless and *we* are free!"

Ho!

"Our frustration is our determination!"

Ho!

"*We* will not be tamed!"

Ho!

"*We* will not be reduced!"

Ho!

"*We* are fearless and *we* are free!"

Ho!

"Our pain is our inspiration!"

Ho!

"*We* are uncontainable forces of nature!"

Ho!

"*We know* who we are where they know only what they're told!"

Ho!

"*We* are fearless and *we* are free!"

Ho!

"*We know* why we fight where they know only their orders!"

Ho!

"*We* are free where they are not!"

Ho!

"*We* are fearless where they are terrified!

Ho!

"*We* are fearless and *we* are free!"

And at this a raucous huzzah roiled up from the assembled as Flaming Jane repeated her refrain, "*We* are fearless and *we* are free! *We* are fearless and *we* are free!" until all were chanting up a gale and a stomp and a rhythm rocked the boat and after their sweat was glistening good Crow hefted himself up atop a barrel and with Noa and another pirate named Ian drumming beneath he began to shout a shanty like only the seraphim can roar the holy hosanna:

Sailor seaman, drunken demon
Take care you don't sink into that drink
Watch for the rum rotgut gets you done
Watch out you'll fall
You're dying
Whippin' out your pistol

Waitin' for that fateful hour
Eager belly goddamn killing for the blam blam
Christ, you should'a died a saint
You could'a seen it all

O, why are you and why am I
Dancing with this madness till we die?
Like sunset's blush our hearts will hush,
No time to lose,
No time to rush!

No time to lose,
No time to rush!

Gnashing devils, grumpy fellows
My you look so stupid when you kill
Go grab your gun go ruin all the fun
You're bound to fall
You're dying
Heaven for the hellbent
Floating like a paper sailboat
Folded out of pretense gaudy phony defense
Hey, we're gonna go to war
We're gonna have a ball

O, why are you and why am I
Dancing with this madness till we die?
Like sunset's blush our hearts will hush,
No time to lose,
No time to rush!

No time to lose,
No time to rush!

Grinning skullface jolly roger
Lead us to our gratitude of death
Bring on the fun let's reach for the sun
Bring on the fall
We're dying
Eden for the exploit
Hoisting up our Babel steeple
Slaughterhouse of old cards stamping like a yard guard
Man, they should'a seen the joke
They should'a let us be

O, why are you and why am I
Dancing with this madness till we die?
Like sunset's blush our hearts will hush,
No time to lose,
No time to rush!

No time to lose,
No time to rush!

And *Eleusis* sailed across the face of the blue-green sea, a sea that had swallowed untold hundreds of ships and drowned untold thousands of lives, a sea of merciless mood and passive reclamation, a sea, after all, that reflected the moon by night and the sun by day, a sea pulsing with the gravity of celestial bodies, by god, and a sea whose wisdom was so vast that it forever failed to notice the flimsy sufferings quarreling upon its surface. This was a sea, this was *the* sea, and the sea has seen it all, but it had never seen anything quite like this band of outlaws howling toward the horizon, riotous with the sort of music that can only be born from the screams of murdered ancestors, celebrating not their stupor but exuberating in their freedom, seeking not the weight of gold but savoring instead a life outstanding, and the sea could only agree with the chorus of exalted voices caressing across its sun-kissed surface like the tongue of an unhurried lover:

> *No time to lose,*
> *No time to rush!*

> *No time to lose,*
> *No time to rush!*

37

SITTING QUIETLY in the captain's quarters the next morning with Flaming Jane still sleeping at his side, Crow reflected upon his fever dream as he ran his finger across the curious warning tattooed across the bottom of the goatskin treasure map: *Prends Garde au Pré des Merveilles*—Beware the Meadow of Marvels. The meadow of marvels, it appeared, was their destination, but there was little by way of direction to this meadow of marvels. The coordinates on the map itself only pointed to a sizable island disconcertingly surrounded by treacherous waters, and the island itself displayed a single tree surrounded by a white snake eating its own tail, and flanked by an angel scowling angry and a devil grinning friendly. There was a black sun drawn along the top of the map along with the constellation Orion, and the warning was scripted across the sea.

Crow puzzled his brow. How could anyone possibly locate a meadow of unspecified marvels on an island of that size? They could easily hack through jungle for a year, find a hundred meadows, and miss a hundred more. And assuming they ever came across this marvelous meadow, how would they recognize it and what were they supposed to look for even if they did? Making matters yet more impossible, the map itself did not bother to point to a specific bay or inlet of the island, surrounded as it was by treacherous waters. An arrow shot from Orion's bow merely pointed to the island where a cycle of arrows turned an infinite circle around it.

Crow might have worried that they were on a fool's quest if anxiety was at all in his nature, which it was not. As it was, since he'd dreamt something of the basic details of the map before ever seeing it, he felt confident that this map somehow pointed the way forward.

Flaming Jane stirred awake and snuggled against his waist as Crow whispered, as he did every morning, "I'm so glad you're alive." She smiled sleepy, sat up, reached for her wineskin, and immediately drained it of its liter of water. Her morning thirst quenched, she gasped refreshed, mussed her tangled wild of hair, and gazed wide-awake and loving at Crow as he continued to study their map.

"I know what the treasure of all treasures is," Flaming Jane announced through a yawn.

"Ah, good," Crow greeted her gaze good morning. "I've been wondering at that myself."

"Your dream said it was worth more than even gold, right?"

He nodded.

"Have you ever heard of the Stone of the Philosophers?"

He nodded again as a smile began to canter about the corners of his mouth. "The alchemical quest? The stone that can turn any metal into gold?"

Flaming Jane's lips cantered right back at him. "What else could the treasure of all treasures be? The Stone of the Philosophers is worth more than any quantity of gold."

Crow fell silent as a considerable smile absorbed his face. "You stole this map from Goldtooth, didn't you? Along with all these sea charts?"

Flaming Jane shrugged.

He shook his head. "That's how he's been able to find us. He knows the map we're following."

"I know," she shrugged again.

"You realize, my love, that the treasure of all treasures cannot rest long undisturbed. As we have already discovered, it casts echoes of itself through the dreams and visions of those who seek it."

"You think Goldtooth knows what the treasure of all treasures is?"

"There is no doubt that Goldtooth knows what he's after. Vengeance alone cannot compel a man for long. But a greed such as this could compel an entire lifetime."

Flaming Jane smiled smug. "That's good," she said. "Because I have a plan."

38

AVING WITNESSED Flaming Jane already outwit Goldtooth firsthand, and having heard the tales of how she mutinied the *Queen Elizabeth*, Crow harbored no lack of faith in Flaming Jane's ability to plan. Still, Crow could not help but feel alarmed when he learned that she planned to divert their ship off its course toward the Lesser Antilles and dock at Boca Diablo, a port on an otherwise wild island off Puerto Rico notorious throughout the Spanish Main for being a pirate haven. Crow scoffed at that description, for a haven it was not. Boca Diablo was actually little more than a roaring swarm of mercenaries, and they'd be lucky to leave with their ship, if not their lives.

Eleusis, after all, was a lightly populated vessel operating with a crew of not more than fifty sailors, half of whom were women, and which included Crow and his Arawak brothers, Flaming Jane and the escaped African slaves, and a random assortment of runaways and outlaws who had somehow earned a place aboard. This made it a delightful ship upon which to sail: spacious, clean, organized, lightweight, and swifter on the water than most vessels that might threaten it. In close combat, however, this advantage would quickly be ceded against an overwhelm of firepower and manpower, so their very survival depended on keeping their distance and their wits about them. Sailing into Boca Diablo seemed an invitation to mishap and general misadventure.

Crow voiced these concerns only once before Flaming Jane overthrew them. "I've been to Boca Diablo before," she narrowed her eyes. "And I am not ignorant of its nature. However, we are being followed, and I know that bastard well enough to know that not only will he not risk following us into Boca Diablo, but there's also an even chance that he will continue on to the Lesser Antilles. Nevertheless," she began gathering the maps and sea charts into a bundle that she would slide into a hollow bamboo tube, "the plans of man are the pranks of God, so you can assist me in telling the crew to leave nothing on board of irreplaceable value."

Crow wanted to protest that the price on Flaming Jane's capture was sure to inspire malice as soon as she stepped off the boat, but he knew better than to press his point. When Flaming Jane wanted counsel, she asked for it, and when others gave it, she listened carefully. This was not one of those occasions, and Crow could only reckon that if she seemed headstrong in her convictions, she must have good reason for being so.

"As you wish," Crow got up to leave. "But let me be perfectly clear: I consider every pirate aboard this ship a brother and a sister, and I'll die before I see a single one of us captured or hung in a gibbet."

"Yes, I know," Flaming Jane smiled authentic. "That is why I love you."

39

TWO DAYS AFTER he'd first alerted Crow that *Eleusis* was being followed, Moby delivered a black vulture feather directly into Crow's hand. Crow accepted it and praised Moby for his apparent scrabble with Goldtooth's vultures, and Moby responded, "Three ships! Three ships!"

Crow considered Moby's reconnaissance. Since they had left the *Damnation* aflame in the midst of the Crown's shipping lanes, Crow had guessed that the Royal Navy might manage to rescue Goldtooth from the ruins of the *Damnation*. Now, Moby had confirmed not only that it was indeed Goldtooth who was following them, but that he'd also succeeded in diverting three ships into pursuit of them. Despite any reservations he held at their course into Boca Diablo, Crow had to admit at least for the moment that he preferred it to a hasty course toward the meadow of marvels. The Stone of the Philosophers was the treasure of all treasures, after all, and Crow understood that an item of such power would not hesitate to trade its quest for a seeker's life.

As the port of Boca Diablo came into view, however, Crow again felt compelled to question Flaming Jane's decision. Glassing the docks, he spied several ships and a crowd several times the size of their crew already observing their approach. As Flaming Jane was most of the way up the mainmast, her red hair billowing in the breeze beneath their Jolly Roger snapping at the masthead, it was evident that everyone ashore knew well who was arriving, and their stature and demeanor broadcast that they had more lynch than love upon their lips—that and the redheaded effigy that was already hanging off the dock. Aggravated at the apparent carelessness of Flaming Jane's maneuver, Crow climbed the masting to consult with her.

"Is it so difficult to trust me?" Flaming Jane greeted him as he made his way toward her.

"I'd sooner sail into a cyclone than any closer to that horde of depravity! They'll take our ship as soon as they can reach it!"

"That's the plan, my love."

Crow paused, vaguely annoyed. "It is clear that you derive delight from your ability to scheme—"

"*Tremendous* delight," Flaming Jane laughed.

"But I am neither a follower nor a fool," Crow continued. "I'll do anything, my love, but give me a reason, not a rule."

Flaming Jane regarded him a moment, considering. "That's a smart turn of phrase," she cackled, "but not as smart as a woman!"

Crow shook his head. He had never known a person so reveled by themselves, a thoroughly conceitless confidence that disregarded the approval of others as quickly as it did their condemnations. Crow sighed as he surveyed the assembly of avarice and villainy awaiting their arrival. "We'll likely die," he observed.

Flaming Jane laughed out loud. "We'll likely not," she sassed. "And even if we do, I'll have you know that I intend to enjoy every merry second until then."

"You'll find no argument from me on that," Crow assured. "But my gut tells me to fire our cannons into those docks. Can you tell me why I shouldn't do that?"

"Patience, boy howdy! That'd simply make a bloody mess and a hound of mortal enemies besides!" Flaming Jane disgusted. "Tell your brothers to spit in their ugly faces, to show their defiance, but to let them take the ship. They're more greedy than bloodthirsty, and once they have the ship they'll be happy to leave us stranded. This ship is worth far more to them than any price on my head."

"We're just going to *give* them *Eleusis*?"

Flaming Jane shook her head. "We're going to *give* them a boat," she said, gesturing to the ship. "*Eleusis* is not this pile of planks. *Eleusis* is this crew, and every man and woman aboard this ship will leave with us, if it be their will."

"And then what?"

"And then you'll have to trust me," Flaming Jane glared into him, "because I know *exactly* what I'm doing."

40

CROW WAS NONE too happy about having to trust another with his life, but if ever there was another worthy of his trust, it was Flaming Jane. After assenting reluctant, he made his way down the ropes, resigned at first, then relaxed, and ultimately curious to discover how it would all unfold. Crow understood, after all, that even when he was in charge there was never any reason to believe he was in control. Crow knew Flaming Jane understood this as well, and so he didn't have to trust her plan—such as it was—he only had to trust the light shining from her eyes, and that was as easy as trusting the sunrise.

Thus assuaged, Crow set about organizing the rest of the crew to gather their effects and weapons. If someone resented (and very few did), Crow simply reminded that one neither obtains nor retains one's freedom by playing it safe, and that— given the manner in which known circumstances were closing them in—venturing into unknown circumstances was bound to reveal new opportunity. In the end, all aboard agreed with ease, and unflinching unhesitant they all together faced the waiting mob and sent a shuffle of knees unnerving and a stammer of chins stumbling throughout the horde ashore, for though the horde had numbers they were each of them alone, and though they had their steel it was enfeebled by their fear.

Then Crow dispatched a single flaming arrow, embedding

it in the redheaded effigy and engulfing it in flames as all aboard roared upon their approach. They may as well have been a tropical thunderstorm bearing down upon the horde, their unmistaken ferocity shrimping shoulders, wincing eyes, and eroding the edges of the crowd as craven after coward slinked off shaking his mercenary head no goddamned way. It was not until they were well past hailing distance that Flaming Jane offered salutations to the man who had doubtless aggravated this throng together with promises of their own ship, a man who himself had once sailed with *Eleusis*, and a man she'd pitched overboard the last time she was here after he tried to organize a mutiny against her—an ill-advised plot that backfired upon him immediately after he attempted to hatch it to another member of her loyal crew.

"Half-Ass McJanky!" Flaming Jane yelled across the narrowing water. "Still as arrogant as you are stupid, I see!" Half-Ass was not his given name, Crow later learned. Half-Ass had earned his sobriquet after half his hindquarters were blown off by case shot in a skirmish at sea. The case shot, it turned out, were actually doubloons that had been pounded into brads, and though Half-Ass was lucky to have survived where many of his crew were torn to pieces, he nonetheless made sure to cut the coins out of their corpses before dumping the bodies of his mates at sea.

"Flaming Jane," Half-Ass McJanky called back. "Stills as arrogant as *yers* stoopid!"

Flaming Jane smiled. "Pleasantries aside, old comrade, and though you are not worthy to kiss the tip of my boot even if it found its way to your lips by way of a kick, I come offering you a gift!"

Half-Ass McJanky raised an eyebrow. "I hopes yers gift is worths more than *yers head*!"

At this, Flaming Jane pulled a line that unfurled a white flag beneath their Jolly Roger. "Our ship is yours if you want her, but only if you take her without a fight!"

Half-Ass McJanky brayed a bad-mannered laugh across the bay. "Thar's a fines idea, Flaming Jane, but why don'ts I just fights you and takes her anyways?"

"Because you know that each person on my crew can kill five of yours before we fall, and we do not fear to fall!"

Half-Ass McJanky's mob shifted, and he momentarily fumbled for words. "And why woulds you surrenders yers ship?"

"We must come ashore for water, rest, and provisions, and you are obviously in a position to prevent us from doing so. But this ship has served our purpose, and anyway, our sister ship will not be long in fetching us," Flaming Jane lied. "Besides, if giving you this ship buries any blood between us, then that's a fine turn for us both, and despite the grotesque warts in your character, you were a fine seaman, and I wish you wealth upon your way."

"Yers sister ship?" Half-Ass McJanky was covetous in his words, as Flaming Jane knew he would be. "How fars behinds is she?"

"Three days away, I reckon, maybe less," Flaming Jane called back.

Half-Ass McJanky paused long, the wind hushing silence as Flaming Jane stared him down. She knew it wasn't the strongest bluff in her bag, but she also knew Half-Ass McJanky wasn't the smartest dog on the sea. "Whats do you wants?" he asked at last.

"Clear the docks of your men, and permit us safe harbor. Then the ship is yours. Even an unwashed simpleton like yourself ought to be able to understand that."

Half-Ass McJanky paused again, aggravated by her insults,

but Flaming Jane knew there was no further decision to be made. There was no way Half-Ass McJanky could compel these men to fight for something they were being given. The mob was already nervous and muttering impatient, its edges eroding faster as men made the decision for themselves. This fact was not lost upon Half-Ass McJanky, and he hastened to bellow, "Very wells!" in order to seize the credit for his men's departure. "Clears these docks, men! You'll haves yers ship in ones hour!" Then to Flaming Jane he boasted a warning: "Ones hour, Flaming Jane! Any man lefts aboard yers ship in ones hour wills be hanged froms the yardarm!"

41

STRIDING SINGLE FILE past what remained of the line of Half-Ass McJanky's men, the Eleusinians spat, shoved, and skirmished any man who scowled their gaze longer than a split second. Flaming Jane was at the end of the line, wearing a sash of pistols across her chest and a pistol in each hand, flanked by Crow ahead of her and the giant Noa behind with Catface seated upon his shoulders, and Flaming Jane easily stared down any man who dared to glance at the pirate woman who rumor held could bite a chunk out of your neck and spit it back in your face before you could gargle *yar!* Only one man was fool enough to think he was cool enough to take a stab at Flaming Jane, and by the time Crow caught his offending arm Flaming Jane had the attacker poising upon his tiptoes with the barrel of a pistol elevating his chin. Catface hissed a wicked swipe at the attacker while Noa slapped him off his ballet backward and sprawling head over hindquarters, and thereafter the rest of the line gave them an eyes-avert and wide berth.

At the end of the line stood Half-Ass McJanky, and the gloat of his grin was almost enough to cause Crow to forget about any unrevealed plan of Flaming Jane's and spank the piss out of him right there. Handing their ship over to an unrepentant idiot like Half-Ass McJanky stretched the limits of his tolerance for human stupidity, but Crow held his tongue and his sword as the foul of Half-Ass McJanky's breath assaulted him, moving to stand behind Flaming Jane as she paused to address him.

"You always were as charming as the devil, Half-Ass, and just as untrustworthy." Flaming Jane bowed with circumspect respect. "But the ship is now yours, as you have long wished her to be."

"She shores is," Half-Ass McJanky agreed, accepting her courtesy. "As she woulds'a beens anyways. But I must says," his voice wheezing with the glee of its own self-congratulation, "I can'ts helps but bes amused at our turns of fate. What comes around goes around, I supposes."

"Yes," Flaming Jane smiled. "And all one has to do is wait as we play out our parts. Everything in time."

Half-Ass McJanky nodded, mystified by her reply. Some part of him suspected that Flaming Jane had an angle, but a much louder part only permitted him to brag his victory. "Well," he shrugged. "I supposes thar's rilly nothing left to says but... *I wins.*"

"Yes, Half-Ass McJanky," Flaming Jane affirmed, resisting an impulse to split the sneer of his lip with the tip of her boot. "You wins."

42

MERLIN AWOKE to find a ring of blackfoot daisies woven about the head of his penis. Not knowing whether to be confused or annoyed at this, he scarcely had time to fling the cockwreath of flowers across Lila's bedroom before a squelch from an undiscovered walkie-talkie on the bedside table demanded his befuddled attention.

"Little Smoochie to Big Smoochie," Lila's voice blared from the radio. "Come back, Big Smoochie."

Merlin smirked at her chosen CB handles and reached for the walkie-talkie. "Uh, Big Smoochie here," he spoke into the transmitter. "Nice daisies there, Little Smoochie."

"They're not just daisies," Lila corrected.

"Sorry, black-eyed daisies."

"Black*foot* daisies," she corrected him again.

"Yes, black*foot* daisies," Merlin indulged her whimsy. "So, what's your ten-twenty, Little Smoochie?"

"Cut the chatter, Big Smoochie," Lila responded officiously. "I need you to be my dispatcher this morning."

"All right," Merlin puzzled. "Whatever that means, Little Smoochie."

"I'll explain over lunch. For now, I just need you to radio me at *exactly* 11:20 from the top of the grand staircase of Alta Plaza Park, in Pacific Heights. Do you know where that is?"

"Yeah, I've been there before." Merlin checked the time. It was 8:30. "So you mean like three hours from now?"

"Two hours and fifty minutes from now, at *exactly* 11:20, and it *has* to be from the top of the grand staircase of Alta Plaza Park to be in range. Just radio me and say, 'Unit 505, can you confirm pickup?'"

"Exactly 11:20," Merlin responded. "Do we have to synchronize our watches or something?"

"What do you think this is, amateur hour?" Lila's voice crackled over the radio. "Use your cell phone, of course, they're already synched via satellite."

Merlin chuckled. "Ten-four."

"So what are you going to say at exactly 11:20?" Lila said after a moment.

"Unit 505, can you confirm pickup?"

"You have to sound administrative, like a radio dispatcher. Try again."

"Wait, where are you now? And what are you picking up?"

"Cut the chatter, Big Smoochie. I'll explain over lunch. Now let's hear your radio dispatcher."

Merlin sighed and imitated his best radio dispatcher. "Unit 505, can you confirm pickup?"

"Perfect. Then I'll confirm and you'll ten-four. That's it. If I don't confirm right away for some reason, just wait thirty seconds and radio me again. But just make sure you're at the top of the grand staircase at Alta Plaza Park, and maintain complete radio silence until then. I'll meet you there afterwards. Ten-four, Big Smoochie?"

Merlin looked amused at the walkie-talkie in his hand. "Ten-four, Little Smoochie," he said, playing along.

"And remember," Lila said. "Möbius! This isn't really happening!"

43

T HE RANGE on Lila's high-powered walkie-talkies was supposedly thirty-five miles, but that was hilltop to hilltop
and free of obstructions. In the thick of the city with all
its insane hills and buildings, Lila didn't trust her walkie-talkies any farther than a couple of miles, and for her purposes, the
top of the grand staircase of Alta Plaza Park was less than a mile
from Ivan's gigantic house in Presidio Heights, and nearly the
same elevation and a straight line of streets at that.

Merlin had done as instructed, radioing Lila at exactly
11:20 from the top of the grand staircase of Alta Plaza Park
and saying, "Unit 505, can you confirm pickup?" to which
she'd responded, "Unit 505, confirming pickup," and he'd said,
"Ten-four," and that was that. Now, after running up and down
the grand staircase a couple of times just to thrill time while he
was waiting for Lila to appear, Merlin enjoyed the magnificent
views of the city and bay that the park afforded, till his walkie-
talkie again broadcast the sound of Lila's voice:

"Little Smoochie to Big Smoochie, come back."

"Big Smoochie here," Merlin drawled in his CB voice.
"What's your ten-twenty, Little Smoochie?"

"Right behind you, Big Smoochie."

And as Merlin turned around he spotted Lila walking
toward him, unmistakable in the confidence of her stride,
though curiously hidden beneath some mirrored sunglasses
and a chestnut brown wig. She carried a vinyl deposit envelope in her grasp, and smiled when they made eye contact,
vaguely stern in her approach. "Let's go," she said, brushing a

kiss against his lips with all the severity of a Soviet defector, and they hustled without speaking down the grand staircase.

"So you picked up a vinyl deposit envelope?" Merlin inquired after he could no longer contain his curiosity.

"It's actually real leather," Lila smiled sly. "Let me buy you lunch," and she led him into a high-ceilinged eatery crowded with urban professionals yakking across their overpriced business lunches beneath the exposed and polished ductwork. Once they were seated and they'd ordered, Lila passed the leather deposit envelope to him. "Open it," she invited.

Merlin tried but the zipper had a combination lock. "Do you know the combination?"

"Try six-six-six," she smiled.

Merlin entered the combination and unzipped the envelope, where his widening eyes discovered it stuffed with cash, mostly hundred-dollar bills, with a few dozen fifties and twenties scattered throughout. "Jeezus!" Merlin fanned through the bills beneath the tabletop. "How much is in here?"

"Almost ten thousand," Lila's eyes flared wild. "And all courtesy of the Holy Company of Beautiful People."

Merlin was momentarily speechless. "What?"

And thereupon Lila explained how Ivan hosts abundance rituals every full moon, during which time his disciples are supposed to donate money in order to stimulate the flow of abundance in their own lives—and the more money they donate, the more abundance they could anticipate in the following month, hence all the hundreds. Lila knew that Ivan had contracted with a private security firm to pickup the abundance offerings every twenty-eight days, the morning after the full moon abundance ritual, at 11:30 a.m. sharp, not a minute later and not a minute sooner, so as to minimize disruption to the dozens of disciples still basking in the afterglow of the previous evening's abundance ritual, or what they called the Adoration. The Adoration essentially consisted of them lounging around in saffron togas, massaging one another with various essential oils, and taking turns anointing and kissing the feet of the Master as he loafed upon his dais nibbling grapes in pharaonic splendor. The armored truck typically arrived early and parked in the shade of a tree in front of the neighbor's house, the security guards paying no attention at all to Ivan's house, just waiting till the specified 11:30 to make the pickup, their dispatcher confirming it over the radio. Having once been in the Holy Company of Beautiful People herself, Lila had seen it happen this way several times.

Lila had simply purchased an identical rent-a-cop uniform from a uniform supply house, dressed the part with wig and sunglasses, and showed up ten minutes early, at 11:20, while the armored truck was still waiting in the shade of a tree in front of the neighbor's house. The squelch of her radio and the voice of a dispatcher, "Unit 505, can you confirm pickup?" both completed and compelled the illusion. Lila knew that Chris Bliss would be the witless doorman and that he resented his selfless service, terribly annoyed to be distracted from the Adoration. And so, glistening with massage oil and wearing nothing but a hasty toga, Chris Bliss handed over the leather deposit envelope without a second thought, scribbling his signature on her tablet computer and eager to return to the Adoration. By the time the actual security guard showed up ten minutes later, Lila had already abandoned her rent-a-cop uniform and was long gone.

Lila pointed her walkie-talkie's antenna at Merlin. "It's all about the walkie-talkie, yo. People automatically think you have some sort of authority just because you squelch a radio."

Merlin blinked, confused or amused, as if Lila had just pulled a fistful of rose petals out of her panties and flung them in his face. "Jeezus!" he astounded at last. "You're totally a con artist!"

"I am a *consciousness* artist," Lila replied, a full-blast smile drenching her face. "Didn't I already tell you? Life is performance art. And besides," she blew him a sultry kiss as if she were blowing the smoke off the barrel of a warm handgun, "even if by *con* you mean confidence, then you should know that confidence comes from the Latin *confidere*, to have full trust, and for whom does an artist have full trust if not their very own spirit? By that meaning, mustn't *any* artist worthy of their birth be a con artist?"

Merlin shook his head, still flabbergasted. "When did you come up with this?"

"I've actually been fantasizing about doing it for months," she replied. "Ever since I left that stupid cult. But I never thought I'd actually do it!" She shuddered with exhilaration. Then she added, under her breath and mostly to herself, "I can't believe this!"

"You'd better believe it," Merlin assured. "And if the shine in your smile is any barometer, this is a very good move."

"You're with me, then?"

"Of course I'm with you," Merlin snorted. "You do remember that I've been possessed by an imp since I was eight years old, yes?"

"Some kind of a jaguar, wasn't it?"

"That's right," Merlin nodded. "But all its spots were like eyes."

44

A N HOUR LATER, Lila and Merlin were riding the BART back
to her apartment in Berkeley, exhilarant. Both of them were
silent, consumed by their own thoughts, eyes occasionally
glancing off each other's but generally avoiding this for fear of
busting out into yowls of laughter.

Merlin studied the grin cavorting across Lila's lips as she gazed
out the window at the passing landscape. Some part of Merlin
clapped distraction and hollered caution, but these were muffled
beneath the elation soaring through his heart. Everything about
Lila was just absolutely exactly. Merlin was certain he'd met the
female version of himself, and he was *in love*, baby, in love like a
fool in fretless free fall off a blackfoot daisy–bedazzled cliff, and
my is that breeze refreshing! Sure, he was now an accessory to
grand larceny, but that was nothing compared to this infraction.
They had broken *the* rule, the rule from which all other illusions
derive, the rule that reality is only to be consumed and never to
be created. Merlin could no more turn away from the thrill of
that than he could turn away from the rest of his life.

Lila, too, was untamedly in love, and had yet to realize that
for the longest time since her childhood, her soul was not serenaded by that faraway cacophony of music boxes. When Lila was
a child, you see, her parents were terribly inconsiderate of her
innocence, and their yelling bellowing sometimes crashing argu-
ments so terrified her that she would hide in her closet with her
ballerina collection, each of which had a music box mounted in
its base. She would wind up all her ballerinas and set them pirou-
etting, unleashing a chaos of plinking music boxes that banished
the banshees of her parental discord.

The soundtrack of this trauma had echoed throughout her life, but now, watching the crowded urban landscape whiz past, a pleasant depersonalization eased her point of view. What had begun as a sort of gamesome reminder—Möbius, this isn't really happening—had assumed an unanticipated reality now that she had actually crossed the line and taken the dare. Looking out at the city itself, Lila felt as if it were already nothing more than the ruins of some foolhardy civilization. She'd felt this way only once before, walking across the National Mall on a trip to Washington, D.C., where the sheer scale and solidity of the various monuments give the impression that it was stacked together with the precise intention that it would one day be the masonry ruins to some ancient empire. But today, riding the BART train, there was nothing grand at all, just cars metabolizing into rust, neighborhoods pulsing between decay and gentrification, and stores full of carefully organized goods destined to be dusted for a decade before being consigned to a tangled pile of inglorious flotsam in a sneeze-achieving thrift store.

And here was a warehouse, an air-conditioned personal storage facility crammed with yet more of the same inglorious flotsam. Lila once read that there was over seven square feet of such personal storage space for every man, woman, and child in the United States. She couldn't imagine why anyone would wish to stow so much stuff, let alone produce it in the first place, and she blinked at the hubris of the enormous sign, Climate Controlled, seeing it through the fierce eyes of some lingering survivor to catastrophic climate change scavenging her way across an absurd landscape of abandoned automobiles. Lila smirked at her decontextualized vision, pleased at least that irony would survive the collapse of humanity's civilizations.

And here was a distant congress of homeless people gathered under a highway overpass, looking from a distance just exactly like a troop of monkeys. Musing upon her curious perceptions, Lila's vision abruptly detonated to encompass all of humanity, costumed monkeys disputing territories, eking out survival, laying down rules, acting out roles, and everyone just trying to get safe. Lila bit her lip in a moment of regret. Prior to a couple of years ago, Lila had gone out of her way to avoid the homeless, the way they harassed drivers at intersections with their despondent signs, the way they lurched hopefully toward open windows, the way she felt compelled to dodge eye contact lest she inadvertently invite further beggary, but mostly the way they reminded her of how she herself was almost homeless once.

It was, ultimately, a gigantically gregarious homeless man on Telegraph Avenue named Big Abe (short for Abendroth, he was proud to point out, which is German for the red afterglow of the evening sky) that finally shone his way through Lila's defenses when he convinced her one afternoon that Ronald Reagan was the Antichrist. "There are six letters in each of his names!" Big Abe had exclaimed, displaying an additional finger for each name: "Ronald. Wilson. Reagan. Six-six-six! It's all right there in front of you! And when he ran for governor of the state in 1966, promising to 'clean up the mess at Berkeley,' he cleaned up the hopes and dreams of a generation by gradually eliminating state-sponsored higher education and laying the groundwork for today's indentured students! And they've been tightening the screws ever since, haven't they? Can't change the world if you can't make rent, can you?" Big Abe settled down. "Anyway, everyone knows all about this in Hollywood. I mean, Reagan's house in Bel Air was at 666 St. Cloud Road until they had the address changed to 668." Big Abe nodded, satisfied at the self-evident truth of his assertions. "Like I said, it's all right there in front of you."

Big Abe had bragged to Lila about how he got seasonal work

in the three months prior to April 15 every year as a dancing Statue of Liberty doing roadside publicity for a local chain of tax preparation services, and although Lila had cringed at the total lack of dignity of such a job, this had never even occurred to Big Abe. In Big Abe's mind he got to dance for a living, and dancing was all he'd ever really wanted to do. But then last year, the entire chain of tax preparation services invested instead in motorized mannequin Statues of Liberty for their roadside publicity, and on the eve of April 15, Big Abe's spirit faltered and he lost all hope, placing a noose around his neck, tying the other end to the railing on the side of an overpass, and jumping. Big Abe was big enough that the weight of his body decapitated him on the noose, and the remains of his body were discovered early the next morning and hastily removed, that which passes for human civilization proceeding heedlessly along without him.

Lila remembered all this today in that split second that became the rest of her life. She fathomed the socially corrupt truth of the homeless predicament, their abandonment by the minions of the middle class, those who still imagined that the world of their egos was really happening, that their retirement plans would save them, that their granite countertops would protect them, and that life was ever something other than monkeys lost and lonely in cataclysmic mystery. Releasing a sigh, Lila determined right there to find a way to overthrow the delusions that defeat humanity, and a breath she'd been bracing her entire life finally found its relief.

45

L ILA'S MOTHER DIED when she was barely eighteen, and having an estranged father and neither extended family nor
inheritance to support her, Lila might have stumbled into
homelessness herself if not for her wits. As it was, she managed
to survive and eventually even to establish herself sufficiently to
enroll at UC-Berkeley by running various scams across the city
for a couple of months. Several times, for example, dressed as a
waitress and always being careful to disguise her red hair, Lila targeted the most expensive restaurants in the Bay Area during the
lunchtime rush, moving through the bustle of wait staff looking exactly as if she belonged there, and approaching table after
table, smiling hectic in her greeting, gushing pleasantries, asking
how their meal was, and either prompting their payment or collecting the vinyl folders already containing their cash and credit
cards, exiting in under two minutes. A grift born of the utmost
desperation, Lila was nonetheless alarmed to discover how good
at this she was.

The cash she collected from this she then invested by showing up at a few high-end jewelers, always being careful to disguise her red hair and otherwise dressing and acting the part
of some overprivileged and entitled debutante. After trying on
a few pieces of choice jewelry and charming the sales staff with
her hoity-toity conceits, Lila would leave a gold credit card she'd
obtained from one of the restaurant tabs with the saleslady before
excusing herself to the restroom, leading the saleslady to believe
that she would decide upon her final selection once she returned.
Lila would then return with a Louis Vuitton handbag that she'd
allegedly found in the restroom, revealing it to contain several

hundred dollars in cash and involving all the sales staff present in attempting to identify its owner and some means of contacting her that it might be rightfully returned. Galvanized by her Good Samaritan honesty, the sales staff was thereby dutifully distracted while Lila helped herself to the selection of thousands of dollars of jewelry they'd laid aside for her on a jewelry tray, simply wandering out of the store while they brainstormed how they might somehow reach the owner of the handbag. The jewelry she'd then sell off at various out-of-town pawnshops, the sole exception being an irresistibly fascinating Möbius band pendant.

Far from being some sociopathic swindler, however, Lila suffered a terrible guilt for these stunts. She tried to tell herself that the yuppies on lunch had probably sold their souls to some corporation committed to systematically undermining the planetary ecosystem and all human dignity in the process. She tried to tell herself that the restauranteurs were forever serving up diminishing portions anyway, substituting cheaper ingredients in their quest to gouge a greater profit from their customers. She tried to tell herself that the jewelers were essentially complicit with the entire corrupt history of colonialism, that their blood diamonds left a crutch of amputations and other war-torn atrocities in their wake, that their prices were wildly inflated anyway due to the diamond cartel's violent domination of world markets, and that the jewelers themselves cynically concocted fictions of love and romance in order to con their customers into even desiring such gaudy baubles in the first place. She even tried to tell herself that it was important to break the law occasionally, if only to remind herself that her compliance was not compulsory and thereby to ensure that she'd never be herded onto any cattle cars.

Yes, her thefts were justified, she tried to tell herself, but in the end she was incapable of ignoring the fact that there were indeed real people victimized by her actions. If necessity is the mother of invention, Lila realized, then desperation is the father of deception, and in a society as ruthlessly selfish as the United States of America under late capitalism, Lila came to understand that *everyone* was desperate, that *everyone* was forced into the same isolated corner, the same corner that caused them to believe that they could count on only themselves, and that they must therefore deceive one another—and their very own selves—in order to survive. As a consequence of this epiphany, once Lila had established herself at UC-Berkeley, she resolved to retain her humanity and leave that terrifyingly cunning side of herself forever behind—forever, that is, until the day she bounced with the abundance offerings from the Holy Company of Beautiful People.

Realizing this, Lila slid a twenty-dollar bill out of the leather deposit envelope and examined it. After turning it over in her hands a few times, feeling increasingly guilty, she fished a lighter out of her handbag as well. "We should make an offering," Lila said, flicking a flame alive under a corner of the bill.

"That's a fine idea," Merlin agreed as he watched the flames crawl across the White House printed on the back of the bill. "Odd that we care at all, isn't it?" he mused aloud, noting his own attachment to the vanishing value.

"Isn't it, though?" Lila turned the bill to direct the flames.

"A grimy, crumpled piece of paper," Merlin observed. "Too dirty to wipe my ass with, actually."

Lila smiled, the flames reflecting in her eyes as they sparkled entranced. When she could hold it no longer, she let it drop to the steel floor in front of them. "Look," she pointed as she whispered the last phrase visible on the bill before it all curled into ash:

"In God We Trust."

46

L
ILA PULLED the cable to signal the BART train to stop. Merlin smiled at this development, sensing her intention.

"In God we trust," Lila averred. "I suppose there's really no sense in gathering more than we need."

Merlin watched her shift about as the train slowed to a stop. "You are so goddamned sexy."

Lila stood and restated her position. "I want to redistribute most of this cash."

Merlin leaned forward and kissed her belly. "I want to make love to you all night long."

Lila blushed as she waited for the doors to open. "So," she hesitated. "Are you with me?"

"Why do you keep asking me if I'm with you?" Merlin stood. "Do you imagine that your generosity of spirit should frighten me off?"

Lila shrugged. "That or reckless larceny."

Merlin snorted as the doors to the train opened. "You'll find you've met your match in me, ol' Bonnie. I'll have you know that I scammed dozens of banks into funding my world travel." He took her hand as they exited the train. "Why, you're holding hands with the very reason you can no longer buy traveler's cheques on credit cards."

"*Oh really?*" Lila led the way toward the highway underpass. "I can't wait to hear *this* story."

As this story happened to be one of Merlin's favorite brags, he didn't wait for a second prompt. "Well you know how credit cards have those rewards programs, where if you spend a hundred dollars you get a dollar back, or one percent back on gas, or groceries, or travel, or computer rebates, or whatever else? Well, I applied for every card I could find that had a reward program and then I'd spend my credit limit every single month on every single card. The only thing I bought, though, were traveler's cheques, which you used to be able to buy fee-free at any AAA office if you had a membership. What I figured out is that even though traveler's cheques are the same as cash, they showed up as purchases on my statements and not as cash advances, meaning I wouldn't lose any money to fees or interest as long as I paid off my balance in full every month. So, I just maxed out all my cards every month. I'd walk out of the AAA office with thousands of dollars in traveler's cheques, which I'd then immediately deposit into my checking account and pay off all my credit cards.

"See, my only goal was to accumulate rewards. At first, I was only doing like twenty thousand dollars at a time, but because I was spending and paying off my credit limit every single month on every single card, my credit limits skyrocketed. Within six months I was walking into AAA with a *deck* of credit cards and lining them up across the counter, buying twenty thousand dollars in traveler's cheques on every card and walking out of there with a quarter-million dollars in traveler's cheques. Do the math: a one percent rebate on two hundred and fifty grand is twenty-five hundred bucks. Then I'd do it all over again as soon as the payments had cleared, so I was cycling the money through three times a month. I eventually bought a date stamp and a signature stamp to rubber-stamp all the cheques with, and the folks at the AAA office loved me since they earned a commission on the sale of traveler's cheques. In fact, they even won an award for selling more traveler's cheques than any other AAA office in the country, though that was ultimately my undoing—"

"How's that?" Lila interrupted.

"I was living in a small town up in Mendocino at the

time—not exactly a tourist destination—and I think the award alerted some actuary somewhere that something curious was occurring. One day, the clerk at AAA let me know that I wouldn't be able to buy traveler's cheques on credit cards much longer, so I just amped it up before the loophole closed. I started going to AAA every other day, walking out with a quarter-million dollars, depositing it in my bank, then going online and paying off all my balances electronically. My credit would be open again within a day, and I'd do the same thing all over again. I did that for almost a month until some banker named Chad from Visa called me and demanded to know what I was doing. I wouldn't tell him, and I kind of just taunted him, so Chad canceled all my credit cards right there, and shortly after that the loophole closed. But it was never illegal, my credit rating remains stellar, and I've lived very well off those reward points, cash-back bonuses, free gas, free computers, free groceries, free airfare, free hotels around the world, you name it." Merlin grinned triumphant. "In fact, I still have a few hundred gallons of free gasoline rewards to use up if you're ever in the mood for a road trip." After a moment he added, "But it has to be *after* the total solar eclipse."

"Wow," Lila was impressed. "You really are possessed by an imp."

"Some kind of a jaguar," Merlin nodded. "But I confess I enjoyed a raucous satisfaction in ripping off the loan sharks and their debilitating interest rates, their late fees, and their worthless reward programs that are only ever there to get people to spend more money that they don't have and thereby thicken their shackles. I found a loophole and channeled tens of thousands of dollars away from a usurious system of vacant greed that serves nobody but the lords of the manor. An anemic drop in the bucket, I know, but my only regret is that I blew the money on myself, on my own hedonistic explorations instead of what you're doing."

"And what am I doing?"

"Service."

"Nah." Lila slowed into sadness, shaking her head. "At least you targeted the real thieves. This," she held up the leather deposit envelope, "this was a terrible sin. I shouldn't have done this. These were just other people, peasants the same as me. Maybe they're lost in their own narcissistic fantasies and spiritual ambitions, but they're just trying to get safe. All anybody ever wants is to feel safe."

"They want to feel *love*," Merlin corrected. "And you're on your way to karmic zero, by the way, giving what you've taken, redistributing what they would happily give away anyway the moment they attained the enlightenment they're supposedly seeking. And besides, you're just donating what Ivan would otherwise have stolen, right? Maybe we try not to see it, but it's a crime against humanity to greed what others need. There's not a goddamned Christian anywhere who could argue with that, although, paraphrasing Nietzsche, there was only ever one Christian, and they crucified him."

Lila stopped, tugging Merlin's hand to grab his attention. "I don't know whether it's your pheromones or your philosophy," she said, "but I adore you, Merlin."

Merlin sniffed his armpit. "It's probably my pheromones." Then, a nervous chuckle later, he met her shining eyes. "I adore you more, Lila."

And thereby they commenced upon a long and fondling kiss, unchaste in its expression and terrific in its abandon, and when they ceased the world was quiet, the air was still, and Lila whispered into Merlin's ear, "I can't *wait* to see what else we get into."

47

Rue to Crow's misgivings, Boca Diablo was little more than a roaring swarm of mercenaries, and the taverns and brothels that dominated the townscape offered little by way of diversion and much by way of threat. After purchasing two mules to haul some of their effects and enduring a slurring onslaught of harassment, Crow and the rest of the Eleusinians stood sentry outside an inn while Flaming Jane went inside to reserve accommodations for the night. Crow met the eyes of all who observed them and shook his head in disgust. Whatever the histories of these dregs had been, they had sunk so deeply into their own depravity that there was nothing left upon their countenances but an ogred and ugly vulgarity, and the glares seeping sallow from their bloodshot eyes offered only dim hatred for this band of Injuns, outlaws, niggers, and *women*. Nary a pirate in sight, Crow observed, a brother or sister to the free spirit, the code of equality and honor, a friend of God, and an enemy of the world.

This is brilliant, Crow groused to himself as he gripped his sword. Let's proclaim our location so that every liquor-lit mercenary looking for bragging rights will know exactly where to attack us in our sleep. Crow sighed impatient in the dusking light, knowing that there would be little by way of rest tonight. Soon after, Flaming Jane emerged and loudly announced that she'd secured most of the second floor for them (there was vacancy aplenty due to the egress of Half-Ass McJanky and his crew), and at this audacity Crow finally understood that Flaming Jane was merely offering diversion for the injurious intentions surrounding them. After securing their donkeys in the alley behind, the Eleusinians filed inside, past the brandy-nosed drunk of an innkeeper, up the staircase, and down the hall. Instead of occupying the rooms she'd just rented, however, Flaming Jane led them toward the end of the hall where they crowded unobserved into the last room, the one she'd made certain the innkeeper knew was to be hers. There, Flaming Jane directed Crow and Gabriel to lead their brothers to occupy rooms in the neighboring inn. "Pay for nothing," she directed. "And let no one know you're there."

Hidden by the alley, Crow and Gabriel quietly roped their way down to the ground, followed by their Arawak brothers. Skilled in the arts of quietude and surprise, they wasted no time locking the innkeeper in a closet, securing the front doors, and occupying the set of rooms directly across the alley. It wasn't fifteen minutes before Crow had lit a kerosene lantern, illuminating their grins and inviting the remaining Eleusinians to follow.

An hour later, the Eleusinians were asleep and at ease, knowing that their morning would come before dawn. And indeed it did, after the last of the patrons had passed out and the snore of the seashore sated the silence before dawn, the predictable lynch posse arrived at the inn Flaming Jane had checked into, where the brandy-nosed drunk of an innkeeper could hardly be bothered to open his jaundiced eyes before pointing the way to Flaming Jane's room at the end of the hall on the second floor. Crow was already awake—he had been so for half an hour— awaiting their enemies' expected arrival from the open window across the alley and contemplating the cowardice of humanity. He held a bow in his hand and an arrow tipped with oilcloth at the ready. A single candle illuminated Flaming Jane's sleeping form, and Crow contrasted the perfect beauty of her curves with the lumpy mound of bags and a gunpowder cask stuffed under the blankets in the room across the alley. Not very convincing, he thought, but drunken cowards are easy enough to fool.

Crow was considering what poison motivates those who seek only to harness the freedom of others when a shaft of light suddenly illuminated the room across the way as the door opened. Sighing himself ready, Crow watched as a dozen corrupted shadows shushed and hushed their way into the room, weapons drawn, everybody wanting their own stab at Flaming Jane. As they crowded tiptoe and clumsy around the bed, Crow drew back his bow with his breath and waited till they stabbed at the kindling. Then he lit the tip of his arrow off the candle, and the sudden flare awoke Flaming Jane, who sat up grinning in the window just in time for her would-be assassins— diverted also by the arrow's flare—to see her firelit smile flicker ghostly magnificent at them as Crow watched them puzzle and confuse for a moment before he squinted the pity from his eyes and released his arrow roaring into the bedridden barrel of gunpowder as he delivered them to the flames they were chasing.

48

THE EXPLOSION quickly consumed the rickety inn, the blaze waking the entire town and offering ample distraction for the Eleusinians to depart Boca Diablo undetected. Thus it was that the legend of Flaming Jane grew. Rumor maintained that the gang who attempted to ambush her in her sleep at Boca Diablo had burst into flames, and this—combined with her flaming effigy and their flaming booby trap of Goldtooth's *Damnation*—convinced sailors across the sea that Flaming Jane was no mere name, that she was the devil incarnate who could burst into flames when attacked and carry her attackers back to hell with her.

"You can always trust people to be themselves," Flaming Jane explained to Crow as she led their party down a jungled road two hours beyond the port settlement of Boca Diablo.

"My mind is weary and my body needs rest," Crow responded, pissed at their predicament. "I trust that my head will not rest upon a rock tonight." In fact, Crow had already begun to piece together Flaming Jane's plan, although since he'd yet to have any of his suspicions confirmed he saw no reason not to warn her that she'd better not disappoint his trust.

"Take you, for instance," Flaming Jane continued. "I can always trust you to be loyal and cantankerous. It is in your nature as much as it was in Half-Ass McJanky's nature to be so invincibly stupid and covetous."

"Yes, my lovemuff, and I can always trust you to be reckless and quick-witted, I suppose?"

"Indeed, my lovestallion. But the point, as I said, is that you can always trust people to be themselves, and seeing the truth of an enemy's character lends a terrific tactical advantage."

Crow harrumphed. "So you're counting on the bottomless idiotism of Half-Ass McJanky to barrel headlong into Goldtooth's squadron?"

Flaming Jane nodded.

"And you're counting on the black-hearted vengeance of Goldtooth to think he is you and thereby to attack him relentless?"

Flaming Jane continued nodding.

"So our enemies will kill one another, reducing their numbers and raising our chances?"

Flaming Jane concluded her nod, and Crow paused. "And since I can trust you to have a plan, I can trust that you would not have surrendered our ship and led us down this tangled trail if you didn't have another ship hidden somewhere off this island?"

"It's true that we overtook more than our share of ships before you came aboard," Flaming Jane conceded. "And we certainly didn't sink them all."

Gabriel abruptly interrupted their conversation, having pushed his way to the fore of the line to halt their progress. Speaking to Crow in his native tongue, the other Arawak gathered around, their eyes narrowing as they looked warily about. Crow nodded. "The jungle ahead has been disturbed," Crow reported. "There are traps about."

Flaming Jane raised her eyebrows at Gabriel. "How can you possibly know that?"

"I spent years living off the jungle with these men," Crow responded. "And the only traps they couldn't spot were the ones they set themselves."

Flaming Jane grinned impressed. "We set a series of traps near here last summer. But *I* haven't even spotted our markers yet."

Gabriel spoke as Crow translated: "The jungle only appears chaotic. Once you understand its principles, everything is exactly where it needs to be. Any disruption of the underlying order is perfectly apparent." Gabriel pointed ahead, all eyes following his finger. "That branch," he said. "Why do its twigs turn away from the sun?"

Flaming Jane was quiet, consternation distressing her composure. "Ah yes," she observed at last. "A trip line interferes with the natural growth of the twigs, I presume?"

"And what of your markers?" Crow inquired, alarm raising his voice.

"I haven't spotted our markers," Flaming Jane shook her head, looking apprehensive for the first time since Crow had known her. "Because these are not our traps."

49

T HE ELEUSINIANS fell into battle position, circling their backs and holding their weapons wary. No one made a sound; indeed, the entire jungle seemed to clench itself silent. Crow studied the line created by the disturbed twigs, discerning that it led deep into the forest, which likely implied one thing. "An arrow trap," he whispered to Gabriel, and Gabriel nodded. Somewhere out of sight, Crow guessed, an array of bows were leveling their hair-trigger arrows upon this road and ready to loose upon the unsuspecting. Doubtless a decoy tactic, intended to maim, but its imprecision made it useful primarily for creating the illusion of an ambush and thereby distracting from the real danger.

Gabriel examined the ground. "Reeds and leaves litter the road unnecessarily," he observed, nodding up ahead. "It's a pit trap."

Crow nodded and translated, seeing the full intent of the trapper. Trigger the arrow trap, maim a few, panic the rest into the pit trap ahead, itself covered with a net stretched across the top and hidden with reeds and leaves. Crow looked to Flaming

Jane, her eyes piercing the forest for any sign of activity before settling upon Crow.

"I'm sorry," she stated, absent regret and as a matter of simple fact. "I underestimated Half-Ass McJanky. He must have spent the last couple of months searching for our hidden ship. He probably had some lackeys trigger our booby traps, which told him he was close, and when he still couldn't find her, he set these vengeful traps for us upon our return."

"It doesn't matter," Crow replied. "Gabriel can guide us through any trap field. Do you have any sense of where we are?"

Flaming Jane nodded. "What we're looking for is maybe fifty yards ahead, around that bend."

"That's where the ship is at?" Crow confused, for fifty yards ahead was nothing but thick jungle.

"No," Flaming Jane shook her head. "That is where the one thing that everyone else would avoid is at."

50

AFTER HAVING EVERYONE lie down and shield each other and themselves, Gabriel crept ahead to locate the trip wires. This he managed without difficulty, and after lying down himself, Gabriel triggered the trap. Instantly a flash of arrows sliced the air above them, embedding themselves into trees or receding into the forest. Standing, Gabriel then picked up a large branch and swept the ground in front of him until— just as he'd predicted—he found the netting covering the pit trap. After Gabriel pulled the netting aside and called the all clear, the crew made its way forward, collecting arrows from the trees on their way, and surrounded the pit that had been intended for them.

Extending fully across the road and some ten feet across, the pit was half as many feet deep. Its bottom was lined with stakes, their sharpened tops waiting to pierce the flesh of anyone misfortunate enough not to have noticed the trap. Flaming Jane regarded the trap in silence, though her incense at Half-Ass McJanky's treachery was palpable. At last she turned to Gabriel and thanked him, then asked him to lead the way forward.

Flaming Jane fell into step with Crow and took his hand. "I'm grateful that you and your brothers joined our crew. We surely would have stumbled into these traps on our own."

The severity of Crow's brow softened as he heard Flaming Jane's words. He glanced at her and nodded.

Flaming Jane continued. "I'm sorry I've been less than forthcoming with you about my plan. Your presence is clearly providential, and I appreciate your patience and trust."

Crow nodded again, accepting her apology. "Perhaps you could tell me then what it is we are looking for out here in the bush?"

"Ah yes," Flaming Jane sighed, slowing to a stop. "Though I don't suppose you will enjoy the answer." She gestured ahead, where a circle of scattered skulls surrounded a flat parch of earth that seemed to swirl its surface curiously toward a center.

"What's that?" Crow asked.

"That's the one thing that everyone else would avoid," Flaming Jane answered. "Quicksand."

51

ORTIFIED BY HIS blunder in managing the secure delivery of the abundance offerings—and baffled as to how the scam had even happened or who might have been behind it—Chris Bliss had decided in a panic not to reveal his blunder to anybody, least of all to Ivan. Thus it was that he plunged himself into paranoia, and a day later Chris Bliss found himself nervously humming *Oo-fa-kay-fa-lay-lay* as he unfolded Ivan's chair at the nail salon while Ivan waited outside in the air-conditioned Range Rover.

Ivan required that his chair be brought along for him wherever they went, lest his spine be thrown out of its sacred adjustment. Aside from the seats in the Range Rover, which were all programmed specifically to conform to his body (and whose suspension also had an automatic leveling option), this chair was the only chair in which Ivan ever sat. After Chris Bliss had carefully calibrated the chair with a digital level and adjusted the sliders under its legs until it was perfectly level across every orientation, he guided Ivan inside for his weekly manicure and pedicure. Ivan sat experimentally upon his chair, complaining after a moment that the cushion felt a little thin, at which point Chris Bliss hastily mollycoddled its thickness by adding a few additional layers of tissue from a box of Kleenex he always carried with the chair. Ivan sat upon it again and sighed princess and the pea at last.

The Korean immigrants who eventually set to work on Ivan's fingers and toes were accustomed to this ritual, and since their English was more or less limited to anything having to do with nails and cuticles, at least while working, Chris Bliss felt free to speak to Ivan uncensored, offering his report on being attacked by bottle rockets as well as his failed attempt with the wormwood poison. But of course he said nothing about the abundance offerings, and in an effort to distract from his failures, he enthusiastically described how Lila had not fallen after all, and how stricken with grief she'd been at her behavior.

"She chased you off with bottle rockets?" Ivan shook his head incredulous, dismayed with this loyal half-wit upon whom he had to rely for his intel. Ivan should have guessed that Chris Bliss would make such a blundering mess of things. "And Rukmini loves coffee. Since when does she drink matcha lattes?"

"I don't know, Master." Chris Bliss paused. "But matcha has a hundred and thirty-seven times the antioxidant potency of regular green tea."

Though he consumed fistfuls of antioxidant vitamins every morning in his vain efforts to forestall the aging process, Ivan had never heard of this. "Really? A hundred and thirty-seven times?"

"Because you're consuming the whole powdered tea leaf, not just the water it's been steeped in."

Ivan considered this. "Put that on my grocery list."

"Of course, Master."

"Watch it!" Ivan suddenly yelled at the pedicurist and yanked his foot away from her massaging hands. "Tickling," Ivan grumbled indignant, gingerly offering his foot once again to her apologetic hands.

"I believe her," Chris Bliss announced after a minute of silence, as if his assessment of Lila was born of a supremely discerning intellect. "I think she knows that she's been in her mind, and that she's fallen from grace. I think she wants to see you." In truth, Chris Bliss really had no idea what he thought, any more than he had any idea that he had no idea. His was not a self-reflective mind, after all, and he just wanted to help the Master relax, if only that he might be willing to once again offer him the Wisdom.

Ivan nodded. "Rukmini is still with this Merlin, then?"

"Unfortunately," Chris Bliss sighed. "He must be the source of her dark energy."

"Not so short!" Ivan barked this time at the manicurist, transferring his frustration and triggering paroxysms of murmuring obeisance from the technician. The thing is, Ivan could trust exactly zero of Chris Bliss's analysis of the situation. He'd made Chris Bliss his lieutenant precisely because he was easily the stupidest man he had ever encountered, ever eager for others to define his point of view and utterly incapable of exercising anything resembling a critical intellect. This made him perfectly suitable for witnessing Ivan's backstage machinations, and reliable for carrying out any black hat activities without question, but Ivan had met stray dogs that possessed a greater insight into human social psychology. Ivan sighed impatient. He would have to observe Rukmini and this Merlin himself.

"Master?"

"Yes, my child?"

"I've been thinking about the Wisdom."

"Remember, my child, that the Wisdom cannot be spoken."

"Yes," Chris Bliss agreed. "It's translinguistic."

Ivan smiled, anticipating face-fucking this moron again later. "Perhaps I will try to offer you the Wisdom again."

"I would like that, Master."

"We'll see." Ivan closed his eyes and relaxed into his foot massage. "We'll see."

52

VAN SNEEZED three times in rapid succession, fumbling his tweezers into the toilet in the process.

"Fucking christ," Ivan muttered, rubbing his nose to relieve its twitch. He'd been plucking his nose hairs in between the gargantuan fits of sneezing it triggered, and he'd finally just completed his right nostril. Looking over his nose at his reflection, he grimaced at the bouquet of black hairs still tangled amidst the snot of his left nostril. As if that weren't ghastly enough, two of them were silver, and he also noticed a single follicle on his eyebrow growing straight out, perpendicular to the rest of his brow. "Oh *god*," Ivan moaned, licking his finger and trying to smooth it flat. Failing that, he tried to pluck it with his fingertips, also to no avail.

Exasperated, Ivan leaned on the sink and regarded the tweezers lying at the bottom of the toilet. Shaking his head, he failed to grimace his Botox-paralyzed brow as he considered how all of this was Lila's—*Rukmini's*—fault. *That cuntwhistle is determined to expose me as some kind of a fraud,* Ivan thought, *sending out that mass email accusing me of being a narcissist. Of course I'm a narcissist,* Ivan glanced up at his reflection. *I mean, look at me! It's hardly my fault that enlightenment makes a person incredibly attractive, is it?*

Ivan looked away, trying to hide from the fact that he was worried. However she'd done it, Rukmini had succeeded in imbalancing him, and he simply could not permit that to persist. An anxiety he had not known for years had been taunting at his aplomb ever since, a nagging, nameless terror not only that he would someday die, but also that it would be as if he had never really existed at all. It's dark energy, Ivan determined, and Ivan had already let all his followers know that Rukmini was the source of this dark energy he'd been sensing. But slander-mongering wasn't going to be sufficient in this case. Regardless of his idiot lieutenant's assessment, Rukmini needed to be eliminated. Rukmini needed to be destroyed.

And soon, too. Ivan was losing his hair, and what kind of deity does that? Rogaine had delayed it, but it turns out that Rogaine also breaks down the collagen in skin, which meant that not only had Ivan's porcelain face begun wrinkling but also that he had to get more frequent collagen injections in his lips lest they wither to their razor-thin natural state. He'd already started wearing a Sikh turban sometimes to hide his thinning crown, but really, he just needed to get away, schedule a hair transplant procedure, and lie low somewhere while his hair grew back.

For now, though, Ivan had to retrieve his tweezers. Flushing them seemed an invitation to plumbing hassles, which was absolutely out of the question with this toilet, and he couldn't very well leave them there. Besides, he still had a nosegay of boogered nose hair to deal with and an idiotic eyebrow follicle on top of that. Holding his breath, Ivan tried to psych himself up to plunge his hand into the toilet water, but even though as a breatharian Ivan claimed to never have to sully the water with poo, and even though Chris Bliss's selfless service included cleaning the toilet once a day, Ivan had yet to follow through after several lunges. Recollecting his enlightenment at last, Ivan sat down on the bath mat, pulled his legs into a half-lotus asana, straightened his spine, and focused on his breathing. Meditate, yes. Breathe in, goddammit. *Sat-Nam.* Truth is my identity. Breathe out.

Before he could successfully center himself, however, Ivan spied a scuff on the side of the lid of the toilet tank, virtually out of sight and nearest to the corner. Meditation forgotten, he scrambled onto his knees to inspect it more closely, running his index finger across the scuff, frowning. Sure enough, a shard of porcelain enamel had been chipped off, revealing a luster of gold beneath. Gold, yes, as Ivan had converted most of the millions of dollars he'd collected from all his various guru scams over the years into gold, having it cast into a two-hundred-pound toilet coated in porcelain enamel in order to hide it. After carefully examining the remaining surface of the lid and the entire rest of the toilet, Ivan satisfied himself that that was the only imperfection in its surface, and leaned back against the wall to consider. He could not imagine how that chip had occurred, since he was the only one who ever used this bathroom. Located off his master bedroom, Ivan considered the bathroom his corporeal sanctum, and kept it locked with an electronic combination that only he and Chris Bliss knew. Chris Bliss thoroughly cleaned his corporeal sanctum once a day in selfless service, but was only to use an exceedingly soft microfiber cloth upon any of its surfaces.

Alarmed, Ivan fished a small bottle of porcelain enamel repair compound out from under the sink. Touching up the imperfection, he resolved to change the combination to his bathroom and only to clean it himself henceforth. Even if Chris Bliss had somehow chipped the toilet lid, and even if he had noticed that he had done so, Ivan felt confident that it would never remotely occur to Chris Bliss why it revealed a luster of gold beneath. But still, Ivan wasn't comfortable taking any chances with his golden commode. Between his creeping hair loss, Rukmini's impertinence, and now this chip upon his toilet, the signs seemed to be pointing to an endgame. He was going to have to abandon the Holy Company of Beautiful People soon, and take his solid gold throne with him. Ivan had been talking about ascending under the solar eclipse only in order to keep his disciples' attachments to him high and thereby to stimulate greater abundance offerings, but perhaps it was time for him to make his exit after all.

But first, Ivan had to retrieve his tweezers and finish plucking his nose hair. Returning to his breath, he meditated upon his enlightened divinity, and after a few minutes abruptly plunged his left hand into the toilet, instantly yanking it out as if the water had been boiling. But his fingers succeeded in laying hold of the tweezers, though they flew out of his recoiling hand and clattered across the floor as Ivan began retching in realization of where his hand had just been.

Retrieving the tweezers at last, he pulled himself up and caught his reflection in the mirror—eyes bloodshot and caved in from dry heaving, skin blotched and sallow, and blue veins bulging from his forehead and neck as if he were about to transmogrify into some preternatural beast. Gasping at this wreckage of his visage, he hastened to refresh his face with water a fractured second before horrifying that he'd not yet scrubbed the hand he'd sullied in the toilet. *O christ jeezus*, he panicked goddammit the desperate fucking hell.

Half a bar of soap and a Silkwood shower later, Ivan emptied a bottle of peroxide over his tweezers before satisfying himself that it was safe to resume his nasal grooming. An hour later, when at last he'd finished preening, Ivan carefully swept every nose hair, nail clipping, eyebrow, cuticle, pube, and hangnail into a dustpan and emptied it into a glass jar. To this he added the contents of the electric razor with which he shaved any errant body hair in between his bimonthly full-body wax. Then, outside on his patio, he incinerated his collected corporeal detritus in a toaster oven, setting aside the scant ashes to be offered as relics for his disciples.

Vibhuti, he called the ashes. Vibhuti, Ivan explained, was a physical manifestation of his divine presence, and just one of the *siddhis*—spiritual powers—over which Ivan claimed passive mastery. Every full moon, Ivan would manifest incredible quantities of vibhuti out of nowhere, cascading the holy ash over a jewel-adorned bust of himself as his disciples chanted mantra and contemplated the magic. A chosen disciple from his inner circle would hold aloft an obviously empty upside down earthenware jug while Ivan stuck his hand inside and manifested a miraculous cascade of vibhuti for minutes at a time, much more than the jug could possibly hold. All this vibhuti was distributed to the disciples, who collected it in pendants and peppered it across the thresholds of their homes and such as a means of attracting abundance into their own lives.

Ivan stimulated this massive manifestation of vibhuti simply by sprinkling into the jug a little of the original vibhuti he'd incinerated from his own bodily debris. "The universe rewards generosity," Ivan explained. "With an offering, we stimulate the flow of abundance." In this way, the full moon vibhuti ritual was a demonstration of Ivan's central teaching: that anyone can manifest anything they want into their life. After all, if the Master could summon vibhuti into existence, then surely they could manifest greater wealth into their lives. Hoping to compel abundance, wallets were emptied and Ivan's collection basket overflowed, for on full moons it was perfectly evident that their guru was truly possessed of supernatural powers toward which they could only aspire.

And Ivan made certain they never forgot this.

53

ONTRARY TO CLICHÉ, the danger of quicksand lies not in getting sucked under, but rather in getting permanently cemented within it. Victims of quicksand die of exposure and starvation, and only rarely of drowning or suffocation. But facts such as these are irrelevant to the superstitions and fascinations of wild-eyed imagination, and Crow was as incredulous as anyone that Flaming Jane had, after all this, led them to a pit of quicksand.

"Quicksand?!" Crow took a step away from Flaming Jane. "After all this, you led us to a pit of quicksand?!"

Flaming Jane looked idly around. "We had traps all around here, but it appears they've all been sprung. Half-Ass McJanky probably assumed the quicksand was just another trap."

"What is the meaning of this?" Crow demanded.

"You have to trust me this one last time," Flaming Jane answered as Noa and the other Eleusinians poked cautiously at the quicksand with various sticks, smirking and chattering excited.

Crow looked at them puzzled, and Noa grinned. "It's safe," Noa reassured, but Catface for one obviously did not concur, jumping off his shoulders and taking off into the forest, never looking back.

"Safe?" Crow snorted, watching Catface's exit with some dismay. "Is that what they're calling quicksand these days?"

"I've done this before," Noa answered.

"Done *what* before?" Crow demanded, and Flaming Jane could not help but gush into a grin when he looked to her in disbelief. "And what about Catface?"

"Catface can take care of himself," Flaming Jane assured. "And this really is quite something," she continued as her Eleusinian crew went about fastening up their belongings, releasing the mules, and forming a queue. "There's an underground river beneath us; that's what saturates and destabilizes the sand here and creates the quicksand. If you dive in, your momentum will carry you all the way through the bank of quicksand and into the underground river. Then the river will carry you to the cavern where we hid our sister ship, and our collected treasure." She paused, and added, "It's quite a ride."

"And how the bloody christ did you manage to discover that?" Crow raised his voice.

"It was Noa, actually. The last time we were at Boca Diablo, Noa was kidnapped. The lynch mob dragged him out here, unchained him, and were going to force him into the quicksand while they jeered his slow death—"

"No man jeers my death," Noa interrupted. "So I dove headfirst into the quicksand to escape this world quickly." He grinned. "I was surprised to find myself alive, and after I found my way back to Boca Diablo, I led the crew to the cavern I had found, where we hid our sister ship. Then I showed them this secret entrance."

"Half-Ass McJanky had already been ostracized," Flaming Jane anticipated Crow's next question. "He'd obviously captured some loose rumor, but he had no idea where we had hidden our sister ship. That's why we require," she paused, choosing her words deliberately, "a trial of trust before we reveal too many secrets to new crew."

"I will see you on the other side, my brother Crow!" Noa called out just before huffing a deep breath and diving headfirst into what appeared to be the center, defining a clear swirl on the surface of the quicksand as it swallowed him, splashing muck everywhere, erupting the Arawak into cries of alarm, and rendering Crow speechless.

"There's a convection current, like a whirlpool," Flaming Jane explained as Crow and his brothers proceeded to watch one Eleusinian after another dive fearless into the center of the spiral. "The center will take you directly to the bottom, but beware of the sides. The river pushes up against the quicksand on the sides, and the current will resist you there. Not that it's ever happened, but if you don't dive directly into the center, you could theoretically get stuck midway down."

Crow listened as his brothers talked out this turn of events in their native tongue. Azriel maintained that this was a shamanic portal leading to another dimension and reminded that even if death were the portal there was nothing to fear in any event. A consensus emerged around this, attended as it was by the ongoing parade of the rest of the crew diving in unhesitant, and the Arawak too began securing their effects. Crow—contemplating the quandary that if all his friends jumped into a pit of quicksand, would he?—at some point turned to Flaming Jane and asked, "How deep is it?"

Flaming Jane shrugged. "Maybe fifteen feet before you release into the current of the river. But like I said, the center will suck you directly to the bottom, like an hourglass. Then you'll be holding your breath for every bit of a good long minute before that tunnel empties into the cavern, so take a deep breath." Flaming Jane smiled as she cut to the front of the line and began fastening up her belongings and ensuring that the bamboo tubes that contained all their charts were properly watertight. "The important thing is not to hesitate. You're going to need your momentum to carry you all the way through the quicksand and into the water."

Crow shook his head. "You're a merciless wench."

Flaming Jane pouted at this assessment. "My dear, a relationship has nothing if it hasn't any trust." Sighing, she continued, "But I suppose I could hardly blame a man for declining an invitation such as this."

And they fell into a long stare, scanning each other's features for signs of truth or dare. It was Crow who finally released his gaze, taking Flaming Jane's hand and guiding her two steps and graceful away from the quicksand. Stepping forward, Crow then bowed and kissed her hand, took a deep breath, gazed again into her eyes, and commanded, "Marry me then," a moment before he turned and dove into the center of the spiral.

54

THE SUCK OF THE MUCK was immediate as the vortex enveloped Crow's body. The quicksand's swallow boggled his senses but it was nonetheless clear not only that he was moving but that he was being pulled, and pulled *hard*. Crow had but a moment to wonder why the sensations of his body being squirmed through a wormhole carried a curious familiarity before the texture of the fluid around him shifted and the force of a rush of cold water grabbed ahold of him and flung him headlong and hell-bent through an absolute and drowning darkness. Earsplittingly disoriented, instinctively protecting his head and aborting every impulse to gasp aloud panic, Crow could discern no direction whatsoever excepting an unrelenting momentum forward and trusting still waiting his lungs began to urge and urge more and still there was nothing but a blind and bubbling velocity nothing to do nothing to try only to trust that marvelous and merciless wench who had fascinated him into so helpless a situation and every beat of his heart insisted upon his breath and he reckoned he couldn't resist another beat but then he did and the throbbing whomp of his pulse overwhelmed his awareness of everything but an immense and unmistakable gratitude for the life he had lived and he sensed his own death as he knew his own life and there stalking out of the blindness some kind of a jaguar lunged toward him and relaxing relenting at last Crow released his spirit and surrendered his gasp just in time to feel his limbs flail into the atmosphere that came roaring into his lungs as his body broke free from the gushing plummet of a waterfall and his eyes found a light at the far end of an immense cavern as his ears found the cheers of his shipmates abounding around and Crow would later tell tale of how his gasp reached down from the bottom of his balls to fill his lungs but right now his breath was his being and his being was drenched in a spirit so thorough that somewhere back in the blackness some kind of a jaguar lost its nerve.

The seventy-foot splashdown might have injured a less exhilarant man, but Crow's body simply displaced the water as if it were nothing more substantial than his very own self. No sooner had Crow surfaced than he saw Flaming Jane sail out of the waterfall, her belongings starbursting all around her perfectly sleek body as the swan of her dive hung impossible precipitous like the devil defiant but if she was ever the devil then the devil was wailing wahoo and when she dove into the water she arrived seconds later into a long and slickened kiss upon Crow's lips and then, beaming like a dream and smacking her lips poppysmic, Flaming Jane said yes, yes of course.

55

A CLEAN-SHAVEN, suntanned man in a business suit stood motionless on the sidewalk in front of a diner, facing the *Bank of America* across the street and resting his right forearm on a newspaper box, extending his middle finger. He had held this position motionless from nine to five on weekdays and nine to noon on Saturdays for the past six months, and as a result had earned the local nickname of Fuck You Fred. The word in the diner was that Fuck You Fred had lost his home when Bank of America bent him over a barrel with a two-year nightmare of bullshit loan modifications before repossessing his house, although this was idle gossip. In any event, primarily due to Fuck You Fred, the diner was Lila's favorite, and she'd initially found it because it was right around the corner from the section of Golden Gate Park that Ivan always used for the Holy Company of Beautiful People's outdoor activities. This is where Lila took Merlin for breakfast the day after she'd bounced with the abundance offerings from the Holy Company of Beautiful People and donated most of it to the homeless.

"Now, I have a bullshit detector like a dog has a nose," Lila explained to Merlin after telling him all about Ivan's full moon vibhuti ritual over breakfast. "And Ivan stank like a pasture. I thought it was a pretty cool trick at first, the way he manifested all that vibhuti out of that jug, and I couldn't figure out how he did it—"

"How did he do it?" Merlin interrupted, after they exchanged smiles with the waitress who collected their tab.

"Patience, boy howdy," Lila smiled, pausing to check the time as she observed an armored truck pull up to the *Bank of America* across the street. "Let the storyteller enjoy the story, too."

"Did you just call me boy howdy?"

"So," Lila continued, "the only thing that ever made me doubt that it was just a trick was that everyone else really seemed to believe that it was bona fide, that Ivan was possessed of Jesusian powers and we were all the chosen people. I think that's Ivan's real magic: crafting an illusion in which everyone's identity is invested."

"Sounds like society at large," Merlin observed as he sipped at his tea.

"It sure does." Lila sipped at her tea in turn. "And once identities are invested in an illusion, people get angry—really angry—at anyone who questions whether the illusion is real, because if the illusion isn't real, then neither are they, or at least, they're nobody like who they thought they were."

Lila fell silent along with Merlin, smirking identical and staring faraway, cupping their teacups as if they carried a sacred and soothing broth. Lila was imagining how she might trigger such an identity crisis for every member of the Holy Company of Beautiful People, while Merlin was wondering how he might do the same for the entire human race.

"So wait," Merlin's fantasy of global dis-illusionment vanished. "How did he do it? How'd he make all that ash fall out of the jug?"

"Right, the vibhuti. Well, I asked him once why he had to

put his hand in the jug, right? What was he hiding? Why not just summon it out of midair?"

"What'd he say?"

"First, he chastised me for doubting, told me how disappointed he was in me. Then he went on about the light created by his manifestation magic being much too bright for the naked eye to bear."

"Ah, that makes sense."

"But then I noticed the vibhuti actually smelled familiar."

"What'd it smell like?"

Lila hesitated. "Well, you remember that I've slept with Ivan, right?"

Merlin shook his head. "Such an unfortunate trauma."

"Well, anyway, the ash smelled like him."

Merlin blinked. "I don't understand. What does that mean, the ash smelled like him?"

"Like him," Lila repeated. "You know," she gestured toward Merlin's nether regions. "Like his—"

"What?" Merlin grimaced. "Like his—" Merlin gestured himself about his nether regions.

Lila smiled huge, wrinkling her nose as she nodded.

"But why?" Merlin mystified. "Why would the ash smell like *that*?"

"I too was puzzled at first, and for a second I even believed that maybe the vibhuti truly was a manifestation of Ivan's divine presence, but then I remembered that Ivan had this habit of powdering his privates."

Merlin shook his head. "I don't really want to talk about Ivan's privates anymore."

"Oh relax," Lila chided. "Just follow me on this. Basically, Ivan nurtures a view of himself as having not only attained physical perfection, but of having ascended beyond the physical.

Basic bodily processes revolt him. I mean, he even admonished his disciples for their grotesque dependence on carbon-based food, mocking their atavistic mastications. He claimed to be a breatharian and to never even have to go number two, although I've smelled maple bacon in his house, and he has a colonic irrigation every other day."

"Truly a god among men," Merlin nodded. "What's a breatharian?"

"Draws all his nutrients from cosmic micro-food in the air, you know. When you're enlightened, you see, you can subsist on nothing but pranic light."

"Ah, right."

"But anyway," Lila continued, snickering, "Ivan was particularly horrified by the very *concept* of smegma—"

"Smegma?" Merlin interrupted. "Wait, what the total heck are we even talking about here?"

"*Listen,*" Lila continued, giddy with her stories. "Ivan was particularly horrified by smegma, so every time he went to the bathroom he dusted his privates with baby powder. *That's* what he smelled like, and *that's* what the ash smelled like. Baby powder."

"Baby powder?" Merlin furrowed his brow and contemplated his tea. "So the vibhuti was actually baby powder? Where was all the baby powder coming from?"

"Talcum powder, specifically, which is a mineral, and which if you combine a quantity of with enough water to form a paste you can spread all around the inside of a clay jug and then dehydrate it into a crust. Then, when Ivan swept his hand around the inside of the upside down jug, hocus-cadabra! Vibhuti! You can compress quite a quantity of talcum into a paste, and it becomes much more voluminous once it's re-powdered."

"You've got to be kidding." Merlin leaned back and

shook his head. "What a cheap trick. What an unbelievable fucking charlatan."

Lila nodded. "Ivan lies as easily as you and I breathe, and he lives very well off it, but he's still just a small-time sociopath who's managed to charismatize a couple hundred people into supporting him. He's exactly nobody compared to the real lords of the manor." She gestured toward Fuck You Fred outside on the sidewalk. "Those who've bamboozled billions of us into believing that money has value, and thereby presume the power to dictate everything from a person's self-worth to their state of health. *Those* are the unbelievable charlatans." Lila shook her head, gazing at the bank across the street as the armored delivery truck pulled away. She checked the time again and watched as Fuck You Fred also checked the time and made a quick note of it on a pad of paper before resuming his human statue.

"And what was *that*?" Merlin demanded, following her gaze. "What, are you casing armored trucks with Fuck You Fred now?"

"It's really more like an informal study," Lila smirked. "Remember roshambo? Humans are utterly incapable of making a truly random decision. Well, supposedly armored trucks deliver and pickup at random times."

"Do they?"

Lila shook her head. "Not according to Fuck You Fred."

56

"DON'T LOOK NOW," Lila smiled. "But Ivan's watching us."
"Oh?" Merlin stretched and yawned, feigning nonchalance. "Are you sure?"

"Of course I'm sure. Seeing him causes my entire being to sigh, like the sole of my shoe relaxing into a pile of dog shit."

Merlin laughed and glanced about. "Where is he?"

"Don't look!" Lila insisted. "I just saw him walk by the bank across the street."

"But I need to see what kind of a guy calls himself Ivan Humble." Merlin held his smiling eyes on Lila.

"Patience, boy howdy." Lila held his eyes the same, licking her lips. "Did I ever tell you that Ivan used to call himself Adonis?"

Merlin raised his eyebrows, grinning. "*Adonis* Humble? Why doesn't he just call himself Adolf Goldstein while he's at it?"

Lila laughed, and pointed at Merlin and snapped. "Nice one, boy howdy."

"Come on, where is he?" Merlin glanced toward the street. "I really need to get a look at this oxymoron."

"I know, dear," Lila shook her head, "and you will, but here's what's going to happen next. Ivan knows I like this diner, that's why he's here, and he's going to linger about in order to orchestrate accidentally running into me as evidence of some kind of an irresistible spiritual connection between us. He needs to do this because he's a clinical narcissist, and his insatiable insecurity compels him to ensure that everyone views him in the same light as he needs to view himself."

"He needs to know that you still think he's the messiah," Merlin summed.

"Exactly," Lila nodded. "And I have an idea."

"Uh-oh."

"I'm going to let Ivan think that I still think he's the messiah until we can unveil him."

Merlin nodded. "You want to unveil Ivan Humble?"

"Ivan is a person who ventures a position of leadership and

not only uses it to enforce the precise opposite of truth, but also to aggrandize and enrich himself on the pretense of service. Leadership is a sacrifice, not an ambition, and leaders who mislead are the very worst among us. Don't you think it's about time we the people cease suffering tact while the demons rig the show?"

"He's rich?"

"He lives in a gigantic house in Presidio Heights owned by a realtor in the cult, and everything from his Range Rover to his groceries to his colonics to his twice-daily chiropractic adjustments come to him via the selfless service of the Holy Company of Beautiful People."

Merlin wrinkled his nose. "He gets his back cracked twice a day?"

"He has to," Lila explained. "Massaged too. Such is the force of his kundalini rising. And add to that swag the thousands of dollars in abundance offerings he collects at every full moon vibhuti ritual for the last seventeen years, not to mention placing himself in the dessert position of countless Ponzi schemes he's organized over the years, and he's sitting on a fortune."

"Ponzi schemes too?"

"Abundance gifting circles, he calls them, though I call them *grifting* circles. Gets his disciples to recruit eight people not in the Holy Company of Beautiful People to give five grand to their grifting circle in order to stimulate abundance in their own life. Then the recruits have to recruit eight more suckers to move up the pyramid, and on and on it goes. A standard pyramid scheme, and every time it inevitably failed down the line it was only because the people involved were too fearful to surrender themselves to the flow of abundance. He got forty grand from every grifting circle he successfully launched. I'm telling you, he's sitting on a fortune."

Merlin mulled Ivan's wicked financial prowess. "How much?"

Lila shrugged. "Who knows? A million, probably way more. And he keeps all of it in gold."

"What, he showed you?"

Lila shook her head. "No, but he was always going on about the instability of fiat currencies and advising everyone to transfer their money into gold."

"And you want to relieve Ivan of the terrible burden of his gold?"

Lila shrugged. "If I knew where he hides it, which I don't. Mainly I just want him to quit stalking me, and the best way to do that is to expose him as the lying sociopath pretending to be a holy man that he is."

Merlin smirked. "Well gawdamn, aside from fretting over my vain plot to ensure my own impossible security, I don't really have any other pressing obligations. Besides, beating back bullies is my life's work, and antagonizing narcissists is my hobby. A third eye for a third eye, a wisdom tooth for a wisdom tooth, that's what I always say."

Lila smiled. "I suspected as much. But I want to be sure you understand what kind of a person Ivan is."

"Stalker, fraud, liar, grifter, narcissistic sociopath… I think you've painted a pretty good portrait."

Lila shook her head. "Perhaps. But Ivan is also the kind of person who surreptitiously doses his disciples with LP9 and then takes the credit for the heart-expanding experience it elicits. Claims that's what it feels like to sit in the presence of a guru."

Merlin blinked into humorlessness. "What's this now?"

"Do you know anything about LP9?"

Merlin squinted at Lila as he considered his earlier years as a bicycle courier. Then he shrugged and looked away. "Only that it's an urban legend."

"It's not an urban legend," Lila assured. "It's *real*."

Merlin shook his head dismissively. "There's no such drug—or medicine—as LP9."

"Yeah, but I've *seen* it," Lila insisted.

After assessing Lila for a few moments, Merlin leaned back. "Do you know what LP9 stands for?"

Lila shook her head.

"LP9. It stands for love potion number nine."

Lila smiled. "How did I not see that? I always just assumed that it was just some designer club drug."

"That's what everyone assumes. But according to the chemist who discovered it, it isn't a drug at all. It's a love potion. And he called it number nine because nine is the cabalistic number for the Holy Unspeakable Name of God."

"How do you know all this?"

"Because," Merlin hesitated. "Not that I'm particularly proud of it, but I used to distribute it throughout the Bay Area."

57

I N 1858, as Merlin told it, a fourteen-year-old peasant named Bernadette was gathering firewood in a grotto outside of Lourdes, France when she was possessed of an apparition that ultimately identified itself as the Immaculate Conception. A series of eighteen apparitions over the next two months instructed young Bernadette to build a chapel and to drink from the spring where the Virgin Mary pointed. As the story goes, though no spring was evident, Bernadette dug into the muddy ground, going so far as to swallow the mud and smear it about her face in oblivious ecstasy while a crowd of disgusted onlookers declared her insane. Within days, however, a clear spring began to flow, and those who drank the water claimed it had miraculous healing properties. Bernadette was later canonized a saint, and not only that, but a member of that elite cadre of saints known as the *incorruptibles*, saints who were allegedly so holy that their bodies did not decay after their death, and even moreso, that their incorruptible corpses gave off a positively floral *odor of sanctity* rather than the typical bile-gargling retch of bodily decay.

"Ivan's incorruptible," Lila interrupted Merlin's hagiography, snickering.

Merlin considered this. "Of course he is."

"*Technically* he's an ascended Master," Lila clarified. "Claims he'll simply dematerialize once his dharma is done, which, according to him, will be during the upcoming solar eclipse."

Merlin shook his head as if clearing his ears. "So anyway," he sighed. "Lourdes now hosts five million pilgrims and tourists a year, and the entire economy is supported by this little spring. So basically this itinerant chemist I met in India set up a little business bottling the holy water from the spring in these little one-ounce Our Lady of Lourdes jewel-cut glass bottles and selling them online to Blue Army Catholics overseas. Turns out that was an honest living all by itself, but a few times a year he'd also send a few dozen bottles of his legendary love potion—disguised as Our Lady of Lourdes holy water—to me, which I'd then distribute to my bike courier crew, who then delivered them via bicycle to all their respective clients throughout the Bay Area, half of whom were Silicon Valley entrepreneurs who thought LP9 was the ultimate nootropic and that it would somehow turn them into a visionary billionaire, but that's a whole other story. Anyway, I basically brokered between the chemist and the distributors and used the profits to fund my travels." Merlin paused, his brow furrowed as he considered his past.

Lila leaned forward. "Who was the chemist?"

"No idea, really, but he called himself Goa Joe. That's where I met him, in Goa, India, where all the Western backpackers converge and party. He'd meet travelers like myself and set us up in his global distribution network. He used to bounce around there in a rattletrap pickup, blithely smuggling his love potion inside of live beehives—"

"Beehives?" Lila interrupted.

Merlin grinned. "Yeah, apparently bees represent Aphrodite, and so he figured he was calling upon the protection of the goddess of sex and love by hiding his potion inside beehives. The authorities certainly waved him along past their checkpoints as fast as they could wave the swarms of angry bees away from them." Merlin laughed. "Funniest guy I've ever met, though. He had this manic, charismatic enthusiasm, where no matter how ludicrous his latest crackpot idea was, you'd get all excited about it too just hearing him blast on about it. I mean, he didn't have to do anything but look you in the eye to make you laugh up a cartoon, like you suddenly realized that you were both in on some kind of a cosmic prank."

"Wow," Lila flabbergasted at Merlin's autobiography. "You have something of a checkered past, mister. Why'd you stop?"

Merlin shrugged. "The delivery drops stopped, and I had grown disenchanted with it all anyway. Besides, you really don't ask any questions in that trade. LP9 is so ridiculously illegal that the government won't even admit that it exists. Where do you think this whole notion that it's just an urban legend came from? I mean, seriously, a *love potion*? Love would undermine the premise of our entire civilization! And you have to understand, we're not talking about some meth-lab ghetto chemist here. Goa Joe considered himself an alchemist seeking to unleash the divinity hidden within humanity with his love potion. He even showed me once how the pure crystals emit flashes of light when you shake a vial of them in the dark. Piezoluminescence, I guess it's called in physics, but to him it was simply proof that he had discovered a magic potion. He had this earnest notion—and if you ever heard him tell it, you'd believe it just the same as if he was telling you that the sun is bright—he had this notion that LP9 was *sent* here direct from the godhead, that it was actually the prophet Elijah heralding the dawn of Christ consciousness. The greatest story never told, he called it. He even claimed that his little potion of love and liberation was the karmic antidote to nuclear weapons. I mean, when you think of it that way, it *is* some kind of a cosmic prank—"

"Yeah, but it can also be used for manipulation," Lila interrupted, thinking of Ivan. "I've seen it happen."

"I know all about it," Merlin nodded. "It's a razor's edge between vision and delusion. That's another reason I walked away from it all. It was undeniably a thrill to play a character in Goa Joe's wild-eyed narrative of human liberation, but ultimately that's all it was, a really good story, and there was bound to be a dark side, and I used to worry about that. Goa Joe just shrugged and insisted that we were dealing with an impassive force of evolution, a vast active living intelligence system breaking free from the black iron prison of human history, and that life at large can't be concerned with the limited experience of an individual any more than the ocean can be responsible for somebody drowning."

"That's kind of harsh," Lila observed.

"I know," Merlin agreed, looking suddenly far away. "But it's also maybe kind of true. And besides, that's probably the best that humanity can hope for anyway."

"What's that?"

"A really good story."

Lila shrugged her chin touché. "So, do you have any left?"

Merlin shook his head emphatic. "I stopped messing around with that stuff years ago. The last time I tried it, it was of an unanticipated potency, and I inadvertently discovered that love is as large as the entire universe—which can actually be an unsettling thing to realize. Anyway, after thinking that I'd died and been reborn about a hundred times over the span of nine eternities, basically burning rubber with the wheels of samsara, I was left with an indefatigable gratitude for sobriety."

Lila burst out laughing, immediately covering her mouth. "I'm so sorry, that's not funny."

"Sure it is," Merlin grinned. "It also totally ripped me out of the social fabric, and I couldn't help but see people as monkeys after that. Everyone just seemed like they were desperately pretending that they weren't these grunting chimps pulsing with lust and feces, flailing about in their oblivious presentations of self. It was totally ludicrous, and probably accurate somehow, but ultimately not real useful for getting along in the world, right? Thankfully it faded after a few days, at least in the immediacy of its perception, though I still sort of sense that the major difference between humans and monkeys is that humans are sexy."

Lila nodded, reflecting upon her own entirely sober perceptions of the world, and after another furrowed pause, Merlin continued. "But anyway, to be totally honest, I had stashed a few vials of it before then, but I'm *done* with that stuff. I've never even been back to see if they're still there—"

"Still where?" Lila interrupted, eyes twinkling as the first intuition of a plan began to take shape in her mind.

Merlin shrugged. "I always hid it in various public places. I was a bit of a paranoiac back in the day."

"But you still know where it is?"

Merlin nodded. "It was supposedly Goa Joe's finest material. Apparently, he'd noticed that LP9 takes on and vastly magnifies the qualities of other substances. I guess he discovered this by accident when he stored a small quantity of liquid in an empty bottle of peppermint oil. According to him, when he eventually sampled it, he was astonished to find that his entire body felt minty fresh, and the sensation lasted for weeks, like the love potion had carried the essence of peppermint into every cell of his body."

Lila chuckled. "And you tried this peppermint love potion?"

"No way," Merlin emphatically shook his head. "Like I said, I was done with it by then, but he insisted it was *every* cell. His lips, his eyes, his hair, his tongue, his *urethra*. He even claimed the inside of his rectum was minty fresh. See, Goa Joe's theory— which somehow sounded a lot more plausible when he said it— was that LP9 is a hyper-homeopathic carrier molecule, that it transcends the illusion of matter and amplifies the subtle energetic vibrations of other substances, anointing your body at the quantum level of its DNA, if that even means anything. So he researched herbs and mushrooms with anticancer properties and then combined extracts of the best of them in another empty bottle of peppermint oil—I guess just because he thought it felt so fantastic to have a minty-fresh asshole. Then after letting it sit for a week he emptied the bottle and filled it with his love potion, on the theory that it would amplify the anticancer vibrations and deliver them directly into a patient's DNA. That's supposedly the potion I stashed, but I don't know what to think of Goa Joe anymore. I'm not convinced that a person can even sustain an expansion of their heart when they have to return to an economic system that enforces uncompromising self-interest, which is necessarily a contraction of the heart." Merlin shook his head. "It doesn't matter in any event. Like I said, I had a pretty serious falling-out with it." Merlin paused. "But Goa Joe really did believe he'd discovered the cure for cancer."

Lila considered. "Damn, that *is* a really good story. Did he ever actually test it on anyone?"

"Nobody knows," Merlin shrugged. "The day he told me he'd discovered the cure for cancer was the last I ever heard from him."

58

A GRATEFUL FIRE was already beginning to crackle by the time Crow and Flaming Jane made their way out of the steep and rocky shore of the cavern's lagoon. Lanterns lit the sleek frigate that would serve as their new ship and illuminated its immense, opalescent king cobra figurehead, enormous serpentine shadows flickered across the walls of the cavern, and bodies glistening mostly naked rummaged dry clothes from a sea chest they'd removed from the hull. Slaps of glad congratulation greeted Crow, for he had taken their test and survived, and if they were shipmates before, they were brethren now. Then, once Crow's brothers and the rest of the exuberant crew who'd followed Crow and Flaming Jane into the quicksand found their way ashore—rumors of Crow's proposal swelled instantly into boisters and bellows of uproarious approval, for though this group of adventurers needed nothing more than their next breath to elicit celebration, news of Flaming Jane's acceptance kindled the sort of jubilation that only true love can spark.

Nonetheless, there was work to be done, and no one needed to be told what it was. Having been at anchor in this cavern for months (and whose lagoon, Crow marveled, must be uncommonly deep not to have run this frigate aground), there was barnacle to be removed, pitch to be patched, rust to be remedied, and a general tidying throughout before they could launch seaworthy. Someone speared a few sea turtles and began roasting them over the fire, Catface somehow reappeared, having found his own passage into the underground cavern, and soon there was wine and hardtack and even some terrifically salty jerky to be had from the ship's carefully stored provisions. It was as cool and humid as a root cellar in the cavern, Flaming Jane explained to Crow as she handed him a perfectly fresh carrot, and all they had to do was store their dried provisions in wax paper and with piles of dry salt to keep the humidity down.

Crow nodded, looking again to the opal-encrusted white golden king cobra figurehead gilded on the prow of the frigate. Their new ship was superior in every way to their former ship. "This ship—" he began.

"*Eleusis,*" Flaming Jane cut him off. "This is the real *Eleusis*. I always knew our other ship was disposable. *This* ship is the fastest frigate in the Caribbean."

"*Eleusis,*" Crow agreed. "You've noticed of course that her figurehead is a white cobra—just like on the map, and in my dream?"

"Indeed I have noticed that," Flaming Jane nodded as she kindly wiped a smudge from Crow's cheek. "I told you I knew *exactly* what I was doing."

59

T HEIR NEW SHIP, Crow learned as he assisted Flaming Jane in arranging their quarters aboard *Eleusis*, had originally been captured from some Scottish pirates—who themselves had hijacked the ship from some Barbary corsairs who'd abandoned the Mediterranean (hence the Greek name of the ship) for the more profitable seas of the Caribbean—the last time they'd visited Boca Diablo. Despite this early success, these Scottish pirates were widely regarded as the stupidest crew afloat, and under Half-Ass McJanky's leadership they had snuck aboard Flaming Jane's other vessel while they assumed the crew was asleep in an inept attempt to commandeer their ship. In the end, however, all they succeeded in doing was surrounding themselves with the pissed-off pistols of the Eleusinians, who disarmed them and locked the lot of them in their brig. Half-Ass McJanky had offered to trade ships in exchange for his own release. Flaming Jane accepted his offer, and was not surprised when she learned two days later that he was attempting to organize a mutiny against her in order to regain control of both ships. Thus were Half-Ass McJanky and his men pushed off a plank a mile offshore of Boca Diablo, and thus did he lose his ship.

"But there's a white snake drawn on the treasure map," Crow pointed out. "Why didn't you set sail for the treasure straightaway in this ship?"

"I wanted to lay this ship low for a few months, along with our collected treasure, and besides, I hadn't yet found the map. Goldtooth had sewn it between two other charts. Plus, there's a black sun pictured on the map, and according to the Royal

Navy's ephemeris, there's supposed to be a solar eclipse next week, which is why we're here now."

Crow paused. "So when did you find the map?"

Flaming Jane hesitated before answering, unsettled by her own perplexity. "I found the map a few hours before you awoke from your fever dream."

60

IT WAS A HEAVY TOIL navigating *Eleusis* through the narrow and meandering passage of unforgiving rocks that led out of the cavern lagoon. All sails remained tied, and the Eleusinians had only the strength of their oars to move their ship out of its hiding place and into open water. As it was, they had to wait for the afternoon high tide so that they wouldn't run their ship aground on the jagged bottom of the inlet, and it rather seemed to Crow that if *Eleusis* were a plank larger then they would have found not only the passage but also the choppy waters of the cliff-covered cove it opened into to be impassable. But with Noa leading with his oar and acting as coxswain, the basso boom of his voice held everyone tight to their tasks, and before long they were safely into open water. After Flaming Jane had set their course toward the Lesser Antilles and a watch-standing schedule had been arranged, most of the members of the crew retired for some much-needed sleep.

"I do not like love," Flaming Jane murmured, resting across Crow's chest after they had settled into their new quarters, snuzzling sleepward. "Like war, it has an uncertain outcome."

"Nonsense," Crow replied. "The outcome of love is perfectly certain."

"Is it?"

"It is. And no amount of cunning can save you from it."

Flaming Jane was silent awhile as she puzzled over Crow's words. "What are you speaking about?" she asked at last.

Crow smiled, stroking her hair and sighing into his sleep as he whispered, *"Surrender."*

61

WHATEVER THEIR ENEMIES' fates may have been, Flaming Jane did not wish to overtake either Half-Ass McJanky or Goldtooth's squadron. To avoid this, she plotted a course that arced broadly eastward before settling onto its direct course toward the island indicated on the map—an island that Crow shortly noticed did not appear on any of their other charts. Where it should have been, presuming the accuracy of their treasure map, were only various warnings, ranging from Biblical references to Job 41 (which, Crow found, described a hellacious sea monster called the Leviathan) to maelstroms and dangerous waters to sea serpents and medieval *here there be dragons* dread.

And now, from halfway up the rigging, Crow smirked, immensely pleased that the fortunes of life had placed him among such a wild tribe and in love with a woman whom he privately suspected to be smarter than his own considerable self. He watched as Flaming Jane fenced her cutlass with another woman of their crew, Zahara, a West African as fierce as she was beautiful, and possessed of a wicked shock of dreadlocks decorated with sun-bleached seashells spiraling off their tips, as well as various feathers and gemstones throughout. Near the bow, his brothers were exchanging the fundamentals of their native tongue with some attentive others, while another group busied themselves war-painting one another's bodies under the tutelage of Rafaela, a natural-born artist who'd also ditched her indentured servitude and discovered a latent talent for revealing the wild spirit seething beneath the faces of domestication.

Crow drew a breath deep with gratitude, for never was there a finer band of companions with whom to share life, and if it so be, death. Marveling at the unabashed beauty that propelled every one of them, Crow saw that this was what set the Eleusinians a class apart from other buccaneers, and why they were feared by pirate and lawful seaman alike wherever they went. Rebelling against the sumptuary laws that forbade members of lower classes from dressing in the manner of the nobility—and as if to claim the class privileges afforded a gentleman—the typical pirate dressed like a flamboyant aristocrat and called himself a gentleman of fortune. The Eleusinian crew, by contrast, cared nothing for imitating the affectations of the upper classes, and Crow had even heard tell of how they'd heaved stinkpots and slop buckets into trunks of such finery. They dressed instead as wild-born warriors, and in the face of their ferocity they rarely found resistance.

"Hell's bells, Crow Smarty!" arrived the voice of Moby, alighting upon the rigging above Crow.

"Someday you'll have to tell me how you manage to find us," Crow answered, grinning.

"Hell's bells, Crow Smarty!" Moby repeated. "Be wary! Be wary!"

Crow quickly scanned the horizons but saw nothing. "How many?" he grunted as he climbed toward the crow's nest.

"Three ships, Crow Smarty!" Moby answered after alighting again above Crow. "Surrounding surrounding!"

"Much obliged, Moby," Crow answered, hefting himself into the crow's nest as he continued scanning the horizons all around. He saw nothing but open water, but did not doubt Moby's warning. Presumably, as Flaming Jane had arranged, Half-Ass McJanky had sailed straight into Goldtooth's squadron. Goldtooth had doubtless delivered them to Davey Jones's Locker, but if he'd managed to gain some intelligence on the existence of Flaming Jane's new ship, he may well have navigated ahead of them, anticipating their course and lying in wait. Crow guessed that Goldtooth's three ships would be ahead of them and glassed the leeward horizon, only to discover that a fog was gathering there. In these latitudes, sea fog indicated breaking water, and breaking water with no storm on the horizon could only indicate land.

"Land ho!" Crow bellowed through the speaking trumpet, but instead of chimping his way back down the masting ropes, Crow threw a belt over the topmost rope and leapt from the crow's nest. The *deathslide*, others aboard had called his innovation, though few had dared a ride. Only slightly slower than freefall, Crow flew toward the forecastle and into the netting he'd rigged to catch himself, and Flaming Jane was already at his side as he untangled himself.

"Land?" she confirmed, knowing that they were nearing the island every other chart indicated only with dangerous waters.

"Sea fog," Crow nodded. "And as Moby tells it, three ships."

62

MERLIN WATCHED as Lila tucked her hair discreetly under her corduroy cap—the kind of baggy cap that can conceal a full tress of hair—pulled on her black leather roshambo gloves, and affixed her sunglasses before she made her way across the street, permitting Ivan to orchestrate running into her just as she had predicted. She gushed in greeting, covering her mouth, touching her heart, throwing her arms around him, an impressive display of affection. Ivan himself did have something of a striking appearance, Merlin considered, certain to stand out in any crowd, doubtless facilitated by his permanent eyeliner tattoos Lila had told him about. Everything about him was much too much: too coifed, too smooth, too sharp, too straight, too perfect, and from a distance, his paralytic Botox face made him look like a puppet when he talked. It would be fun, Merlin thought, to antagonize this guy, to fracture his mannequin facade.

But for now, Merlin had nothing to do but imagine Ivan slipping on a patch of ice and catching his fall in a fresh pile of bumshit—not that there was any ice in the perfectly temperate San Francisco Indian summer. Anyway, Lila had told him to wait for her while she ran into the bank to make a deposit. Ivan or his bodyguards, she said, would probably eyeball him, and if they did, then Merlin should just ignore them and meet her at another café around the corner in a few minutes. All of this came to pass as she described, and it wasn't until Merlin, sitting at the café around the corner and utterly innocent in his expectations, heard distant sirens approaching that he began to suspect what had just occurred.

63

OR MAYBE NOT. When Lila appeared she did not seem the least bit flustered, certainly not as if she had just robbed a bank, as Merlin had momentarily feared. Her hair flew free of her cap, no sunglasses shaded her eyes, and her absence of jacket and jaunt of her stride suggested a woman utterly without fret. But when she grinned upon seeing Merlin, it was a grin he had seen before, the same full-blast smile that saturated her face shortly after she'd revealed that she'd bounced with all the abundance offerings from the Holy Company of Beautiful People.

"Hey, lover," she sighed as she plopped her pack onto the booth and slid into the seat across from him.

"Hey there." Merlin smirked. "Something got your giddy?"

"My what?"

"Your giddy," Merlin repeated, gesturing about her countenance. "Your face exhilarates an uncommon glee."

"Ah yes, well, life is god." She licked her lips. "That's funny. Life is *good*, I meant to say, naturally, though perhaps my malapropism is appropriate as well."

Merlin nodded. "What uh, whatcha got in your back-pack there?"

"Na-thing," she pronounced, puddles of mischief overflowing from her dimples.

Merlin glanced about, but no one was nearby. He leaned forward anyway, lowering his voice. "What'd you go and do now?"

"I'll tell you later," Lila grinned and grabbed his shirt. "Just as soon as you take me home and have your way with me."

64

OT SEX and thirty thousand dollars later, Lila described to Merlin how she'd greeted Ivan, told him how amazing it was to see him, how she'd dreamt just last night of his ascension under the upcoming solar eclipse, and how she was so sorry for being in her mind and not trusting him as her Master. Then she asked Ivan if he would mind sticking around for a couple of minutes just to keep an eye on that man across the street at the diner and make sure he didn't try to follow her into the bank. Ivan agreed yes of course and gallant, whereupon Lila entered the bank, approached a teller, and voice quavering implored upon the teller for help, because, you see that man in the mirrored aviator shades standing outside the bank with two goons now looking around and glancing inside suspicious? He's kidnapped her friend and told her if she doesn't come out with thirty thousand dollars in hundred-dollar bills within two minutes then she'll never see her friend again. The teller complied, alarmed but compassionate, and when Lila thanked her for the three bundles of hundreds and begged her to call for help but please to wait a couple of minutes first so as not to startle her captors, the teller promised her in solidarity and sisterhood that she would.

"Then I left, walked away with Ivan's arm on mine in full view of the bank's windows, turned a corner, promised to call him later, watched as his bodyguards drove him away, then took off my gloves and hat and sunglasses and jacket and walked back in front of the bank's windows on my way to meet you." Lila shrugged as simple as that.

Merlin was stunned, and not at all amused. "What the... what the *fuck*, Lila! What if they recognize you?"

"Who? The police cruisers whizzed right past me, and Ivan was busy thinking he was guarding me from you. Besides, all anyone really registers when they see me is my long red hair, and that wasn't on the camera."

"Uh, what about your Fuck You Fred friend?"

Lila laughed. "Do you honestly think that Fuck You Fred would care if somebody robbed that bank? He's been casing that bank himself for months, and he vanished as soon as the police arrived anyway."

"This is crazy," Merlin shook his head adamant. "You can't be doing this."

"Excuse me?" Lila was indignant. "I can't be doing what, *living my dream?*" She grabbed the parchment Merlin had given her off the nightstand, the one that bore Flaming Jane's signature and her exhortation to Live Your Dream. "You *encouraged* me to do this. You *reminded* me that this is all a dream!"

"Robbing banks is your dream?"

"*Freedom* is my dream!"

"I didn't realize money was freedom."

"Whatever," Lila waved him off. "You can't possibly be that daft. *Action* is freedom, the ability to make freeborn decisions, and as far as I'm concerned I just reclaimed the indentured student loan I was conned into when I was barely eighteen years old in exchange for the luxury of an education. And anyway, the only thing that was 'robbed' was an illusion in the first place. Besides, who are you to pussyfoot, mister international drug smuggler?"

"Promise me you'll never do something like this again," Merlin insisted.

"Promise me you'll never say something like that to me again," Lila retorted.

Merlin shook his head again. "I just don't want to see you get caught, or hurt."

"I've been *caught* and *hurt* my entire life!" Lila raised her voice. "My parents lost their marriage, not because they didn't love each other, but because they were mangled by these social systems! I witnessed their spirits shred under the spur of a society that puts everything from health care to a place to live just barely within reach!" Lila held up the three bundles of hundreds. "This is *worthless*," she emphasized. "People work at jobs they *loathe* for this fool's paper, trading their priceless life, day by forgotten day, for nickels and agitation. Work should be the source of our greatest satisfaction, not this hypertensive indentured servitude traffic jam drudgefest." She displayed the bundles again. "This is *life*, life that was mortgaged, appropriated, and directed long before any of us even realized what was happening." Lila shook her head, inflamed. "I mean, look around, Merlin. The only difference between today and feudalism is the glossy *illusion* that our world is just, that there are no alternatives, and that our conformity isn't ultimately compelled under the threat of banishment. I'm alive, and I won't always be, but as long as I am my mind is my manor and I'm *nobody's* serf."

Merlin shook his head in perplexity and sadness. "I know," he replied. "I can't argue with a thing you're saying."

"Listen," Lila continued, "I'm not just some reckless twit with poor impulse control. I know *exactly* what I'm doing."

"And what is that?"

She paused. "My father scraped his way into owning his own home at last. Then, after ten *years* of house payments, the majority of which went only to pay the *interest* on the mortgage, by the way, his home value cratered when this casino economy collapsed. Then he lost his job, and he desperately tried to get another job he'd hate just so he could keep making payments on a house that had lost most of its value anyway, lose his home in the end, have a massive heart attack from all the stress, age twenty years in a single month, and die when he was barely fifty years old." Lila paused, anger masking her grief. "So pardon me for getting angry, but anger is the sound of the scars on my heart." She paused again. "Besides, did you know that mortgage literally means 'dead pledge'? Pay it off and you've *bought the farm*. This system stole my father's life long before he died, Merlin, just like it does everyone else's. Ten years of payments on a house he'd never own, working for some corporation with the contempt to refer to him as a human *resource*, transforming his life into money just so these bankers who produce nothing but debt can park their Maseratis beneath the helicopter pads on their Mediterranean yachts. It's not about money, Merlin, it's about *life*. The evil call themselves elite, and they steal life like Palpatine vampires, extending their capacities at the expense of everyone else's, and it's a dark, dark alchemy. I'm just bringing some balance to the equation, and Ivan is just the beginning. You can hop off this train anytime you like."

Again, there was nothing Merlin could say. He knew Lila was correct. He'd known it when he manufactured fake IDs in college to avoid going into student loan debt. He'd known it when he scammed dozens of credit cards in order to fund his own world travel. And he'd known it when he participated in an international smuggling operation. The system protects those who have and prevents those who have not, and the only way to keep your life from being stolen—as any entrepreneur can testify—is to ignore the rules. Merlin sighed. "I just want to live life with you, a nice community, some land."

"I know," Lila agreed. "That's all *anyone* really wants. But the game is rigged, Merlin, the deck is stacked. The simple satisfactions of life are effectively prohibited in order to compel our participation in these corrupt, techno-feudal arrangements, turning us into desperate, lonely, angry, hopeless consumers of someone else's dictated culture instead of visionary creators of our own experience. Remember what you were telling me about those incorruptible saints?"

Merlin nodded.

"Well, you realize that shares the same root as *corruption*, right? Comes from the Latin *corruptio*, which means to decay, or to come apart. Supposedly those saints didn't decay, but our corrupt economic system is sure as hell falling apart, and the banks are just the tapeworms consuming every last ounce of life from us. Why should I donate my sacred life to sustaining a decaying corpse? It's disgusting." Lila paused, inflamed. "I mean, haven't you ever noticed that *culture* shares the same root as *cult*? This culture compels our compliance by controlling our access to resources—that's what debt has always been about. The only real difference is one of scale." Lila settled her voice and took Merlin's hand. "Listen, I can see that my presence in your life has inspired you to provide a home and protect, but all our hopes and dreams will curdle into resentment within this system, and you know it. I'm not interested in living out the abject script we've been handed, exhausting our adrenal glands chasing some illusion of security." She shook her head. "Chronic financial insecurity is not security. That path has been trodden into a ditch nobody can steer out of, and the best anyone can hope for is to be an overfed and undernourished worker. All the world's a cage, and all the men and women merely hamsters. I'm sorry," she shook her head, "that's not the story of me. Or on second thought, I'm not sorry at all."

Merlin chuckled. Arguing with Lila was like arguing with the forgotten ferocity of his own heart. He had sought the ecstatic fantastic wow of existence his entire life, and while there was perhaps something to be said for dancing all night long on a candyflip rave on a remote island beach in the Gulf of Thailand and watching the sunrise like it was soaring a roar of song through his soul, he had known all along that such experiences were only reminding him what he was seeking, and now that she was holding his hand he was trying to tug away. "Yes, well," Merlin smirked, relaxing his hand. "You're telling Noah about the Flood here. As you know, I've never really been much of a worker for someone else's enrichment."

Lila smiled, flushed and dewy.

"You know," Merlin sighed reflective. "I met this German guy once on the Kalalau Trail, on the island of Kauai. I don't remember his name, but he was a memorable guy, in Hawaii for his honeymoon, hiking this eleven-mile, cliff-side, grueling, exhilarating switchback trail with his beautiful new wife. The three of us talked for a half hour or so at the eight-mile campsite at sunset, commending the tremendous beauty of Kalalau and our privilege to witness it, and I remember being impressed because they both looked so young and inspired and really just as happy a couple as you'll ever meet. Anyway, they hiked on earlier in the morning than me, and by the time I got down to

Kalalau Beach there was this big commotion with rangers and helicopters and all that, and I find out that the body on the stretcher they're lifting into the helicopter is his, that he and his wife had been so ecstatic at having finished such an amazing hike that they threw off their packs and boots and dove into the ocean." Merlin paused. "But I guess a riptide caught hold of him, and they didn't recover his body for over an hour."

"Oh," Lila covered her mouth.

Merlin paused again long, avoiding eye contact. "Anyway, it was like an existential bomb went off after that. Kalalau Valley is this insanely beautiful place, as close to Eden as you'll ever see, and the juxtaposition of such a horrifying tragedy was just maddening. Everyone who was in the valley when that happened changed their lives after that. You can't come face-to-face with that sort of nightmarish randomness and maintain the illusion that you have any control. You also can't help but have compassion for everybody who's caught in such a ruthless circumstance as life." Merlin's gaze now touched Lila's. "Point is, beautiful Lila, you hold me to my own truth even as I cower from it, and for that I am grateful. And whether it's a day or a decade, for as long as it's right now I'm with you." Merlin leaned forward and they kissed upon his gentle oath, and when he leaned back he smiled. "Plus," he said, "you're sexy as fuck."

65

DESPITE APPEARANCES, the heart of every Eleusinian wished to avoid battle, not only because powder and steel present a terrible assault upon human flesh, but also because battle itself presents a terrible assault upon the human heart. The Eleusinians' flaunt of war paint and ferocity was intended to intimidate, and in this way they typically navigated their way through threatening waters relatively unchallenged and unscathed.

This tactic worked well with Half-Ass McJanky, but with Goldtooth, the dispute would not be so easily dissuaded. As far as Goldtooth was concerned, Flaming Jane and her company of bandits had upended everything he needed to believe about himself and his mastery of life, and nothing short of their slaughter would ever assuage his rage. The Eleusinians understood this, of course, and they also understood that no matter how many times they smacked him down, he would continue to pursue them until they finished what he'd started.

And now, as Moby flew about announcing "Three ships! Three ships!" and an uncommon sea fog gradually enveloped them, Flaming Jane winced in a moment of regret. Twice she could have dispatched Goldtooth from his miserable state, and twice she had let him live, preferring to punish him rather than release him into the forgiving beyond. But here, their advantages were quickly diminishing. *Eleusis* had been retrofitted to be far swifter than other vessels, and the crew had just completed their latest design upgrade, but they possessed no edge if they could not see their enemies' approach, and in a close battle with three ships outnumbered by hundreds of hands, triumph receded into impossibility.

Speed was a liability under these conditions, and so the crew tossed a bank of thirty empty barrels overboard behind them, all of them secured to the ship by an immense and hempen rope. Checking the rope now, Flaming Jane found it as taut and as rigid as a bar of steel, and the drag of the barrels allowed them to maintain full sail while slowing the ship by a factor of at least one half. From there, Flaming Jane checked to ensure all riggings had been cleared from the launching path of the catapult, their newest innovation. The catapult—so gigantic that it ran most of the length of the ship—had taken half a day to crank into launch position, and so was only designed to be sprung once in battle. In addition to delivering its payload, however, the sprung catapult arm would also act as an additional mainmast, locking into its standing position against its stopwall near the bow and already rigged to a second set of loosely bound sails ready to seize the breeze as soon as the catapult was sprung.

Crow and his brothers, meanwhile, were preparing *the dragon*. The dragon was a tremendous cannon that fired directly from the bow of *Eleusis*, mounted where the forecastle had been and whose barrel was concealed within the mouth of the king cobra figurehead. Because ships located their guns broadside, the dragon's location on the bow—combined with the catapult's trajectory—provided them with an uncommon tactical advantage.

But none of these advantages would mean anything in this thickening sea fog. Their only assurance was that they were as invisible to other ships as other ships were to them. A minute ago, Crow couldn't see the stern of the ship from the bow, and now he couldn't even see across the deck. Looking up, the sky was indivisible from the atmosphere in front of his face, although that failed to prevent him from seeing a buzzard cut the clouds just a couple of feet over his head. Neither did the sea fog fail to prevent Catface from seeing that buzzard, and Catface all of an instant leapt unpremeditated and nimble upon the buzzard, tearing it out of its flight in a flail of fur and feathers as he sank his teeth into its neck and landed deft upon his feet, unperturbed at the suddenness of his own actions. Grinning fuck yeah, Crow immediately punched the arms of those on either side of him, their silent signal to ready for battle, and they in turn passed the punch forward. The punch was hard, intended to inspire aggression, and as it slugged its way across the ship all eyes narrowed, stomachs seizing. Lanterns were lit, powder was tamped, pistols were cocked. And then they waited, waited in silence against the muffled creaking of their own hull and the gentle slosh of sea, all senses on full blast, seeking to pick up anything that could tell them what was about to happen.

Peering over the gunwales was peering into white blindness. There was nothing to see but the mist drifting above one's own nose. It was a maddening fog, merciless in its uncertainty, but it was in this uncertainty that Flaming Jane found some relief. Flaming Jane knew her enemies were as maddened by this fog as were she and the crew, but she also knew the Eleusinians' patience could outlast any adversary. The game was simple. Wait for one of their softheaded enemies suffering the worse of drink to snap under stress, to cry out, to fire a pistol, to signal their position, and then attack. Privately, she wagered it wouldn't be more than five minutes, but she won her wager within one.

"Bloody fog!" a sodden voice suddenly cursed directly off

their starboard side, sounding close enough to have been aboard *Eleusis*. But it was much too close for Flaming Jane's comfort, for in firing they would have revealed their own position as well. At this range a return cannonade could devastate them. No, far better to wait for better odds.

And so *Eleusis* drifted, and before long a breeze began to blow, and as the fog began to lift, Crow sent a second slug across the ship to ready once more. And it was good that he did, for there it was now, the ship they had heard, now a hundred feet off their starboard side, and lo, another one just slightly further off their port side. Flaming Jane cursed, seeing the Royal Navy's flag, and, still searching for the third ship, she screamed a preemptive "Fire!"

Eleusis immediately fired its cannons from both sides, and if Flaming Jane were desperate it did not show on her face. Their cannons hit their marks, tearing into the hulls and through the sails of both ships. She figured they had less than a minute before Goldtooth and the Royal Navy returned fire, but then they heard his voice before they saw his ship.

"Yar surrounded!" bullhorned the voice of Goldtooth, his command ship—the *Damnation II*—dead ahead of them a hundred and fifty feet, blockading them broadside. "Surrendar ere 'e slaughter ye!"

Flaming Jane looked expressionless to Crow. "Fire the dragon."

Crow touched a flame to the fuse. "This should be something," he smiled, covering his ears.

Seconds later, when the dragon fired, their entire ship lurched backward from the tremendous force of the blast, scattering Eleusinians across the deck. When they regained their balance, they found a smoldering hole cut clear through the upper deck of the *Damnation II*, but there was no time to rejoice at this before they were met by a cannonade from both sides. Splinters shivers blood and screams, the battle raged as *Eleusis* returned fire on both sides, and as Crow and his brothers reloaded the dragon and lowered its aim, Flaming Jane raced to the stern of the ship, her cutlass already drawn to release the drag barrels slowing their sails. *Eleusis* lurched again as the dragon fired, causing Flaming Jane to slip in a pool of a shipmate's blood. Pulling herself up in the midst of the horror of finding bits and pieces of human flesh all around her, she finally saw Goldtooth's tactic. *They're not attacking our ship*, she realized. *They're firing case shot across our deck, trying to kill us all and take the ship intact!*

"Take cover!" she yelled to her shipmates, watching as the ships on either side of them drew ever closer. Another shrapnel sweep across their deck at this range would savage the most of them. "Everybody below deck!" she screamed, and seeing Noa, she called to him, "The catapult, Noa! Light the catapult!"

Noa nodded, his face twisted hideous by the rage of having seen one of his mates torn to pieces by a blast of case shot. Reckoning the diminishing distance, he adjusted the bowl for a high trajectory, then grabbed a lantern and heaved it into the bowl of the catapult, now loaded with several hundred pounds of oil-soaked and chain-bound timber. The payload burst into flames and black smoke as soon as the flames touched it at the same time that another blast from the dragon tossed them all off balance once again.

"Get below!" Flaming Jane yelled, pulling herself up at the stern of the ship. "They're firing across our deck!"

Crow and his brothers never heard this, but it wouldn't matter anyway, since unless they planned on sailing their bow broadside into the *Damnation II*, they were going to need to keep firing the dragon until they cut Goldtooth's ship in half. Crow barricaded some barrels to provide cover for his brothers. "Load the chain!" he commanded, and his brothers Seraph and Malakai nodded, smirking as they loaded an immense chain shot—two cannonballs attached by a chain—into the dragon.

"Noa!" Flaming Jane raised her cutlass. "On my mark!"

Noa leveled a battle axe at the rope holding the catapult.

Flaming Jane looked at the ships closing in on either side of them, not forty feet away. "Now!" she screamed, severing the dragline with a single slash from her saber at the same time that Noa axed the catapult's pull rope. The release of the dragline along with the catapulting ascent of a second set of canvas snapping into full sail sent *Eleusis* surging forward seconds before both broadside ships fired another round of case shot. With *Eleusis* suddenly free from their line of fire, however, the broadside ships managed to fire only across one another's decks, to their considerable death and detriment. But with the speed of *Eleusis* having suddenly tripled, its bow was now bearing down on a collision with the broadside of Goldtooth's own ship.

"Fire!" Crow roared, and *Eleusis* lurched as an immense chain shot kerblammed and cartwheeled across the diminishing distance, tearing into the bulkheads and timbering the mainmast. But it was not nearly enough to split the ship, and as they braced for collision and close combat the high arc of their catapult's fireball finally found its target, careening like a meteor into the *Damnation II*, splitting it entirely in two and engulfing both sides in flames seconds before *Eleusis* barraged through the wreckage unchallenged.

Flaming Jane, however, would not witness this success. The recoil of the taut dragline caught her off guard, clubbing across her head with the blunt force of a log as it knocked her overboard moments before a sniper's arrow murdered the air where she'd been standing.

66

T HE DAY PASSED, the fog creeping in and rolling back several times but never dissipating completely, and always alarming the crew with the fear of another attack. They had sprung their catapult and revealed all their tricks to escape the last skirmish, and they knew a second encounter would not turn out so well. However he had managed it (and it was suspected the buzzards had some kind of a hand in it), Goldtooth had somehow surrounded them despite the whiteout fog. Though his ships were wounded and now counted only two, there was every reason to suspect it might happen again, and grieving over their own fallen agonized them all the more. Perhaps worst of all, Flaming Jane was missing, and though none dared say it, Davey Jones was the dread.

Desperate discussion surrounded a decision to abandon these treacherous waters and find a safe haven in which to recuperate and rebuild. Crow and his Arawak brethren abstained from these discussions, instead fevering upon a project that had been occupying them since they first came aboard *Eleusis*, modifying some metallurgical tools they'd found in its hull. Gabriel finished running a bronze siphon up the mainmast to the crow's nest while the rest of them constructed a brazier to house a fire made scorching by the continual blast of a bellows. Atop this they placed a massive copper cauldron whose joints they'd sealed with tin, attached via valve to the bronze siphon running up the mainmast.

"What's in there?" Noa asked Crow, who was heaving on a pump to further pressurize the contents of the copper tank, which was already so hot that Noa couldn't come within ten feet of it.

"Greek fire," Crow answered. Greek fire was a legendary weapon of the Byzantine Empire, whose technology had been lost to history but eventually rendered obsolete anyway with the advent of artillery fire and its longer range. But all sailors had heard tell of it, and naval historians consider it humanity's first flamethrower. In fact, Gabriel's Greek fire was a mixture of pine resin pitch and petroleum, heated under extreme pressure. "As likely to blow us all to hell as to actually work." Crow continued heaving on the pump, working nonstop to distract himself from Flaming Jane's having gone missing. "And a Hail Mary sure as hell wouldn't hurt us here."

Meanwhile, the remaining crew studied the treasure map and found no indication of how to bring their ship to safe anchorage within the shoals of an island that shrouded its perimeter in this deadly fog. For all anyone knew, they were as close to suffering another attack as running aground upon a sandbar or tearing into a reef. It was foolish to drift near uncharted coastlines in a deepwater vessel, and absent a plan for a forward trajectory here, there was no reason not to abandon the quest, or at least to sail away from Goldtooth's ships skulking somewhere in this sea fog.

It was in the middle of their vote—a vote that was, against all reason, thus far unanimously in favor of staying their suicidal course until they determined Flaming Jane's fate—that a warning artillery shot tore through the sails above their heads. The sea fog had broken apart and they dismayed to discover Goldtooth's two remaining ships less than a hundred feet off starboard. A bile-gurgling roar greeted their sudden exposure, and all stomachs turned to lead as their eyes fell upon the body of Flaming Jane, strung prone beneath the bowsprit off the prow of the ship recently rechristened the *Damnation III*, ropes crisscrossing her body and binding her limbs, her head hanging lifeless off her torso, and her flame of hair flogging hopeless in the breeze.

67

IVAN SIGHED into the face cushion of the massage table while two of his aspirants massaged his body to ensure his afternoon chiropractic adjustment held—a *massage-a-trois,* they called it. At some level Ivan was relieved that Lila had reached out to him. Her outspoken apostasy and his own angered reaction had startled some of his followers, but he was ultimately able to explain that Lila was the source of all the dark energy he'd been sensing, and had succeeded in getting dangerously close to him. Always are we under threat, Ivan soothed, and must be ever vigilant against attacks from the spiritually dead.

Now here was Lila reaching out to him, dreaming of his ascension under the total solar eclipse, and even wanting to be with him again. It was perfect. As satisfying as it might have been to tie her to his bed one last time and give her what she deserved, poisoning her once and for all with a strong dose of wormwood oil seemed a more permanent punishment. And since everyone already knew that the Master might dematerialize under the total solar eclipse in two weeks' time, Ivan would make Lila's dream come true, use the eclipse indeed to disappear, dematerialize under the maximum eclipse, dump the Holy Company of Beautiful People, and lay the blame for his exit on an incapacitated Lila, saying that her attack upon him with her tremendous dark energy had necessitated his ascension to the higher realms. It made him giddy just to think about, and his entire body suddenly relaxed.

"Ah, good!" spoke one of his masseuses.

"*Very* good!" agreed the other.

68

"MAGIC," Lila replied after Merlin inquired how she planned to unveil Ivan. "The human brain receives over eleven million bits of information per second, but the conscious mind can only interpret about two hundred bits per second." Lila tapped his forehead. "The reality you experience, then—the world of your conscious self—is a *vast* reduction, approximately fifty-five thousand times less than what your senses are actually receiving, which is really another way of saying that in any given moment there are fifty-five thousand other realities you might just as easily inhabit."

"I get it," Merlin leaned forward. "The magician simply redirects attention to one of these other fifty-five thousand realities, thereby distracting others from the reality they're manipulating."

"Pretty much," Lila nodded. "It's actually not that complicated. What's amazing is that people aren't aware that they're immersed in the midst of such magic *all the time.*"

"Like right now," Merlin gestured toward her. "You're directing my attention with your words, and implicitly distracting my attention away from whatever else the full-blast flow of life might have to offer my senses in this moment."

"For sure," Lila grinned. "And you're doing the same thing.

The difference is that a skillful magician is fully aware that they are crafting a reality. There's an intentionality behind it."

Merlin sat back and nodded. "So Ivan is a magician."

"He sure is," Lila replied, "and a dark magician at that. Dark magic," she defined, "is directed toward enhancing your own self-importance. Light magic is directed toward the liberation of all beings."

"Says who?"

"Says nobody," Lila shrugged. "Says me."

69

MERLIN HAD BEEN trying to grow up most of his adult life. Pathetic, he knew, his desperate Peter Pan complex, but honestly, it just didn't seem like the so-called grown-ups were actually enjoying their egoic games of ruthless self-promotion so much as miring themselves and each other within them. Merlin kept waiting for some epiphany that would make it all sound suddenly sensible, abandoning his love for life at large and reducing himself to the soulless promotion of his own insignificant self-interest, but in the end it just sounded an uninspired and insipid path, certain to kick the tickle out of any child's funny bone. It wasn't that he loathed responsibility, not at all, but if responsibility meant pointless careerism working for someone else's profit, and especially if responsibility meant consenting to some necktie noose and further reducing the supply of oxygen to his brain, well, that decision just wasn't apt to happen.

But the day after he agreed to help Lila unveil Ivan, standing on his hands in Golden Gate Park and watching a mischief of magpies dive-bomb an orange tabby that kept stalking beneath a nest, Merlin began to wonder if capitulation might not be such a bad idea after all. He already considered himself something of a dilettante locksmith—he'd enjoyed solving the puzzle of locks ever since he was a child—so maybe he should just get a straight job, plug his soul into a standardized socket on the suburban circuit board, and spend his days whizzing to and fro the crumbling culs-de-sac of consumerism in a futilitarian frenzy like everybody else. Probably he could find a locksmith willing to take him on as an apprentice, for starters, maybe go to law school eventually or something? Maybe careers weren't as thankless as he imagined, slaving rather than seizing the day in order to secure one's future death and decrepitude. Maybe his outlook was fundamentally arrogant, maybe there was some satisfaction to be found in the rat race. Maybe the multitudes of consumers weren't just gorging themselves on illusions in their desperate attempts to slake their spiritual starvation, like the dream that presents a feast that vanishes as soon as you try to taste it. Maybe, after all these years of wandering, he hadn't been being true to his spirit so much as fleeing his own maturation.

Whatever the case, anything was starting to seem preferable to ending up as one of those hollowed-out lunatics forever haunting the Haight and Telegraph Avenue, taking bumperdumps in between parked cars and waiting to raise their fists for some forgotten revolution. On the other hand, Merlin considered, given Lila's recent shenanigans, he might even end up arrested. And Lila, ah Lila, the beautiful Lila, she was a firecracker for certain, and while she thrilled him, she also kind of freaked him out, and sexpot or not, he couldn't help wondering if she might be his femme fatale.

But then a putrid odor curled up his nose, preceding the

presence of some jackass turning his head upside down and spewing a crippling halitosis all over Merlin's olfaction.

Alas, it could only be Chris Bliss.

70

WE NEED TO talk to you, *Merlin*," Chris Bliss blasted his breath in Merlin's face, emphasizing that he already knew his name just before shoving him off center, which was mostly unnecessary, as the carcass of Chris Bliss's breath alone would have eventually sufficed to perish Merlin's balance.

Merlin tumbled expertly to the ground, dismaying to discover that he was now obscured from public view by a substantial hedge and confronted by five guys besides, all of them wearing identical mirrored aviator shades as if they were a goon squad. "Jeezus christ, man!" Merlin hollered nonetheless, waving the air in front of his face as he crawled onto his knees. "Your breath smells like Alpo and open ass! Go brush your teeth, for chrissakes!"

Chris Bliss was momentarily taken aback by this effrontery, but then one of his accomplices grabbed a fistful of Merlin's hair and yanked his head back. "We need you to listen very carefully, *Gandalf*," the other man menaced.

"Mmm," Merlin smiled. "I've never heard *that* before. But I'm right, though, aren't I?" Merlin turned as much as possible to the guy pulling on his crown of hair and gestured at Chris Bliss. "Alpo and open ass. Must we suffer silent tact in the face of his belching breath of slow death?"

"It's very simple, *Gandalf*," Chris Bliss regained after darting his eyes around to the others and incorrectly assuring himself that

Merlin was bluffing about his bad breath. "We need you to stay away from Rukmini."

"Who's Rukmini?"

"Lila. We need you to stay away from Lila."

"And I need you to irrigate your nasal passages, yuck-mouth, but we can't always get what we want, can we?"

A slap stung across Merlin's cheek, and Merlin smiled. "It's called a neti pot, death breath." Another slap stung his other cheek, and Merlin burst out laughing.

"What's so funny?" Chris Bliss demanded.

"The very concept of you!" Merlin continued laughing. "Let us dispense with the thin veneer of civilization! *Force* me to accept your point of view! That always works!"

"One way or another, *Gandalf*," Chris Bliss persisted in his imagined insult upon Merlin's name. "You're going to see the light—"

"My right testicle hangs lower than my left testicle," Merlin interrupted.

Chris Bliss blinked, confused. "Excuse me?"

"Only slightly lower," Merlin reassured.

Chris Bliss looked perplexed at the others. "What the hell is he talking about?"

"I'm telling you this now as a courtesy," Merlin continued, "so that you'll know what to anticipate when I invite you to kiss the underside of my ballsack." Merlin smiled as two of Chris Bliss's henchmen broke into chuckle at this remark.

"Listen, *smart-ass*," Chris Bliss pulled his fist back and leaned in fetid. "We're doing you a favor here. Rukmini is dangerous, a total lunatic, and this is as friendly as we're ever going to get with you. We need you to stay away from her!"

"Listen, *dumb-ass*," Merlin snarled right back, inflamed. "Why don't you go tackle a cactus? I'm real sorry that your black-winged brujo of a guru has swirled you into the sewers of his own self-absorption and conned you into thinking that you're the cream of the crap, but if you imagine that you can compel my compliance, then here's the big moment when you commence kissing my ass. You're nothing but a wound of weak-minded simps permitting a tin god tyrant to dictate you in exchange for the tenuous identity he grants you. You mistake who you are for your social location, you trade your spirituality for your narcissistic ambitions, and you've committed yourself to the most diminutive version of human consciousness conceivable." Merlin paused. "In fact, egos like yours are probably the reason our species is failing itself so spectacularly—"

"Okay," one of the other goons interrupted as the man clenching a fistful of Merlin's hair yanked Merlin to his feet. "Let's go for a walk then, shall we?" And the others immediately surrounded them as they hustled Merlin the forty or so feet to a jet-black metallic Range Rover with privacy glass parked on the street next to Golden Gate Park.

"Namaste," Merlin smirked as he read the vanity plate on the Range Rover aloud. "If only words were not so meaningless, eh?" And they honored the divinity within him by banging his head on the doorframe as they shoved him inside the backseat. "And nice hairline, by the way!" Merlin called out just before Chris Bliss slammed the door behind him, the others standing sentry directly outside every door as Merlin examined his circumstance. The interior had been modified to contain all the comforts of a limousine, with two rows of rear seats facing each other, as well as a video screen and a wet bar. Baffled at this, Merlin found himself sitting directly across from another man, a man who after a moment snapped off his mirrored aviator shades and grinned a gold cuspid, revealing himself to be none other than Ivan.

71

"**I** DON'T BLAME YOU," Ivan opened, dashing off a smile and leveling what he imagined to be his overwhelmingly powerful gaze upon Merlin. "That Rukmini, she's a wankworthy cockthrob of the highest caliber." Ivan gestured to some invisible caliber above his head. "But she's also dangerous, and we can't have her anywhere near us."

"A *what?*" Merlin flabbergasted at Ivan's crass language as he rubbed the smart on his head where they'd banged it on the doorframe. "First of all, jackass, her name is Lila, and second, maybe if you quit stalking her all over the city she wouldn't be anywhere near you."

Ivan continued piercing his gaze. Without a word, he pressed a button on his remote control, illuminating the video screen displaying some random pornographic video, specifically a close-up of some rude fellatio with the volume turned down. Without a breath of explanation, Ivan pointed at Merlin. "You see, that sort of thing is exactly what bothers me." Ivan paused. *"Insolence,"* he pronounced. "A puddle of gonorrheal discharge like yourself, you really have no idea with whom you are speaking."

Merlin was rendered temporarily speechless by Ivan's breathtaking crudity, glancing from Ivan to the video screen and back again, unsure whether to grin or to grimace.

"And quit makin' 'em hang about a witty-bitty bump on your head," Ivan continued, gesturing at Merlin's head.

Merlin ceased rubbing his smarting head. "Makin' 'em hang?"

Ivan looked directly at Merlin. "What's the matter, does your pussy hurt?" he taunted, kissing the air. Merlin blinked at Ivan's ludicrous verbal assault, and Ivan smiled in supreme condescension. "How about you rub a little aloe on your asshole and quit acting so butt-hurt about it already?"

"Umm," Merlin hesitated, then gestured to the pornography on the video screen and attempted to match pace with Ivan's blitzkrieg vulgarity. "Listen, I didn't mean to barge in if you're about to make a deposit to the spank bank or something. It's really no problem for me to wait outside."

"Don't be disgusting," Ivan reprimanded, returning to the graphic details splaying across the video screen. "It doesn't surprise me that you cannot see beyond the illusion here. I am engaged in a process of tantric transmutation. By stimulating my lower chakra, I am ultimately able to raise the kundalini to my crown chakra. But I wouldn't expect you to understand the esoterica of consciousness. As I said, you have no idea with whom you are speaking. You should be grateful I have even granted you this audience."

"You have my apologies," Merlin responded, imperceptible in his sarcasm. "It is an honor to sit in the presence of an incorruptible saint, an enlightened Master who will dematerialize once your dharma is done."

Ivan looked to him and sat back. "So Rukmini has told you."

"Lila," Merlin corrected. "And it's really no sweat off my sack what story you need to tell yourself to get through life, as long as you leave us out of it."

"This is not a story," Ivan replied, looking back to the video screen.

"On the contrary," Merlin rejoindered. "*Everything* is a story. The only ones who claim it's not a story are those who are trying to cast you into *their* story."

Ivan cocked his head, studying the new position adopted by the performers on the video screen. "Hmm," he replied, gazing at the screen. "You must think you are smart."

Merlin shrugged. "I'm smart enough to see that the world is

made of nothing but stories, and that the vast most of those stories try to cajole us into being dependent on concepts and systems that don't have our best interests at heart, not even remotely."

"Listen," Ivan looked away from the video screen, earnest in his equanimity. "You have my apologies for how my disciples have treated you. They're at various stages of their spiritual journeys, and sometimes they can be a little passionate." Ivan held open his palms. "I'm only here to guide them, not to control them."

"The shepherd can't herd his own flock?"

Ivan's eyes narrowed. "I'm trying to give you fair warning here. You need to understand that you are poking a stick at some very wealthy, very powerful people. Silicon Valley entrepreneurs, high-powered attorneys, they even have a couple of city councilmen. They'll harass you right out of the entire Bay Area." His eyes returned to their placidity when they fell again upon the video screen.

"First of all," Merlin corrected, "it's not *they*, it's *you*. *You're* the one poking at us. And second, power is the ability to define another's situation, and nobody defines my situation but me."

"That's naïve," Ivan pronounced, clearly pleased at the angle the video afforded him. "You honestly believe they can't define your situation—as you call it—right into prison if they want to? You sound just like Rukmini."

Merlin fell silent, considering a few moments before leaning back and sighing. "You know in cartoons where there's a little angel whispering in the character's right ear and a little devil whispering in his left?" Ivan did not respond, and Merlin continued. "Well, I'd like to share with you my process right now as I contemplate my response to you. On the one hand," Merlin held up his right hand, "this little angel is whispering for me to throw myself prostrate upon your mercy, to kiss your feet and beg forgiveness from thy saintly perfection." Ivan smiled, and Merlin paused a moment before switching hands. "While on the *other* hand," Merlin raised his left hand, "since you've so inspired me with your vulgarian talents, this little devil is whispering for me to explain to you that I care more for the fate of an asswipe of toilet paper I flushed into the sewers this morning than I do about a grody ogre such as yourself's point of view." Ivan again did not respond, and Merlin went on. "But the little devil is also suggesting, as a less vulgar alternative, that I remind you that you'll always be a politician and I'll always be a prankster, and the archetypes that animate us have *never* gotten along, not once in all of human history, so why don't you just kiss my ass and call it a sundae?" Merlin dropped his left hand and shrugged. "So I don't know, what do you think? I'm kind of leaning toward the left-hand path myself."

But no, Merlin didn't really say any of that, not at all, not really. He certainly thought it, or at least something resembling it that he further refined in private reflection across the days following, but just before he unleashed his fury of words, Merlin flashed on something his father once said to him in third grade after he was served with a detention for mouthing off at his teacher. *Dumb like a fox*, his father had said, tapping on his temple and nodding knowingly, though Merlin never understood what the heck that was even supposed to mean. *But foxes aren't dumb*, Merlin had thought to himself as a child, privately questioning his father's faculties, who by the way also had a lifelong mumpsimus of saying *discernment* when he meant *disagreement*. But today, trapped in the back of this Range Rover with a megalomaniac, surrounded by five deranged cultists and with dehydrated bullshit billowing all about him, Merlin at last fathomed his father's wisdom: Tell them what they want to hear, yes sir right away sir, let them think they're in control, and then do your own thing anyway.

So rather than visiting his altiloquent damnations upon Ivan, Merlin just squinted and after a moment nodded downtrodden.

"You know, you're right," he admitted glumly. "I do sound like Rukmini." He shook his head. "Crazy bitch, she *is* dangerous."

Ivan grinned and slapped Merlin's knee. "Attaboy! I *knew* you'd see the light, my child." He pointed at him smirkingly. "I *knew* it."

Merlin smiled weakly, feigning the feeble. He'd seen the light all right, found the purpose of his entire existence, as a matter of fact, and he couldn't wait to get started.

72

I F MERLIN NEEDED any more motivation, he found it when he returned to his apartment in Oakland. His keys were unnecessary as the door was already ajar, and upon entering Merlin was compelled into an immediate contemplation of impermanence, as every item of ceramic or glass—including the windows—had been shattered, now crunching beneath the soles of his shoes like hard candy. Every surface had been swept clear of its contents, every drawer was upside down on the floor, and all furniture had been overturned for good measure. Indeed, his entire bed was upside down, his mattress mortally wounded, its stuffing spilling out everywhere like the entrails of a nightmare. It also appeared as if the walls had been attacked with a hatchet, slathers of blood-red paint dripping grisly down the largest wall, declaring, Dark Energy!

"Motherfucker," Merlin at last observed once the rubble of his room had settled upon his eyes. He kicked at some debris here and there, but as he had retained his paranoid habit of hiding his cash and valuables in public places, there was no real loss except for a sense of order, and maybe his security deposit. Smirking Mona Lisa, he picked up one of the overturned drawers, fished around through the contents spilled out everywhere on the floor, located a Phillips-head screwdriver, flipped it around in his hand, and turned away. "Welcome to my warpath, Ivan," he muttered as he descended the stairs.

73

A s IT TURNS OUT, there is only one flesh you can wound, and so the path of war is necessarily suicidal, casting increasingly long shadows along its path into the valley of darkness. Merlin understood this, and even after having his apartment trashed he may have eventually chilled out and turned the other cheek by way of walking away if he hadn't happened aghast upon an ambulance outside Lila's apartment and witnessed a pair of paramedics come busting out of the front door wheeling a gurney with a jaundiced and convulsing Lila strapped upon it.

Reeling under the unreality of alarming upon such a traumatic scene, it took several moments before Merlin had grappled the situation into comprehension. Running to the back of the ambulance, several hands prevented his access as he demanded what's happening. There was Lila, hyperventilating and foaming at the mouth, unconscious on the gurney, her skin strangely jaundiced. Distressed entirely outside himself, Merlin explained that he was her boyfriend, please tell him what's happening. One of the paramedics replied that it looked like a poisoning, sir, we can't allow you to ride with us, sir, you can find out more at the hospital, sir. Lila moaned unconsciously, swiveling Merlin's panicked head toward her as she mumbled, unmistakably through her convulsions, *"Mö-bi-us."*

Merlin's mind unraveled as the ambulance sirened away, leaving him stumbling beneath a ceiling of solitude caving in all around him. A shivering breeze hollowed upon his ears as he stood in the street helpless, heartsick, crossing his arms desperately around himself as if trying to hold his heart intact, but there was neither assistance nor avail to be found in this gesture, only a hole widening, an abyss awaiting. Stepping out of the street at last, a bleak of grief overtook him, a wherefore this alone all by myself, and Merlin heard his mind begin to panic but there in the center of his breakdown he found a single candle unflickered by storm, and blurring beneath his tears it became two candles, both of them unflinching, unafraid, a perfectly passive presence emerging like the eyes of some kind of a jaguar, and then Merlin spotted Moby, who fluttered to rest atop the nearest parking meter.

"Namaste," Moby spoke, nodding and bowing at Merlin and cawing about as he fluttered to maintain his balance, and then, just before flying away again, Moby advised, "The heart can only break open."

And Merlin entranced upon the parrot's flight, massaging his heart, quelling his fears, till the ignition of an engine some distance behind startled him present. Turning, Merlin discovered the jet-black metallic Range Rover with privacy glass and its unmistakable namaste vanity plate, driving slowly away.

74

"**Y**AR!" hailed the phlegm-gargling voice of Goldtooth's speaking trumpet once the roar of his crew had slaked its vengeance. "Sarrendar or 'ee 'inish 'er!"

Eleusis fell silent in the face of this assault. All breath was forgotten and the wind drained the waters dead calm. The creak and moan of their hull echoed the strain of their own breaking hearts as they watched Goldtooth's two surviving vultures jockey for position on the bowsprit beneath which Flaming Jane's body hung. And then Crow, having spied a vague of breath in Flaming Jane's chest through his spyglass, confirmed to the crew that she was still living, and then added, mocking Goldtooth's speech impediment, "Any'un 'eel like *sarrendaring* this e'ening?"

"We may die today," Zahara answered, "but we're not leaving her like that."

"If any of us dies today," Noa confirmed, "then we damn sure die free."

"All right, then listen tight." Crow's eyes were as ferocious as an owl's, his voice was boiling, and every sinew in his body was drawn as taut as a bow. "Send up the white flag, lower our cannons, and let them think we're surrendering. And take bloody cover, mates! Goldtooth knows better than to try to board us till he's savaged our numbers and our spirits again with case shot across our decks. Our only shot is to strike first, with Gabriel's new weapon. On my mark, we unleash hell upon him. *Eleusis* will need to keep a safe distance and engage the skirmish, and I'll go after Jane. And if it all goes wrong, then we board *them* and fight to the death. Not one among us survives a prisoner. Are we all aye?"

Everyone nodded, and someone asked, "What's your mark?"

"Fire is our mark," Crow answered just before he stuck a smoldering cigar in his teeth and began making his way up the masting ropes, and his eyes swore the oath of his words.

75

ABRIEL SPAT on the bronze siphon pipe running up through the bottom of the crow's nest, watching as it instantly sizzled into vapor. His design appeared to be working. The bottom valve was already open, and on releasing the top valve, the heated and pressurized oil and pitch *should* gush maybe fifty feet out of the nozzle, not accounting for their height. Unless, of course, the whole system burst first and covered them all in boiling oil. He grinned nonetheless at Crow's arrival at the barrel, handing him a pistol and checking that his grappling hooks were at the ready.

Gabriel adjusted the swivel of the nozzle toward the rear of Goldtooth's new ship—the *Damnation III*—as this was both nearer to the second ship and farthest from Flaming Jane— and secured it into its position as he estimated their distance to be seventy feet and closing. Still too far, he reckoned, but then he saw Goldtooth's men begin to aim their cannons across the decks of *Eleusis* despite their white flag. Gabriel gestured to Crow to ready himself, which for Crow meant unfastening his belt for use on the deathslide.

"Brothers till the end," Crow whispered to Gabriel, and they grabbed one another's wrists in solidarity, their grins wringing tears from their eyes. Neither had nurtured any delusions about how they'd chosen to meet history, and had always known that someday their lives would catch up to them—there is after all insufficient expanse in the narrow minds of man for lives of true freedom—but they prayed that day was not today. A nod sufficed to express the truth in their hearts, and Crow immediately aimed his bow and retired the guard standing at the ready to kill Flaming Jane at the first sign of any resistance. Then, before anyone realized what had happened, Crow grabbed the cigar out of his teeth and, wincing, held it in front of the nozzle as Gabriel turned the top valve open. The force of the gush of boiling oil immediately blew the cigar clear out of Crow's gloved grasp, but not before the oil married the cigar's smoldering tip and roared into a screaming arc of hell and spitfire, howling like the devil stubbed his cloven toe, splattering fire all across the rear deck of the *Damnation III* like a vomiting dragon, scattering panic and billowing a black and choking smoke everywhere it landed.

It was wickedly effective, and desperate to get away from the blast furnace of heat themselves—and alarmed at how the bronze piping was banging under the release of its pressure— Crow and Gabriel swung themselves over the side of the crow's nest. Hanging on with one hand, Crow grabbed a grappling hook with the other, twirling it until it had enough momentum to carry it across the distance. But the pitch of the ships distracted his aim, the hook landing just inside the gunwales off the prow of the *Damnation III* and grappling useless into a barrel. Wasting not a moment to curse misfortune, Crow tossed the useless rope aside and grabbed a second grappling hook, repeating the process but this time matching his release to the metronomic pitch of the ships. His aim found its truth, grappling onto a beam of the forecastle on the *Damnation III*, just behind the prow. Gabriel immediately secured the other end of the rope taut off the maintop while Crow whipped off his belt, swung it over the top of his improvised deathslide, grabbed the other side of his belt, and at Gabriel's go, jumped to his death or to Flaming Jane's deliverance.

Unlike the deathslide aboard *Eleusis*, however, there was no netting to catch his breakneck free fall, but as soon as Crow spotted Goldtooth himself rushing reckless across the deck to secure the murder of Flaming Jane, Crow aimed for a collision. Releasing one hand from his belt burning its way down the deathslide, he flew full-force body blow into Goldtooth, crashing both of them across the deck and scattering both of their weapons in the process. But by the time their tumble had scrambled past its somersault, Crow's belt was already tight around the neck of the man determined to make slaves or slaughter of them all. He glared unforgiving into Goldtooth's bulging bloodshot eyes, Goldtooth's tongue lashing about monstrous macabre as Crow choked the life out of him. But Goldtooth himself was not untrained in the arts of physical combat, and finding his fists he delivered them solid and repeated into Crow's face, ultimately succeeding in tussling out of his grasp. Retrieving his saber Goldtooth slashed it desperate and gasping, separating Crow from the pistols and scabbard and cornering him against the prow, with neither weapon nor means of retreat. Unwilling to leave Flaming Jane undefended from Goldtooth's menace, Crow glanced about and pried his first failed grappling hook from the barrel it had hooked into, swinging it as a club and temporarily preventing Goldtooth's advance. But a strong tug on the grappling hook's rope told Crow that its other end was tangled amidst some wreckage, and a flash of his eyes told him that a burning mast was about to timber upon the rope. Dropping his guard at this realization, Crow allowed Goldtooth to take a clean slash at him, ducking successfully as he swung the grappling hook sidearm into Goldtooth's leg, fishhooking it into his thigh. Goldtooth buckled screaming under this blow but pulled his saber back nonetheless to finish Crow, who was now standing there perfectly defenseless. Their eyes connected as Goldtooth lunged for the kill while Crow only grinned and raised a genial wave, offering him a heartfelt "Fuck you, my brother," a split second before the burning mast hit the far end of the rope and the grappling rope yanked Goldtooth's leg out from under him, dashing his face against the deck before it flung his body into the sea.

76

FIRE WAS EVERYWHERE across the *Damnation III*, and the sea betrayed its traditional reprieve, coated as it was with floating puddles of Greek fire. Pandemonium overwhelmed the ship as attempts to douse the flames with water only spread the oil farther across the decks. Battle stations were abandoned as every man fought to escape the flames and secure his own rescue aboard their sister ship, itself struggling to keep the flames at bay, all the while the surviving Eleusinians—keeping as far as possible from the flames but raging nonetheless with the roar of war—picked off their numbers with bows and flintlocks and traded cannonades with the floundering second ship. Billowing black smoke mingled with the creeping sea fog to hang a choking smog in the atmosphere, an umber sunset poisoned across the sky, and circumstances were growing worse.

Crow waited for the pitch of the ship to slacken the rope before unprying the second grappling hook from where it had dug into a beam on the forecastle. Then he ran it up to the fore of the ship as far as the rope would allow, securing the hook on the prow before venturing out the bowsprit toward Flaming Jane. The ropes had abraded badly across her flesh, but she was clearly breathing, albeit shallow. "Jane!" Crow hollered, but he could scarcely hear himself over the chaos now engulfing the *Damnation III*. He hollered her name again, though he may as well have been bleating, as it had no effect whatsoever. Squirming out on the bowsprit now, he pulled a small blade out of his boot, a blade he kept sharp enough to split a shaft of hair drifting across its naked edge. Touching this blade to the ropes that bound her caused them to sever with scarcely a saw, but it was going to be a trick cutting her completely loose without losing her to the burning sea. Looking behind him Crow saw that Greek fire had now splashed everywhere across the ship and was fast approaching the forecastle. Out of choices, he fastened his grip around Flaming Jane's wrist and set about severing her remaining ties. When her body dropped, it was all at once, but his grip upon her wrist was solid, for the moment.

Crow continued hollering her name, to no effect. He couldn't lift her, he had no leverage; he couldn't drop her, the sea was angry and churning with patches of fire; and he couldn't remain this way, the ship itself was burning. "Jane!" Crow hollered yet again, panic twanging his voice and echoing desperate into whimper but he grit his brow against his fear and tightened his grip and there was no way he was failing no there was no way he was losing her but no he could not do this alone no not this moment not this life and as his grip began to slip he dismayed to realize that he'd been arrogant in all his self-assured imaginings of moments such as this where he always assumed that he would never fail but the power of will is limited by its capacity to command matter and the unfair fatigue in Crow's fingers conspired with the wicked slick of sweat and seawater and no he simply could not hold her weight and she slipped again as his screams of "Jane!" met no mercy.

"Jane!" again Crow hollered, his thoughts snarling promises of how he'd dive in after her, he'd save her, he'd save himself, he'd save them all, for as we the living are reluctant to recognize, life is an impassive witness to tragedy, and bloodthirsty besides.

A tremendous explosion shook the *Damnation III* as the fire greeted its first barrel of gunpowder. Moments later, the ship lurched some thirty degrees sideways, taking on water now and spinning Crow to the underside of the bowsprit. "Jane!" Crow hollered again, struggling to secure himself, and then, readying himself for their inevitable plunge into the churning burning sea, roared, *"Flaming Jane!"*

And yes crescendo her eyes snapped open with nary a blink of grog, whirling about as they soaked in her circumstance. Fixing upon Crow, she broke into a smile unsullied by their surroundings, and without a word she met the occasion, using her other hand to pull herself up his arm till she could herself lay hold of the bowsprit. Her weight released, Crow scrambled to the base of the bowsprit, pulling himself onto the prow and pulling Flaming Jane into safety, the burning ship notwithstanding.

"Good evening!" Flaming Jane yelled ebullient over the roar of the nearby flames. "Pray tell, my love, how is it that we find ourselves here?!" She continued to grin despite the inferno of their situation.

Crow shook his head at her ludicrous enthusiasm, the traumas of the day weighing heavy upon him. "Hang on!" he commanded, pulling her in tight as he entwined his other hand as high as he could reach through the taut rope still securing the grappling hook on the *Damnation III*'s bowsprit to the maintop of *Eleusis*. Then, lifting his leg to his hands, he again grabbed the blade out of his boot and yes of course paused to kiss Flaming Jane swashbuckling heroic, after which she spoke into his ear, inexplicably and just as Crow severed the rope above the grappling hook:

"Go with the flow."

Whatever that was supposed to mean, Crow had no time to consider it as the severed line yanked them off the burning remains of the *Damnation III* to pendulum across the distance to *Eleusis*, their feet kicking at the licks of flames as they skimmed the surface of the sea but as *Eleusis* heaved aside from the release of the grappling line's tension it lifted them safe and moments later they narrowly cleared the gunwales of their own ship and fell at last upon the deck of *Eleusis*.

77

FLAMING JANE had been unconscious throughout the day, and after Crow had tended to her bruises and burns she'd slept through the night as Noa navigated them away from the scene of the battle. In the morning, the crew debriefed her on the events of the previous days. Flaming Jane tried to smile at their hard-won successes but could only frown, lips trembling, eyes misting. "Who's dead?"

Crow paused, looking away as he spoke. "Jurakán, Impulse, Hosanna, and Dayenu."

Beneath her trickling tears, Flaming Jane's eyes roared more ferocious as each name was spoken. When Crow finished she closed her eyes. "I'm so sorry."

"It's not your fault—" Crow began.

"Twice I could have rid us of that bastard, and twice I've only taunted him."

"It's your better nature," Crow compassioned. "Besides, I finished him myself yesterday."

Flaming Jane sat up, glancing at the two remaining buzzards circling the sky above their ship, and brushed their gentle hands off her. "Goldtooth lives!" She pointed at the sky, getting up and sauntering toward her quarters. "And better nature or not," she promised, "I won't let him live again!" Then she slammed and locked the door behind her, where she could only be heard to sob inconsolable throughout the day and into the night.

78

MÖBIUS, Lila had mumbled through her unconsciousness in the back of the ambulance. *Möbius*, Merlin thought as he made his way to Highland General Hospital. *Möbius, this is not really happening.* Why did she say that? What was that supposed to mean? What *exactly* was that supposed to mean? Was she delirious? Was she speaking in the universal sense, or the local sense? Something was pretty clearly goddamned happening in the local sense, Merlin thought, and there was no question but that the Holy Company of Beautiful People had something to do with it.

After a couple of hours observing a purgatory of misery parading its way through the emergency room waiting room, Merlin was permitted to see Lila. Evidently, Merlin was told, Lila had ingested some as-yet-undetermined neurotoxin. The jaundice was an indication of its hepatotoxicity, and though her condition had stabilized, she remained mostly unconscious, and they feared permanent brain damage. Holding Lila's hand then, somber by her bedside, wincing uncertain at how the cruel thorns of fate are masked by the sensual vulnerability of roses. Merlin was thereby terrifically startled when Lila winked open her left eye, its whites yellowed under jaundice, and scanned about the room.

"Are we alone?" Lila whispered.

"What?" Merlin startled, bewildered by her abrupt lucidity.

Lila blinked open both of her yellowed eyes and smiled. "Möbius, silly. I tried to tell you."

"What?" Merlin frowned confounded. "You're okay?"

"I'm *fine*," Lila insisted, sitting up, though the jaundiced tone of her skin and the yellowed sclera of her eyes did not reassure Merlin. "Help me remove this IV."

"Uh," Merlin hesitated. "You don't *look* okay. Like, not at all."

Lila held up her arm, displaying its skin. "I dyed my skin with turmeric, and I put iodine drops in my eyes. Then I took a bunch of yohimbe to elevate my blood pressure for the paramedics, and put a couple of effervescent vitamin C packets on my tongue so I'd look like I was frothing at the mouth. Didn't you hear me say our safety word? But we have to get out of here before anyone shows up and *really* starts asking questions. I'm already a few thousand dollars into this prank just for the ambulance ride."

"Prank?" Merlin's face fell at last into flabbergast. "Turmeric? What?" Merlin raised his voice. "Jeezus, Lila! I thought you were dying before my eyes! Why the hell didn't you tell me?"

"Shh!" Lila reprimanded. "I *tried* to tell you, and you weren't even supposed to see me anyway. I was just going to call you afterward."

"Yeah, well, I thought you were goddamned delirious!" Merlin protested. "I mean, you were jaundiced and frothing. It was pretty goddamned convincing."

"It was *supposed* to be convincing," Lila said. "Besides, this just makes us square for that fake argument prank you pulled."

She smiled, muttering, "Look who flipped the bitch switch... Remember that?"

Merlin slumped into the bedside chair, shaking his head. "No, no way. That ain't cool, Lila. I really thought I'd lost you. You totally freaked me out."

And as soon as Lila saw that Merlin had been hurt she immediately crawled into his lap to cradle him. "I'm so sorry," she cooed, petting his hair. "It's okay, baby. We're safe."

And Lila hugged him till Merlin let go, at which point he asked, "So can you please just tell me what the hell's going on?"

"It's Ivan," Lila answered as she stood. "He's been trying to poison me. I wanted to make him think he succeeded."

"Poison?" Merlin horrified as he stood as well. "Are you *serious*? And how do you even know that?"

"Because his idiot lieutenant Chris Bliss left a bottle of pure wormwood oil on the table at the coffeehouse that day he was spying on us. Do you know what wormwood oil is?"

Merlin shook his head.

"It's the herb they used to spice absinthe with, at *very* low doses. But it's a potent nerve toxin at high doses. I think he wanted to slip it into our drinks at the coffeehouse."

"Why didn't you tell me any of this?"

Lila sighed. "I tried to tell you what kind of a person Ivan was, but I just didn't want to freak you out any more than you already were by telling you that he was trying to murder me."

"Golly," Merlin responded, still pissed. "How gallant of you to withhold information from me."

"I'm so sorry, baby. I'm just trying to get these lunatics off my back, and I really need your help."

"You have my help," Merlin reassured. "But you can't be keeping secrets like that."

"I promise," Lila promised.

Merlin nodded. "So that Range Rover was at your apartment again, by the way."

"I know," Lila sighed. "And thanks to my nanny cam, I knew someone had been inside my apartment as well. That's why I put on this whole charade, to make them think they succeeded. They saw the ambulance take me away?"

Merlin nodded.

"Perfect," Lila smiled. "Now they think I'm incapacitated or dead, and will quit bothering after me."

"That makes one of us," Merlin responded. "Ivan tried to have his goons rough me up earlier today."

Lila's eyes went wide. "What happened?"

"They told me to stay away from you," Merlin shrugged. "I just played it dumb like a fox and agreed." He fell silent for a moment. "Did you know that Ivan watches porn while he talks to you? Says it raises his kundalini."

Lila laughed helpless. "I know, you can't make this stuff up. I told you he was a lunatic."

"Yeah, but you didn't tell me he was a shit-spitting fuckmouth." Merlin shook his head. "I mean, that guy's a whole other species of vulgar."

"Wow," Lila nodded, impressed. "You actually got to see the real Ivan."

"I guess." Merlin idly pulled the screwdriver he'd retrieved from his apartment out of his pocket and tapped it on his palm. "Anyway, they also trashed my apartment."

Lila cringed, wrinkling her nose in compassion. "Are you okay?"

"I'm actually great," Merlin smiled genuine. "Now that I know you're okay. A month ago I didn't know what the hell I was doing with my life, and now that I've met you, and thanks to Ivan, I've found the purpose of my entire existence."

"Oh?"

Merlin pointed his screwdriver at her. "Unveiling Ivan and the rest of that brainless cult with you."

Lila smiled. "What's with the screwdriver?"

"What, you think you're the only one with a plan here?"

"Well, you'll be happy to know that I already have a vacation rental set up for us to use as a safe house for the next two weeks. Dogface is already there."

"A safe house?" Merlin raised his eyebrows. "My, you *have* been planning. What happens in two weeks?"

Lila shrugged. "Ivan is going to ascend under the solar eclipse, of course."

79

"L*A PETITE MORT,*" Merlin murmured as Lila relaxed across his chest at the safe house, both of them contemplating the stupendous intensity of their heart-healing orgasm.

"La *what*?" Lila lifted her head.

"It's a French idiom for orgasm," Merlin yawned. "Literally means 'the little death.'"

"Oh yes," Lila smiled and snuggled her head back across his chest. "I've heard of that."

"So I was thinking," Merlin went on. "If an orgasm, even one as stupendous as we just shared—"

"Stupendous," Lila purred.

"Yes," Merlin stroked her hair and continued his post-coital pontifications. "So if even a stupendous orgasm like *that* is a little death, then death itself must be an unbelievably *gigantic* orgasm, right?"

Lila lifted her head again grinning. "A mad philosopher drunk on your own oxytocin, that's what you are."

"Every bit of it." Merlin grabbed firm hold of her hips. "But listen to this, baby: If death is an unbelievably gigantic orgasm, then that makes life the foreplay, right? And just as the more untamedly you approach foreplay, the better the orgasm is, so it is with life and death. The more courage you bring to your life, the more fantastic will be your death."

Lila laughed at his extrapolations. "Careful with your philosophical masturbation there, mister," she toyed with his lips, "you'll get your syllogism all over the sheets."

80

I T IS AN unfortunate artifact of narration that some characters
seize the foreground of our attention while others recede into
the invisible background, not out of irrelevance, mind you,
but out of the simple limitations of storytelling. Consider, for
example, how engaged you are with the struggles of the story of
your own life, and the stories of those near and dear to you, and
how oblivious you are to the struggles of every other story passing you by. No less than you are they, for certain, captured in
the selfsame life-and-death struggle, as a matter of simple fact,
and yet, who has time to regard that?

And look now, four pirates—all of them brothers and sisters to the free spirit, all of them true to the code of equality and honor, all of them friends of God and enemies of the
world—four pirates have here perished under extreme prejudice. Their names were Jurakán, Impulse, Hosanna, and
Dayenu, but who in the name of Davey Jones were they? If
every life is its own story, and each person is thereby their own
stouthearted hero or cravenly enemy, it can only be with deep
regret that we are unable to record the lives and swashbuckling
adventures of every Eleusinian who once feasted their feet upon
those fair sands of the Caribbean Sea. Despite these failures, as

the surviving crew of *Eleusis* releases the remains and effects of their shipmates to the indifferent depths of the sea, let us at the least pull the deceased's index cards from the akashic records, that universal library of all experience, and salute them so long as their souls sail away across the cosmos.

Let us begin with Jurakán, a mestizo sailor of Spanish and Mayan descent, and a good Christian man who'd tried for most of his life to make an honest go at it. Raised in a colonial mission, he believed in the teachings of Christ until the day he died, even though life had long ago dismayed him with the garish hypocrisies of his fellow Christians. Jurakán had first encountered the Eleusinians on one of their earliest plunders, when they overtook the galleon upon which he was serving, hauling Aztec treasure from the Yucatán to a Spanish fort in Cuba, there to assemble in a convoy for the voyage to Spain. Though their approach had been bare teeth and bloodthirsty, once the Eleusinians were aboard and all weapons had been secured, the pirates idled the morning away chattering on about the breathtaking beauty of that morning's sunrise, sharing tobacco, pointing out the schools of fish silvering along in the crystal-clear waters, and in general being the most genial people Jurakán had ever encountered.

As it turned out, the Eleusinians had been seeking a sparkle in the eyes of another in order to swell the ranks of their own crew, and while everyone else met their eyes with resentment and murderous intent, when they met the eyes of Jurakán they immediately invited him to join them. Jurakán took one last look at the corrupted souls populating his vessel, not a man among them having appreciated that morning's truly spectacular sunrise as anything other than a stab upon their collective hangover, and tossed in his lot with the Eleusinians. And never for a moment did Jurakán regret it, having finally found among their community the Christ he'd been seeking his entire life shining right there within his own heart, and when he died shielding Noa from a blast of case shot across their deck (and thereby permitting Noa to successfully light the catapult that assured their escape), Jurakán's soul burst out of his body as if it'd been holding its breath its entire life, and his last words—gasped only to himself—were, "I had no idea how much I existed."

And then there was Impulse, a German adventurer. Temple von Impulse was the full sobriquet he'd devised for himself, and Impulse was a bounty hunter by trade, a bounty hunter who ultimately realized the outlaws he was hunting were leading far more adventurous lives than the obese elite who dangled fat bounties over their heads and sought to enslave every last outpost of freeborn humanity. As Impulse considered adventure to be the highest ambition of the human experience, he could no longer in good conscience capture those whose only crime appeared to be the adventure of freedom. Impulse had even had Flaming Jane in his sights during the Eleusinians' first visit to Boca Diablo, and could have taken her head and collected the bounty, but true to his name, Impulse was keen on following his impulses as the surest path to high adventure, and it was just such an impulse that caused him to adjust his aim at the last second and snipe instead the daggered hand that was just then about to stab the heart out of Flaming Jane. It'd been one of Half-Ass McJanky's assassins, and after relieving the assassin of his last breath and properly introducing himself to Flaming Jane and her comrades, Impulse expressed the philosophy that moved his life and wondered if he might accompany them toward a life of higher adventure.

The charm of his philosophy—and the delight with which he articulated it—guaranteed his acceptance, and Temple von Impulse was thenceforth known to spend his days holding breathlessly forth upon whatever topic had most recently fascinated him, having mostly to do with notions of the body as a temple and the consequent importance of consuming various kelps, seaweeds, and algae toward achieving a maximum vitality. And in between *Eleusis*'s occasional skirmishes, Impulse had a knack for regaling in detail every random happenstance that occurred as well as how following their impulses in the heat of their battles had guided them through flawless and unscathed.

But alas and of course, Temple von Impulse would not live to retell his final skirmish at sea, though it was nonetheless an impulse that compelled him to hit the deck just before the sweep of case shot, and another impulse that compelled him then to stand and take a shot at a sniper he'd spied in the enemies' crow's nest, winging him only but hesitating the sniper's arrow just long enough for him to miss his mark upon Flaming Jane. In taking the shot, however, Impulse undefended his torso, and when an arrow thwacked through his heart, Impulse staggered to the deck, astounded that death had found him. Glancing begrieved upon the arrow's ruination of his bodily temple, the cries of battle fell faraway and fast, and as *Eleusis* surged forward from the release of its dragline and the snapping ascent of its second set of sails, Impulse felt his soul surge forth from its temporary temple, and as his point of view expanded he saw all at once how his impulse was true, how it saved another's life and served the greater good, how his death would deepen the hearts of his mates, and opening his dying eyes he discovered the setting sun and staring into it he saw how this moment was in fact the greatest adventure of his entire life, and as his spirit roared Valhalla he soared into that great white light, and whatever last words he might have mustered could only surrender under the fathom of his newborn smile.

And finally, there was Hosanna and Dayenu, sister and

brother, fraternal twins born in a Cimarron settlement in
Panama, among a community of runaway slaves that took
its name from a native Taino word meaning "flight of the
arrow." Hosanna was the older sister, born fist first, and her
name expressed an adoration of her existence. Dayenu was
the younger brother, born with his grip firmly upon his sister's ankle, and his name expressed overwhelming gratitude, as
Dayenu is a Hebrew word literally translated as "it would have
been enough for us."

Hosanna and Dayenu fought an inseparable tangle until the
age of five, when sick of their incessant bickering one day their
mother grabbed ahold of them and made them stand across from
one another, directing them that they were to take turns slapping
each other. Terrified, their slaps were timid and feathered in the
face of this frightful maternal command, and all the more so as
their mother heckled them to slap each other harder. "Now why
ain't you slappin' on him harder now gawdammit? Go on now,
slap the crooked right outta his teeth!" she goaded Hosanna,
and to Dayenu, "Now go on then, boy, give it to her good now
gawdammit!" Hosanna and Dayenu soon began sobbing under
their cruel circumstance, blubbering eventually, till their mother
shook her head severe and wagged a stern finger in front of their
tearful faces. "Now you remember this now next time you take
to bickerin' gawdammit!" she reprimanded. "There'll be plenty
enough fools in this world that wants to fight you, and there ain't
no sense to be found in fightin' on each other. Now you remember this now. You're brother and sister and you love each other
more than you even understand. Now go on then now, Mama
loves you now, give each other a hug now."

And their hug was tearful and true, and never again would
they be found fightin' on each other, for it wasn't a year before
slave traders raided their Cimarron settlement, kidnapping

them and selling them both into slavery, but they were never separated and so they never failed to defend each other brother and sister. Thus it was that many years later they found themselves aboard the *Queen Elizabeth* when Flaming Jane organized their mutiny over Admiral Jasper. For Hosanna and Dayenu, that mutiny was the reclamation of their kidnapped childhood, and no one glared a more ferocious gaze than them as they circled their backs in battle, vowing that no one not ever again would cross the perimeter of the soul they shared.

And they kept this vow till the day that they died, when manning their cannon under fire, Hosanna and Dayenu were savaged by the sweep of case shot across their deck. Dayenu realized what was about to happen and leapt to shield his sister at the same instant that Hosanna leapt to shield him.

"Brother!" said she.

"Sister!" said he, and neither of them succeeded in shielding the other as the shrapnel seared across their profile in embrace, and moments later when *Eleusis* lurched from the force of its dragon cannon firing from its bow their torn bodies toppled, Dayenu keeling overboard first, and Hosanna catching a final grip upon her brother's ankle as they fell not into the churning sea but into the luminous arms of their ancestors, welcoming them into the Garden that never once knew the sweat of a slave, and cheering their lives louder than the sun could ever shine.

PART THREE:

BEWARE THE MEADOW OF MARVELS

81

"DO YOU BELIEVE in reincarnation?" Lila asked Merlin as they sat on the screened patio of a coffeehouse in the Mission twelve days before the solar eclipse, cradling their matcha lattes, watching the other patrons hunch over their coffee, sipping on gossip and snapping on caffeine, and patiently waiting for all of them to leave so that they might have the patio to themselves. Both of them were wearing implausible blond wigs by way of disguise.

"Nah," Merlin shook his head, idly tapping the screwdriver he'd retrieved from his trashed apartment on the tabletop, eyeing the industrial refrigerator located just outside the door that opened to the patio from the inside of the coffeehouse. "That's never really made much sense to me."

"So what about all that business about pirates on Halloween?" Lila protested. "Crow and Flaming Jane, wasn't it? And that message in the bottle you found?"

"With full apologies for my cheesedick approach," Merlin grinned, "I was only trying to find the path beneath your panties that night." He paused, eyes gleaming inscrutable. "Although that message in the bottle from Flaming Jane was an uncanny synchronicity. And anyway, I just don't like the notion that life is something from which we're supposed to escape, which is what reincarnation seems to imply." Merlin paused. "I *like* being alive. I love it. In fact, I daresay it's the greatest thing I've ever done."

"Ah, but now the moon has possessed your tongue," Lila teased.

"True enough." Merlin peered through the screens at the crescent moon waxing ghostly magnificent from beneath a gossamer of clouds. "The might of the moon may have mauled my mind into merry-hearted madness." Merlin looked again toward Lila. "But I've donated some time thinking about it, and it just doesn't make any sense to me. If the ultimate reality is undivided unity, then where does reincarnation fit into that? Who's reincarnating if it's all undivided unity? My greedy little ego, my pathetic social identity? Who gives a crap about that in the cosmic scheme of things—"

"Your *spirit* reincarnates," Lila interrupted.

"See, right there," Merlin pointed at her. "You said *your* spirit. Whose spirit?"

Lila shook her head. "That's just an artifact of language. Try this: the spirit that animates your physical existence."

"Same same but different," Merlin shrugged. "Again, *whose* physical existence? But I see your point, I suppose. Maybe you're right and language is inescapably built around the ego. That's a very good point, but even if I grant that, we still have to remember that the ultimate reality is undivided unity— a lonely fact that stretches all the way from mystical philosophy to quantum mechanics. Given that, just exactly *who* is this spirit that animates my physical existence, and how is it distinct from undivided unity? Who's the actor, remember that? It has to be the same spirit that animates your existence, right? And everyone else's too. So if the undying love of God animates me and everything else, then fine, the Great Spirit incarnates all over Creation as the simple flip side to its undivided unity. But nobody walks around inhabiting their supreme identity, do they? When we talk about reincarnation, we're not offhandedly acknowledging the inexorable eternity of God. We're typically talking about our own spiritual ambitions, a pairing of words which actually doesn't make a jot of sense, by the way."

Lila smirked. "I didn't mean to get you so worked up."

Merlin watched as the patrons at a nearby table left, leaving only one other occupied table on the patio with them. He shrugged and sipped his tea. "Probably it's just that the people most into reincarnation are usually implicitly congratulating themselves on their own station in life, like your guru—"

"He's not my guru," Lila interrupted.

Merlin continued. "Fair enough, but do you know what I mean? The ego will do anything to convince us that it exists."

Lila smiled. "The devil too."

"Touché." Merlin flipped his screwdriver and pointed it smartly at her. "The greatest trick the devil ever pulled was convincing the world that he exists."

Lila sighed a broader smile. "It's all just another day in the lie—I mean, life."

Merlin's eyes went wide at the smartness of her remarks. "Holy jeezus!" he called out to the nearby empty tables. "Somebody get this girl a drink!"

Lila smiled on. "I think you're wrong about reincarnation, though."

Merlin leaned back and scratched his chest cocky. "That's only because you haven't understood me."

"Oh, I understand you," Lila assured. "I even agree with what you've said, but I think you've overlooked a crucial detail in your ontology."

"Oh *really?*" Merlin grinned garish and mocked her phraseology. "I've overlooked a crucial detail in my *ontology?*"

Ignoring him, Lila continued. "How is it that you exist as an individual in a universe of undivided unity?"

Merlin's gaze sparkled as he shrugged. "It's all just another day in paradox—I mean, paradise."

Lila clicked her tongue, pointed at him, and winked. "*Touché, monsieur.* But I wonder if you've considered the possibility that your spirit—possessive pronouns notwithstanding—is an isomorph, which is to say, a microcosm of the macrocosm?"

"What's an isomorph?"

"It describes a similarity in form across every stage of a life cycle, similar to how fractal geometry looks the same no matter your level of magnification."

Merlin was silent, considering her comment. "Huh," he said at last. "So my spirit is God microcosmic?"

Lila nodded. "And God is your spirit macrocosmic. Fundamentally the same, though distinct at its own level."

Merlin leaned back in his chair. "That's interesting," he murmured amused, watching as the folks at the last remaining occupied table got up to leave. "That would make reincarnation a sort of cosmic koan, wouldn't it? Its truth lies not in its concept, but in its contemplation." Merlin nodded for a while, watching as the folks at the last remaining occupied table exited through the noisy screen door on the patio, its hinges meowing like a hungry cat. As soon as the screen door banged shut Merlin slammed the front legs of his chair to the floor. Standing, he grabbed his screwdriver off the table, strode over to the industrial refrigerator just outside the door to the interior of the coffeehouse. Opening the refrigerator, Merlin immediately set about unscrewing a screw that held the interior molding in place along its top. Once accomplished, he pulled the molding down and stuck a couple of fingers under it till he succeeded in fishing out a plastic bag with several small bottles inside. Dropping this into the cargo pocket of his pants, he screwed the molding back into place and returned to the table, drawing a deep sigh before resuming his nodding at Lila's last remark. "Well, my dear, it appears that you've inspired an epiphany on my part."

Lila smiled, way more interested in the contents of Merlin's cargo pocket than in any idle notions of reincarnation. "What uh, whatcha got in your pocket there?"

"What, this?" Merlin fished the small plastic bag out of his cargo pocket, opened it, and placed a small, glass statuette bottle of Our Lady of Lourdes on the table. "Just some holy water for your guru."

82

ESPITE THE CREW's relief at Flaming Jane's rescue, and despite her belief that she needed to press on, the mood of *Eleusis* had shifted with the death of four of its mates. Flaming Jane probably could have insisted on them following her course, but that was not her way. Instead, she made preparations to depart for the island in a rowboat, on her own.

"What's your plan?" Crow asked, in their private quarters.

Flaming Jane shrugged. "For the first time since I took Goldtooth's ship, I don't really have one."

"So what are you doing, then?"

"I'm doing what I must."

"Which is what?"

"Preventing Goldtooth from finding that Stone!" Flaming Jane raised her voice. "According to the Royal Navy's ephemeris, the eclipse is only three days away! Can you imagine an object of that power in his possession? The ability to create wealth out of nothing? He'd enslave the entire world and turn us all into brainless workers for his own conceit!"

Crow paused. "But what makes you think you can find it before him?"

"Do you remember what I said to you just after I came to?"

"You asked me how is it that we find ourselves here?"

"No," Flaming Jane frustrated. "After that, right before you cut the grappling line."

"Something about going with the flow?"

Flaming Jane pointed at him. "Exactly!"

"But what does that even mean?"

"Look," Flaming Jane pointed at the treasure map spread on the table. She traced the arrows shot from Orion's bow turning an infinite circle around the entire island. Crow blinked, not comprehending. "The map is telling us not to steer the ship or direct its course," she explained, "but to simply trust the currents to bring us ashore." She pointed to the whirlpools surrounding the island. "That's the only way through these stormy seas."

"To go with the flow," Crow murmured as his face grew a smile. "Why don't you explain this to the rest of the crew?"

Flaming Jane shook her head. "I will not expose this crew to any more risk. I know them well enough to know that they would follow me to my grave, and I know myself well enough to know that I can charm my point of view onto most anyone, but this is neither their path nor their best interest."

Crow drew a deep breath. "Then I'm coming with you."

Flaming Jane nodded. "You'd bloody well better be."

83

THERE WERE MANY among the crew who protested Flaming Jane's decision to pursue the quest alone. As much as she wanted to protect them, after all, they wanted to protect her just the same. But Flaming Jane could not be persuaded from her position, and insisted there was no sense in risking beaching their entire ship in the shallows of the uncharted island. The only solace for the crew was Crow's promise to watch over her. Flaming Jane rolled her eyes at this gilded insult, then she promised to watch over Crow as well.

Once Flaming Jane and Crow had set off with their provisions in a rowboat and a bank of sea fog once again overcame them, Crow set the oars aside and took the opportunity to let Flaming Jane know that *Eleusis* would rendezvous with them in five days' time a mile offshore of a bay on the far side of the island. Flaming Jane was momentarily incensed at this perceived betrayal, but Crow waved her off.

"Yes, well, whatever on that, my love. You're mad with grief, and while I love you forever and respect your willingness to go with the flow, as you call it, I'm not about to spend the rest of my life marooned on an uninhabited island with you."

"And yet you're willing to cast off into the open ocean in nothing more substantial than a rowboat?"

"I couldn't let you go it alone," Crow replied. "Besides," he examined the water off the side of the boat as if he could read its currents, "the flow will lead us safely ashore."

Flaming Jane smiled, pleased with his faith in her dream. Without saying a word, she retrieved a scarlet wine bottle from her pack, made certain the cork was good and tight, and flung it into the ocean.

"What was that?" Crow asked.

Flaming Jane smiled without answering, and instead began to gentle a song:

> *Flow, flow, flow your boat*
> *Gently down the stream,*
> *Merrily merrily merrily merrily,*
> *Life is but a dream!*

Crow listened as she sang it a couple of times, learning the lyrics, then joined in midway through the third time, singing the verse in round with her. They continued this for several minutes, varying octaves and tempos and Crow eventually finding a couple of chords to accompany with his cavaquinho. They had a marvelous time of it, and when Flaming Jane finally sighed her last round and Crow completed his in basso, they pitched into peels of laughter.

"Outstanding!" Crow complimented. "Where did you learn this song?"

Flaming Jane shrugged. "I dreamt it right before I came to."

"When you were unconscious?"

Flaming Jane nodded.

"What else did you dream?"

Flaming Jane shook her head. "Nothing. Just that song, over and over, exactly like we just did, only it sounded like every child in the world was singing it. And when I finally woke up, 'go with the flow' was echoing through my mind."

Crow shook his head impressed, then glanced at the currents of water around their rowboat. "You know, the current does seem to be picking up."

Flaming Jane looked around, not that there was anything to see in the fog. "Yes," she agreed. "I thought I felt a quickening of the breeze."

"Do you hear that?" Crow referred to a distant roar.

"The surf?"

"No," Crow shook his head. "Too constant. Sounds more like a waterfall."

And with that assessment, the fog bank broke apart into a suddenly clear sky. Looking port side, there was a tumbling whitewall of sea fog from whence they had just broken, towering above them, occasionally licking into the open air only to sparkle into countless sundogs evanescing into sunshine. The whitewall stretched wide in both directions, eventually curving back around itself like the inner wall of an immense coliseum across an expanse of open water. The current had them cruising alongside the whitewall at a good clip, and for a full minute they did nothing but gape at this oasis of ludicrous beauty.

"What is this!" one of them exclaimed, or perhaps they astonished nothing at all. Regardless, their wonder soon found its exclamation as they realized what was happening, and when they did, they most certainly shouted simultaneous: "Maelstrom!"

Their clip accelerating now that they had crossed the event horizon of the whirlpool, the whitewall of fog drifting farther away, and a whitewater roar growing in their ears, there was nothing to do but try to steer clear of the whirlpool with their oars. But it was fruitless, and when they first caught sight of the vortex at the center, they found themselves dumb, and after recovering their wits, Crow and Flaming Jane looked at one another and erupted into howls and wild. Flaming Jane began to sing again, this time shouting her song:

Flow, flow, flow your boat
Gently down the stream!
Merrily merrily merrily merrily,
Life is but a dream!

Crow joined her immediately, holding her hands and neither of them never more happy than this moment this death, their lives of defiance and daring having brought them after all to each other, and life now ravishing them with a scene of such epic spectacular that it could only have been crafted exclusively for their eyes.

Their rowboat now slanting as it was drawn into the whirlpool, Crow noticed something. It might have been an unexpected motion, an unnatural shading of light, a subtle discontinuity—some intuition told him that things were not what they seemed. Remembering the medieval warnings of dragons and serpents on some of the charts, Crow interrupted their song, pointing at the eye of the whirlpool and—still smiling for all the glory of Creation—shouted, "That's no maelstrom!"

Flaming Jane looked just as a preternatural light dazzled from the deepest recess of the vortex, cascading lawless colors across its coursing waters and spotlighting beams across its turbulent mist. "What is that?!" Flaming Jane thrilled.

His eyes are like the rays of dawn... The descriptions Crow had read in Job 41 after seeing the passage referenced on one of the sea charts now shuddered alive in his mind. There was no time to recite any of this, however, and Crow could only holler its biblical name: "Leviathan!"

"What?!"

"Leviathan!" Crow repeated, incredulous. "It's a goddamned sea monster!"

Flaming Jane looked to the whirlpool and back to Crow, but it really didn't matter much to her whether it was a maelstrom or a monster. Their fate seemed certain in either event. "Perfect!" she laughed. "What do we do now?!"

Eyes blazing, Crow did not answer, but only leaned in to kiss Flaming Jane.

84

F ACED WITH the immense imminence of their earthly demise, Flaming Jane would offer no coyful parry to Crow's passionate kiss. Flaming Jane easily captured his lips and at his further prompting they soon untangled eager and agreeable from their breeches and suaved themselves together with a yes and nectared sigh. Seized by the ferocity that defeats all fear, their rowboat would surely have capsized under their passion if not already in the thrall of the hellmaw of some sea monster. As it was, their craft was perfectly stable as it circled the vortex in ever tighter circles, and once they felt to be angled near forty-five degrees, Crow yelled his love over the roar of the water and Flaming Jane yelled hers right back and it was never more true as they found in this universe the eyes of another oneself and their hearts soared with the joy of a trillion tragedies and it might have been forever if not for something else.

How it happened cannot be known, but it was as if the maelstrom suddenly vanished its own vortex in a split and single instant. The next moment found the rowboat drifting an idle circle in a sea of silence, Crow and Flaming Jane swiveling their heads what the heck as a sea fog tumbled toward them upon the dead calm like mist upon a mirror, and then the entire sea seemed first to swallow and then to swell as a single large wave appeared in the distance.

The wave was silent in its coming, a force within the ocean sweeping toward them, and a wall of water growing taller by the second. Neither spoke a word as they scrambled for the oars, aiming to give their rowboat sufficient momentum so as not to be simply swamped by this rogue wave. Pulling hard on the oars until they felt the wave begin to lift their craft, Crow then leapt to the rear of the boat and anchored his oar into the wave as a skeg, seeking to fin their position and ride the wave toward whatever shore it sought.

It worked, after several unsteady seconds and a near topple, and they soon found themselves surfing the wave's crest. Flaming Jane wahooed at this and Crow grinned, though not as mighty triumphant as he felt since he was focused on holding their position stable as they carved their way across the shoaling face of the wave. "Take your oar and do what I'm doing!" Crow yelled, and Flaming Jane immediately consented to his direction.

"How did you know to do this?"

"My brothers and I used to play at something similar along the shores of Haiti."

Flaming Jane's face was absolutely at peace. "It's marvelous!"

"Pay attention to the oar," Crow cautioned. "This wave is about to get a hell of a lot higher, and faster."

Flaming Jane fell silent. "Was that really a sea monster?"

Crow laughed as the wave began to rise more rapidly as it approached the shallows of the shoreline. "Here we go!"

The sea fog shrouding their view broke apart and the long shoreline of an island emerged in its place. The beach was enthralling in its beauty, but there was time neither to notice nor appreciate this as the wave towered ever higher behind them.

"Close your eyes!" Crow yelled as they skimmed down the face of the growing wave. Closing her eyes seemed ludicrous, but Crow already had his closed, so she followed suit. Immediately she understood his meaning as the celestial oceanic forces of the wave possessed her remaining senses, relaxing her grip on the oar as she fathomed that there was nothing at all to be done to control this overpowering chaos, but only to hold steady and to trust that this wave would see them safely home.

She soon sensed it growing darker through her closed eyelids as her ears began to roar hollow, and couldn't resist snapping open her eyes only to discover a pipeline of water surrounding them as they shot through its collapsing center and toward an awe of sunshine beyond. Crow's eyes remained closed as he held their position, smiling gently as his eyes softened open, a minor adjustment to his oar skimming them out of the tube and angling their race down the face of the wave, escaping its forward velocity into a receding lagoon as they ground to a halt upon the sand of new land several moments before the rogue wave crashed monumental on the shores beyond.

85

"THE LEVIATHAN," Crow explained as they dried their provisions around a fire later that night, "is a sea monster in the Bible—"

"There's a sea monster in the Bible?" Flaming Jane interrupted.

Crow nodded. "The Book of Job was referenced on one of the charts, and I looked it up. Basically, Leviathan is too large to comprehend. It's absolutely indestructible and inconceivably ferocious. Legend says it survives by eating an entire whale every single day."

"That beggars belief," Flaming Jane shook her head. "Why didn't it just swallow us then?"

"Leviathan is king over all that are proud." Crow poked at the fire and smirked. "And its mouth is supposedly the mouth of hell. If that thing was Leviathan, I think it was repulsed by our love."

"Repulsed by our love!" Flaming Jane guffawed. "What an insufferable fucking puritan!"

Crow grinned. "Indeed, and I think that mumbo about eating a whale a day is mostly nonsense. Leviathan actually feeds on fear—that's what makes it so enormous, since humanity is riddled with fear—so I figured we'd better make ourselves as unappetizing as possible."

Flaming Jane was quiet for a few moments, watching fireshadows flicker across his features and falling all the more in love with him. "I knew there was a reason I let you come along."

Crow snorted. "As if there were any question. I was coming along with or without your consent. If a maelstrom and a sea monster can't dissuade me, I don't know how you imagine that your stubbornness could."

Flaming Jane said nothing, but she snuggled closer and Crow wrapped his arm around her. They smiled at one another and nuzzled their faces, breathing deep against one another's skin. Flaming Jane's eyes wandered across the star-flung heavens as the distant surf purred impermanence and the moments relaxed into eternity. Suddenly struck by an overwhelming sensation that the night sky was actually nothing but stars and that there was no real darkness anywhere, her eyes retreated to the prominence of Orion's Belt shining above the southern horizon. As she contemplated this constellation and its presence upon the treasure map, a shooting star streaked forth like a flaming arrow from Orion's bow, tracing an impossibly slow descent above the tree line of the island as Flaming Jane smiled, knowing now the morrow's direction toward the meadow of marvels.

86

"DO YOU EVER wonder if you are shadow puppets of some much larger theater of experience?" An unknown, unexpected, and terribly deep voice very suddenly resonated from the far corner of the screened patio.

Merlin and Lila startled upon this interruption—having believed themselves after all to have been alone on the screened patio—and whirled toward the voice before his second syllable had satisfied. "Puppets what?" Lila responded after they'd confused for several moments at the silver-haired gentleman delicately sipping at his espresso from the far corner of the patio. He wore a striking white double-breasted suit and flaunted a spectacularly opalescent white snakeskin tie that matched his white snakeskin shoes. His silver hair was slicked back, emphasizing the widow's peak of his receding hairline and suggesting the outline of horns at the top of his high forehead. Generally speaking, his was not a presence liable to be easily overlooked.

Merlin was less polite than Lila. "Where in the *hell* did you come from?" he demanded as he quickly stowed the small glass statuette bottle of Our Lady of Lourdes back in the cargo pocket of his pants.

"I assume that your colloquial usage of 'hell' intends merely to emphasize your interrogative," the silver-haired gentleman responded. "But I nonetheless suggest that its literal—or more to the point—its etymological usage lends a far more interesting inquiry. Deriving from the Old English *helan*, the term *hell* properly refers to a veil. Veil of course is the illusion, the mask of the divine, in which case I can only nod appreciative and concede that yours is a very good question, and one from which all wisdom proceeds."

Merlin and Lila exchanged glances. "With full respect for the deliberations of your diction," Merlin attempted to match the silver-haired gentleman's bombastic articulation, "the question was neither rhetorical nor philosophical. Where did you come from? You were not here a moment ago."

The silver-haired gentleman sipped again thoughtful at his espresso. "That is a most peculiar allegation. Tell me, do you commonly accuse those around you of violating object permanence?"

"I don't know," Merlin responded. "Do you commonly sneak up on people and bark fresh questions at them?"

"Ah, at last I see." The silver-haired gentleman shook his head and clicked his tongue. "Most regrettable. In that case, I beg for your pardon and bow disgraced upon bended knees. Age, it seems, depraves me of my manners. I pray as time soothes all wounds that you may one day forgive this accursed dementia which ails against my etiquette, and Lord willing and the river don't rise, may we one day speak again." The silver-haired gentleman paused and gestured toward the screen door. "Specific to your initial inquiry, though, certainly you can see the screen door."

Neither of them having seen nor heard anyone enter through the noisy screen door, Merlin and Lila exchanged eyes of wide confusion before Lila spoke. "Puppets," Lila said. "What were you saying about puppets?"

The silver-haired gentleman bowed. "My gratitude is eternal for the ease of your absolution. Difficult to dance in the sludge of a grudge, as is certainly clear to souls so magnanimous as yours."

"Yes yes," Lila drolled, gesturing a papal sign of the cross with her hands. "All is forgiven. Now what about those puppets?"

"Of course," the silver-haired gentleman nodded as he removed a tobacco pipe from his jacket. "And a thousand weeping apologies for these infernal digressions, as if I have nothing to offer but this tangle of tributaries. *Shadow* puppets, I repeat. Shadow puppets of some much larger theater of experience. Do you ever wonder if this is what you are?"

"Well, naturally," Merlin responded. "The archetypes are the puppeteers."

"Archetypes," the silver-haired gentleman repeated, assessing him momentarily as he prepared his pipe. "An intriguing designation—"

"What was your name again?" Lila interrupted.

Having lit his pipe, the silver-haired gentleman paused, contemplating the smoke rings he had blown. "Pardon me," he responded at last, "but it simply *staggers* me to realize that my manners are so boorish! What kind of an illiterate lout embarks upon an encounter without a proper engagement of the pleasantries of introduction? What a calamitous circumstance! You must surely disgust to witness this ancestral disgrace, and hardly to mention the comprehensive abandonment of decorum it necessarily implies! I may just as well be a belching barbarian who waves a fresh femur in my fist, isn't that quite right?" He shook his head in mirthless sorrow. "Oh dear ones, listen to me now. I fear I cannot pretend to repair this error if I hasten to introduce myself in some graceless froth of regret. Nevermore, I must bear this failure as Prometheus bears the eagle who feasts daily upon his liver, and fade forever into obscurity as the nameless brute who interrupts private conversations, and speaks of burps besides."

Merlin and Lila laughed, for lack of any other response. "How about we just call you Professor Fresh?" Lila suggested.

"Professor Fresh." The silver-haired gentleman nodded. "Even if it be mockery, I accept your appellation with bottomless humility, for I am forever grateful that you even deign to continue to converse with a cretin such as myself."

"Jee-zus," Merlin observed. "Your bullshit is unparalleled."

Professor Fresh's eyes twinkled as he nodded once again. "Balderdash, to be precise, though I appreciate your vulgarism nonetheless. But now I wish to tell you something true," he announced, placing his espresso cup back onto its saucer and straightening as he held his hand at arm's length, squinting as he pinched a millimeter of sky outside the screened patio between his thumb and forefinger. "The truth, dear ones— or at least something it resembles—the truth is that when we focus the Hubble Space Telescope on this random pixel of sky betwixt my thumb and forefinger, this one random dot on the overwhelming vault of heaven, we discover *thousands* of *galaxies*." He paused, gesturing his arms broad. "*This* is the cathedral of eternity in which we find ourselves, and this magnificent insignificance is what we fail to see so long as we inhabit the smallest, most loudmouthed point in the entire universe, the arrogant and lamentable dream of ego. Inhabiting such a mudhut in your otherwise celestial mind, by the way, inevitably makes you *liars*." Professor Fresh smiled, as if savoring the lilt of the word across his tongue. "*Liars*," he said again, pointing his pipe stem at them.

Lila and Merlin glanced at one another. "Hmm," Merlin hesitated. "That's vaguely rude."

Professor Fresh frowned, shaking his head begrieved. "Oh dear ones, how can I bear witness to the continual dolt of my demeanor? Here I level inadvertent insults upon you, and assault you with an indelicate stab of my pipe stem as well." Professor Fresh adjusted the placement of his espresso cup upon its saucer. "Prostrate am I before you, and if your ears are yet attentive despite my mortifying discourtesies, pray may ye hear that when I call you a liar, I speak in the plural, referring to *all* of you and everyone, everyone who pretends that they exist distinct from the universe at large even as someone somewhere right now panics at their last gasp, all because some voice in their head fools them into the belief that it exists. Oh, the truth offends conceit, dear ones, but you are not who you think you are. Your ego remains a lie, a big lie, a whopper so colossal that no one ever questions it, for who can imagine that anything can have the audacity to distort the truth so monstrously? And yet you do, day by lonely day as you play at your vast conspiracy of egotism and plug your ears against the cavernous echoes of your own determined solitude, you are *liars.* Just like every other homeless, runaway ego, you lie to each other, you lie to ourselves, and deep down you *know* that you lie, and that makes you paranoid, fearful of your own fraud, and drives you into further pretense and manipulation, and all of it in service to that phantom in your mind who desperately pretends that it exists, that its pretense at life is real—"

"Oh we know *that,*" Lila interrupted. "The greatest trick the ego ever played was convincing the world that it exists." Beaming, she turned to Merlin and joined him in mouthing *Möbius.* "But what of love?"

"Ah, love," Professor Fresh smiled, preparing to light his pipe again. "The only truth there is." He pointed his pipe stem at them again. "Love is a prank the spirit plays on the ego to teach it the one lesson it tries not to learn." Nodding, he satisfied himself with another puff upon his pipe.

"What lesson is that?" Lila asked.

"That it is not in control, of course," Professor Fresh responded after blowing a couple more smoke rings, which Lila momentarily thought were actually Möbius bands, but upon double take the rings had already dissipated too much for her to be sure. "Love is the solution to being human. Without love your ego loses itself forever in its own lies," Professor Fresh went on. "Love is the universal solvent, the only force in the universe with the capacity to dissolve the walls of ego and teach you that you are indeed one another's keeper."

"The ego will do anything to convince us that it exists," Merlin responded, reiterating his earlier remark to Lila.

"Yes, I know," Professor Fresh responded. "The devil too. It's all just another day in the lie," he paraphrased them, nodding as if in approval. "I mean, life."

Merlin was again incredulous that they had somehow overlooked Professor Fresh's blinding white presence. "Exactly how long have you been sitting there?" he demanded.

"Ah dear ones," Professor Fresh shook his head. "As I obviously cannot sustain any semblance of suavity, I regret that this encounter is simply untenable. Not only do I eavesdrop on your conversation, itself a heinous crime against all civility, but now I am so tactless as to taunt you with your own words. Nay, I must accept a smart rap across my knuckles before I can bear the shame of another faux pas. These gaucheries must cease posthaste this time."

"This time?" Lila intrigued.

"And look!" Professor Fresh tossed up his hands. "Now I go enigmatic! I presume to wield hidden knowledge over you like some overbearing demiurge, nay, that is neither my name nor my nature, and I overstay my welcome." He stood. "Dear ones, lest I bare my soles soon upon this tabletop and establish my ill-bred pedigree for certain, I must be on my way." Bowing, he turned to go. "But it is good to visit with you again, and I am forever grateful for your patience with my philistine manners. And though life is little more than a dramatic loop through a garden of nothingness," he turned to go, "my only point is to remind you to remember."

"Remember what?" Lila called out.

"That nothing matters," Professor Fresh responded as he opened the screen door to the patio, its hinges meowing like a hungry cat. "It matters very much indeed."

87

A KICK OF SAND in their faces spat and startled Crow and Flaming Jane awake under a dewy dawn, coals still smoldering from last evening's fire. Both of them scrambled and reached instinctive for their weapons, but were ultimately prevented from doing so by a level of blades upon them.

"Gotchas, bitches!" It was Half-Ass McJanky who greeted them good morning, his eyes evil with vengeance and his teeth sneering with tobacco, and flanked by four of his equally foul compatriots.

"Oh ferchrissakes," Flaming Jane rolled her eyes.

"I thought I smelled you," Crow added in disgust. "Why don't you go floss the maggots out of your remaining teeth?"

"Focks you!" Half-Ass McJanky drew in close to Crow's face, spittling his face and wilting his eyelids with the wind of his rotgut. "Wee fixin's to delivers yee to Davey Jones's Locker, sees! But not until wee rapes yee and yers woman proper!"

"How sensual," Crow sassed, at which point Half-Ass McJanky slapped him.

"Ties them up!" Half-Ass McJanky yelled, then slapped Crow again, getting giddy hysterical about it and humping his own pelvis. "Wee gonna gits our rapin's right on!"

Crow glanced at Flaming Jane as their hands were being twined behind their backs, winking and sharing a grin as he nodded toward a wineskin lying amidst his supplies. Crow then looked at Half-Ass McJanky till their eyes met. "Please," Crow said, allowing his eyes to dart again to the wineskin. "Permit a pirate a right taste o' rum?"

"Rum?!" Half-Ass McJanky roared, scrambling to seize the wineskin Crow had indicated with his glance. "Sees here now, gents! We jus' wons us some rum for our rapin's!" Thence followed a snot and gargle of cheers as they tightened the twine fast before pushing past one another to get at the wineskin.

"Hangs on thar, mateys!" Half-Ass McJanky held the wineskin out of their grunting reach. "Fockin' hell now, each man in turn!" At that, he uncorked the wineskin and held it aloft as if it were some torch of sacred liberty and offered his guttural toast: "To rapin's!"

"To rapin's!" his men roared in unison as Half-Ass McJanky guzzled five swallows from the wineskin, finishing only when the others wrestled it from his lips, and then each of them in turn, the others taking great care to count the bob of each man's Adam's apple to make sure no man got more than his fair share of swallows, and periodically regurgitating their salutation. "To rapin's!"

"How did you get on this island anyway?" Flaming Jane inquired after their first round was finished.

Half-Ass McJanky turned to her and mocked her falsetto. "How dids you gets on this island anyway?" This caused great gusts of inexplicable hilarity among them, until finally, after having another swig and smearing the filth on the back of his hand across his lips, he answered. "Goldtooth attacksed us and taksed us prisoner, sees, and human sacrificed us to a sea monster, but he throwsed us up like Jonah the whale!"

"Jonah wasn't a whale," Crow interrupted.

"Yes we was so!" Half-Ass roared at Crow. "And anyway, Goldtooth'll takes us back when wee shows up with *yers heads*!"

"Why would you want Goldtooth to take you back?" Flaming Jane asked. "Didn't he human sacrifice you to Jonah the whale?"

"Don'ts matters!" Half-Ass McJanky yelled. "That don'ts even enters into it! I'll bes seccin-in-comman' when I comes back with *yers heads*! Betcha gits my own ship back, too!"

"Whoa!" one of his foul compatriots suddenly roared, causing Half-Ass McJanky to wheel about. "Dids you sees that? I almost felled right over!"

"Yers drunken!" the others roared right back. "You never moved!"

"I almost felled right over!" he insisted, eyes again agog. "Whoa!"

"Shuts yers stoopid!" Half-Ass McJanky snarled, drooling copious as he hastened to unfasten his own breeches. "Let's quits all this conversatin's and gits our rapin's right on," he muttered, staggering backward and almost losing his balance on his gimped leg. At that, Crow swept his foot under Half-Ass McJanky's lame leg, toppling him off balance and atop the smoldering coals.

Half-Ass McJanky scrambled coughing out of the coals and back to his feet before lifting his scalded palms before his face and screaming. "Gits him!" he howled. But it did not appear there was an ounce of sense to be made of anything for the lot of them.

"Wuz happensed?" one of them gawked, the others crouching low, careening about disoriented as if the earth itself were quaking.

"Have you ever contemplated the depths of your own stupidity?" Crow asked Half-Ass McJanky once Flaming Jane had succeeded in squirming free of their hasty twining of her hands.

Seizing her cutlass, she freed Crow's hands and the both of them stood, arming themselves and taking care to secure their supplies from the pitch and lurch of the five drunkards.

"Huh?" Half-Ass McJanky grunted, his eyes alternating between squinting at his own hands and wild glares of suspicion at his compatriots.

"Something tells me there was more than rum in that wineskin," Flaming Jane observed.

"Wormwood poison," Crow answered, taking a step back from their mayhem. "From the barrel that Goldtooth hoped to deliver to your ship, remember? Azriel saved us a wineskin for just such an occasion."

"What a bunch of tosspots," Flaming Jane squinted. "They're completely delirious."

"It's going to get worse," Crow predicted, eyeing the buzzards beginning to circle the skies above. "Let's get out of here and not look back."

And it was good that they did, for shortly after they stepped away a chorus of screams curdled the sky, Half-Ass McJanky and his men setting upon one another with such gruesome rampage that it wasn't ten minutes before the buzzards were settling in for an early-morning breakfast.

88

*B*EWARE THE *MEADOW* OF *MARVELS*.
      Several beaches over, being careful to walk in the wet sand and surf so as not to leave any footprints, Crow and Flaming Jane examined the map together after leisuring over a

brunch of spitchcocked eel. Although the map seemed to caution them *against* this meadow of marvels, there was—aside from the angry angel and the grinning devil that flanked the island—no other obvious direction which they should seek. And after Flaming Jane revealed the aeromancy of last night's shooting lodestar from none other than Orion's bow, there remained no possible dispute as to their direction.

After they had hiked across several more beaches and scrambled around the rocky cliffs eroding between them, they came to the spot Flaming Jane believed the shooting star to have indicated. And sure enough, there where the forest met the beach was a neat trail, though a ten-minute tread upon it unsettled them on a fork in the path. They stopped and stared in silence for a while, peering as far as they could down both directions. The right-hand path seemed infinitely more inviting. It was flat and apparently well trodden, briars and brush barely interrupting the course. The left-hand path, by contrast, quickly disintegrated into a diagonal treachery of tangles and thickets and loose stones and ravines, to where there really didn't seem to be much of a path at all.

"What say you?" Crow inquired at last.

"It's perfectly obvious, isn't it?"

"It certainly is."

"Shall we step off, then?"

"Perhaps a kiss for luck?"

"A kiss for love," Flaming Jane corrected him upon her kiss. "And whatever will be, will be."

At that, they grinned and drew their swords, immediately setting upon the task of clearing the tangles of the left-hand path.

"Never been much for the beaten path, have you?" Crow grunted as he hacked his machete.

"It's a simple matter of principle," Flaming Jane agreed.

"Of course," Crow nodded. "Had you considered the angel and the devil on the map, then?"

Flaming Jane paused her slash and machete. "How do you mean?"

"The devil was on the left side of the island on the map, and we have chosen the left-handed and sinister path." Crow gestured with his blade. "*Sinister* means left-handed in Latin, and of course it also means ominous, unlucky, and evil, but that's probably just a prejudice against intuitive thinking. It's the devil, after all, that's smiling on the map."

"Ah so," Flaming Jane nodded, impressed, "I suppose this then is the path of the devil?"

"I suppose," Crow sighed. "But I'd follow a grinning devil over an angry angel any day."

89

T WAS A HEAVY, sweaty business hacking their way up the sinister path. Footing was uneasy, thorns were merciless, and it was relentlessly uphill without a switchback to ease the incline. The only consolation was an abundance of passion fruit vines, which Crow and Flaming Jane snacked upon any time the fruit was within easy reach. They gloved their hands to protect against blisters and took turns carrying supplies and hacking the path. Hours passed in this exertion, they guessed they'd climbed over two thousand feet, and by late afternoon when the path at last peaked an endure of mosquitoes finally began to argufy their moods.

"These blasted bugs are bound to leave us with fever!" Flaming Jane lamented.

Crow agreed. When they considered perhaps turning back, however, they discovered to their dread that the forest had already recovered from their hack and slash, now masking whatever vague path there once was entirely.

"What enchantment is this?" Crow cried, eyes scanning the foliage, now seeming closer than ever. Spotting a familiar leaf, he followed it to its trunk and began hacking at the bark.

"What are you doing?"

"Here," Crow commanded, handing her some bark. "Chew on this." He continued to hack a quantity from the tree, being careful to avoid its aggressive thorns. "The bark resists the fever. Azriel showed me."

Knowing Azriel's faculties, Flaming Jane immediately rolled the bark into a quid. "Delicious," she drooled, grimacing at its profoundly bitter and astringent taste, though she noticed immediately how her thinking cleared. Crow soon joined her in grimace, and before long their grins defeated their disgust as they marveled at how incredibly remarkably bad it tasted.

"It was foolish of us to look back," Flaming Jane concluded after some rumination. "We've only one direction, and we ought not exhaust ourselves rethinking decisions made."

"True enough," Crow nodded thoughtfully. "And there's no time to tarry. But I have to say," he continued, suspecting around. "I'm beginning to wonder if this truly *is* all a dream."

"Oh yes?" Flaming Jane intrigued. "Whose dream is it, then, yours or mine?"

"As far as I can tell, it's mine."

"Hmm," Flaming Jane considered. "It rather feels like *my* dream."

"You *would* say that."

"I'm some character in your dream, am I?"

"Nah," Crow shook his head. "That hardly makes a jot of sense. I couldn't have dreamed you up if I tried."

"But I do know what you mean." Flaming Jane looked around, softly singing, "Merrily merrily merrily merrily, life is but a dream…"

Crow nodded. "And what did I say after I awoke from my fever?"

"That life wasn't really happening?"

"Exactly." Crow surveyed their surroundings, his suspicious eyes at last capturing the flash of Moby's wings above them just as Flaming Jane asked,

"Where *are* we?"

90

MOBY FLUTTERED to rest upon a branch above them, immediately announcing, "Möbius!"

"Moby!" Crow called out a greeting as Flaming Jane delighted. "I might have expected you!"

"Wake up, Crow Smarty." Moby blinked and chewed on one of his toes.

"Crow *Smarty*?" Flaming Jane asked, looking at Crow.

"Crow Smarty," Moby repeated. "Wake up, Crow Smarty."

Crow ignored the heckles upon his name. "Indeed a dream it seems, but what riddle is this?"

Moby ceased chewing on his toe for a moment, as if considering, and then repeated, "Wake up, Crow Smarty."

"I'll get right on it," Crow sighed, annoyed at the simplicity of the advice. "But in the meantime, old friend, how do we get out of this thicket? And have you seen a meadow?"

Moby cawed, bobbed his head, then ruffled his feathers. "Meadow of marvels, Crow Smarty. Be aware. Wake up, Crow Smarty!" Then he took off, fluttering upward through the branches till he was free of the canopy and gone.

"How in the hell did Moby know about the meadow of marvels?" Flaming Jane immediately asked. "And why does he call you Crow *Smarty?*"

"I have no idea," Crow answered both questions. "But I don't doubt his advice, even if I don't really know what it means."

"Crow Smarty," Flaming Jane snickered.

"Shut up about it already."

Flaming Jane looked around, feeling lightsome. "Have you ever realized you were dreaming in a dream before?"

"Of course."

"And what do you do when that happens?"

Crow shrugged. "Whatever I want, I guess."

Flaming Jane nodded. "So if this life is really a dream, we ought to be able to do whatever we want, correct?"

Crow considered. "And what we want is to get out of this jungle and find the meadow of marvels."

"Right. So let's do that." Flaming Jane fastened up their provisions.

"Okay." Crow looked around, uncertain about how to proceed.

"Puzzling, isn't it?"

"It's goddamned confounding," Crow agreed. "Now I can't even tell which direction we came from."

"Any direction is a direction," Flaming Jane offered.

"True enough." Crow lifted his machete and gestured ahead where the sky seemed to filter more readily through the jungle.

"Let us find this meadow then, my lovemuff," he announced as he began hacking through the vines and brush.

Flaming Jane readily followed, reveling into gratitude for Crow's companionship as she watched him tirelessly bushwhack a path out of the jungle ahead of them. *Life is but a dream*, she hummed sotto voce, an ancient and familiar grin scampering across her lips, a grin that had not relaxed upon her face since a childhood so distant that it felt like she was remembering someone else's life. *Curiouser and curiouser*, Flaming Jane wondered to herself, enjoying this newfound manner of not feeling like she had to control every damn situation, of surrendering to the flow of life.

And at just such a thought as that, a sear of pain punctured her left calf above the leather of her boot. She let out a cry as her eyes caught sight of a tremendous white snake slithering aside like a whiplash of panic as Crow pivoted in alarm just in time to suffer a selfsame snakebite. Curses snarled their tongues as the tremendous white snake vanished into the underbrush, and before any sense could restore itself the path upon which Crow was agonizing collapsed, spilling into a tumble of gravel and dirt and sending him skidding slip-sliding down a steep ravine where he vanished off a silent chasm before Flaming Jane shocked and blinking realized that she was alone, or perhaps she was screaming no as shadows deepened and the jungle maddened like cicadas serenading insanity. A sword through her heart would have staggered her less mortal, and Flaming Jane stumbled to the ground, clutching her calf and scrambling for her own footing trembling abandoned alone as an avalanche of solitude tore into her, churning her stomach and disgorging every wince of grief she'd ever suffered but never permitted, a wretched relentless demon wringing unforgiving the bile from her soul.

A few minutes and an eternity of catharsis later, Flaming Jane found herself emptied and strangely lucid. Sensible now, she tied a tourniquet above her calf, then dug a length of rope from her cache of supplies, tied it around a tree, and—limiting its length to about forty feet—harnessed the other end around her hips. Then she gingerly determined made her way down the precipitous ravine, spreading her limbs wide to maximize her traction on the pebbled and eroding surface. Her estimate on the length of the rope proved sound, and when she reached the bottom she had just enough length to permit her to lean peering precarious over the briary edge where she witnessed herself never smaller, and never more alone, than upon this surround of colossal cliffs soaring thousands of feet above a marvelous meadow.

91

"THERE IS NOBODY easier to manipulate than a narcissist," Lila explained to Merlin the day before the total solar eclipse, in between munching thoughtfully on a broccoli sprout salad seasoned with Himalayan salt and unfiltered raw apple cider vinegar that he'd prepared for her. "Flattery gets you everywhere, in the first place, but on the other hand, if you ever cross a narcissist by questioning their self-presentations," she pointed with her fork, "you need to be prepared for a backlash of narcissistic rage. Their demonic egos can only sustain themselves with constant adulation and praise, and the slightest disagreement or challenge so terrifies their cataclysmic insecurity that they'll never forego the opportunity to destroy the person who tried to suggest to them the terrifying truth about themselves."

"That's how you knew he'd try to kill you?"

Lila nodded. "And that's how I know he's going to pretend to ascend tomorrow."

"You're absolutely sure?"

"There is no question about it. He was already planning an eclipse ceremony in Golden Gate Park, and hinting that his ascension was imminent, and now I've raised too many questions about him. Ivan is going to ascend under the solar eclipse tomorrow and blame me for having to leave, and my presumed debility or death will just be my obvious karmic comeuppance." Lila toyed with her broccoli sprouts. "You can always trust people to be themselves." She pointed her fork back at Merlin. "Any gesture of reconciliation from him was never anything more than a manipulation. In fact, he was already trying to undermine me before I ever even challenged him, because deep down, narcissists know they're full of shit, and they can sense the individuals who are not so easily deluded. They'll make scapegoats out of them, inviting the group to project their sins upon them, thereby distracting everyone's attentions from their own failures and cementing their position of tyrannical leadership. A tyrant requires a scapegoat, and vice versa. One cannot exist without the other."

"Diabolical," Merlin shook his head. "How do you know so much about narcissists?"

Lila laughed. "What, you mean aside from being one myself?"

Merlin grinned. "Ah, I was wondering at that."

"Narcissism is the human condition," Lila explained, "at least insofar as we derive our self-worth from the opinions of others. I'm no exception to that damnation any more than you are. But I'm talking about *clinical* narcissists, those who chart their course according to a remorseless megalomania and lack anything resembling empathy. Sociopaths, really." She gestured back and forth between them. "We obviously take some degree of pride in ourselves and care what others think about us, but not to humblebrag, we're also capable of exercising restraint, of feeling remorse, and of holding our values intact."

"It's interesting," Merlin considered, "that a clinical narcissist would craft a delusion of himself as being an ascended Master."

"Well, what else could he possibly be besides the highest

possible attainment of humanity? A cokehead oil brat turned crack-smoking male prostitute? Because that's what he was."

"Seriously?"

Lila nodded. "And I don't mean to badmouth crack-smoking male prostitutes, by the way, but that's frankly not a path that leads to enlightenment ever, if only from the ego-deranging effects of cocaine. This whole cult, inflating his ego to salvific proportions, all of it, it's all to escape from his own self-loathing; that's my psychoanalysis."

Merlin shook his head. "That's the whole problem with people, always identifying with their egos."

"Right?" Lila smiled. "As if any of it is even really happening."

92

LATER THAT NIGHT, being careful to stay to the side of a closed-circuit security camera's viewfinder, Merlin aimed his paintball gun at it and fired a pellet of black paint directly onto its lens. He'd always been annoyed at these Orwellian, panopticon surveillance technologies anyway, desperately propping a broken system of egregious inequality, and he could not resist a cheesy grin as Lila congratulated him on his shot.

"Nice shot!" Lila whispered, unnecessarily, as the streets were quite empty. "Eat paint, Big Brother!"

Merlin holstered his paintball gun. "Have you ever heard of Hakuin?" he inquired unwhispering as they strolled toward the next security camera they had identified along their route.

"No," Lila replied, glancing admiringly back at the splotch of black paint that now coated the eyes of the camera. "Who's Hakuin?"

"I thought of him when you were talking about Ivan earlier today," Merlin responded. "Hakuin was this Zen master from way back in the day. He lived up on a hill outside a village, and was widely regarded as a holy man. So one day, the daughter of a wealthy merchant in the village turns up unexpectedly pregnant. Her parents are mortified and demand to know who the father is, but she resists telling them until she finally relents and confesses that Hakuin fathered her child. Outraged, they march up the hill to accuse Hakuin. He's planting his cherry tomatoes in his garden and he pauses his gardening and listens politely, and when they are finished, he smiles and says, 'Is that so?'"

Lila touched Merlin's arm and pointed ahead to the next camera. Merlin readied his paintball gun as they took care to avoid its angle of view, and once they were within range, Merlin took aim and fired off another paintball pellet.

"Nice shot!" Lila commended again.

Merlin regarded the anarchic mess ruefully as he again holstered his paintball gun. "So anyway," he resumed their stroll, "several months later when the child is born, the parents march back up the hill with the entire village now in tow and the wealthy merchant presents the child to Hakuin, saying that because he illegitimately fathered this child that it was his responsibility to raise it. Hakuin's harvesting cherry tomatoes in his garden and he pops one in his mouth as he listens, wincing at its delightful tartness, before he politely replies, 'Is that so?' as he accepts the child. Then each of the neighbors steps forward in turn and shakes their heads and wags their fingers and basically tells him how much he sucks and how disappointed they are in him, and how he is no holy man. Again, Hakuin replies, politely to each of them, 'Is that so?'"

Lila gestured ahead to their final target, and Merlin nodded, continuing his story as they drew stealthily closer. "So a year goes by, and Hakuin is raising the child as if it were his own, and finally the wealthy merchant's daughter breaks down and confesses that Hakuin is not the father after all, that the father is the fishmonger's son. So now her parents are mortified and filled with regret, and they make their way up the hill to apologize and retrieve the child." Merlin paused, took aim at the camera, and fired off a final paintball pellet before resuming. "So Hakuin looks up from his gardening and listens politely, and when they are finished, he pops a cherry tomato into his mouth, wincing again at its delightful tartness, and says, 'Is that so?' as he gives them the child back. And then they thank him and tell him that he is truly enlightened, a holy man, a saint, and Hakuin's only reply to all of this is, 'Is that so?'"

Lila smiled goose bumps. "So a true Zen master cares not at all what others think of them."

Merlin holstered his paintball gun. "Entirely indifferent to both condemnation and praise. Basically the perfect opposite of Ivan."

Lila nodded appreciative and regarded his handiwork. "Nice shot, by the way."

Merlin grinned a grand ego. "Yer gawdamn right it was a nice shot."

93

CROW HAD BEEN pleased at least at how easily his blade had been severing the stalks, but he'd been troubled nonetheless over the riddle and fix in which they found themselves. It had just occurred to him that the closer they came to the Stone of the Philosophers, the more uncommon their experiences became, as if the Stone itself were at the center of a mystical maelstrom. Before Crow had a chance to voice this notion, however, the tremendous white snake bit him just as his footing promptly collapsed and he crashed scrambling down the steep and graveled ravine and before he could gasp or lay a grasp on anything he pitched through a bed of brush and burst limbs gesticulate into a wide-open and weightless sky. A sickening free fall of lurching panic pulled hold of him as Flaming Jane's receding resound of "Noooo!" was swallowed by the roar of the wind and the rush of the rockface and though it felt far too much more than real Crow remembered yes he realized that he must be dreaming after all and his body relaxed and his soul released and his heart shone sacred supernova as his gloved hands reached instinctive for the immense vines dangling from this hidden cliff and he found a grip and tightened upon it tearing crashing snapping gashing breaking raking a jolt a snarl and flailing swinging salvation till the creaking pendulum of his momentum slowed into silence and drifting slowly turning the panorama of a marvelous meadow settled upon his eyes.

94

I T WAS A minute before Crow began to recover from the shock of his fall and realize his position, dangling from a vine a thousand feet from the top and a couple of hundred feet from the bottom of an immense cliff. Still dazed, he wove an arm and a leg around the vine to stabilize and assess. All things considered, he was relatively intact. The palm of his right glove was completely shredded and the skin underneath thoroughly tenderized, rendering its grip upon the vine an excruciating endeavor. Aside from that, the muscles in his right shoulder seemed to resent any weight whatsoever. But he managed to switch his gloves with each other, pulling them on palms-up so as to protect both of his hands, even if the fit was awkward. After that, he tore a strip of fabric from his shirt with which to tourniquet his snakebite, and then, unnerved by the crick and creak of the vine under his weight, he began the long squirm down the vine, eventually pulling a second backup vine into his grasp once it was within reach.

As for Flaming Jane, she had been scanning the face of the cliff for some time before her eyes captured a murmur of motion near the bottom. It was much too distant to discern what she saw, but it summoned enough hope for her to bellow "Ahoy!" into the combe, echoing upon itself for several seconds before the chasm resumed its emptiness.

Ho there! a distant echo of Crow's voice soared into her ears, followed by *Watch your step!*

Flaming Jane laughed despite her tears. "You too!" she yelled, and then, "I love you!"

It was an uneasy span of time before her ears captured Crow's *I love you!*, and when she did the liminal echo was yet more faint, sounding as if it were straining from another dimension. Flaming Jane deduced they could only hear the echoes of one another's calls, and hence there was little permission for jest and intimacy when a gust of wind could blow their words forever out of earshot.

"Where are you!?" she yelled, and held her breath till she heard his unbearably indistinct reply, *Meet me at the tree!*

An enormous and solitary tree occupied the center of the meadow as if in sentry. There was no missing it, and Flaming Jane immediately began making her way back up her rope. She would have to find another way down, she resolved simple as that, although she was envious of the straightforward efficiency of Crow's path. It wouldn't matter in any event, for once she had clambered about halfway up she froze at the sight of two vultures picking at the fibers of her umbilical rope as if it were the gristle of a carcass. The fibers of the rope were already breaking and snapping apart, and there was scarcely a second for Flaming Jane to drop her gear and snicker sonovabitch before the rope snapped and sent her skidding after her sack of provisions out of control down the face of the graveled ravine and vaulted her into the same wide-open and weightless sky for a split second of silent ecstasy as the world entire rotated around before the hurling berserking velocity of her earthbound plummet seized hold and a song sung by every child on earth soared through her soul like sunshine:

Merrily merrily merrily merrily,
Life is but a dream!

And Flaming Jane understood what was happening not just in that breathless moment but beneath every moment of her life and it was a treasure so tremendous that it vanished forever banished all sadness all suffering and death was no match and certainly no threat because, after all,

Death is but a dream!

Sailing now flying fantastic phenomenal Flaming Jane spied the vines climbing the sides of the cliff and she knew how Crow survived and if a man could do it then bloody well so could she and as she reached toward them she saw one no wait two vines arc away from the cliff wall intersecting her path and lo it was Crow who'd alerted to the preceding plummet of her pack and easily tracked her flaming hair streaking out of the sky like a comet and their eyes seized their grip a moment before their bodies careening collided in an oof and tumble cracking crashing fumble cursing clusterfuck.

"Goddamnit!" Crow roared. "I told you to watch your step!"

Flaming Jane was still laughing hysterical wahoo when the first vine snapped. The ten-foot drop before Crow's second vine yanked taut jolted her more than the thousand-foot one had, and watching the remnants of the first vine curl away beneath them sobered her to the tasks of survival. As soon as their arc reached the cliff wall they were both reaching for second and third vines.

"You okay?" Crow grunted through his exertion.

"Never better!" Flaming Jane gushed.

"What happened?"

"Goldtooth." Flaming Jane gestured skyward, referring to the two vultures, then shook her head in disbelief. "Let's just get to the ground."

95

A MIST CHILLED the air as they squirmed their way down their vines, the result of a slivered waterfall cascading silent in its distance down the far wall of the combe.

"Unreal," Crow assessed as he finally planted his feet on the floor of the meadow.

"Marvelous," Flaming Jane added, just before she jumped her remaining distance.

"Bloody snake," Crow cursed as he seated himself to inspect his calf. "We'll be lucky to survive the hour."

Flaming Jane joined him, inspecting her own calf. "At least we've gotten somewhere. The map pictured a white snake, don't forget."

"Hmm." Crow furrowed his brow, running his finger over his snakebite. "There's no heat or swelling. How are you?"

"No pain, no redness," Flaming Jane offered. "Perhaps it wasn't venomous?"

"I'm inclined to agree." Crow stood and loosened his tourniquet. "If only not to lose all hope. I suppose we'll find out one way or another soon enough."

Flaming Jane stood as well. "We should make camp here, in case we need to lie low for a spell."

"Let us tread carefully," Crow advised as Flaming Jane began retrieving their scattered provisions. "And is that what I think it is?" He was referring to a small, gallon-sized barrel that Flaming Jane was examining.

"Gunpowder," Flaming Jane affirmed.

"Where did that come from?"

"Probably from him." Flaming Jane pointed to the remains of the skeleton collapsed upon the meadow.

Crow examined the skeleton, the brokenness of its bones implying a selfsame fall. "I'm amazed the cask is still intact."

"Indeed," Flaming Jane observed, stuffing the cask into her pack. "Perhaps his body saved it from the fall."

Crow fished the map out of another satchel and unrolled it. There was no question that they had arrived at the meadow of marvels, of course, but if he required confirmation, the single tree drawn upon the island certainly sufficed. Crow squinted at the actual tree, attempting to estimate its enormity across the rolling distance. "Well," Crow concluded. "Here we are."

"Yes," Flaming Jane nodded. "That's what I always say."

96

"**H**AVE YOU NOTICED," Crow at last voiced his suspicion, "that the closer we've gotten to this Stone of the Philosophers, the more peculiar our experiences have become?"

"Indeed," Flaming Jane nodded, furrowing her brow and shaking her head as she examined the map herself, turning it sideways and upside down. "What do you make of this crazy map lately?"

"Eh?" Crow reached for the map. Glancing at it, he found himself peering at a surface enchanted. His gaze bedazzled upon the white shimmering ouroboros rotating and swallowing upon itself, and from there every element of the map danced into a kaleidoscopic flux, turning unfolding such that he could not get a fix on any of it. Fascinated, Crow only reluctantly rolled the map and cleared his throat.

"So?" Flaming Jane smiled huge.

"It would appear," Crow chuckled uneasy, "that we ought not mistake the map for the path it's intended to indicate."

97

THE EVENTS OF the day exhausting upon them, Crow and Flaming Jane took advantage of the waning daylight to gather their remaining scattered provisions and prepare their shelter for the night. Sleep soon possessed them, summoning seraphic dreamscapes of merciless beauty.

Flaming Jane found herself falling far faster than she had fallen off that cliff, falling so fast that she feared her flesh was about to be blown right off her skeleton. Despite a panic born of this hellbound velocity, there did not appear to be anywhere to fall, indeed, there did not appear to be anywhere at all. It was all just black, as black as a hardened heart, and Flaming Jane's alarm turned merely curious as she maneuvered herself face-first into the hurtle. As soon as she did there appeared a point of light beneath and before her eyes, and as it grew upon her approach she saw that it was a maelstrom of celestial proportions, a spiraling vortex of stars surrounding another eternity, and as it engulfed her senses surrounded a cacophony of new-born sensation glaring clamor cloy till the tumult tumbled into an emergent harmony and her eyes bewildered toward a vim of color coalescing into the writhe of a snake braying rainbows across the opalescent surface of its skin and as the spectrum

soothed its colors cooled into a white so bright it was only light
and the snake opened its eyes onyx devastation and just before
drawing its tail into its mouth it looked toward Flaming Jane
and intoned,

Who makes whom first?

And Crow found himself on the edge of a severe precipice, relaxing, legs dangling over a thousand-foot drop on three
sides and a woefully steep incline behind. Examining the slope
behind him, Crow could not imagine why or how he got himself into this predicament, let alone how he would get out of it
without kissing the chasm, though he was at ease at least for the
moment. But the moments kept passing and the sun kept setting and the warm rock felt increasingly cold against his body as
he gradually admitted that his was not at all a sustainable position. Shivering first from cold and then from fear Crow gradually terrified immobilized as any move seemed a certain fall but
the longer he waited the more his body stiffened and shivered
until he heard the smallest most feeble most helpless part of
his existence whisper *help* and upon this entreaty his paralyzed
body suddenly determined and his face snarled in defiance of
death and he gently very carefully scrambled around in his narrow precipice, turning himself to surmount the slope behind
but then he glanced up and twenty feet away looking down
upon him was some kind of a jaguar. And Crow knew he had
seen this jaguar before and he knew it was his death and as the
jaguar began to pad its way expertly down the slope Crow has
never seen such noble such graceful ferocity and Crow knew
that this was it that there was no way out and that he was about
to die and the echoes of his last words resounded throughout
the chasm as he called out to those he has loved wishing them

to know that he will always love them and as he turned to face his fate the night has fallen and the jaguar is in front of him but the spots on its coat are blinking open like eyes and the jaguar lay down somehow somewhere before him and Crow astonished to hear his own death speak:

I pray for you.

The jaguar reverberated basso profundo enormous as its fur shone golden divine illumination and Crow choked oh my god as his heart burst tremendous and his hand reached forth and his fingers slid into the silken fur of the scruff of the jaguar's purring neck as Crow—and Flaming Jane—awaken.

98

"WAKE UP, Crow Smarty," Moby called out to the sleeping forms of Crow and Flaming Jane.

Sitting up simultaneous and without startle, Crow and Flaming Jane looked at one another golden under a dawn of orange sunshine.

"You look incredible!" Crow was first to speak.

"Stunning!" Flaming Jane agreed in turn.

"Not that you didn't look incredible before today," Crow hastened to add.

"Of course."

"But today you are even more," he paused, *"radiant."*

Flaming Jane moved her limbs, examining herself. "I don't think I've ever felt so supple."

"It's true," Crow added. "Neither ache nor stiff assaults me, no groan gnarls within my throat, and nary a grain of sand grits upon mine eyes."

Flaming Jane was silent awhile, gliding her fingertips across the skin of her forearms. "I feel like I've been baptized in the tears of God."

Crow smiled, not knowing how he understood her meaning. "Tell me, did you dream?"

Flaming Jane looked up, considering. "Not that I remember. Did you?"

Crow shook his head. "No. But then again, I'm uncertain whether we're dreaming right now. Remember that map yesterday?"

Flaming Jane reached for the map and unrolled it, shaking her head quizzically before passing it to Crow. Crow took one glance at the map before smirking at its continued animation and rolling it up. "Let us be upon our way and discover this day." And they buoyed themselves standing, lithesome and lighthearted like children at play.

Flaming Jane explored the limits of her limbs. "I don't think I could stretch if I tried," she marveled.

Crow confirmed this just as Moby fluttered to rest on his outstretching forearm as if he'd been waiting all morning for just such a perch. Moby regarded them, bobbing to and fro, and seemed himself to grin as he bid glad day and good tidings before vaulting feathers sprawling toward the waterfall:

"May your days dare delight with your dreams."

99

ON THE MORNING of the total solar eclipse, and the day they planned to unveil Ivan, Merlin was brushing his teeth, watching the subtleties of faraway expressions breeze across Lila's face. Merlin guessed Lila was anxious about their caper, but in fact she wasn't thinking about it at all. Rather, she was thinking about lentil beans.

As a child, shortly after her father had left, Lila lived for a time in a cramped apartment with her mother. They were broke, flat broke, powdered milk and government cheese, having the gas turned off in favor of the electric, shallow baths of cold water made tepid by adding a pot of water that had been boiled on a hot plate, basically just not-quite-homeless broke. Lila was vaguely aware of the situation, the enthusiasm of her childhood somewhat distracted, and one afternoon after school came blasting in the kitchen door, managing to hook her back-pack on the dangling power cord to the Crock-Pot in the process, yank it off the counter, dump its contents of lentils and carrots all over the kitchen, and shatter the glass lid and ceramic crock upon the floor. Lila's mother flew squawk and startled in from a nap, gasped at the damage, and shrieked at Lila that that was their food for the week—"What are we supposed to do now?!" Then she stomped into her boots and slammed out of the apartment, tires squealing, all that.

Crestfallen, Lila then spent the next hour and a half meticulously separating every piece of broken glass and ceramic from their food, placing the lentils and carrots in one bowl and the shards of ceramic and glass in another, then cleaning the floor. When her mother returned home—as it turned out, with a box of groceries she had obtained from a local food bank—Lila meekly showed her how she had salvaged their food for the week. Her mom did not respond, but instead sat down on the couch and wept softly. Lila could still feel the sinkhole in her heart that had opened as she watched her mother cry, struggling to sustain some semblance of dignity to their existence.

"I read about this tribe once," Lila said to Merlin, who was swishing the toothpaste from his teeth. "They were well fed and wealthy, and didn't really have any immediate enemies. Nevertheless, whenever one of them was injured or fell ill, others would surround them and steal their money, going so far as to put them into debt for the rest of their life—unless that person had paid their protection racket in the first place."

"Sounds familiar," Merlin said, after he spit the toothpaste lather into the sink.

"Well, yeah, that was the point the writer was making. He wasn't actually describing a tribe at all, he was describing American society as if he were an anthropologist alien to it. From that point of view, national identity is nothing but some cartoon mascot masquerading as we the people, and absent all the political puppeteering, it all just seems absurd. Nobody would count themselves a member of a tribe that treated its people that way, because that's actually not a tribe. It's something else, a system of slavery or indentured servitude, because if you not only can't count on your tribe to educate you, but if you also can't count on them to help you when you're injured or sick, then *it's actually not your tribe.*" Lila shook her head, disgusted at the stupid pretense of a civilization gradually devouring the lives of everyone she knew, abandoning them, diminishing every individual to look out only for themselves, for their own impossible safety, and blaming anyone who stumbled on their own bad decisions, on their own poor planning.

"So this stupid pretense of a civilization we're supposed to identify with," Lila went on, "is really just the darkest spell of all. It's obviously not our tribe; it's mostly just a system for harnessing life and hogging resources. The only reason people behave themselves at all is because the illusion pretends itself inevitable, having effectively deskilled us all from the simple tasks of living."

Merlin walked over and kissed Lila with his peppermint fennel lips. "My my," he smiled. "Aren't you the anarchist this morning?"

Lila grinned and bared her teeth ferocious, snarling outstanding.

100

I T WAS A two-mile hike to the tree at the center of the meadow of marvels, and thoroughly distracting. Every footfall into the grass and wildflowers of the meadow unleashed a splash of grasshoppers scattering in every direction like the shrapnel of genesis. Butterflies drunk on pollen fluttered around in clumsy perfection while bees revved about high on their own honeycomb. Dragonflies dueled and flirted, hovering and darting every which way while wildflowers flaunted their unabashed spectacular. Sunbeams sliced from beneath tremendous cumuli and any given moment found three distant waterfalls and a vaunt of gratuitous rainbows. Crow and Flaming Jane could scarcely take a step without pausing to marvel over this meadow indeed.

At some point in the midst of their amble, Flaming Jane and Crow approached one of the hundreds of deep brown boulders distributed throughout the meadow. It was not until they were less than fifty feet off, however, that they discerned that the boulder bore an impressive fur coat, and that it was breathing. More than that, it was eating—grazing—and the crunch and thwack of their approach finally caused this undetermined beast to lift its massive head lethargic, a cowbell jangling as it leveled a masticating gaze upon them.

"What *is* that?" Flaming Jane whispered as they halted their approach.

"Some kind of cattle, or ox?" Crow replied. "It's gigantic."

Flaming Jane studied the animal. "I've heard stories of such beasts, massive creatures that roam the grasslands of the North American interior. Trappers call them buffalo."

"Buffalo," Crow pronounced. "Why is it wearing a cowbell? And what are they doing here?"

"Grazing, it appears."

"Its head is bigger than both of our torsos combined," Crow astounded. "That thing must weigh over a ton."

"We should give it a wide berth," Flaming Jane cautioned, beginning to lead an arc away from the beast. But their motion alerted the bull, which moved itself to face them as it clawed at the earth. Simultaneous to this, every formerly motionless buffalo they had mistaken for boulders strewn about the tremendous meadow fell into motion as well, moving as one as they adjusted their positions in a rumbling cacophony of hooves and cowbells.

"Whoa," Crow murmured, automatically reaching for his flintlock. "We are rather exposed out here, aren't we?"

"Indeed," Flaming Jane agreed as the bull snorted and shook its horns at them.

Crow raised his hackles and his eyebrows at this display. "Beware the meadow of marvels, I suppose?"

"Don't look at him," Flaming Jane warned, tremble tightening her voice. "Let's just keep walking away." Despite this circumspection, the bull continued to snort and claw at the earth, and even threatened two steps toward them. Dark clouds roiled across the sky, wildflowers shuttered their petals, a bracing breeze began to blow, all beauty drained from the suddenly grayscaped meadow, and their bodies grew tight with fright.

"Hold on." Crow ceased their panicky retreat. "Just hold on a moment. That map, and this meadow, it's all enchanted."

"Oh yes?" Flaming Jane breathed hopeful.

"The meadow reflects our point of view, and nothing more," Crow continued as he ignored the buffalo and simply embraced Flaming Jane. It proved to be a sound hypothesis, for after their hearts had relaxed their rhythms and they felt the atmosphere begin to breathe itself anew, Crow and Flaming Jane gazed amazed at one another timid with smile, intoxicating upon one another's pupils shining like solar eclipses as they witnessed each other age a thousand years of grin as their flesh fell away and their grinning Jolly Roger skulls swept into dust as they revealed themselves to be something far more beautiful than flesh could ever contain. And then the vision blinked and there they were, shining like the dawn upon Eden's dew as great sun-scapes beamed again across the heavens brimming with songbirds and the bull and every buffalo returned to their idle grazing.

"Holy God," Crow whispered and Flaming Jane tittered as eyes alive they kissed electric and resumed their amble across the meadow of marvels.

101

"WHO'S HAPPENING?" Crow heard himself confuse some unknown steps later, his voice warbling molasses as his footsteps chuckled into genuflect. He glanced disoriented toward Flaming Jane, who grinned eyes wide for several moments before the both of them burst into nympholeptic roars of laughter storming into heaven like the drunken angelic.

"Everything is slightly out of weird," Flaming Jane eventually managed to mumble vibrato once she regained herself, whimper she laughed imbalanced before stumbling into tears and Crow's embrace as they descended to the earth like shadows stretching into dusk.

"I have a dream in my eye," Crow murmured meaningless, and thereupon, deep within the gentles of meadow, where clouds billow voluptuous everlasting, where breeze whispers and secrets sing through leaves of grass, where death blossoms and life decays as maggots frenzy across a rot of flesh, where flowers sprout from skulls where eyes once witnessed the sufferings of stars, where moonlit mushrooms crest mounds of shit while time marches men like tocks on a clock, where song strangles into scream as the bang of war echoes back to song, where memories evanesce into eternity and identities vanish into infinity, where the furl of mind fails at last to find anything other than everything as the solitude of divinity grieves across forever like the terror of joy like the audacity of youth sobbing into sorrow, thereupon Crow and Flaming Jane discovered the source of all love.

Hearts unbroken, their eyes mist open heads together amidst the shade of an immense banyan, itself enveloping a yet larger tree of undetermined species, as dozens maybe a hundred vultures soar and circle the sky. Still recollecting their senses, Crow and Flaming Jane neither moved muscle nor made a sound as they fascinated over the meditative hush of the vultures' flight and soon their ears caught a plummet of dew cut the air as it dropped from a branch high in the tree and as it hurled in they witnessed the meadow entire including their grins reflected within its surface before it shattered upon and baptized their foreheads with a thousand chimes of water each still containing a universe its own and before they could gasp hallelujah there came another and another again and again anointing them both with these waters most holy.

Crow and Flaming Jane might have been content to marvel away the rest of their life under this Elysian spell if not for the distraction of the vortex of vultures' continued descent. "We're not dead yet!" Crow bellowed at last, much to Flaming Jane's boister and mirth as the vultures' every next circle was wider and higher as they watched all the flock disperse, all the flock except for two.

"You're not dead yet," an unknown, unexpected, and terribly deep voice answered Crow's exclamation. "But you may be soon."

102

CROW AND FLAMING JANE scrambled into a sitting position to discover a tremendous white serpent wound within and around the tangle of banyan trunks forming the base of the tree. As the serpent moved, shades of rainbow shimmered across the opalescent surface of its skin, yes, and if they were uncertain whether it was the serpent that had just spoken it dispelled any doubt by continuing.

"Please forgive the depth of my voice," the serpent went on, pausing to lick a sparkling drool of venom from its glistening fangs. "I am not nearly so serious as the gravity of my voice may otherwise indicate."

"What is this?" Crow spoke, indignant at the startle and

not yet recovered of sufficient faculties to think to question how a serpent was even speaking in the first place.

"I intrude upon your moment," the serpent admitted, blushing rainbows along the length of its neck. "Another pardon upon me, for it is not often that the unsullied soul discovers paradise in a droplet of water." Slithering into a fresh position above them, the serpent dangled its head near eye level with Flaming Jane and Crow, who instinctively drew themselves back. "In my feeble defense, however, those villainous buzzards precede my bother upon you, though this is surely no excuse for the absence of my manners."

"You're the serpent on the map," Flaming Jane grinned, pointing at the serpent.

The serpent merely blinked its onyx eyes. "What can be the meaning of this accusation?"

Flaming Jane held up the map as evidence, which the serpent lithely commandeered with its tail before tucking it between the fork of a branch well out of their reach.

"What did you mean when you said we'd be dead soon?" Crow interrupted, drawing his sword and rising onto one knee, pausing only due to a lingering dizziness. "Do you mean to bite us again?"

"It is an unwelcome relief to discover that I am not the only one among us with abominable manners," the serpent sighed. "But let us not suffer the collective indignity of graceless conversation, hmm? Without some semblance of civility, it is surely a slippery slope to adolescent fart noises with our armpits, though I myself am without the necessary arms."

Crow and Flaming Jane puzzled at one another while the serpent continued. "Ah, but now I fracture your porcelain ears with shards of vulgarity, and this after I taunt you with black visions of imminent death." The serpent shook its head as it muttered to itself. "The onomatopoeic fart is nearly as offensive as a fart itself, and fundamentally a scatological, classless syllable. Whenever did I become such a bloody bandersnatch?" The serpent drew a long sigh. "A thousand pardons for this grotequerade of grunts that pretends at proper comportment. I merely assume you are a son of Adam and a daughter of Eve and carry the knowledge of death in any event, but even in that case it *is* a terrifically boorish topic for me to introduce. Alas, I fear the years coarsen my once-genteel courtesies." The serpent again dangled itself near eye level with Crow and Flaming Jane.

"Stay back, serpent!" Crow leveled his guard, placing himself between Flaming Jane and the serpent.

The serpent regarded Crow's sword. "What a shiny stick you carry, dear one. How clearly it reflects the meadow."

Crow, remembering his lesson with the buffalo, sheathed his sword cautiously, still unsteady on one knee. "Why did you bite us then?"

"*Bite* you?" The serpent shook its head. "A welcome home kiss, and you believe it a bite? What are we now, a bad manners convention—"

"What newfound nonsense is this?" Flaming Jane interrupted. "You punctured our skin with your venomous kiss, serpent. It burned like the devil and caused us to fall off that bloody cliff!"

The serpent looked at them as if perplexed before gleeking a mist of venom from its fangs across their faces. "Dear ones, how else am I to give you my potion?"

"Potion?" Crow and Flaming Jane spoke in unison, hurriedly wiping the mist from their faces.

The serpent nodded. "Love potion, to be perfectly precise. And a cliff-side tumble is necessary, I am afraid. After all, surely you know the phrase *falling* in love," the serpent went on. "Love, dear ones, love is a good deal more ruthless than your poets imagine."

"Enough nonsense!" Crow charged. "You said we'd be dead *soon*."

"*May* be dead soon," the serpent corrected. "And in either event, death *is* sooner than most expect."

"You're the devil, aren't you?" Flaming Jane pointed again. "The serpent of Eden! Admit it!"

The serpent tested the air with its tongue for a while before speaking. "A devil imagines itself to be separate from the source of all love and alone against the universe. If this describes you— and I think it describes most of your kind—then it is *you* who are the demons of Eden. There is no hell worse than human-ity—and no heaven better, mind you—but until you wake up from your history you must meanwhile mistrust the men who mean to rule your hell. And anyway," the serpent continued, "I am beyond all binaries. When you release your fear the dev-ils become angels. Yin and yang, after all, is a false dichotomy."

"Yin and *what*?" Flaming Jane stood at last, unsteady on her feet, followed by Crow. "What the devil are you even speaking about?"

The serpent lifted itself level with their eyes at the same time that its tail secreted their map higher up in the branches. "Suspicions slant thy lovely eyes," the serpent observed as it appeared to lengthen and stretch, dazzling rainbows across the opalescent surface of its skin. "A slander precedes me, hmm? It should be perfectly obvious that I bear nothing but light, and yet you permit rumors and hearsay to dictate your point of view—"

"See here," Flaming Jane interrupted, suspecting the ser-pent's cunning and wishing to discover how this encounter was relevant to their quest. "Are you going to swallow your tail or what?"

The serpent regarded its tail, looked toward Flaming Jane, then back to its tail, and back again. "This is a most unexpected inquiry. Pray tell, why suggest such an abomination among our otherwise polite company?"

"The map," Flaming Jane began. "The map pictures a serpent swallowing its tail."

The serpent again regarded its tail, disgust curling around its nostrils. "The slander is worse than I know. What sort of a map pictures me in the act of fellatio with my own tail? Ah, but please reprieve me of that last remark! I lower my brow once more, and antagonize you with anachronism besides." The serpent turned to Crow and lowered its voice to a whisper. "But ask me later about fellatio, my good fellow." Then it winked as it gestured its head toward Flaming Jane.

"The Stone," Crow replied, attempting to stern the face of the serpent's absurdity. "We seek the Stone of the Philosophers."

"Ah, the Stone of the Philosophers, yes." The serpent smiled as it wound itself into a helix around a single branch. "At last we arrive at the fruit of this encounter. Tell me—and please pardon my presumption—but do you in fact know what the Stone of the Philosophers is?"

"The alchemical quest, of course," Flaming Jane responded. "The stone that can turn any metal into gold."

"A very good answer," the serpent nodded. "And I trust you realize the allegory?"

Flaming Jane blinked uncertain at his words. "Of course."

"Yes of course," the serpent repeated. "Then let us not delay another moment." Retrieving their bundled map with its tail, the serpent proceeded to tear a bite off its edge and swallow it ruefully before continuing. "High in the branches of the tree this banyan protects there exists a single perfect apple. As it requires a thousand years of sunshine to generate this singular fruit, this tree produces but one perfect apple every millennium. And further—and this is most important—only if you open it under the moonshadow of tomorrow's sun can you find that which you seek."

"Moonshadow? There *is* to be an eclipse, then?" Flaming Jane inquired. "The black sun on the map pictures an eclipse?"

"What is this?" the serpent responded, snapping the remaining map open with its tail and proceeding to examine it at length, never mind that the map was facing away, and upside down besides. "Ah so," the serpent nodded, idly tearing and swallowing another piece off the goatskin map, "this must be the Frenchman's map."

"The Frenchman?" Flaming Jane demanded. "Who is this Frenchman?"

"An unworthy soul." The serpent adjusted its position so that it was again dangling at eye level in front of them. "But pay attention, dear company, for there is one vital proviso: You must *eat* the apple to find the Stone of the Philosophers. If you simply tear the apple open, there is nothing to discover but a common core."

"Ballocks!" Crow responded. "Trickery!"

"I hasten to add," the serpent assured, "that you need not be so gluttonous as to eat the *entire* apple, as it is a rather large specimen. A single bite will suffice to secure your Stone."

"You expect us to eat a piece of fruit at your suggestion?" Flaming Jane laughed. "Do you suppose us fools?"

"Ah, loathsome regret!" The serpent hung its head. "I insult your intelligence with my ill-chosen words, or perhaps the cunnilingual taunt of my tongue inspires your mistrust. Ah, but heavens again!" The serpent recoiled. "Listen to me! I possess the politesse of a common cad! What becomes of my decorum?" Turning to Flaming Jane, the serpent lowered its voice to a whisper as it winked and gestured its head toward Crow. "But ask me later about cunnilingus, my fair lady."

"See here," Crow insisted. "You called me a son of Adam and her a daughter of Eve, so you must know we know the same scripture—"

"Some call it slander," the serpent interrupted. "Libel, technically."

"So you say," Crow continued. "But surely you must know that we cannot possibly follow your advice."

"Surely I must," the serpent agreed, tearing off another piece of their map and swallowing it. "Perhaps I merely protect the apple, and see to it that it remains forever uneaten. After all, since I know you suspect me a knave, if I truly wish you to eat the apple," the serpent snickered, "I surely must tell you to *not* eat the apple."

Flaming Jane stepped back and examined the branches soaring above the banyan. "Tell us, serpent, what tree is this?" she asked.

The serpent craned its neck and looked to where Flaming Jane was looking. "A pertinent question, of course, and it is terribly rude of me to tease you with this pretense of roguish prevarication. This, my dear ones, this is the very Tree of Life, and if you eat of its fruit you live forever. I can hardly blame you for your disbelief, but it is not my nature to lie."

Crow snorted. "Come now, serpent! You beguiled Adam and Eve into eating the fruit of the Tree of Knowledge!"

"Ah yes, a damn fine prank." The serpent smirked and finished consuming their map. "History is not kind to the fork in my tongue, that much is certain. But I dare you to discover even in the slander where I lie. They consume the fruit, their minds open to knowledge, and they gain the freedom to choose their reactions. I bear them nothing but light."

"And condemned humanity to a life of suffering," Crow added.

"Reread your slander," the serpent responded. "*I* condemn no one. And besides, you deserve your suffering."

"Oh? And who are you to dictate suffering?"

"Dear me," the serpent shook its head. "Please pardon my infinite inarticulation. What I intend to indicate is this: Your suffering is your birthright, and suffering is only another way of saying passion, which of course is only another way of saying love. Passion compels your existence, though there may come a time when your societies think your passions dangerous and seek to protect you from yourselves, and in the process rob your lives of any meaning, derail your destiny, and make brainless consumers of you all."

Crow had no idea what the serpent was speaking about. "You still got Adam and Eve kicked out of the Garden," he grumbled.

"Your indignation is understandable, with such hideous slander against me," the serpent soothed. "But the deepest expression of your freedom to choose between good and evil is love. In that case, the Garden is absolutely everywhere—"

"Then pray tell, serpent," Flaming Jane interrupted. "Why are we not there? What on earth happened?"

The serpent paused, looking as if it might have shrugged were it possessed of any shoulders. "It is you who abandon the Garden, all of you, moment by forgotten moment."

"Abandon the Garden?" Flaming Jane repeated. "Why would we do that?"

"You tell me," the serpent sighed, slithering its way onto the ground and moving into the tall grass. "Anyway, it's a long story."

"A long story?" Flaming Jane repeated. "How long?"

There was no answer as they watched the serpent's tail disappear into the meadow, though after some moments its voice echoed from a distance:

"As long as history."

103

OFFICER COBB checked the video monitor and squinted out the narrow cross-window on the back door of the armored truck. Officer Cobb was not really an officer, not anymore. He used to be a police officer, but he had been fired after a cell phone video of him using his Taser on a seventy-eight-year-old woman he had pulled over for rolling through a stop sign was widely circulated on the internet, replaying the part where her dentures shot out of her mouth over and over again in slow motion. Now Officer Cobb was an armored truck guard, though he did legally change his first name to Officer shortly after being fired from the police force. Despite these indignities, Officer Cobb still got to carry a loaded gun, and was even authorized to use it in the event of robbery, the thought of which never failed to rouse a half-mast in his underpants. Though Officer Cobb was unaware of the unconscious motivations compelling his behavior, this was why he was vaguely careless in handling the satchels of cash he was charged with transporting as the hopper. Officer Cobb *wanted* someone to try to snatch one.

Thus it was that he set the two satchels of cash he intended on carrying into the bank on the pavement while he secured the back door of the armored truck. Security protocols dictated that the satchels never leave his hands between secure locations, and that he carry only one at a time. This might have made a difference in the outcome of his day, but probably not. When automatic gunfire erupted from the alley diagonally across the street, Officer Cobb immediately returned fire on the masked robber concealed in the dumpster. He emptied all his rounds, never coming close to hitting his target, and it wasn't until the last echo had ceased to resound that he realized his target was a plywood cutout with a bad guy masked robber painted on the face of it, similar to the kind used at the police academy. Later, his colleagues would mock him for this, jeering its complete lack of even a nick upon its edge. Later still, Officer Cobb would be suspended and ultimately fired for his failures to follow protocol, resigning him to living out his authoritarian fantasy surfing internet pornography all night long as a graveyard shift security guard at a warehouse no crook even cared to case.

There was no automatic gunfire, either, by the way. The plywood cutout of the bad guy masked robber was rigged to set off a strip of firecrackers. The masked robber sprang up from the dumpster at the same time as the strip of firecrackers went off, and it was all just a diversion. Meanwhile, a couple of saffron-robed and turbaned Hare Krishna–looking cultists sporting mirrored aviator shades that had been chanting and zilling down the sidewalk nearest to the van deftly snatched the two satchels of cash, stashed them under their voluminous robes, and ducked down an alley. Officer Cobb was still squinting what the fuck at the plywood cutout across the street when his partner came hollering out of the cab of the truck pistol drawn and bellowing something about Hare Krishnas. His partner had seen them in the side-view mirror, and had to grab Officer Cobb by the epaulets to seize his mystified attention from the dumpster across the street.

"It was the Hare Krishnas, jackass! Call it in!" his partner yelled in Officer Cobb's face and gestured down the alley. "I'm going after them!" His partner took off down the alley, squinting and waving his arms to clear the clouds of smoke billowing from a smoke grenade the Hare Krishna–looking cultists had left in their wake, and ultimately spotted a corner of saffron fabric sticking out of one of the steel doors at the end of the alley. He flung the door open pistol first, finding nothing but a concrete and cinder-block rear hallway accessing the various businesses in the building and the torn corner of saffron fabric that had been caught in the door. He retrieved the fabric and ran down the hallway, past the back doors to three businesses, and exploded out the door ajar on the far side, dropping his arms oh shit when he found himself across the street from Golden Gate Park, where there were over two hundred saffron-robed and turbaned Hare Krishnas or something in mirrored aviator shades, chanting and dancing in the gradually eclipsing afternoon sun.

All the commotion around the armored truck was observed by Fuck You Fred, the stillness of his human statue having at last been fractured when the firecrackers went off and Officer Cobb discharged his weapons down the street. Smiling satisfied, Fuck You Fred relaxed the middle finger on his right hand, shook his hand awake, and walked away.

104

WITHIN MINUTES a dozen police cruisers had converged upon the scene and cordoned off the entire area of Golden Gate Park and all its adjacent streets with a police line. The Holy Company of Beautiful People hardly took notice—certainly no more so than of the report of firecrackers and whatever else around the corner a few minutes ago—so swept up were they in the ecstasy of the oncoming solar eclipse and Ivan's imminent dematerialization, not to mention the love potion with which Ivan had covertly dosed all of them when he shared his final Eucharist with them that morning. It was a dose sufficient to facilitate a highly suggestible state of mind and a magical feeling of uncontainable enthusiasm, but not enough to expand anyone's heart into cosmic visionary experience.

Ivan's high-end medicine carrier had unexpectedly turned up a couple of vials of this material two weeks back—Lila had anonymously hooked up the dealer with some of Merlin's hidden LP9 stash, knowing that Ivan had a standing order for it, for which he was willing to pay five times its already considerable market value. After carefully sampling it himself, Ivan concluded that it was exactly the missing piece he'd been waiting for to wrap up this monkey business. With all the pieces now in place (Ivan had accumulated over four million dollars and wanted to retire while he was ahead...), Ivan announced to the Holy Company of Beautiful People that his dharma was done. The assault of Lila's tremendous dark energy, Ivan explained, combined with the inexorable expansion of his own crown chakra—which even his turban could no longer contain—demanded his dematerialization at the peak of the solar eclipse, just as he had been predicting for the last several months. Chris Bliss would ascend to the rank of Master in his place, Ivan assured, and Chris Bliss, incidentally, was alone in receiving a triple dose of LP9 that day, and was currently writhing screaming high upon the grass, undergoing apotheosis as his heart expanded to messianic proportions.

Ivan himself sat lotus and alone upon a flower-bedecked table, sporting his own set of mirrored aviator shades, and despite the emerging disorder, he managed to focus on not allowing the unfolding chaos to distract him from his own plan. The presence of the police force and SWAT team was obviously not accounted for and was certainly worrisome—Chris Bliss had assured him yesterday that he'd turned in all the paperwork to officially permit their use of the park, and even showed him the permit—but if nothing else it lent credibility to the delusions of persecution he was forever laying on his followers. Yes *of course* the state would interfere and attempt to prevent his dematerialization, just as the Roman Empire had crucified Christ. Ivan wondered momentarily if everyone's LP9 experiences would turn bad once he'd disappeared—not that he actually cared, mind you. The only reason he was putting on this whole charade rather than just skipping town wasn't only to ensure that no one would realize that they'd been conned, though that was obviously important. More than this, Ivan *needed* them to believe in his divinity—it allowed him to imagine the same—and so long as he dematerialized the illusion would persist. But Ivan wondered nonetheless what all this fuss was about, plus it sure would be fun to witness the ensuing havoc.

Owing to Ivan's imminent dematerialization, devotees were not permitted inside a three-foot perimeter of five thousand dollars' worth of specially treated flame-retardant roses encircling his altar. Ivan warned them that his light would soon become unbearably bright, possibly even resulting in blindness, and so to look at neither him nor the solar eclipse, even though everyone was already sporting identical mirrored aviator shades. Many had draped themselves prostrate along the ground around the roses in adoration. All farewells had taken place on the evening prior, and all had taken a vow of silence along with the Eucharist in the park late that morning, a silence that apparently did not extend to include the glossolalic ululations now jubilating from the lips of most everyone. The stage appeared to be set, Ivan reflected, and even better than he'd planned with the police in such a presence.

Everyone was properly peaking and feeling the fervor, and the sun was already half obscured. A cool wind was kicking up, and Ivan couldn't see any reason to wait till the peak of the eclipse to disappear and risk additional interference from these cops, whatever business they thought they were into. There already appeared to be some necktie detective readying himself with a bullhorn.

All right then. Ivan brought his hands above his head, elevating the cries of his devotees as he masked his face with his voluminous sleeves, deftly switching his mirrored aviator shades with an identical pair of welding goggles he'd attached to his forearm and hidden up his sleeve. Then he pressed a trigger button on a small remote strapped to his other wrist and brought his fingers into a perfect guyan mudra, touching his forefingers to his thumbs and settling the backs of his hands upon his knees. Five seconds on the fuse, *om-mani-padme-hum*, and though Ivan could scarcely see anything through his welding goggles, he certainly saw the sizzling flash of white flare all around the table and amidst a chorus of cries of exaltation—and knowing nobody could see anything but the blinding white light—he slid off the table and slipped out of his turban and robe, leaving them with the original aviator shades he'd been wearing in a pile upon the altar to make it seem as if he'd dematerialized right out of his clothing. He'd dressed for the stealth of it in a black outfit beneath his robe, and ducked beneath the heavy cloth shrouding the table. There he removed his welder's goggles and readied his escape.

Ivan had left the manhole cover slightly ajar from its lip two nights before. This had required a special hook to remove the hundred-pound plate, and now he pulled on some gloves, slid the hook out of his belt, dragged the manhole cover two-thirds off, and crawled down the ladder. Scanning around once more to make sure he hadn't left anything behind, and satisfied that the magnesium fuses he'd rigged throughout all the flame-retardant roses were still flaring spectacularly bright, he slipped on a head-lamp and made his way down the ladder into a utility tunnel, pausing only to lock the manhole cover back into its position with his hook. Then it was about a half a mile through a network of underground tunnels before Ivan fit a dark wig over his own thinning blond hair and fixed a phony mustache in place, climbed another ladder, opened another manhole beneath the rear bumper of his Range Rover he'd parked early that morning on a nearby residential side street, and—having previously raised the vehicle's suspension to its extended profile option—squirmed out easily, replaced the manhole cover, retrieved the keys from a magnetic key locker behind the rear bumper, checked his reflection in the tinted rear window of his Range Rover, and chuckled at his own magnificence.

105

THE EFFECT OF Ivan's magnesium flares was nothing short of pandemonium. His devotees threw themselves into an absolute frenzy—their ascended Master had just dematerialized in a sustained flash of blindingly bright light, after all—and cries found their ways to words oh my god the glory how holy it's true so spiritual and so forth. Nobody knew whether to hug each other or to beat on their breasts with ecstasy, but all blundered backward several feet in shockwave to the miracle. The police, meanwhile, also flew into a frenzy, multiple bullhorns barking orders like a pack of dogs around an errant deer, resounding cavernous off the nearby buildings and sounding for all the love potion like the tremendous reverberations of the Master's dematerialization.

A magnesium fuse will stop burning as suddenly as it starts, like a flashbulb, and so it was that when the miracle had spent itself after a full ninety seconds, the blindingly bright light vanished as suddenly as it had begun and those few who had been agog and gawking screaming how beautiful the light suddenly found themselves temporarily flash blind. Cries of "I can't see!" panicked among them as the eclipse continued to creep toward its maximum umbra, while others surrounding them hugging and soothing reassuring it's only temporary, like Saul of Tarsus on the road to Damascus don't you know, and much tearful rejoicing such wonder of wonders the Master's ascended oh the miracle.

And as the siren of a fire engine slowed into silence the cacophony of police bullhorns at last surrendered to some semblance of rank and a single voice commanded, "Remain Calm!" And Chris Bliss, who up until that moment was still melting his face off and utterly in the grip of an ecstatic clear white light experience triggered by the love potion and Ivan's magnesium flash, heard these words as Moses heard the Ten Commandments and snapped open his eyes Mount Sinai, the constipated ick that typically dominated his countenance having transformed into the cherubic beam of, of… the Wisdom! Remain calm! Yes of course! This was the Wisdom! Remain calm! So simple!

Yes he sat up angelic, radiant becalmed, and standing enlightened, heard the voice of God further command, "Raise Your Hands Above Your Head!" And thusly he did so, a hallelujah chorus rising celestial crescendo, and look, his flock followed suit, murmuring uncertain at their new shepherd, but following nonetheless! Chris Bliss raised his face to the sky, dreams streaming down his cheeks as ecliptic sunbeams soared out from beneath God clouds, and hallelujah hosanna the Vastness the vision, he was an ascended Master!

"Nobody Move!" Chris Bliss blinked through his tears at this latest holy commandment, the first note of confusion stumbling his ecstasy, but remained as still as a statue in order to properly channel the Wisdom to his followers, ultimately deciding that he was supposed to relay this message to his flock as well. "Nobody move!" Chris Bliss loudly repeated, hands and face still heavenward but momentarily startled at the hallucinatory reverberations of his own voice. That must be what it sounds like when you channel the voice of God, he determined, and once its dozen echoes had hammered themselves into silence, he repeated himself to the same effect. "Nobody move!"

"You Will Be Taken Into Custody For Questioning!" the steely voice of God continued, and Chris Bliss nodded in gratitude for the foresight he was being given, followed by "Freeze!" at which point Chris Bliss ceased nodding obedient under God. Three police officers, meanwhile, tackled one of the Holy Company of Beautiful People—Dalai, it was, terminally ill with metastatic breast cancer and with absolutely nothing to lose—who had suddenly freaked out and decided to make a run for it. This commotion sent a jostle through the assembled, a jostle that ultimately slammed into Chris Bliss and succeeded in swerving his attention at last away from his own messianic delusions and toward sustaining his own balance. Glancing around wildly disoriented, he found himself baffled way beyond what the fuck by the situation he all at once discovered.

His followers, his flock, they looked so fearful, so frightened. Shoulders hiked, anxiety crowding their brows, black helicopter of the apocalypse assaulting the heavens above, and all of them penned in by a line of yellow plastic tape and a phalanx of dark energy, outsiders, *the dead*. Early afternoon shadows confused under the dusking light as a cold wind born of the maximum eclipse met his face, and all Ivan's warnings swarmed in on him at once. That the Holy Company of Beautiful People was a mystery school by necessity, that they were a chosen people and their light shone uncommonly bright, and that they would attract the envies and resentments of outsiders, *the dead*, those who knew nothing of the sacred mysteries. That Christ had been crucified, that the early Christians had to hide in the catacombs or be fed to the lions, that others just like them had been persecuted all throughout history, and that the shepherd must protect his flock. Chris Bliss closed his eyes against this collision of reality, his solar plexus roiling with bile and emotions uncertain as he hallucinated that they were surrounded by porcine demons slurping drooling trampling their light and upon spying a bullhorn it realized upon him that the words alleged by God—Remain Calm! and all the rest of that jazz—were actually spoken by these blasphemous pig demons, and that the Wisdom in its translinguistic ways must of course be the opposite of this imperative, and so his open eyes greeted the scene of three police officers still struggling to contain a supernaturally elastic Dalai, and when Chris Bliss found his voice at last the hammer of Thor never sounded a thunder so tremendous as the transcendental bellow that hurled forth as he roared, "R*uuuuunnnnnn!*"

106

OWING TO THE highly suggestible state of LP9 intoxication, the entire Holy Company of Beautiful People—over two hundred of them—did immediately and exactly as the bellow of Chris Bliss highly suggested. And they didn't just run, they roared forth a full-on fury, scattering and trampling over and past the police and their cruisers like Viking berserkers, and one officer later swore he heard them screaming "Valhalla,

I am coming!" and his comrades nodded no shit it's true, even though they knew it was not.

It was an absolute riot that the police—numbering all of fifteen, some flash-blinded themselves—were utterly unprepared to meet, least of all under the dusk of a maximum eclipse. In the end, the police succeeded in detaining exactly three people, and Dalai was not among them. Rather, it was three who had been flash-blinded and had lost contact with their comrades guiding their way, ultimately settling for singing "The Battle Hymn of the Republic" at full volume:

> *Mine eyes have seen the glory of the coming of the Lord!*
> *He is trampling out the vintage where the grapes of wrath*
>   *are stored!*
> *He hath loosed the fateful lightning of His terrible swift sword!*
> *His truth is marching on!*

Such it was that by the time the bellow of their retreat had receded and the Holy Company of Beautiful People had vanished, abandoning their saffron turbans and robes across the city along the way, the only echo that lingered from this bedlam were three ebullient voices, continuing to sing, again and again:

> *Glory, glory, hallelujah!*
> *Glory, glory, hallelujah!*
> *Glory, glory, hallelujah!*
> *His truth is marching on!*

107

A S IT HAPPENED, the herd of buffalo had found their way
to the meadow of marvels a dozen years ago by way of a
French captain who'd sought to retire to the hidden island
he'd found, build a ranch populated with buffalo calves captured during his post in the Louisiana territory, and ultimately
claim the entire island as his own kingdom. Fate intervened
once he succeeded in landing the buffalo, however, and a dev-
astating maelstrom destroyed his ships and drowned his entire
company. Ruined and marooned, it was not long before the
meadow of marvels drove the captain mad, and after drawing
the map and stuffing it inside a large bottle which he heaved
into the sea, the French captain threw himself off a cliff clutching a barrel of gunpowder, though he did survive a second long
enough to suffer the windblown regret of this suicidal decision.

Crow and Flaming Jane knew nothing of this history as they
surveyed the herd of buffalo peppered across the twilit meadow
from the top of the tree. There were at least two hundred head
of buffalo, though their numbers appeared sparse across the
immensity of the meadow. Flaming Jane watched as Goldtooth's
two surviving buzzards ceased their apparent reconnaissance and
drifted toward the open end of the meadow.

"Goldtooth will be here soon," Flaming Jane observed. Crow looked to where she was watching the buzzards and nodded.

"Yes, well," Crow pointed to a grapefruit-sized green apple bedazzling by the light of the sunset a third of the way out from a branch just above them. "The apple is right there. Whether the serpent's words are true or not, we're going to have to thwart Goldtooth from obtaining the Stone of the Philosophers."

"True enough," Flaming Jane agreed. "Nothing says we have to eat the stupid fruit. All we have to do is keep it from Goldtooth during the light of tomorrow's eclipse." She hefted herself up to the next branch and pulled her way toward the fruit. At first reach it was just out of her grasp, but after adjusting her position her fingers captured the apple and the gentlest tug upon it released the branch from its pregnant weight with a considerable rebound. Its pluck, however, seemed to reverberate across the entire meadow as any trace of a breeze immediately ceased and as the song of every bird and the buzz of every bee fell suddenly silent only to be momentarily replaced by a jangling symphony of cowbells as every buffalo interrupted its graze to gaze toward the towering tree at the center of the meadow.

"Momentous," Crow chuckled.

"It's *heavy*," Flaming Jane responded, weighing the fruit in her palm and offering it to Crow.

"Indeed," Crow agreed. "Feels more like a pumpkin than an apple." He joined Flaming Jane in quizzical contemplation as he handed it back to her.

Flaming Jane weighed the apple again, measuring it with both hands as she shook her head and grew into a grin. "I'll be damned if there isn't a stone inside."

There was little time to celebrate the success of their quest as a volley of gunshots echoed in the distance, startling the buffalo into a halfhearted stampede till they had assembled at the opposite end of the dusking meadow, shifting about uneasily. Without a word, Flaming Jane wrapped the apple in a kerchief and placed it in her pack, and she and Crow began descending the tree.

"Do we have a plan, then?" Crow asked once they were hidden within the banyan that surrounded the lower portion of the giant apple tree.

Flaming Jane squinted through the tangle of trunks. "Those shots came from over there."

"I know," Crow nodded, checking to see that the combe of cliffs still surrounded their every other direction. Then he added, unnecessarily, "Our only way out of this meadow."

"Yes." Flaming Jane pursed her lips, examining every direction. "So it appears. But those shots weren't for us, and nightfall is upon them anyway. They won't near us till the morning sun." She resumed descending the banyan.

"Meaning what?" Crow puzzled.

Flaming Jane looked up at him, radiant in her smile. "Meaning we have one more night together, of course."

108

THUS DID Flaming Jane and Crow make camp at the base of the banyan, preferring to bask in the satisfaction of a day well-worn than worry for the morrow.

Crow raised a wineskin "to the single finest day of my life, my pussywhistle."

"'Tis true, my lovemuscle." Flaming Jane kissed the wine from his lips.

"And we've had some good days," Crow added.

Flaming Jane smiled. "Each one better than the last."

Crow enjoyed a long sigh. "Ah, but tomorrow we may die."

"What a lot of rot," Flaming Jane chided. "Death is but a dream, don't you know?"

"So you say," Crow nodded appreciative, then shrugged. "The serpent did say we may be dead soon."

"Since when do you listen to talking serpents?"

"Since when do serpents talk?"

Flaming Jane did not answer, but instead crawled on top of him, kissing him all over. Crow soon aroused against her as they grew heavy with passion like a couple of elegant animals really good at caressing, drinking their breath off the winesweat of one another's skin and eventually sharing in the delights the serpent had earlier taunted. Crickets cheered in waves across the meadow as the lovers' bodies undulated beneath the galactic ejaculate of the Milky Way like a couple of rabid cherubs frothing at the genitals, and as the night wore on every star in the moonless sky illumined them sleeping limbs tangled as if it were the night before the morning of the fall.

109

A MILLION DOLLARS in hundred-dollar bills weighs approximately twenty-two pounds. Merlin knew this and, having already glimpsed that his satchel from the armored truck contained bundles of hundreds, figured that his satchel alone held at least half a million dollars, which meant that if Lila's were the same as his—he shook his head and focused on their getaway. Once he and Lila were inside the other steel door at the end of the alley—which is to say, *not* the door in which he had earlier that morning fixed a torn corner of a saffron robe in its doorjamb—Merlin dropped his satchel, pushed the door open slightly, and plucked a wad of paper out of the door's catch. To prevent either door from locking shut, Merlin had jammed a wad of paper into the catch of their locks early that morning after impressing the hell out of Lila by successfully picking their locks. Now Merlin loosened the crumple of the paper, itself a grocery store receipt, tossed the paper to the pavement outside the other door, and let the door close again, satisfied by the certainty of its latch. Then, in the back of a single unoccupied storefront, they slipped out of their turbans, robes, and sunglasses, jammed these into a stuff sack, and crammed the two satchels of cash inside two backpacks. Then they sighed, and looked at one another, grinning at the swimming caps they were wearing beneath their turbans to prevent any stray hairs from turning up as forensic evidence and possibly linking them to any of this mischief. Can't be too careful.

"Wigs!" Lila whispered, fetching them out of her pack. The swimming caps had been her idea; she'd purchased them when she purchased their latex gloves. "People lose between forty and a hundred and twenty hairs each day," she'd pointed out as a matter of fact when she presented them to Merlin.

Once they had their blond wigs in place—Merlin's being a Billy Idol cowlick, and the only men's wig that Lucy in Disguise, a costume store that Lila suggested, had in stock—they gathered their effects and moved to the front of the store, watching from the shadows out the front window as police cruisers arrived and surrounded the park across the street. Lila checked her watch; noting that they had about ten minutes until the maximum eclipse, which is when she figured Ivan would dematerialize, while Merlin rehearsed their route in his head—having tagged any security cameras along their route with his paintball gun late last night.

Sighing simultaneous, they settled in for a wait, sharing a silent smile that was neither exhilarant nor terrified, and were therefore as startled as anyone at the blinding flash of white light that all of a sudden engulfed the perimeter of Ivan's altar as he prematurely dematerialized, illuminating the shadow that concealed them as well. But this mattered not at all, as *everyone's* attention was now riveted great thunder and holy god upon the white blaze of glory at the center of the park. Lila whispered "Now!" and they shielded their eyes as they exited the building through the front, making their way unobserved away from the chaos in the park, about twenty paces apart so as not to look like they were together, unhurried, unworried, and even occasionally pausing to regard the ruckus or the sky exactly the way a vaguely interested pedestrian might.

110

T WO BLOCKS LATER, they arrived at Ivan's jet-black metallic Range Rover with privacy glass, unmistakable for its NAMASTE vanity plates, and Lila reached under and behind the rear bumper to retrieve the car keys—this was where Ivan kept his keys, as he claimed the electromagnetic frequencies of the keyless entry remote control interfered with his spiritual vibration. Finding the key fob (the jet-black metallic Range Rover with privacy glass had only a keyless entry and ignition system), Lila popped the hatch, Merlin lifted it, and they slung their backpacks onto the rear row of seats. There they pulled the satchels from the armored truck out of their packs and left them right next to the paintball gun, a saffron robe with a corner torn off, and a sack of groceries they'd left there earlier that morning after locating where Ivan had parked his Range Rover, carefully spilling several bundles of hundreds onto the rear seat. Reclaiming their backpacks along with a few bundles of hundreds they'd planned to anonymously give to Fuck You Fred, Merlin was about to slam the hatch on the vehicle when Lila stopped him.

"Hang on," Lila said, leaning inside and pulling a corner of a blanket aside, a blanket that was covering something on the center of the expanse of floor between the two rear seats facing each other. "I wanna see what this is."

"What is it?"

Lila puzzled a long moment. "A toilet?"

Merlin blinked, impatient. "And why are we mesmerizing over a toilet?"

Lila continued staring at the toilet as various lateral memories recollected themselves, how she'd glimpsed this toilet once before, how Ivan had strictly forbade anyone from using his master bathroom, how Ivan had an electronic lock on the door to his "corporeal sanctum," and how Ivan repeatedly advised his cult to convert their wealth into gold. "It's Ivan's toilet!" Lila stood up ebullient. "Hurry! Help me move it out onto the sidewalk!"

"What?" Merlin flustered. "Why?" But he immediately set about helping heft the various parts of the toilet onto the sidewalk outside the Range Rover. "Jeezus *christ* this is heavy!" Merlin snarled as he wrestled with the weight of the toilet, and he was right. The average toilet weighs between thirty-five and fifty pounds, whereas Ivan's toilet weighed every ounce of two hundred pounds. The only reason it was even possible to move it by hand at all was that it was already dissembled into its component parts, so no one piece weighed more than a hundred pounds.

"Careful, don't chip the finish," Lila instructed as together they set the heaviest piece, the throne itself, upon the pavement.

"Right." Merlin glanced at the sky to gauge their timing. "Remind me again why we're straying from our perfect plan to move this goddamned toilet? Ivan should be back any minute now!"

"This isn't just a toilet." Lila radiated with the light of a thousand suns as she grabbed the last piece, the toilet tank lid, from the Range Rover. Even the lid seemed unreasonably heavy, and after purposefully chipping its edge against the pavement, Lila triumphantly showed Merlin the luster of gold beneath. "Ivan's gold!" Lila elated. "That's why it's so heavy!"

A blink later, and Merlin understood. "I'll go get our Range

Rover," he volunteered as they covered the pieces with the blanket, pulses pounding. Merlin locked Ivan's Range Rover, tossed the key fob to Lila, and they began jogging away. "You take care of his." Once they were a block away, they turned a corner and Merlin watched the lights on Ivan's Range Rover as Lila experimentally pressed the unlock button on the key fob. "Clear," Merlin said, indicating that the keyless entry remote was out of range, whereupon Lila commenced pressing the unlock button repeatedly and methodically, counting under her breath and aiming to press it at least 257 times in order to desynchronize the pseudo-random number generators and thereby disable the keyless entry and ignition system, just as Merlin had taught her. Merlin, meanwhile, jogged on to retrieve their SUV, and at one point a smirk nearly unswallowed him, threatening to hurl a braying bwa-ha-ha of laughter, for Merlin was no Zen master, and was the kind of chess player who had to resist his grin growing into guffaws whenever his tactics were about to reveal their checkmate. But he held his gentleman's composure firm and furrowed his brow, prohibiting nevermore a smirk.

It took Lila about ninety seconds to accomplish her task—she went ahead and pressed it an even three hundred times just to make sure—just enough time for Merlin to retrieve their SUV, an identical-to-the-year jet-black metallic Range Rover with privacy glass they'd rented from an out-of-town, high-end car rental agency using one of Merlin's fake IDs and a prepaid credit card. Immediately, they parked directly in front of Ivan's Range Rover and commenced moving the various parts of the toilet into the cargo area of their Range Rover, still under cover from the dark of the eclipse. They hefted the last and largest piece—the throne itself—together, grunting and shuffling across the fifteen feet till they had it in the rear cargo area of their rented Range Rover.

"This is fun," Merlin said as he stepped back, still disciplining his glee, and sounding for all his sternness like he was saluting.

"Yeah baby," Lila agreed, their solemnity succumbing to snickers as she experimentally pressed the unlock button on Ivan's key fob and satisfied herself that they had indeed succeeded in disabling it. She replaced the key fob in the key locker under and behind Ivan's rear bumper while Merlin double-checked their license plates to be sure their false tags were still intact. He'd taken a high-resolution photo of Ivan's namaste vanity plate last week using a telephoto lens, and printed it out life-size and full-color on photo paper. This he laminated to render it stiff and waterproof, and mounted these false tags in front of the original license plates with double-sided tape. Everything was as it should be, they dusted off their latex gloves that's that, and upon getting in the car their lips met in a hallelujah and spontaneous kiss.

Pulling away from their kiss simultaneous wow and shuddering, Merlin started the engine as strains from the Beatles' "Across the Universe" came alive. Lila smiled at Merlin's gesture—he had assembled a Beatles mix for her to soundtrack the occasion—and grabbed a map out of the glove box before crawling into the backseat in order to hide from any traffic cameras. Merlin lowered the sun visors to hide his face from the same, and Lila examined their map; their route was drawn in red, and the location of every traffic camera along their route was circled. Off they went, with Lila navigating, and every time they approached an intersection with a traffic camera, Merlin would slow until the light turned red and once the coast was clear they would blow through the intersection, thereby triggering the traffic camera to flash a picture of the vehicle and its false namaste vanity plates. They hit four traffic cameras in all, ultimately circling back such that they passed the residential street where Ivan was parked, all to create a record of the illusion that Ivan had split in a hurry and then mysteriously returned to his location.

And indeed, shortly after Lila had jumped out and tore off their false tags at the close of their loop, when they glanced past the residential street where Ivan had parked his vehicle— and just as "Hey Bulldog" came on Merlin's Beatles mix—there was Ivan, disguised in a dark wig and a fake mustache, standing confounded outside his Range Rover, repeatedly pressing the unlock button on his key fob.

111

CROW AWOKE to find a ring of blackfoot daisies woven about the head of his penis. Not knowing whether to be amused or annoyed at this floral assault upon his manhood, he glanced around for the culprit but could not see Flaming Jane anywhere.

"Wouldn't've been very funny if I'd been stung," Crow grumbled to himself as he tossed the cockwreath aside, standing as he pulled his breeches on. He continued scanning for Flaming Jane as he dressed. Her pack was next to his, and for that matter, all her clothing was neatly folded beneath his. Crow's inevitable conclusion, incredulous though it was, was that Flaming Jane was off on some great and naked romp in the morning, and none too careless a cavort given the gravity of their situation. Crow busied himself securing their provisions, preparing their pistols, and testing his bow. When he was done with these chores, he walked a broad perimeter around the tree but could find neither trace nor trail of Flaming Jane.

Crow considered calling out for her but did not want to draw attention. Instead, he slung their provisions on his back and began climbing the banyan. The only safe course of action, he reasoned, was to try to spot her from high in the tree. He secured their provisions near the top of the banyan, assembled his spyglass (relieved that it had survived yesterday's tumbles), and continued climbing up the giant apple tree. He stopped when he was about ten feet above the banyan and scanned the meadow. The buffalo were still gathered where they'd rustled to last night after the volley of distant gunfire. Glassing the opposite end of the meadow, the open end from whence the gunshots had rung last evening, Crow's heart sank. There, not more than two miles distant, a company of British soldiers had formed a phalanx and were advancing across the meadow.

112

AGITATED, Crow descended the giant apple tree until he was hidden by the surrounding banyan and continued glassing the approaching phalanx. They looked haggard, at least, exhausted in their step, and whatever path had led them here had not been easy on their numbers. Nonetheless, they would be upon him in less than half an hour, and trapping himself in the tree seemed insensible. But what of Flaming Jane, naked and defenseless? A morning such as this and she greets it weaving daisy cockwreaths and rollicking across the meadow?

Not knowing what else to do, Crow made certain their provisions were well hidden high in the banyan and made his way down, staying on the far side of the tree to avoid being seen. He had skittered about a hundred paces away from the tree, staying low amidst the grasses and wildflowers, when he heard Flaming Jane whooping from afar. Dumbstruck, Crow stood and watched her sprinting toward him as naked as the air is free, mane untamed and exhilarating behind her as a ferocious grin drenched the distance between them. Crow attempted to gesture her caution and shush, but her shining eyes and her cheering exaltation made it clear he might sooner have calmed a charging tiger.

"Come on, come on, come on!" she exuberated as she approached, showing no sign of slowing down. "Back to the tree! Back to the tree!" Crow could do little more than astound at the lithe vision tearing barefoot toward him, befuddled by her bare-naked directions. But considering that she had about a thousand times more enthusiasm than he, there was little else to do but follow.

Finally catching up to her back at the tree, Crow explained breathless about the phalanx of soldiers approaching, who surely had heard if not seen her commotion, and that the tree would trap them for certain. Flaming Jane listened politely before scampering up the tree.

"Come on, come on!" Flaming Jane urged, glee-stricken. "Trust me!"

Crow resisted the consternation rising within himself. By his reckoning, they had about twenty minutes of life before them regardless, but he wasn't about to blow it on a bicker. And in any event, history had shown that there was no swerving Flaming Jane once a notion possessed her, so why not enjoy it from on high, maybe snipe as many soldiers as they could? Unable to resist sneaking a peak at Flaming Jane's undercarriage as she climbed above, Crow grinned and hefted himself into the tree. Life had been good—it usually is to those who dare—and he was ready for what may.

Flaming Jane and Crow finally embraced in the small enclosure near the top of the banyan where he'd secured their provisions. Their kiss was wet and wild and surely would have proceeded through a thoroughgoing treetop tryst if not for the press of the situation upon them. As it was, Flaming Jane pulled on her clothes while Crow glassed the soldier's approach.

"They know we're here," he reported, extrapolating from one of the soldiers pointing.

"Good." Flaming Jane grinned.

Crow looked toward her. "What exactly are we doing?"

"Giving up," Flaming Jane replied.

Crow blinked. "Uh, no we're not, lovemuff. I wager we can pick off at least ten of them from here."

"And that leaves, what, another forty?" Flaming Jane shook her head.

"So what's your plan?" Crow demanded.

Flaming Jane sighed. "Listen, we knew we were going to die someday, right? So why not today, together, the day after the single finest day of our lives? *We won.* We found the Stone of the Philosophers, and all we have to do to prevent Goldtooth from ever obtaining it is tear that apple open!" She gestured toward the sun. "He can suck on the core for the rest of his vulgar life, but he'll *never* have the Stone."

"That's it?" Crow was incredulous. "That's your plan? Then why the hell were you off racing around stark raving naked?"

"Because I've always wanted to run naked through a field of wildflowers," Flaming Jane smiled. "And now I have."

113

CROW WAS HAPPY that Flaming Jane had had her way with the wildflowers, and he told her so, but he also told her there was no way Goldtooth would survive him.

"I would never deny us that satisfaction, of course," Flaming Jane replied. "I just wish us to greet our death grinning, to die as we have lived."

"Yes, well," Crow chuckled as he handed her a pair of pistols. "There's never been any question as to that. Death has always been the exclamation mark to this sentence, baby!"

Flaming Jane leaned in and kissed him long against these words. "I adore you," she whispered.

"I adore you more," Crow responded, holding her gaze an eternal minute that ceased only when they noticed the sun had begun to shade into its eclipse. Marveling at the eerie light composed of a dusk with short shadows, Crow picked up his cavaquinho and, caressing Flaming Jane's misting eyes as an ovation of surrounding leaves applauded the passage of a breeze, he began to strum his requiem:

Fare thee well my lover like
a rainbow into open sky
It shimmers as it fades
It vanishes into the sun
All my love and all my heart
are open for the world to share
Increasing and releasing me

Fare thee well my love, hmmm...
Always shall we meet again
Always shall we meet again
Always shall we meet again
Always shall we meet again

Echoes of the life we've lived
resound around us like a crowd

that cheers us on and on into the sun
Memories are weeping like a
river flowing to the sea
it trickles into tumbles till
we dissolve into the sun

Fare thee well my love, hmmm…
Always shall we meet again
Always shall we meet again
Always shall we meet again
Always shall we meet again

Visions of your aching beauty
blossom like a butterfly
daring and preparing me
Miracle that moves my breath
must kiss you deep with gratitude
and hold you as we sail away into the sun

Fare thee well my love, hmmm…
Always shall we meet again
Always shall we meet again
Always shall we meet again
Always shall we meet again
Fare thee well my love
Fare thee well my love—

A gunshot interrupted his croon as a lead ball tore through the nearby branches of the banyan. Crow gently wrapped his cavaquinho, secured it on his back, and picked up his bow. "All right then." He smiled genuine and took aim. He paused as he turned to Flaming Jane. "I'll wager you my fortune I can pick off more of these grunts than you."

"That's a bet you're bound to lose," Flaming Jane assured him.

Grinning, Crow turned back to his aim and let his arrows fly. Having hung his quiver within easy reach, Crow felled seven soldiers before he had to take cover under a hail of arrows and gunfire. He had three arrows left. "That's seven," he thrilled. "Best shots of my life, right there."

"Impressive, for certain," Flaming Jane assented. Then, cupping her hands around her mouth, Flaming Jane hollered, "Hey, Goldtooth! Welcome to your death, you lipless twit! You have five minutes to surrender before we finish off the lot of you!"

Goldtooth guffawed, less than a hundred feet away. "Yar-har! It's ye 'oo dies today, Jane!" At that, two dozen soldiers rushed the tree, shields above their heads. Crow and Flaming Jane fired their pistols and managed to fell two of them, but Crow didn't waste any arrows trying to hit them. After some unseen commotion at the base of the banyan, the soldiers retreated to their former position, having left a pile of kerosene and kindling amidst the trunks of the banyan.

"Shit," Crow assessed their situation.

"You've led your men into another trap, you cheerless chump!" Flaming Jane hollered nonetheless.

Crow appreciated her bluff and expanded upon it. "Who do you think set every trap on the trail of bones that led you here?!" he bellowed in turn, buttressing their bluff before picking off two more soldiers with a single arrow. Crow had guessed correctly that the angel's inviting path had been riddled with traps, so why not take the credit for it? It was effective, as Goldtooth did not respond, and the soldiers were visibly unsettled. Crow laid his bow aside, having only two arrows remaining, and retrieved his cavaquinho, filling the air with a wild-begotten shoutsong:

Dear god! Here we go again!
Façade, act without a brain!
What kind of stupid seeks to
lead a line of fools?
You think you own us
but you only own your rules!

Dimwit, common dumb and dull!
Unfit, worthless in your skull!
Your brand of being
only fills this life with death!
Make haste and hurry
and please draw your final breath!

All the world can see!
All the world can see!
All the world can see!
All your failures all the world can see!

Your soul, flaunts upon your face!
Asshole, of the human race!
What kind of loser
chases wealth his whole life long?
You think you're Master
but you haven't heard the song!

All the world can see!
All the world can see!
All the world can see!
All your failures all the world can see!

And thereupon Crow and Flaming Jane fell into gales of wild-seasoned laughter, cackling howls and taunting catcalls while Crow continued to beat out a rhythm on the back of his cavaquinho, periodically bellowing *Heyyyyy Goldtooth!* while Flaming Jane punctuated his jeer with a maenadic hilarity that caused most of the soldiers to marvel at their freedom even as they prepared to murder it.

"You've already lost the treasure of all treasures!" Flaming Jane shouted after their dithyramb had at last exhausted itself in a long-winded howl near the totality of the eclipse. "Beware the meadow of marvels, Goldtooth! You have two minutes to surrender!"

"It's ye 'oo has two 'inutes to sarrendar, Jane!"

"Ninety seconds!" Flaming Jane pressed her bluff, impressing even Crow. "And my name is *Flaming* Jane!"

"Aye, 'tis!" Goldtooth guffawed. "And ye'll earn it today!" At that, a half-dozen archers lit their arrows and took aim at the kerosene and kindling at the base of the tree. "Sixty seconds, Jane!"

Crow took one of the archers out, but saved his last arrow for Goldtooth. Glancing toward Flaming Jane, he was surprised to see her grinning as if she believed her own bluff.

"This is gonna be close," she muttered, shaking her head as she reached into her pack and retrieved the giant apple. Unwrapping it from its kerchief, she offered it to Crow. "Hungry?"

Crow was flabbergasted. "Uh, what about all that talk of surrender, and dying today?"

Flaming Jane waved him off. "Clearly I was drunk off the dew of wildflowers when I said *that*."

"Last chance, Jane!" Goldtooth roared. "Sarrendar!"

Flaming Jane looked at Crow. "Listen, there's no way we're dying today, not like this, not by his hands, and we're sure as hell never surrendering to that bastard."

"So we eat the fruit under the light of the eclipse and live forever?"

Flaming Jane shrugged and sniffed the apple. "We are godless pirates, after all, and it smells simply luscious."

Crow sampled its aroma as well, agreeing. "It *is* the case that we haven't had a proper breakfast this morning."

"Shall we, then?" Flaming Jane lifted the fruit between them and drew her face near.

"'Ire!" Goldtooth roared as the archers fired their flaming arrows and the base of the banyan crackled into a snarl of flames.

Crow licked his lips and drew his face nearer. "We can hardly abide this torment of curiosity, can we?"

"Not for another moment," Flaming Jane agreed and they simultaneously bit into the apple.

114

FLAMING JANE was certain no tongue had ever tasted such glory as shuddered through her body when the apple touched her lips.

"Oh my god," Crow gushed, humbled by unspeakable flavors as its ambrosial nectar dribbled off his chin. "Today have I tasted, and all songs fall silent with awe."

Flaming Jane licked her lips and laughed, squinting her eyes from the smoke and shielding her face from the heat. "I wonder how long it takes to live forever?"

"I don't feel any different," Crow replied, coughing on the smoke as he wrapped the twice-bitten apple and placed it back in the pack. "And forever or not, we need to get out of this tree."

"Wait!" Flaming Jane insisted, scanning across the meadow. "Something's about to happen!" A moment later, an explosion detonated in the distance, its echoes swallowed by the thunder of a thousand tons of buffalo stampeding toward them. Crow swiveled his head toward Flaming Jane and found her grinning unstoppable. "I set a cigarro fuse on the cask of gunpowder we found to trigger a stampede." She coughed, waving smoke away from her face. "I told you that was a bet you were bound to lose."

Crow amazed as Goldtooth and his soldiers alarmed and scrambled retreat from the onrushing stampede. As it drew near, a cacophony of cowbells clanged ever more clear like wind chimes under thunderstorm, but there was ultimately nothing the soldiers could do but fire their pistols pointless and panic. The onslaught of buffalo quaked the very tree as it roared past, charging into over and across the soldiers with neither hesitation nor regret, crushing ripsnorting and trampling upon them like so many blades of grass, and when it had passed neither Goldtooth nor a single soldier was left standing, and when the herd at last becalmed and its beasts had returned to their peaceful ruminations, no buffalo contemplated the meaning of what had just occurred.

115

A s for Crow and Flaming Jane, moments after witnessing the collapse of Goldtooth's line under the unforgiving hooves of the buffalo, choking smoke overtook them. Blinded and unable to breathe, their options became quickly desperate. They hurled their packs out of the small enclosure near the top of the banyan, some forty feet up, and then, unable to descend into the searing heat and facing imminent immolation, Crow and Flaming Jane wrapped their limbs around one another and pressed their faces into one another's, whispering love and sobbing apology as a godsent hush of rain soothed their sorrow, hissing as it kissed the inferno, taming the flames as it quickly rolled into a drenching downpour, whereupon Crow and Flaming Jane managed to slip and blunder their way out of the tree and tumble unconscious upon the blessed ground.

116

Ivan heard the fleeing stampede of his former flock, roaring like the rage against the dying of the light, ferocity swelling the atmosphere like an unchained revolution. Neck hairs bristled instinctive as Ivan fumbled his fob cursing the flaunt of his Range Rover and the infallible security of its keyless entry and ignition systems. The LED on the fob lit up every time he pressed the unlock button, battery's obviously fine, so what's happening?

And the first wave of saffron footfalls greeted the pavement of his street, undomesticated survival compelling their maniacal advance, and Ivan scrambled to take cover from the onslaught of jihadi madness bearing down upon him. None would recognize him, that was certain, if they would even see him, for not only had he ascended into the higher realms as far as they knew, but the sun was dark and he was clad entirely in black and a dark wig and a seventies porno mustache besides, and ultimately presented nothing more substantial than a stammering obstacle for those whose fight or flight was coursing full-blast adrenal madness.

And Ivan tried to run in Pamplona bravado before stumbling hapless beneath the hooves of flailing feet hailing heedless upon him and as his face found the asphalt his head ground itself upon his teeth, fingers were broken, ribs were cracked, and his ass was thoroughly kicked. Pummeled and bruising the stampede passed and his body at last relaxed punch-drunken and peaceful upon the pavement. I just need a little rest, that's all, Ivan thought to himself. Yes, right here is perfect, this wonderful street, ah, this nurturing pavement, so comfortable, like falling asleep in the snow.

And drooling awake, the sun blasting high afternoon with squelching radios and inconsiderate strobes and muffling shadows prodding him rolling him onto a stretcher, and Ivan felt the cold kiss of steel upon his wrist, smacking its lips with a clink.

117

IVAN WAS MERELY being detained for questioning at this point. The police assumed he was one of those crazed solar eclipse cultists who'd fallen under the feet of his fellow faithful, and despite his injuries, he was at least guilty of failure to comply, disturbing the peace, rioting, and of course they'd put the heat on him to point to the perps of the armored truck robbery.

Coming around, Ivan began to fathom the basic outlines of his circumstance, and when asked by one of the paramedics if he was one of the solar eclipse cultists he immediately denied it, saying he knew nothing about those lunatics, look at how he's dressed ferchrissakes (Ivan was unaware that his wig was off-kilter and his mustache had been torn halfway off, now dangling off his cheek like a pupating caterpillar…), and besides, he was only in the street at all because that's his car right there, that

Range Rover right there, and the goddamned keyless entry was jammed, but it was only when he tried to gesture toward his car that he noticed his right hand was handcuffed to the gurney.

"What the hell is this?" Ivan demanded, assuming some sort of authority now that he had demonstrated ownership of his $100,000 statusmobile.

"Take it easy," the paramedic responded, who was in fact not a paramedic at all but a police lieutenant in charge of the investigation into the armored truck robbery. His name was Lieutenant Down, and Lieutenant Down had arrived on the scene while Ivan was still punch-drunk, pushed aside the outranked detectives already on the scene, grabbed a paramedic's uniform, and made sure Ivan was read his Miranda warning before he was fully coherent. High-profile armored truck robberies like this don't come in often, see, and Lieutenant Down wanted to crack this case quick and grab a promotion to captain. Too many perps these days had gotten wise to the gotcha games cops play and were actually remaining silent, but suspects will spill all to their caregivers, especially if they don't fully understand that they're suspects. So he just reassured him. "You'll be all right." Lieutenant Down laid his palm gently upon Ivan's shoulder. "You were pretty wild when you came to is all, not surprising given what you've been through. That's just for your safety. That car right there?"

"Yes," Ivan insisted. "I drive a Range Rover."

"That's a *hell* of a nice automobile," Lieutenant Down flattered, gesturing for a couple of police officers to have a look at it. "Namaste," he pronounced the vanity plate. "You do yoga or something?"

"I do," Ivan assented. "Ashtanga."

"Me too," Lieutenant Down nodded, lying. "Me too."

Anything to keep him talking. "So what's the story with that pendant you're wearing?"

"This?" Ivan touched his alleged Philosopher's Stone amulet with his left hand, the dollop of amber with a mosquito inside that he'd long ago shoplifted while backpacking across Europe. "It's fossilized amber, with a mosquito inside. Supposedly it was found in an anthropological dig outside Hamelin, Germany. That's where I bought it."

"No shit you say?" Lieutenant Down peered at the amulet, curious. "Hamelin, like from that Pied Piper legend?"

Ivan shook his head, wincing. "I don't know anything about any Pied Piper."

Lieutenant Down fell silent for a few moments, coveting Ivan's amber amulet. He decided to change the subject back to the Range Rover. "Man, that's one *hell* of a nice automobile."

"It handles extremely well," Ivan sighed. "A hundred miles an hour feels like forty."

"Ain't that right?" Lieutenant Down nodded. "So do you remember anything else about what happened?"

"Not really." Ivan shook his head and continued to make a show of wincing, never hurts to ploy for sympathy. "I guess I must have blacked out."

"Take it easy, bro, we'll be on our way soon. Just hang on a sec." Lieutenant Down stepped away to confer with the police officers who'd inspected the vehicle. The homing beacon hidden within the satchels of cash from the armored truck pointed to the Range Rover, and despite the privacy glass, the police officers had spotted the satchels from the armored truck in the rear seat, along with the several bundles of hundreds Lila had spilled out. They handed him the fob they'd found on the pavement. Lieutenant Down had a look for himself, tested the remote, and grinned. Trotting back to the gurney, he complimented

Ivan again on the automobile. "One *hell* of a nice automobile," he said. "What a bummer the keyless entry failed, eh?"

"A hundred grand ought to buy a reliable set of keys." Ivan winced again, drawing a dramatically sharp breath. "Know what I mean?"

"Yeah," Lieutenant Down chortled affable, "you'd think. Anyway, we found this for you." He closed Ivan's hand around the fob, just to make sure his prints were solidly on them. He wanted his promotion, and he wanted this case ironclad. "You're right, though, damned thing doesn't work. Go ahead and try it."

Ivan complied, sighing impatiently at its uselessness. "Well, thanks for finding it anyway."

"No sweat, bro, let's get you to the hospital." And another paramedic prepared to push the gurney into the back of the ambulance, just as Lieutenant Down played his Columbo card. "Oh, just one more thing." He again laid his hand on Ivan's shoulder. "Look over there." And he pointed to Ivan's jet-black metallic Range Rover with privacy glass, where two police officers were suddenly brutally prying open the rear cargo door with two gigantic crowbars, doing their duty best to scrape, dent, and just generally bang the hell out of the finish in the process. Lieutenant Down then yanked the amber amulet off Ivan's neck with one hand and plucked the remains of the seventies porno mustache dangling off Ivan's what-the-fuck face with the other. Pocketing the amulet, Lieutenant Down held the mustache up for their mutual examination, grimacing as if it smelled of smegma. "You're under arrest for robbery," Lieutenant Down declared, then tossed the mustache disgusted back in his face. "And nice 'stache, you goddamned lunatic."

118

T HE EVIDENCE against Ivan was overwhelming. It probably would have been sufficient for the loot along with its homing beacon to have been in his car, which he was intending to enter wearing a disguise, but there was also a paintball gun and a sack of groceries that matched every item on a grocery store receipt that had been found in the alley down which the perpetrators had reportedly fled. Moreover, the torn corner of saffron robe that the armored truck guard had recovered from the doorjamb matched exactly a saffron robe with a torn corner that had been recovered from the back seat. And finally, if all this were not more than enough, traffic violation cameras clearly showed his jet-black metallic Range Rover with privacy glass and its unmistakable NAMASTE license plate blowing through several red lights just shortly after the robbery took place.

News media fell all over themselves with competing headlines about the armored truck robbery and the solar eclipse cult riot, but as the authorities were not making public the identity of any suspects or the connection between the two events so long as their investigation was ongoing, the Holy Company of Beautiful People remained dazzled by the delusion that the Master had dematerialized, gathering furtively in their homes to recount their harrowing ordeals and narrow escapes from the law, and also to marvel at how minty fresh they all felt. Chris Bliss did his best to manage the tensions within their group with flaccid platitudes, but was in general finding enlightenment to be incredibly stressful.

Fortunately or not, after ten days of desperately trying to

be enlightened, Chris Bliss was reprieved of this role. It happened when the news reported on the arraignment hearing for the prime suspect in the armored truck robbery, and all of a sudden there was Ivan being hustled undignified in an orange jumpsuit on the television screen, managing only to blurt into a microphone some reporter had poked into his throat, "My toilet,"— which was odd for more than the obvious absurdity, as Chris Bliss had noticed that the toilet was indeed missing from the corporeal sanctum he had inherited from Ivan. But Chris Bliss, blinking hapless at the TV screen, simply could not comprehend what he was seeing as his attendants looked anxiously to their new Master for some reassurance, some explanation of what was happening. Chris Bliss had no concept behind which to hide from the black hole that had suddenly opened in his gut, a wormhole of anxiety threatening to swallow everything he thought he knew about life and his role within it. Obviously, this had to be some kind of a ruse, yes. Though he knew Lila to have been poisoned and probably dead—having seen the ambulance take her away himself—it appeared as if the Holy Company of Beautiful People remained under attack by some kind of powerful dark energy. The Master had a doppelgänger, yes, a demon determined to discredit his heroic life and miraculous ascension. Yes, that must be it.

The next morning an attorney from the Holy Company of Beautiful People visited Ivan in the jail. He reported back that Ivan—inasmuch as he remained—had been exasperated at the Holy Company of Beautiful People's ignorance. Ivan insisted that there was no disappointment to bear, that the highest parts of the Master had indeed ascended, although due to interference from the state he had inadvertently left his bodily space suit behind. The person on the television, the attorney reported, and whom he had spoken with was but a physical echo of the ascended Master, you see. And anyway, the space suit formerly known as Ivan went on, *obviously* an ascended Master can exist in more than one dimension at a time. The Holy Company of Beautiful People was to tend to the Master's abandoned space suit, see to it that it remained comfortable, as it could still function as a medium through which the Master would occasionally communicate with them.

But what of Chris Bliss, their new Master? The space suit formerly known as Ivan shook his head no. Chris Bliss was a fraud, he said, a venom of dark energy liable to spread lies about him, and neither Chris Bliss nor any of his inner circle could argue with this, as they had all been taken in for questioning just minutes after the television broadcast, Chris Bliss literally caught with his pants down, evacuating all twenty-six feet of his hyper-anxious colon into the new toilet he'd just had installed in the corporeal sanctum he had inherited from Ivan.

As it had happened, once the authorities had shown the space suit formerly known as Ivan the security video of him apparently strong-arming some innocent woman into robbing the very same bank for him, the space suit formerly known as Ivan sang the names of everyone in his inner circle in a desperate attempt to take the heat off himself. And who was that woman? they demanded, but the space suit formerly known as Ivan only insisted he had no idea, lest he be implicated in her poisoning as well.

As news of these arrests spread, paranoia infected the ranks of the Holy Company of Beautiful People. Journalists continued to develop the story, allegations of drug use surfaced, stories of sexual abuse, something about magnesium flares masking a dramatic getaway. And as Ivan Humble's bullshit continued burbling out of the sewers of his teetering metropolis of deceit, it overwhelmed the dikes of his disciples one by one, the

mounds of lies upon which they had built their spiritual salvation dissolving beneath their feet as the narcissism they so cher-
ished, the *folie à plusieurs* belief that they were a chosen people,
yes a holy company of beautiful people, failed to float them
whatsoever as a rising tide of truth drowned their egos thrash-
ing in the throes of identity crises that would last for years. Like
rats washed from the sewers they frantically clawed their way
into various rebound fanaticisms, another group, another poli-
tic, another career, another ideology, desperate for anyone to
tell them who they were and what was happening, but always
left shivering, vulnerable like a bum in the winter, alone, yes,
abandoned and alone.

Lost in the wilds of life and sadness alas, yet out of this suffering was born an epiphany, for some, an epiphany decades
in its discovery, the despondent understanding that they were
alone, yes, abandoned and alone, and the heartrending realization that they were nobody special after all, that they were just
like everybody else, that they were just another lost soul feeling
its way through life, and that although everybody dies alone,
that not everybody dies lonely, and there is thereby no greater
service than to comfort another soul, to make another life easier, to soothe another solitude, to serve another oneself, and to
love as large as life allows, and even more.

And though there were some two hundred further fictions
that unfurled from that day, white-knuckle stories of life against
death, of heroes ascending and cowards descending, of families
born, and sometimes torn, stories of sacrifice and success every
bit as gripping as your own life, there is one postscript that
merits special attention here: It was Dalai, struggling against
a disillusionment she had long suspected on top of struggling
against a metastasized breast cancer, Dalai was a month later
confused to learn that her cancer was gone. Not in remission,

her mystified oncologists had emphasized, but *gone*, as if it had never been there at all. And though Dalai had long ago guessed Ivan's chicanery more than most anyone aside from Lila, Dalai was nonetheless left wondering at her own miraculous recovery and the day that presumably occasioned it for the rest of her natural life. Ivan Humble was a fraud, of that there could be no doubt, and yet somehow, burning through his black and heavy veil of deception, something magical had still happened, and for Dalai, at least, there would always breathe the hope that a miracle would one day shine its truth through the lies that shroud humanity.

119

DAWNSHINE DAPPLED through the tittering leaves of the tree, cavorting across the blackened faces of Flaming Jane and Crow like the devil incognito.

"I say," commenced the serpent, dangling nearly its full length from a branch high above them as it chattered directly in their sleeping faces, "I pray I do not offend thy slumber, but I wish to offer you my commendations on yesterday's battle. Certainly, we must contend with a gag of maggots as the meadow reclaims what remains, but what is this Garden if not a stomping ground for your petty human dramas?"

Crow croaked awake only to discover a thirst so great it rendered him unable to speak or even to fully open his eyes. He tried rubbing his eyes but succeeded only in getting soot in them, at which point he staggered standing and stumbled squinting toward their packs to retrieve some water.

"Ah yes, of course you must slake your thirst at the very outset." The serpent followed along, gracing itself through the branches of the banyan. "Pardon me for this presumption upon your attention whilst you suffer such desiccation. I may just as well belch in your face, isn't that quite right? Ah, but listen to me now! My tongue grows vulgar, and can hardly speak without a rape upon your virgin ears. And yikes again! It appears I can do little more than pile profanities upon you. However did I grow so uncouth? A gentleman no more am I, of this much at least I can be certain."

Having hydrated himself, Crow ignored the serpent as he gently roused Flaming Jane and offered her water, which she immediately and gratefully accepted.

"Hydration is essential, of course," the serpent prattled on. "Nothing holier than water, you may say, unless of course it drowns you, in which case it's downright damnable—"

"Quiet!" Crow barked at the serpent.

The serpent swiveled its head toward Crow, looking him up and down. "Heavens to hellfire," it shook its head. "Perhaps I can forgive your grump under the oaf of my churl, but what am I to make of your snarl and snap froth?"

"What's your game, serpent?" Crow demanded, standing as he spoke.

The serpent writhed itself higher in the tree before responding. "I have a name, you know, though perhaps I am at fault for my presumption to speak without the pleasantries of introduction in the first place."

"We know your name, serpent." Flaming Jane sat up.

"Ah, good, my hopes are not in vain," the serpent replied. "So tell me, what's my name?"

"Perhaps we prefer not to speak it," Crow spoke up.

"A senseless superstition," the serpent clicked its tongue. "But I wonder if you know that the name you so rudely—and incorrectly, I may add—presume to project upon me means 'bearer of light,' hmm?"

Crow and Flaming Jane looked at one another, then Flaming Jane responded, "You never answered his question, serpent."

"Can it be true?" The serpent gasped aghast. "Am I truly

so uncouth as to ignore a proper inquiry? Pray forgive me, and remind me what query I inadvertently disdain?"

"What is your game?" Flaming Jane pronounced as she did her best to wash the soot off her face.

"Ah, right-right-right," the serpent nodded. "So that's what puzzles you. 'Tis a fair befuddle, to be certain. You now know the taste of the apple, I presume?"

"You know we tasted the apple," Flaming Jane responded tart. "And you also know nothing happened."

The serpent scratched the skin beneath its mouth with the tip of its tail. "Again I forgive your sass and indignation, if only for the cranky awakening for which I am partly to blame. But tell me, what under heaven makes you say such a thing?"

"We were nearly burned alive yesterday!" Crow hollered.

The serpent nodded. "How nearly horrific."

"You said if we ate the fruit we would live forever," Flaming Jane insisted. "You lied to us, even after insisting that it was not in your nature to lie!"

"Ah," the serpent sighed. "This is terribly awkward, I'm afraid. Let us leave aside the rainstorm of your salvation— although, to be perfectly honest, such rainstorms care little for your salvation and everything for the tree's—but let us leave aside that rainstorm in any event, dear ones, for when I say that you live forever, I never intend to imply that you never die."

"Ah, now there's a treacherous turn of phrase," Crow assessed.

"Indeed," Flaming Jane agreed.

The serpent straightened itself and cleared its throat. "I prefer to believe that there is neither parallel nor peer to my powers of articulation, but it now appears that I am the voice box of utter confusion. But if you permit me to clarify my geometry, dear ones, forever does not move in only one direction, which is to say, one cannot simply *begin* to live forever. On the contrary, to live forever requires you to realize that you *always* live forever." At that, the serpent began sucking pensively on its own tail as if it were a pipe stem.

"What of death, then?" Flaming Jane asked. "You mince your meanings, serpent."

"Not a bit of it." The serpent ceased its sucking and shook its head. "Death is your renewal, and once you realize this, you live forever, as God."

"You speak grammatically correct nonsense," Flaming Jane charged, but the serpent did not seem concerned, instead wrapping itself helical about the base of the banyan.

"Life is a dramatic loop through a garden of nothingness," the serpent responded, once it had completed its sixth circumference.

"And what does that mean?"

Completing its seventh circumference, the serpent yawned and answered, "Probably nothing," just before taking its tail into its mouth and swallowing itself entirely until it had vanished into the gleam of a sunbeam upon the tree.

120

A BELLIGERENT WAKE OF buzzards feasted upon the carrion remains of Goldtooth and his soldiers, bickering bloodthirsty among themselves despite the prosperity of corpses, and periodically puking before returning to their gorge and frenzy.

"Let's get out of here," Crow disgusted after he'd recovered his remaining arrows and they'd regarded the carnage for several moments in silence.

"Yes, let's," Flaming Jane immediately agreed, shaking her

head as if from a trance and hefting her pack. "It's disturbing, isn't it, how a demon like Goldtooth inspires the demon in others?"

Crow nodded grim. "A rotten apple ruins its neighbors," he responded, quoting Chaucer.

Flaming Jane sighed. "All this warfare, these battles, all this death," she continued. "It moves of its own momentum, doesn't it? And it's not until it's all over that you can even begin to feel the weight of the sins you've committed."

"Sins?" Crow frowned. "My entire life has been set upon by a swarm of ogres seeking to enslave me. I've thrown at them anything sharp enough to fend them off, and if I've sinned it was only to meet my mornings free."

"I understand that, of course," Flaming Jane agreed, tears weeping clean down her cheeks. "But it all seems to fracture from a single disturbance somewhere, doesn't it? Some ancient trauma reverberating throughout the lives of history, and for which our cannons offer but the faintest of echoes." She paused despondent. "Evil is infectious."

Crow spat. "I have seen a thousand styles of cruelty in this world, but none more sadistic than Goldtooth's. The wicked locate their self in this world, and the righteous locate their self in their spirit, and I'll remind your righteous spirit that he tried to burn us alive yesterday. Victory may feel like despair to a sensitive soul, but if there's no flavor to savor in vengeance here, that only means he didn't succeed in corrupting us."

Flaming Jane nodded, appreciating his words. "Do you suppose we should forgive him?"

Crow snorted. "Of course we should forgive the miserable canker blossom, now that we've released his soul from the trials of life. What else are we going to do, haul his horseshit around with us for the rest of our days? Forgive and forget, as far as that goes. If evil is infectious, then there's your cure right there. Shake it off like a dog after a fight, and get right back to wagging your tail."

Flaming Jane fell silent at this. After a minute, she sighed. "Even Goldtooth was an infant once." She sighed again and cooed, "Poor Goldtooth."

Crow frowned. "Goddamned right, poor Goldtooth."

"Ah, my Crow," Flaming Jane smirked. "How about you get right back to wagging *your* tail?"

Crow took her hand. "I'll wag *your* tail," he assured as they ambled away from the battlefield, periodically pausing to fondle and kiss, trading smart remarks as their fingertips traced across the tips of wildflower petals, here pointing out minutiae, there gesturing vast, incautious grins pooling across their faces and undomesticated laughter pelting across the heavens as Flaming Jane and Crow reveled their way toward their rendezvous with their crew, their friends, and their family aboard *Eleusis*.

121

"SO THAT'S IT, then?" Merlin sighed, clicking off the TV at the vacation rental where they'd been lying low, once the local news had exhausted its voyeuristic lens a couple of weeks after the heist and returned to its typical taunts of terror and looming pestilence.

"You sound disappointed," Lila observed, scratching Dogface behind her ears as she stood before her wagging her tail. "That was some good television. I mean, the solar eclipse riot? We didn't even *plan* that part."

Merlin shrugged, picking up a ukulele he'd recently purchased at a thrift store and plucking idly at it, tuning it here and there. "A little heartsore, I guess. Do you know what I mean?"

Lila nodded. "Like we're supposed to be clinking smug champagne and dancing on the bad guy's grave, but now that it's all over, I'd really rather that we never had to go to war in the first place?"

"Exactly," Merlin nodded, his ukulele punctuating his words. "War exerts a heavy toll upon the soul."

"Yeah," Lila agreed, and they fell into silent contemplation as Dogface's tail ceased its motion. After a minute, Lila touched the back of Merlin's hand. "You know how the villains of this world win, how they destroy the rest of us?"

"How's that?" Merlin asked, a solitary, abandoned plink mourning upon his ukulele.

"By hurting us. When they hurt us, they trick us into closing our hearts, because once our hearts are closed, life loses all its magic and we become just like them, imprisoned in the solitude of ego, and life is no longer about love, but about getting safe."

Merlin nodded, his ukulele found a few more notes, and Dogface resumed wagging her tail.

"But look at what happens with an open heart!" Lila gestured toward the other room. "We have a golden toilet!"

Merlin chuckled and his ukulele started to find its groove. "A four-million-dollar golden toilet, depending on the raw weight of the gold." He shook his head. "Unreal."

"Unreal? There's a lot more happening in reality than we are led to believe, Merlin. Luck is a force in this universe."

"Is that so?"

"Yes it is, and especially when you're acting from a place of courage, which by the way derives from the Latin *cor*, for heart. God enjoys a good story as much as anyone, and we are nowhere if not within the story of God."

Merlin smirked at her woowoo philosophies and paused his ukulele. "Still, it's kind of hard to wrap my mind around the fact that we're suddenly millionaires. I mean, what are we supposed to do now?"

"Oh, that's easy." Lila grinned. "We'll buy a big house and a couple of luxury SUVs and build us a fence around our lot as tall as local ordinances permit and barely recognize our own neighbors as we isolate ourselves into our own private retreat from the hostilities of the world at large. We'll set up an investment account that will allow us to live comfortably off the considerable interest for the rest of our pampered lives, we'll only associate with others from a place of implicit self-interest, we'll chase away our lonely boredom with garish Caribbean cruises and by jet-setting away to tropical resorts—always first-class and five-star, mind you—and in general, we'll poo upon the little people and ignore the hideous contradictions of the social order as we take care of and protect only ourselves."

Merlin frowned, his ukulele as silent as the death of all music.

"Möbius!" Lila slapped him on the knee with a wild cackle. "I'm just fuckin' with ya!"

"Jeezus." Merlin laughed, relieved as his ukulele resumed its breath. "That sounded awful."

"Can you imagine?" Lila shook her head. "Seriously, though, I figure we'll lie low for a spell up north here in Nevada City, you can practice your lovely ukulele, we can plot our next prank, and we can advance the greater human project in our own small way. Like I said, Ivan was just the beginning, and the edifice of ego that this civilization has built itself upon seems intent upon suffocating every last gasp of free spirit from the face of this planet. We're going to have to help get people's hearts out of that nightmare. Who would want to live in a world where you can't open your heart?"

Merlin grinned, laid his ukulele aside, and leaned forward. "Will you marry me?"

Lila smiled at him and replied, unhesitant, "Yes and nectar."

And they met in a long and languorous kiss, and upon its resolution Merlin leaned back, retrieved his ukulele, and grew a gigantic smile. "I was hoping you would say that."

Lila grew a gigantic smile right back at him. "God, I love you."

"I love you more, Goddess."

"Now there's a prank to plot, isn't it?" Lila Louise enthused. "Love is a prank the spirit plays on the ego to teach it the one lesson it tries not to learn, remember that? What greater prank than love?"

Merlin Otherwise only nodded you betcha as he strummed

his ukulele until the chords found their rhythm and he began
to sing the song that sealed their souls forever entwined:

Tempt me with your outlaw apple
with eyes that flash so wild
Answer me it's oh so good
with lips that dare and smile

> *as we lick yes,*
> *and nectar!*

Cast this day into the night
the wind it shivers cold
Cuddle with me closer trust
our spirit soars so bold

> *as we whisper yes,*
> *and nectar!*

Fend with me the taunt of dark
our fear will find repose
Dream with me discover light
the shining smile that knows

> *as we murmur yes,*
> *and nectar!*

Blinking into mourning sad
at life's forgotten hymn
Must we surely die my love
and fade into the dim

> *as we cry yes,*
> *and nectar!*

Find with me the love that's lost
the song that's long unsung
Sing with me abandoned words
unleashed upon our tongue

> *as we shout yes,*
> *and nectar!*

Kiss me by the candlelight
oh kiss me by the sun
Dance with me like hurricanes
and spin our souls undone

> *as we roar yes,*
> *and nectar!*

This was all Merlin Otherwise had written of his song, but after strumming through the chord progression once more, he began again adagio and crooned a spontaneous epilogue:

Watch me as I live my life
as I shall witness yours
Free our hearts of all our hurt
and open all the doors

> *as we purr yes,*
> *and nectar!*

Epilogue:
In the Beginning

"**H**AVE YOU EVER wondered if you're someone else at the same time, but just don't realize it?" Crow asked Flaming Jane a week later as they strolled hand in hand toward the tree at the center of the meadow of marvels.

"Eh?" Flaming Jane responded as she grinned at their shipmates awaiting the arrival of their nuptials beneath the proscenium branches of the banyan. "What are you saucing on about now?"

"Who knows?" Crow answered. "But life seems a story, doesn't it? And I have heard it said that there are two sides to every story."

"Only two?" Flaming Jane whispered as their fellow Eleusinians encircled them, Moby alighting upon Crow's shoulder.

"Quiet now," Crow whispered back, and they fell silent just in time to be trounced by a hail of whistles and wahoos as their shipmates pelted them with thousands of wildflower petals. Yes, it had been a good week by any reckoning. Crow and Flaming Jane had rendezvoused with their shipmates, hugs and hellos, laughter and glad tidings, able to report not only that they'd salvaged the Stone of the Philosophers and that Goldtooth was dead, but that their elusive retirement from the sweet trade of piracy had finally found them, as the island was abundant, uncharted, uninhabited, absolutely free, and entirely theirs. They'd found a cove in which to shelter *Eleusis*, burned the remains of the Battle of the Buffalo—as it came to be called in their oral history—and planned the wedding that now surrounded them.

At the center of the table set for the afternoon's feast was the grapefruit-sized green apple, now curiously healed with nothing but a couple of flushes of sunrise blush where Crow and Flaming Jane had a week ago bitten into it under the light of the solar eclipse. Retrieving the apple, they held it aloft between them as they spoke their vows in the presence of their tribe: To hold one another to the highest truth, to hold one another to the highest beauty, to hold one another to the highest freedom, but above all else, to simply hold one another safe against the solitude of life. Their vows were short but nonetheless sincere—neither pirate possessed any patience around somber ritual—and when Crow at last announced that he would kiss Flaming Jane now, his grinning bride grabbed the apple and, as if to say not so fast there pussyboy, wedged her teeth into one of the blushes left by the eclipse, displaying the apple buffer and daring him to just try and kiss her *now*, by god. Only momentarily bewildered by this unscripted shenanigan, Crow's eyes kindled at his feral wife as he matched every devil in her grin and without warning lodged his teeth into the other blush on the open end of the apple, growling fierce to make damn sure this untamed pirate understood the truth of their equation. Moby cawed at this development and alit into the branches of the tree as eyes surprised and fast ferocious, Flaming Jane snarled right back, twisting and yanking her head and trying to tear the apple free from Crow's teeth, who managed to match her every gnash and maneuver but found little opportunity to parry as they prowled a circle around one another trading tugs on the apple as their tribe roared a roiling enthusiasm like a misbehavior of angels and out of this rumpus an impulse frothing with the effervescence of all that is sudden found and yes it healed the hearts assembled and Crow understood and surrendering all resistance surprised Flaming Jane with a slack upon his yank just long enough to successfully tear the apple free from her determined teeth, crunching through his end victorious and teasing the apple ha-ha. Gladhearted bellows and bravo huzzah, Flaming Jane chewed her bested bite of apple undaunted as Crow did the same, eyes glaring unswerved by the boister about them, and Crow tossed the apple high and as it spun momentarily eternal at the apex of its ascent, Crow and Flaming Jane at last dared mingle the nectar sweetening their tongues, sealing their union slick across their lips as a sigh of light breathed everlasting, the apple bouncing unregarded off both of their heads and handily caught by Noa like the bridal bouquet that it would turn out to be, who tasted it too and passed it immediately forth, all hearts relishing it in turn till it was consumed to its core and all that was left was the stone, yes, the Stone of the Philosophers, and though words must fluster and forever fail to fathom such a stone, it can at least be said that it was never the stone that could turn any metal into gold, and it was only ever the truth that can turn any lie into light: the truth that our lives are spun from nothing but love

and other pranks.

Postscript

MOBY CAWED and fluttered about from branch to branch of the banyan, avoiding a white serpent coiled among its branches, the gleaming opalescence of its skin camouflaged against the play of sunlight upon the tree, and unregarded by anyone else but Catface, who crept through the branches of the banyan, pawing and batting playfully at the serpent's flicking tail. And though the serpent could have swallowed Catface whole if it had ever cared to, this was not its way, and the serpent's attention was instead consumed by the matrimonial proceedings beneath, and as Crow and Flaming Jane kissed Moby cawed triumphant, and though no one would ever hear the serpent's toast beneath the barrage of their own good cheer—laughing just exactly the way a congregation of pranksters prays—its words would echo nonetheless throughout the hearts of all:

"May you be ever overwhelmed by how many people you love."

Acknowledgments

A ROCKING CHAIR on my front porch beckons silent contemplation. I confess that I enjoy a morning tea from that grandfatherly perch from time to time, and one Sunday morning I turned up the volume on the stereo inside my house so that I might enjoy some music outside on the porch as well. On that particular morning, just as the lyrics of Leonard Cohen's "If It Be Your Will" opened, a breeze awakened the leaves of the sycamore in my front yard. More than that, the breeze seemed to ebb and flow through the leaves as if in response to the music, so much so that by the time Leonard reached the most soulful peak of his prayerful song, it rather felt as if the tree itself were raising up its limbs in a dryadic celebration of all of life. It was marvelous, and I encourage you to try it yourself sometime.

Naturally, it was only my attention that created the apparent synchronicity between the music and the leaves under the breeze, and yet, it is also only our attention that creates any particular aspect of life at all. Attention is the art of directing the mind to a particular object, and attention, my friends, attention is the currency out of which reality is constructed. This is why we say *pay* attention, and this is also why we have multibillion-dollar corporations whose only commodity is our attention.

Given this, I wish to thank my readers for granting their priceless attention to the words I have here woven. Without your attention, this story would have been a tree falling noiselessly in the woods. Without your attention, these characters never would have lived, these ideas never would have been thought, these emotions never would have been felt. With your attention—not just on these words, but on wherever else you choose to focus it in your life—all things become possible. I thank you.

And though the years of writing are solitary, there are numerous friends and collaborators involved in bringing this book—as well as further iterations of my previous books—into existence. Salutes are due to my family, as well as to Todd Albert Jeremy Arthur, Matt Bialer, Trevor Blackann, Holly Bryant-Simpson, Bernard Setaro Clark, Greg Cooler, Owen Egerton, Pilar Garcia-Brown, Jon Gonzales, Casey Holloway, Chris Johnston, Jenna Johnson, Kristin Kalbli, Diane Lasek, Michael Lindner, Dave McCully, David Mizne, Tom Robbins, Dan Seidel, and anyone else whose name I have inadvertently left off this list. I am honored by your assistance and encouragement.

Finally, years ago, in a correspondence with another novelist, he noted how throughout his life he had known individuals whom he privately considered to be better writers than himself. I know this experience well, and I would like to sincerely thank those friends and intimates of mine who enjoy the wonders of the word as much as myself. They continue to inspire me with their flavors of language, but none of them more so than the beautiful Christina, whose blithe, effortless pronouncements a-muse me on a daily basis, and whose company is the grace of all that is good in this universe. To her I can only say yes, and nectar.

Recommend this book to your friends
and explore special offers at
TonyVigorito.com/share.php

Just a Couple of Days, by Tony Vigorito

**"May be the most unusual,
the most original novel I have ever read."**
—Tom Robbins, bestselling author of *Jitterbug Perfume*

"Irreverent, whimsical… Recommended."
—*Library Journal*

Join cult favorite Tony Vigorito in his award-winning underground hit chronicling the party at the end of time. A mischievous artist kicks off a game of graffiti tag on a local overpass by painting the simple phrase, "Uh-oh." An anonymous interlocutor writes back: "When?" Someone slyly answers: "Just a couple of days." But what happens in just a couple of days? Professor Blip Korterly is arrested; his friend Dr. Flake Fountain is drafted into a shadow-government research project to develop the ultimate biological weapon, and an accidental outbreak turns into a merry-hearted, babble-inducing apocalypse that will either destroy humankind or take it to the next step in evolution.

"An apocalyptic vision worthy of Kurt Vonnegut."
—*Kirkus Reviews*

"A lyrical, thoughtful, viral meme of a book. Read it!"
—Christopher Moore, bestselling author of *Lamb*

**Read an extended sample at
TonyVigorito.com**

Nine Kinds of Naked, by Tony Vigorito

"Have a ball with this hyperactive, zany novel."
—*Publishers Weekly*

"A wild stylist... Startlingly original."
—*Chicago Sun-Times*

Join cult favorite Tony Vigorito in his acclaimed, surreal whirlwind of a novel exploring chaos theory. A prisoner spins a playing card into a somersault, stirring a wind that becomes a tornado that takes off the roof of a church in nearby Normal, Illinois. Elizabeth Wildhack is born in that church and someday she will meet that prisoner, a man named Diablo, on the streets of New Orleans—where a hurricane-like Great White Spot hovers off the coast. But how is it all interconnected? And what does it have to do with a time-traveling serf and a secret society whose motto is "Walk away?"

"Almost more musical dance than written word."
—*Sacramento Book Review*

"Channeling the spirited humor of Douglas Adams."
—*Texas Monthly*

"Comic, dramatic, and everything in between."
—*Booklist*

**Read an extended sample at
TonyVigorito.com**

Made in the USA
Middletown, DE
24 November 2018